PRAISE FOR CAROL BERG AND HER NOVELS

"Carol Berg is an absolutely gorgeous writer. . . . She does incredible, intricate world building that moves along like a deep, powerful river: It looks, on the surface, as though it's carrying along at a reasonable rate, with occasional dips and swirls into eddies, but beneath that is an absolutely tremendous current pulling you along toward inexorable rapids, and you barely know it's happened until you're already over your head. And then, just in case ... the same thing with the character de... pe that are also enormously ... characters, but the reader." ...ker Papers series

"Among m... her characters, story, and ... seen in fantasy, and a beaut...

...nd Shadow series ...d *Breath and Bone*)

"Carol Ber... I have run across. Her books ... r against which I measure al... t just books; they are art, an... vriting style gives all of her b... re more real than real, and h... ts as you read, and you learn ... —Bookworm Blues

"Carol Berg has spun a tale of magic and politics, of intrigue and betrayal. Set in a rich world, told through the eyes of a compelling and sympathetic hero, her story twists and turns, building to a conclusion that satisfies while hinting at more adventures to come. I eagerly await the next Sanctuary novel."

—D. B. Jackson, author of the Thieftaker Chronicles

continued . . .

Breath and Bone

"The narrative crackles with intensity against a vivid backdrop of real depth and conviction, with characters to match. Altogether superior."

—*Kirkus Reviews* (starred review)

"Berg's lush, evocative storytelling and fully developed characters add up to a first-rate purchase for most fantasy collections." —*Library Journal*

"Replete with magic-powered machinations, secret societies, and doomsday divinations, the emotionally intense second volume of Berg's intrigue-laden Lighthouse Duet concludes the story of Valen. . . . Fans of Marion Zimmer Bradley's Avalon sequence and Sharon Shinn will be rewarded."

—*Publishers Weekly*

"Berg combines druid and Christian influences against a backdrop of sorcerers, priestesses, priests, deep evil, and a dying land to create an engrossing tale to get lost in . . . enjoyable." —Monsters and Critics

"An excellent read . . . a satisfying sequel." —Fresh Fiction

Flesh and Spirit

"In Carol Berg's engrossing *Flesh and Spirit*, an engaging rogue stumbles upon the dangerous crossroads of religion, politics, war, and destiny. Berg perfectly portrays the people who shape his increasingly more chaotic journey: cheerful monks, cruel siblings, ambitious warlords, and a whole cast of fanatics. But it's the vividly rendered details that give this book such power. Berg brings to life every stone in a peaceful monastery and every nuance in a stratified society, describing the difficult dirty work of ordinary life as beautifully as she conveys the heart-stopping mysticism of holiness just beyond human perception."

—Sharon Shinn, national bestselling author of *Royal Airs*

"Carol Berg has done a masterful job of creating characters, places, religions, and political trials that grab and hold your attention. . . . Don't miss one of 2007's best fantasy books!" —Romance Reviews Today

"It's challenging to create a main character who's not exactly a good guy and yet still elicits reader sympathy. Carol Berg's newest novel, *Flesh and Spirit*, features a man who has committed quite a few misdeeds and yet remains likable. . . . Berg also excels at creating worlds. . . . It's like we're exploring this world alongside its characters, and this technique works remarkably well. . . . I'm eagerly awaiting the duology's concluding volume, *Breath and Bone*. This first installment is an engrossing and lively tale with enough action to keep you hungry for more." —*The Davis Enterprise*

The Daemon Prism

"[Berg's] insight into the nature of human good and evil, the constantly ebbing and flowing relationships among lovers and friends . . . consistently raises this novel above sword-and-sorcery routine." —*Publishers Weekly*

"An amazingly complex and rewarding story. *The Daemon Prism* is certain to reward the devoted students of the Collegia Magica trilogy." —*Booklist*

"One of the best fantasies I have encountered in years. . . . Berg takes chances with her characters . . . that leave them imprinted indelibly in your memory and heart . . . wonderful."

—Science Fiction and Other ODDysseys

"Enthralling and not to be missed." —*Kirkus Reviews*

"Filled with action and feeling, as if it occurs in a Berg version of the Age of Reason; fans will appreciate this stupendous story." —Alternative Worlds

BOOKS BY CAROL BERG

THE COLLEGIA MAGICA SERIES

The Spirit Lens

The Soul Mirror

The Daemon Prism

THE LIGHTHOUSE SERIES

Flesh and Spirit

Breath and Bone

THE BRIDGE OF D'ARNATH SERIES

Son of Avonar

Guardians of the Keep

The Soul Weaver

Daughter of Ancients

Song of the Beast

THE RAI-KIRAH SERIES

Transformation

Revelation

Restoration

DUST AND LIGHT

A SANCTUARY NOVEL

CAROL BERG

ROC

A ROC BOOK

ROC
Published by the Penguin Group
Penguin Group (USA) LLC, 375 Hudson Street,
New York, New York 10014

USA | Canada | UK | Ireland | Australia | New Zealand | India | South Africa | China
penguin.com
A Penguin Random House Company

First published by Roc, an imprint of New American Library,
a division of Penguin Group (USA) LLC

First Printing, August 2014

LIBRARY OF CONGRESS CATALOGING-IN-PUBLICATION DATA:

Berg, Carol.
Dust and light: a sanctuary novel/Carol Berg.
p. cm.—(A sanctuary novel; 1)
ISBN 978-0-451-41724-4 (paperback)
1. Magic—Fiction. 2. Sorcery—Fiction. I. Title.
PS3602.E7523D88 2014
813'.6—dc23 2014004222

Printed in the United States of America
10 9 8 7 6 5 4 3 2 1

Set in Bembo
Designed by Spring Hoteling

PUBLISHER'S NOTE
This is a work of fiction. Names, characters, places, and incidents either are the product of the author's imagination or are used fictitiously, and any resemblance to actual persons, living or dead, business establishments, events, or locales is entirely coincidental.

For artists and historians,
and all who show us truth

ACKNOWLEDGMENTS

Thanks as always to my extraordinary posse—Susan, Curt, Catherine, Brian, Courtney—for keeping me thinking. And to the Fairplay gang—Cindi, Jeanne, Susan, Vicki, and yes, you, too, Michael, Stella, Richard, and all the crew—for enabling words with comradeship and hospitality. To Brenda, for constant encouragement and our days of magic in the Northwest. To my readers, for the connections and insights that keep me going. To agent Lucienne and editor Anne, for your trust and insights. To my mother, for the beginning. And to Pete, the Exceptional Spouse, for all these things and everything else, ever and always.

The blades of winter pierce root and stone, dust and light. Day sky sheened with silver; stars shattered with frost; life burrowed deep. The killing season. A fragile beauty, fraught with danger, hunger, and pain. Stripped branch and barren vine crack and shrivel. My heart yearns for warmth, for companionship, for glory. Yet waking is storm. 'Tis harsh magic to dance on ice.

—*Canticle of the Winter*

DUST

— AND —

LIGHT

Part I
The Blades of Winter

CHAPTER 1

YEAR 1291 OF THE ARDRAN PRINCIPALITY

YEAR 214 FROM THE UNIFICATION OF ARDRA, MORIAN, AND EVANORE AS THE KINGDOM OF NAVRONNE

YEAR 1, INTERREGNUM, MOURNING THE DEATH OF GOOD KING EODWARD

EARLY WINTER

Rumors flew into Palinur on a malignant north wind. After seven bloody months, Perryn, Duc of Ardra, Prince of Navronne, had battled his contentious brother Bayard back into the northlands. While frozen roads and rivers locked Bayard in the river county, Perryn was returning triumphant to his royal city. For better or worse, King Eodward's throne was his. Navronne's brief war of succession was over.

Perhaps.

My unfocused anxieties felt somehow traitorous to my heritage. The politics of ordinaries shouldn't touch me, a pureblood sorcerer, gifted by the gods to provide magic to the world. Were they yet living, my parents would berate me for unseemly distraction and my teasing brothers call me soberskull or grimheart. But the war *had* touched me, and would forever, no matter which prince won the prize.

The frigid air pricked like needles this morning. Another fretful night had left me nervy, as if bowmen stood on the rooftops, arrows nocked and aimed at my back. Ten times in the half quellé from my town house I'd spun around, imagining a pickthief fingering the gold chain about my neck. Now the babbling river of people flowing through the back lane of the Council District had come to a standstill, trapping me between a heavily guarded flock of squalling geese and a rickety tinker's cart headed for some nobleman's kitchen.

The blockage did naught for my composure. I'd determined to reach my studio at the Registry Tower early and had foolishly assumed the streets might be less crowded while the morning was yet dark as pitch. But refugees from the northern battles had swarmed into the city ahead of Prince Perryn's legions. Barons and villeins, freeholders and crofters, monks, practors, and townsmen crammed the streets with wagons and carts, trading their belongings for what provision anyone could offer. What hopes people bore of sustenance in a famine year might be realized only in Palinur—and before the returning troops ravaged the remaining stores.

Fools, all. The new year had not yet turned, and Navronne already lay in the grip of yet another ruinous winter. Market stalls were bare, grain stores heavily guarded. Meat and fish commanded prices akin to rubies.

The poor light—a weedy torch here and a grimy wagon lamp there—scarce penetrated the murk. An escort to carry a lamp and clear my path was a luxury my purse could no longer support, and when my steward had offered to hire a linkboy, I'd refused, unwilling to wait. A poor decision. I was expert at those.

Exasperated, I squeezed past the tinker's cart, only to end up ankle-deep in a stew of ice and muck, blocked yet again. Two men were pounding each other bloody, surrounded by jeering onlookers.

"Move aside!" Magelight blazed white from my hand, quieting the noise in the lane.

Most folk properly averted their eyes at the sight of my mask and claret-hued cloak and squeezed to the sides of the lane to let me pass. I could properly summon a constable to punish those who did not, but that wasn't going to speed my progress.

Unfortunately, neither was the uncomfortably direct assertion of my prerogatives. A rag-topped cart crammed with women and children choked the lane ahead, while three men attempted to repair a broken wheel. The families had painted their foreheads with dung to appease whatever god they believed had brought this doom of war and winter on the world.

I considered reversing course altogether, but an alley sheering off to my left looked more promising.

The alley was certainly no garden path. I stepped over piles of unidentifiable refuse, a bloated cat, and a beggar, either sleeping or dead. But the empty quiet was a welcome contrast to the cacophony that rose again behind me. The wind sighed and whistled through the dark slot.

I dimmed my magelight. I needed to conserve power, rid myself of distraction, and focus on my work today. A portrait done the previous afternoon needed repairs before the Master of Archives inspected it.

Lucian . . . see . . .

I would not look back. *Would* not. The breathy words were naught but wind.

. . . meddling . . . end it . . .

. . . no saving him . . .

I made it halfway to the graying light at the far end of the alley before I whirled about and raised my light again to affirm that the touch on my shoulder and the footsteps—soft as bare feet on green grass—were mere imagining.

At six-and-twenty, I was a man of fit body and intelligent mind, a pureblood sorcerer of honorable bloodlines and with an exceptional magical bent for portraiture. Save for one small failure in discipline five years past, which had borne entirely *un*subtle consequences, my conscience was clear. So why did I have this incessant sense of being watched? My eyes insisted that shadows darted away as I rounded corners and that wisps of colored light glimmered in the dark courtyards outside my windows. Only in the last tenday had my fancy added these whisperings just at the farthest limits of hearing. Warnings, but of what, I had no idea.

Not that I believed in them. That would be madness.

The sensations were not magic. Every day of my life was filled with magic. Nor were they ghosts. Were ghosts real, mine would be only three months raised and so numerous I could not mistake them. These oddities had gone on nigh half a year. Reason could explain none of it.

No matter reason or belief, my fears were undeniable. Reason did not always hold sway, and purebloods were not immortal.

Lucian . . . listen . . .

Without looking back, I raced from the alley into the busy boulevard that led uphill to the Tower.

By the time the city bells pealed ninth hour of the morning watch, I was glaring at the sketch propped on my easel. The subject, an overripe girl of fourteen, had come into the Pureblood Registry the previous day for her biennial portrait, which seemed a silly exercise in the face of such world-shaping events as war and disastrous winter. Instead of the pups and roses she wanted as her background setting, my fingers had insisted on drawing wrecked houses and hanged men. The girl's grandfather Pluvius, Master of the Registry Archives and my own contract master, would most certainly disapprove, so I'd come in early to remove them with an unsatisfactory wash of ink.

Touching my pen to the portrait yet again, I raised the girl's true image, shaped in my mind at her sitting. A quick comparison to the actuality on the page, and my will released the enchantment waiting in my fingers like liquid fire. A few quick strokes instilled a little more of the spoiled-daughter pout so clear in my mind's eye. Better. Truth.

Even so mundane an evocation of magic filled me with awe and divine purpose. No matter personal grief or inexplicable megrims, magic held me centered—an inexhaustible source of wonder.

The fire in the grate had left the tower studio stifling. Blotting my fingers, I hurried across the cluttered chamber to the fogged casements and twisted the latch, welcoming a drift of cold air.

Better to be here than down below. My boots were dry. The air was quiet. A small fire blazed in the *pocardon*, the royal city's ancient market—thankfully nowhere near the town house where my young sister remained secluded with our devoted servants—but I could not smell it. Here in the chambers of those who administered the lives of pureblood sorcerers, all was as it had ever been: serene, unhurried, and well disciplined, separate from the chaos of ordinaries, as the gods intended.

A bitter draft swooshed through the tower room, riffling fifty loose pages before the door slammed shut again behind a rumpled giant.

"Earth's Mother, Lucian! I thought I was never going to get here this morning." Gilles dropped his pen case and sagged onto a stool, puffing and blowing, his cloak muddy and twisted halfway round, his hose ripped, and his mask drooping from the left side of his flushed face. "Some cursed lackwit found a stash of five pigs and let them loose. A thousand beggars were tearing each other apart to get at them."

Despite the grim circumstance, I had to grin. "Pigs. And yesterday it was geese. And the day before—hmm—your manservant spilled your morning posset on your sleeve?"

Though the Albins, the wealthiest of all pureblood families, provided their son an armed escort party, he arrived most mornings in a similar state. Gilles attracted disorder like beggars attracted fleas. Tripping over his own feet or annoying his hound served as well as riot or ill wind.

I appreciated Gilles. He had mentored me when my first contract brought me to the Registry Archives, and he had taken it with grace when I was given a senior commission of six major portraits only a few years later. Although his uncle was a Registry curator, he had never been offered one.

Our skills meshed well; I worked better with younger men and with elders of both genders, Gilles with middle-aged women and fidgety children. We had even supped together several times over the years when our work kept us late. An ordinary might describe us as friends, though such frivolous relationships were discouraged in pureblood society.

"Surely Prince Perryn's victory will settle the city," I said, turning back to the window. "Of the three, he's said to be Eodward's truest son, noble in mind and bearing."

"Bayard's stubborn, though," said Gilles, blotting his broad forehead. "And until he's crushed entire or someone finds Eodward's will saying which one inherits, Bayard won't leave off fighting. But even Bayard the Smith couldn't be a worse sovereign than the Bastard of Evanore or the Harrower priestess, may she writhe in Magrog's chains for eternity."

I actually knew very little of Perryn or Bayard or the third royal brother, the bastard prince who ruled the south, but every day of my life I would beg the gods for some fitting end for the vile priestess, Sila Diaglou. She and her fanatical Harrowers believed our ten-year siege of ruinous weather, the rampant plagues, diseases, famine, and war were humankind's penalty for corrupt living. Harrower mobs had destroyed far too much of worth in their pursuit of *purity and repentance*, ravaging, burning, slaughtering innocents in the name of their vengeful Powers. . . .

I closed my eyes and summoned discipline. Emotions about the unchangeable past, especially when snarled with ordinaries and their politics, only cluttered a man's thinking.

My grandsire had been wise to negotiate my first contract with the Registry itself. A historian of rare gifts, he had warned of the upheaval to come at mighty King Eodward's death. Young and stupid, I had chafed at the limitations of a Registry position. A contract with a town, a hierarch, or a noble family outside Palinur would certainly have fetched better terms—more prestige, wider contacts, a better stipend to fill the family coffers—and surely more interesting work. But youthful folly had already squandered my grandsire's favor that might have allowed my opinion to be heard.

The Pureblood Registry will endure, no matter the shifting loyalties and upsets of ordinaries, my father had said, trying, as ever, to ease the bitter gulf between my grandsire and me. *The world cannot live without pureblood magic, and our survival, as well as our prosperity, is founded on Registry discipline. You'll flourish there.*

Unfortunately, Patronn had not lived long enough to see his own father's predictions fulfilled. Nor had my grandsire, my mother, my brothers, nor any child or elder of my bloodlines—all of them dead in the ordinaries' war. Only Juli and I were left.

"I just hope for order in the streets," I said. "I've not taken my sister out in months. Her tutors have stopped coming; gone into hiding, I think. Yet she insists she should be out rebuilding the Verisonné Hospice or designing an enlargement of the Fullers' Guildhall."

"Rebuilding? Designing guildhalls? A girl of fifteen?"

"Idiot child. No one's building anything until times are more settled. And without serving a proper apprenticeship, she's like to build roofs that will collapse. Though, in truth, it's not just that. . . ."

I let it go. No need to bemoan my inadequacies as surrogate parent. Juli was immensely gifted, and star-eyed about her magic despite our personal sorrows. But her stubborn nature was going to bring us more grief.

"Oh!" Gilles clapped a hand to his head. "Almost forgot. I met Master Pluvius on the stair. You're to attend him immediately in the Curators' Chamber."

"Great gods, Gilles!" I slammed the casement shut and raked fingers through my hair. Tugging my shirtsleeves straight and adjusting my wrought-gold belt, I eyed the blue velvet pourpoint I'd discarded when I began work, weighing the consequences of further delay against the disrespect of casual dress before my superior. Of course, Master Pluvius himself—forever fussing over me—had recommended I work in shirtsleeves to keep my outer garments clean. But he also held the future of a very important commission in his hand, and he was ferocious about promptness.

"Did he say what this was about?"

"No. Just that you should come immediately.

"Sorry, Lucian!" Gilles's call drifted after me, as I abandoned the pourpoint with its hundred button loops and raced for the upward stair.

"Lucian de Remeni-Masson, you've met Curator Pons-Laterus and Curator Albin, the Overseer of Contracts?"

My stomach knotted as I faced three senior administrators, attired not just in customary pureblood formality, but in their official gowns of black and wine-red stripes. I felt half-naked in undertunic, shirt, belt, and hose. Stupid, stupid, stupid not to take the time to present myself respectably.

Summoning composure, I touched fingertips to forehead and bowed deeply to each. "I do have that privilege, Master Pluvius. *Doma* Pons. *Domé* Albin. Pardon my rude attire. My . . . uh . . . current occupations delayed the delivery of your summons."

I would not lie. Yet neither would I excuse my delay by blaming Gilles, even if his uncle weren't sitting in front of me.

Guilian de Albin glared down his long straight nose at me. He himself looked like a sculpted idealization of a pureblood—that nose, the raven hair pulled back severely from a noble brow, a thick-muscled body—and he fulfilled every expectation of such a figure. The Albins were not only the wealthiest, but one of the most powerful, and definitely the most traditional, of families. I'd once heard Albin reprimand a fellow curator for allowing the man's own daughter to address him in public.

And *Pons*, of all people. She knew the worst of me. Her black eyes, so like the pits of olives, had been pinned to my back every day for nigh on five years. Why was she here?

"Sit, Lucian." Pluvius, the white-bearded Master of Archives, the robust historian who directed my work, motioned me to a stool in the center of the room facing the U-shaped table. His sober expression told me nothing. Pluvius could dither like a nursemaid and bellow like a guard commander, all in the same hour over the same incident.

Natural apprehension at sudden formal meetings warred with rising hopes. Rumor said my commissioned portraits of the six Registry curators had won high favor. While following the formal style of previous official portraits, I had distinguished each with a more naturalistic background. Every instinct in me said the paintings marked a major step forward in my skills. They were pleasing in balance and form, and the likenesses excellent as well as true.

Though the portraits were not yet hung, Pluvius had quietly set me to preparations for a portrait of my grandsire and hinted a second senior commission might be involved. I'd been working late on preliminary sketches every night for a tenday, reaching deep into power and memory and grief to touch the truth of a man I had known better than any other living person. Without question, the sketches were the best work I'd ever done.

Curator Albin inclined his head in my direction. "Your family's loss these three months since was a blow to all pureblood society."

Body and spirit grew rigid. His cool reference shuttered excitement and rising hopes as spilled ink blots a sketch.

"The Remeni have been elite for generations. And the Massoni were already so few. Both bloodlines nearly wiped out in a single night. Dreadful, tragic . . ."

Dreadful? Tragic? The words were entirely, grotesquely insufficient. A sudden overload of work had kept me in the city that night, but I could see it all, as clearly as any image my art could produce. The cool late-summer night in the rolling hills outside Pontia, moonlight bathing our beauteous vineyards, still healthy amid the land's failure. Music and laughter bursting from the great hall of our family estate, as my grandsire, mother, father, brothers, aunts, uncles, and cousins celebrate my youngest brother's first contract. Someone—my father? One of my uncles?—would have queried the first hint of smoke that was not candles or hearth fires. And celebration had transformed to panicked horror as they realized the hall was ablaze and the doors barricaded.

Rampaging Harrowers had drowned my family's dying screams with their nonsensical chants about purity, repentance, and corrupt magic, or so the local magistrate had reported. Gleefully, I'd thought. The leering ordinary had worn a telltale of Harrower orange inside his jupon. Madmen were everywhere these days.

". . . and of course, it has left you in a difficult position—only six-

and-twenty, lacking four years until you can be named Head of Family, yet serving a contract that expires in the spring. You will need a negotiator. Second Registrar Pons-Laterus"—he motioned to the woman beside him—"has graciously taken on that commission."

My chest near caved. My worst imagining come true.

In the past months I had pursued every remote family connection, hoping to enlist a competent advocate before the Registry appointed a random official to negotiate my next contract. But the war and the dreadful weather had made the great families wary of entanglements. And now, of all of them, the Registry had given me Pons. *Goddess Mother . . .*

The Second Registrar, a hard, sour woman as gray and blockish as the Tower itself, had served as Registry investigator for the city of Montesard during my years at the university, the years when my indiscretion had brought disgrace upon my family and altered my future.

I exhaled smoothly. *Do not let them see. Albin will think you an undisciplined child, as Pons does already.*

"I am honored by this most generous gesture," I said, bowing in Pons's direction even as my gut churned. "But perhaps . . . Master Pluvius once offered . . ."

"It is entirely inappropriate for your current master to negotiate your next contract," snapped Albin, who'd had the final say on every pureblood contract for twenty years. "He cannot be objective."

Yet one could say the same about any Registry-selected negotiator. Pons would be strictly honest, no doubt, but she made no secret of her despite. She believed family influence had unduly mitigated the consequences of my *unseemly involvement with ordinaries* in Montesard.

"But I'm sure the Second Registrar's duties demand her undivided attention," I said. "As my contract does not expire until almost midyear, I've other avenues—"

"Alas, not so," said Albin. "All next year's contract expirations for Registry positions have been advanced. The stipends already paid will not be reclaimed for the unfulfilled months—an expensive sacrifice on our part. But our attention must be directed toward the new king, affirming our traditional cooperation and prerogatives. Your contract expires at midnight tonight."

Tonight! I could scarce choke out the necessary response. "Yes, of course, *domé*, that sounds wise."

Negotiations without preparation . . . altogether *un*wise. I needed to study my current contract, gather comparisons from other portraitists, convince the Registry to cede a more appropriate income for my skill level and perhaps shorter hours. Tutelage for Juli came dear and I needed to be available to chaperone her lessons. Then, too, this was likely my last chance to shape my future.

The gods had gifted me in exceptional ways, both with power for magic and with a family that indulged and nurtured my particular talents. My grandsire—our Head of Family—had even been willing to challenge Registry tradition for me, and in a moment's lapse of discipline I had thrown it all away. I would forever grieve for my grandsire. My determination to cleanse the stain I'd brought to his name had rested in the hope of more serious, substantial service than anniversary portraiture.

"I suppose Curator Pons and I must finalize a proposal right away and set a contract meeting for this evening," I said. One did not display emotions, especially such private ones, outside the family.

Curator Albin crossed his arms and sat back in his chair, waiting.

Master Pluvius studied the table in front of his folded hands.

Pons planted her forearms on the table and leaned forward. Plain silver rings gleamed from her thick fingers as she tapped a sheaf of documents. "In truth, Remeni, the Registry has made no offer for your service. As we've no time to solicit other offers, I've gathered together what open bids for portraitists we have already. Perhaps one of these will suit."

No offer . . . My mind stuttered and reeled. Of course the Registry wanted me back. My work here had been exemplary. A senior commission while in my first contract. The promise of another with my grandfather's portrait. Never a reprimand. My every moment since my disgrace had been given to improving both my art and the self-discipline my role in life demanded—to becoming a man worthy of the Remeni name. Master Pluvius had long said I could wrestle out details that made my subjects near step out of the canvas, allowing Registry investigators to identify any pureblood inerrantly.

"I don't understand." My voice—properly calm and detached—might have belonged to someone else. "Have I somehow failed in my work or my deportment? Master Pluvius?"

"Certainly not, lad. It's just . . . unique circumstances. These unsettled times."

"First Curator Gramphier knows of this?" To invoke my personal connection with the highest-ranking official of the Registry galled, but Gramphier had been my grandsire's longtime colleague. He had encouraged my Registry contract as a way for me to demonstrate my worth.

Pons settled back in her chair, her face impassive save for the touch of scorn on her thin lips. "Naturally Gramphier knows. But if you wish to let your contract lapse as we solicit new offers for your service, we can halt this right now. You could contact me when your intellect is functioning at some useful level."

Bitter truth quenched my protests. My service *must* be sold. Juli and I had no other income. Our Ardran vineyards had frozen two winters running; who knew if they would ever come back? And, along with every person in the world we loved, our family's treasury had been lost in the Harrower raid. We were nearing the end of the funds my father had provided for my maintenance in Palinur. Juli had brought my last stipend on a visit to the royal city. My work had prevented me from escorting her home in time for our brother's celebration, else we would have burned alongside the rest of them. I needed a contract, and the curators knew it.

"No, no, *Doma* Pons. Certainly I'll hear these bids."

Pons read through each application in her stack.

A Karish abbot sought *a pureblood artist to travel alongside, illustrating prayer cards to enlighten unlettered villagers.*

A customs official on the eastern borders needed *charts of goods carried through the border station for taxing purposes.*

"Your skills at reflecting the inner person would suit this Trimori mine," she said, tossing out an age-yellowed parchment. "The governor wishes to ferret out troublemakers from felons sent to labor in the pits."

"A traveling position is out of the question," I said, "as are those in remote or military outposts. My sister is a maiden of fifteen without other family. I must see to her education."

And the stipends these offered were pitiful. None would support a pureblood household, much less allow me to accumulate the wherewithal to rebuild our family. These bids had gathered dust in the Registry vaults because they were insults.

Swelling anger threatened my composure. Pureblood sorcerers held the power of magic, the greatest gift of the gods to a troubled world, and they sacrificed a great deal to preserve, nurture, and share that gift. Not even

Karish monks lived with more study, rules, and restrictions. Purebloods bound themselves and their grown children into strict service on the assurance that they would be provided the means to maintain the dignity of our calling and to withstand such travails as war and famine.

"Well, then . . ." Frowning, Pons thumbed through the stack and pulled out a yellowed page. "I see only one that might suit. One Bastien de Caton offers a position here in Palinur. He requires *line drawings for purposes of identification.* Compensation left to negotiation. But it is only a one-year contract. Do you wish to interview the master?"

I leapt at the offer before an angry outburst could disgrace me further. "No need to interview him." Identification portraits were exactly what I was doing already. And only a year's contract. In the interim I could find a better advocate and search more thoroughly. "Palinur suits best. If I'm required to live in, I'll at least be able to look in on my sister. As long as the contract meets Registry standards."

Registry contracts were quite strict about personal security, respectful address, comfortable accommodation and sustenance, and permissible penalties for unsatisfactory work. My age left me no standing to disapprove contract terms—only the Registry and the Head of Family, or, in my case, Pons, had a say. But even Pons would not undermine pureblood prerogatives with a poor contract.

"I shall negotiate the best terms possible, given the unsettled times," said Pons. She dipped a pen and scratched a few notes on the page. "I shall stipulate that you will live in your own home, though this Bastien will, no doubt, insist on appropriate hours. I foresee no difficulties."

"Come here, Lucian," said Master Pluvius. Before I could think, I was signing my name where his finger pointed. Curator Albin snatched the paper from under my hand and applied his seal to the bottom. As if the terms were already settled.

Pons rose briskly, her formidable bulk blocking the gray light from the casements behind her. "We shall provide the usual escort party to deliver you to your new master tomorrow . . . if all goes well in the negotiation, of course."

"Yes, certainly. My gratitude for your consideration, *Doma* Pons, *Domé* Albin, Master Pluvius."

The three curators had already reached the doorway as the necessary politenesses stumbled from my tongue. I felt as if I had been trampled by wild horses.

"Go home, Lucian. Whatever you're working on will have to be finished by someone else." Master Pluvius lingered in the doorway. "I'm sorry about all this. Be sure I shall give you good recommendations."

"I appreciate that, master."

Yet why would I expect differently? The Registry required every pureblood to sit for a portrait each year until age twelve, every two years until age thirty, and every ten years thereafter. Each small artwork was magically linked to its subject, and our signatures irrevocably bound the artist and the work. The accuracy imposed by our bent ensured that no ordinary could pass for a pureblood, and no pureblood could pass for another. Gilles and I could scarce keep up with the load. How could they not renew my contract?

"Master, why—?" The doorway was empty.

If this Bastien de Caton was a person of influence, his request would never have been left unfulfilled long enough to gather dust. If he represented a town, a market fair, a temple, or another institution, the offer would have borne that name as well as his. And *Caton*. The man took his name not from a noble seat or reputable family but from some nearby settlement or crossroads so insignificant the name scarce shifted the dust of recollection. He was *no one*.

I hurried after Pluvius, only to see him vanishing down the stair. "Master," I called, "who is this Bastien de Caton?"

The old man looked up, the torchlight reflecting a profound sadness that shook me to the marrow. "He's Palinur's coroner, Lucian. He'll use your portraits to identify the dead."

CHAPTER 2

"Poor *ancieno.* Is the new contract so awful? Who but Registry clerks would even want an ink dabbler like you? And old *Pew-Pons* to negotiate"—my sister's mocking trilled—"the very picking crow who held you to the fire at the university. Now, *that* was ill luck."

Juli posed carelessly in our reception room door as we awaited the arrival of my escort on the morning after my dismissal. She was so slight, so deceptively languid. Very like an iron stanchion garlanded with orchids. Her heavy black-brown hair, gleaming with red lights in the lamp glow, spread loose over the indigo silk of her morning gown.

"I've not met my master as yet," I said. "But this is a fine opportunity and something different from anniversary portraits. My art was growing stale in the Tower."

I'd told Juli none of the wretched details. Our troubles had already changed her. No use making it worse.

My mother had called Juli her angel child, and from eleven years' distance, eldest to youngest, it had seemed true. When I'd lived at home, Juli was a bright and cheery sprite, playing at her beginner's magic. Her bent revealed itself early as she built towers and miniature cities that sprawled across our inner courtyards. She smoothed sticks and chipped stones, teasing them into balance and harmony with her magic. She forever challenged my younger brothers to improve on her creations. At ten, in the same year I began work at the Registry, she applied herself seriously to her drawing. Whenever I went home for a visit, she pestered me incessantly to teach her.

All that had changed. In the months since the horror at Pontia, my sister had prisoned herself in steel and brambles, pricking, jabbing, arguing, defying the rules all purebloods accepted gladly as the price of our gifts. She refused to explain herself. Refused to listen to my warnings or pleas or commands. She screamed that I was not her father, mother, or Head of Family. I felt helpless around her.

"Ooh, la! Mother Samele prevent such talents as yours from getting stale! Perhaps another year at university would *sharpen* you. And this time without your elders to object."

Juli's jabs about the university struck home, as she knew they would. I had been a fool in those days, associating with so many ordinaries in such . . . free . . . circumstances. I had been warned that even conversation with ordinaries could seduce an undisciplined man. But indeed I had forgotten myself, my place, and my responsibilities.

Never could I repeat such a failure. My sister had no one else.

"Lace up your gown, Juli, and bind your hair properly, else go back to your own rooms. I don't know who the Registry will send as escort, but it does our reputation no good for you to appear so . . . untidy."

"Bind your own hair," she snapped. "I think I'll cut mine off today. I hate it."

"Don't. Just don't. Please, *serena*." My sister's hair was supposed to remain uncut, plaited, and wound about her head in the style of a country matron, which indeed looked ridiculous with her tender features. But our family discipline prescribed it, just as it prescribed everything else, from the color and shape of our masks to the particular aspects of our bents that we could practice and the very gods we worshipped. Registry and family protocols shaped every detail of our lives, and investigators noted lapses.

"Four years and I can change the rule to a style you prefer," I said. "Please, just behave until then." I could not bear the thought of Pons sending a minder to supervise us until I came to my majority.

Pons had been livid when I was not publicly whipped, censured, or otherwise shamed after Montesard. She desired me to be an example, so that no pureblood family would dare send their progeny into the libertine world of a university again. Perhaps with her promotion to curator, she had influence enough to get what she wanted. She couldn't know that the price I'd already paid was irredeemable.

For almost thirty years, my father's father had served King Eodward as Navronne's Royal Historian, using his magic to read battlefields or borderlands, for delving into ruins or deciphering ancient texts to extract the sweeping truths of war, migration, and civilization. The king had credited my grandsire with helping him grow Navronne into a healthy, prosperous kingdom renowned in the world—one with some chance to withstand this abrupt decline in the weather. I had longed to follow in his footsteps.

By the age of ten years, almost every pureblood youth displayed a pronounced leaning toward one parent's magical bent or the other's. Yet my talents had remained balanced between the Masson bent for art and architecture and the Remeni bent for history. Though I showed a deft hand at portraiture, inherited from my Masson mother, my preference had ever been for my Remeni father's bloodline magic. I relished the study of history.

Dual bents were extremely rare, and usually displayed each as barely functioning. The family would prepare the youth for a modest future—hired work within pureblood society with severely limited use of magic, forbidden to marry or conceive children. Unfortunately, experience warned that two strong bents led inevitably to madness, and the Registry had long insisted that the lesser one be excised. Yet my talents had both manifested as quite robust, and by age sixteen, I still could not say honestly that one exceeded the other. The divine glory of the magic thrilled and satisfied no matter which I invoked. Even my brothers teased that my only madness was excessive adherence to rules.

With the encouragement of my good and generous parents, my grandsire had allowed me to pursue both talents far longer than usual, even including a university education in history. If I maintained my strong discipline and even temper to the end of my studies, he would petition the Registry to allow me to retain both bents.

Fool that I was, I squandered their indulgence, and my grandsire forbade me to pursue my bent for history further. No matter my pleading never again to stray, he had spent one dreadful day laying enchantment on me to ensure it. It had felt as if he had removed a limb and seared its stump with a cautery iron. It had been clear to all that our Head of Family expended his honor and his considerable influence to save me from additional punishment. He had resigned his royal post within the month, and he—my beloved grandsire, the man I honored above every other on this earth—had never spoken to me again.

The charcoal night beyond our glass window had shifted to winter gray. Incipient dawn brought the noise of boots and voices in the outer courtyard.

Giaco, my manservant, arranged the folds of my cloak, fastened the clasp, and passed me my mask. I slipped the bit of maroon silk over the left side of my face, nudging its spelled edges to settle and cling about eye, nose, and ear, until it felt no different from my skin.

The half mask required of every pureblood when going out among ordinaries signaled the magic that lay hidden within us. In company with the wine-red cloak, it ensured no ordinary could ever mistake us—a certain kindness, as the penalties for interfering with a pureblood were quite severe. The mask served warning to us, as well, reminding us of our need to maintain detachment from the ordinary world and focus on our masters' tasks.

My tasks . . . I'd not even had a chance to read the new contract. A Head of Family usually informed his kinsman of the contract terms before delivering him to a new master. Evidently a Registry negotiator felt no such need. Certainly, Bastien de Caton, Coroner, must have prospered mightily from the war to afford me.

Giaco knelt to dust off my boots, as if that might prevent them from being sullied in the streets . . . or my master's charnel house. Rumor had it that during last spring's famine riots and the summer's sickness, corpses had piled up so high they rotted in the lower streets or were thrown into open pits outside the walls. What would I do in such a place? *Deunor's fire . . .*

"Gods' mercy, Luka. What's wrong?" Juli's rosy skin had drained of color.

I swallowed my gorge. "Nothing. All's well."

Soflet, both steward and porter, glided across the atrium to admit my escort party. I inhaled and composed the half of my features yet exposed.

But Juli, swift as a hummingbird, slipped in between me and the door. "You're not going into battle, are you, serving one of these cursed princes in their war? They're not going to lock you away? You're coming back?"

For that one moment, the brambles fell away and the steel dissolved to very young flesh.

I clasped her quivering shoulders. "No battles, no princes, no traveling, no war," I said softly. "Old *Pew-Pons* assured me I'll be allowed to live here with you. As the city settles under Prince Perryn, we'll dredge up your tutors and all will be as before. Speak with Maia and prepare the sealing feast for tonight when I get home. Have Soflet bring up our best vintage, and send Filip to find us meat, no matter the cost. I'll be bringing home the fee to replenish the Remeni-Masson treasury. Today we begin our family anew."

Her face froze. She whipped her hands apart, breaking my grip. "Maybe I will; maybe I won't."

"*Domé* Remeni-Masson . . ."

The soft-spoken newcomer and his three men, outfitted in black and scarlet and framed by the gilded entry, could not have noted Juli's sneer or heard her insolence. Indeed, as they introduced themselves and motioned me toward the outer courtyard, my sister composed herself, standing haughty and expressionless as was proper for a pureblood woman. The initiation of a pureblood contract was a most solemn occasion.

By the Mother, it was cold! Bitter wind howled through the streets, disguising splintered shutters, scattered refuse, overturned wagons, and charred stalls with dusty snow.

None could recall such winters as had plagued Navronne these last ten years. Those far older than I shook their heads and murmured of a universe out of balance, of the bowl of the sky slid askew, of angry gods or the lost Danae, mythic beings who once tended Navronne's fields and forests. Every baker filled his shelves with feast bread at the turn of the seasons, ready for those who would set it out to lure the Danae back to heal the lands of men. No such beings ever showed themselves, of course. The land grew more ill by the season.

My back itched; sighs teased at my ears. I hitched my cloak higher as we trudged down the hill.

No need to worry about risky impressions. My escorts were but Registry servitors. Purebloods with bents too weak to garner contracts were frequently employed as Registry guards, clerks, or messengers—positions where the presence of ordinaries would be unthinkable. It was respectable service. Leander de Corton-Zia and his comrades were likely skilled swordsmen and well trained in defensive magics.

The blizzard seemed to have calmed the city this morning, chasing the panicked refugees under cover. As we left the broad avenues of the upper city and the sprawling, bright-painted Temple District, hurrying down the sweeping turns of the Riie Domitian into the poorer streets, we spied them crowded into abandoned warehouses or huddled around fires in cramped alleyways. Until the war, Palinur had been an orderly place.

I dipped my head into the wind, wishing our family custom mandated a full mask of wool in winter. Better yet if discipline mandated a lock on the thing when one was young and stupid. It had been a sunny afternoon in Montesard when slim, sure fingers had tugged off my mask so that the most astonishing green eyes in creation could look upon my face. *Morgan . . .*

An aching heat flooded my belly.

In my first year at the university, my youthful eye, craving knowledge of the manly experiences I'd heard whispers of, had fallen on another student who was also reading history. She was a tall young woman of strong opinions and an incomparable eloquence in their defense, of deceptively plain features that took on a deep golden glow when she spoke of the tides of war, conquest, peace, and lawgiving that had made Navronne a model for all kingdoms in the middle continent. Morgan was her name—an ordinary—though the word failed absolutely when applied to her. Against all rule and discipline, I had spoken to her, laughed with her, touched her, and, in time, allowed her to remove my mask . . . kissed her . . . worked magic for her. . . .

"This way, *Domé* Remeni." A firm hand on my shoulder dragged me to a halt. Leander, breathless, pointed back to a lane of deserted alehouses where his men waited. I had raced right past my escorts.

I bricked up the bitter memories in the vault where I'd prisoned them. "Thoughtless of me," I said, and followed him.

The fertile fields and rugged scarps of central Ardra had been occupied for a thousand years, city upon city layered on Palinur's heights, comprising at least four enclosing walls. The two most recent yet stood. The outermost wall, Caedmon's Wall, had been built by the great king himself at the unification of Navronne. The innermost, the Elder Wall, had gone up at least five hundred years before that.

Leander halted at an arch of broken bricks. A steep path led down into an ill-favored warren of rickety houses, sheds, stables, and sop-houses grown up between the two standing walls at the lowest end of the city.

"Traversing the hirudo is our best route, *domé.* Every other way takes us outside the city gates, an hour longer at best, especially in such a wind. Unless you say differently . . ."

He sounded as if he was hoping I would say differently, but a terse message from Pons had told me to report to my new master at eighth hour, and the second quarter bells had already rung. Contracts left no choices. We headed down.

The hirudo was a dangerous, unhealthy place. In constant shadow, forever damp, the unruly settlement festered like an untreated wound, rife with disease and every kind of unsavory activity. Cicerons ruled here.

Cicerons plagued every Navron town and highroad like wandering packs of wild dogs. Skin as dusky as purebloods, bedecked with arm bracelets, earrings, and necklaces of false gold, they bred thieves, smugglers, fortune-tellers, and artists at picking pockets, knife juggling, and sleight of hand. Their knives found human targets, as well, especially any who crossed them. It was hard to tell one of them from another, and when constables ran one band of thieves to ground, they would find another in its place, their quarry long moved on.

We threaded the shadowy labyrinth for half a quellé, dodging diseased cats, racing ragamuffins, and ropes hung with rags. The wheedling gamblers fixed their eyes on their dice cups. The simpering procurer fell silent and looked away. None showed fear or awe. Even the women wore knowing, secretive expressions, and I could not shake the sense that they believed that someday I would walk this path alone and matters might be different.

My escorts kept hands on their swords and raised green magefire around us. In honor of the occasion, my father's ruby ring hung from my neck on a slender chain. I folded my hand over it, the only object of value we had retrieved from the ashes at Pontia.

Too much to hope that my contract included provision for a daily escort. The Registry came down hard on any who interfered with purebloods, but Registry guards, too, were stretched thin with the city so unsettled. My own sword training was scarce more than dabbling, and I'd spent so much time pursuing the two bents that my stock of common spells, including anything useful in combat, was pitifully thin.

The narrow path arced around a pigless sty at the far end of the hirudo, where the land kicked up sharply. A steep, tortuous ascent, including a last series of some fifty steps half a boot wide and almost vertical, brought us to a narrow slot in Caedmon's Wall, laced with iron bars. Neither horse nor armored knight nor even a person particularly well fed would be able to squeeze through. We emerged atop a broad plateau.

The prospect astonished me. Beyond a lumpy field of ice-crusted mud, like a phantasm behind the haze of swirling snow, sprawled a walled compound of stone spires, shed roofs, and chimneys. Atop the gatehouse arch, the twinned images of Deunor Lightbringer and his half brother Magrog, Lord of the Underworld, held pause in their never-ending battle for human souls. A necropolis . . . a city of the dead.

Warnings skittered through my skin like spider feet. Not since my days at the university had I ventured so far from the familiar. Was it that disastrous experience had my gut clenching in such dangerous fashion or was it that the air reeked so foully of endings?

We tramped through the snow-pale emptiness as the temple bells from the city heights called eighth hour. In the distance, a party of villeins dug in the frosty ground and loaded handcarts, their shovels crunching in the quiet. Shivering in my fur-lined cloak, I couldn't imagine what might be worth harvesting so deep in such a winter.

A tarnished brass plate was embedded in the brick above the gateway arch. Etched into it were the words NECROPOLIS CATON. My new master had not taken his name from some scrabbling village or crossroads, but from a burial ground. What kind of man named himself after a graveyard?

Leander rang the gate bell.

Back straight, I composed every expressive aspect of my body with pride. *Capatronn, Patronn, may my service and my life bring honor to our family name. Great Deunor, Lord of Fire and Magic, let my gift not falter.*

The iron gates swung inward. A pale, willowy young woman in unsullied white robes stood in the arch of light beyond the gatehouse tunnel, arms spread, head bowed, as graceful and still as sculpted marble.

"Welc— Oh!" Her eyes flicked wide as we emerged from the brief blackness. Swallowing her surprise, she averted her gaze and stepped aside.

"Where will we find Bastien de Caton?" said Leander. "We have the honor of initiating the fulfillment of his contract with the Pureblood Registry on behalf of the noble family Remeni-Masson."

The girl dipped her knee and near twisted her head off trying to catch a glimpse of us while keeping her eyes down. "'Crost the yard, sirs . . . lardships. Straight past troughs and slabs and up to the deadhouse." Her voice grated like steel on slate. "You'll likely find him inta sargery off right, or round left and out ta the Hollow Ground or the Render. We're plowin' bones today."

Surely such abrasive, awkward diction could not have its origin in one of such ethereal form. And *plowing bones* . . .

Mired in disgust and disbelief, I'd not gleaned the least idea of where we were to go next. I'd never visited a public necropolis. Fortunately Leander kept a clearer head. He led us briskly across a broad, flagged courtyard toward an imposing stone block of a structure. The deadhouse, the girl had called it—a prometheum more like, a hall where the dead could be tended with proper ceremonies. But what was the Hollow Ground, the Render, or a sargery?

On the other hand, *city of the dead* was a more accurate term than I'd ever imagined. Men, women, and children of every sort milled about the courtyard—singly or in groups—babbling, wailing, whispering, clinging to one another in gaudy displays of emotion. Indeed, the noise astonished me. Donkeys brayed. Hammers pounded wood here, hollow metal there. Water dripped and sloshed and trickled through stone sluiceways running under our path and around every side, while somewhere inside or beyond the formidable edifice ahead of us a choir chanted Karish plainsong as serene as divine Idrium itself.

The cart road split to either side of us, while we continued across the flagstone court toward the prometheum. Discipline required my eyes be fixed straight ahead, but peripheral sight hinted at merchant stalls nestled to the walls, where hawkers bellowed the virtues of oils and unguents or touted the skills of Ledru the Coffin Maker or Eason the Stonewright. To either side of us, servitors in russet tunics bent over stone tubs or clustered round a few of the stone tables lined in ranks, dealing with their . . . occupants. Younger boys or girls perched on ladders, tending great bonfires that roared and snapped in stone cauldrons, creating pockets of heat despite the ice wind blowing through the close.

"Hold back, slugwit!" yelled a gaunt, grizzled bald man in a stained apron as we neared the wide steps of the prometheum. He waved at someone behind us, where iron cart wheels rattled on the rough paving.

"Sane man don't drag a deadcart 'crost a processering. Not with magical folk. Cripes!" The willowy girl's grating mumble preceded her own appearance pelting down a side path and up a ramp to reach the prometheum portico before us. She caught her breath just in time to pose beside the door and wave us under the carved lintel. Her draperies fluttered as might those of fair Erit, goddess of clouds.

The incongruities of the girl's speech, manner, and appearance—and this noisy maelstrom in a place of the dead—struck me so hard just then that I came near exploding in laughter. By the Mother, Juli was right. I had acted the lightning-struck ox since walking out of the Registry the previous morning. The humiliation of my dismissal was wretched, and being pawned off on a necropolis was not at all the future I'd planned. Indeed, my duties here must surely be vile and demeaning. But I was not *afraid*. These living seemed no different from crude and noisy ordinaries anywhere. And the dead held no terrors for one of the blood. I believed in neither ghosts nor phantasms, neither demon gatzi nor glowing blue Danae who wandered the wilds and stole ill-behaved pureblood children from their beds.

In much better humor, I marched on as our "processering" swept through the prometheum door.

The thick stone surround silenced the courtyard babble. Trickling water echoed in a profound quiet, and faint strains of the Karish plainchant hung in the rounded vault along with the pungent scent of ysomar, the favored ointment for the dead.

In the way of all edifices built to strike awe in the human heart, the prometheum rotunda was grand. Blazing torches revealed vaulted ceilings, monumental statuary, and larger-than-life murals of gods and angels and human figures of all sorts. Yet the paints that had once shimmered with color were now sorely faded. And the statues were of a crude and common sort, not at all the lifelike renderings pureblood sculptors had produced in the last decades of Eodward's reign.

A strident whoop and a burst of laughter quickly hushed shattered the shabby solemnity. Two young men, the elder dark-haired and lean, the younger short, soft, and fair, ducked their heads. Though their heads were bowed, hard breathing and smothered spasms bespoke an aborted wrestling match in the shadowed niche just inside the great doors. Until they glanced up at me and their jaws dropped.

Leander peered past the two. "Bastien de Caton?"

Customary respect should have had Coroner Bastien awaiting our arrival under the portico. To greet us inside trod the bounds of propriety—a kind of boasting, demonstrating his mastery of a pureblood. But not even to be waiting here . . . The man must be as brazen as a Ciceron pickthief or as ignorant as a brick to put himself so in jeopardy of legal censure.

The elder of the two—a tall, clear-skinned man with a dark, bold gaze—pointed to a corridor that plunged through the smoke-dulled mural before us.

Beyond the mural, we passed a number of private preparation rooms awaiting the noble dead. My attention remained fixed ahead, where the white-clad cloud goddess had somehow got ahead of us. Again posed in a graceful stillness, she held open a door to a vaulted colonnade.

Leander's sharp inquiry resulted in a whispered, "Through here and rightward, lordship. Bastien's ta the Render just now, huntin' dead murders."

Yet indeed we had no need to search out this mysterious Render nor discover what *huntin' dead murders* might signify. Winter daylight streamed through the arches to either side of the colonnade, illuminating a thickset man in a heavy wool shirt, leather tunic, and thigh-length boots. He stood square in our path, fists on hips and scowling at us from amid a tangle of sand-colored hair. Fog or steam or smoke, bearing a stench so foul as to leave me unwilling to take another breath, wreathed him as if he were some gatzi lord from Magrog's netherworld.

"You're late." His voice rumbled the stones.

CHAPTER 3

"I told that Registry woman I required promptness."

My new master rudely stood his ground. No shred of respect before five sorcerers. Indeed, his acid tone likely removed yet another layer of paint from the funereal scenes peeling from the colonnade ceiling.

Leander detached a scroll from his belt and boldly stepped forward into the malodorous fog. "Bastien de Caton, I have the hon—" His announcement dissolved into a choking gag.

The man snatched the scroll from Leander's hand. "I'd best not find some magical skullduggery has changed the words since the terms were agreed. Heard that's been done time to time. But I'm the king's man round Caton, well versed in the law, not an ignorant villein ready to grovel, as you likely think."

"I—assure—you—" Leander's retching coughs near made me gag as well.

"So which one of you is bound to me?" Bastien scanned the contract scroll, glancing up just in time to get his answer. Scarlet-cheeked Leander, incapable of speech, waved a finger at me.

Taking shallow breaths, I stepped out from my escorts.

We were of a height, my new master and I, though his shoulders, arms, chest, and thighs were likely twice my bulk, and appeared . . . solid. Quite solid.

My spirit's momentary elevation was well damped.

"Hmmph." He grunted and dropped his gaze to the contract again. "Take off the mask."

By this time, a blur of faces gawked from the side gates through the nasty fog. I'd no time to feel my way with this fellow. Rules were rules. Best stand my ground from the beginning.

"No," I said. "I cannot. With all respect, Master Bastien." I inclined my head in his direction and touched my fingertips to my forehead.

His head jerked up and he met my gaze. Gold-brown eyes, keen as a lance point, pierced my own. Any idea that this man was foolish, ignorant, or in any way malleable fled.

His curt nod was very like that of a smith judging the quality of raw iron as he decides how to heat and pound it. And then a grin—not at all a friendly grin, to my mind—spread from one side of his broad, hairy face to the other. He tapped the contract scroll across his wide palm. More than ever, I wished I'd had the opportunity to glimpse its terms.

"So that's to be the way of it," he said. "Dismiss your party, *Servant* Remeni-Masson. Take a deep breath and taste your future. Then we'll see how you can profit me."

Matters were not so simple as Bastien's wish. Dame Fortuna was kind, and Leander was able to throttle the urge to vomit. He politely informed the coroner that there was yet one small matter to deal with before his party could leave. To be precise, the fee.

Bastien snorted. "So the Registry must touch my coin first—take its portion before the sorcerer pockets it and accuses us ordinaries of cheating. Very wise. Keeps things in order. We needs must traipse inside to fetch it, though. Not going to risk dropping a purse into a dead-pit, am I? None of you lot would care to fish it out of a five-year bone stew."

Brisk as a storm wind, the coroner strode past us into the prometheum, trailing the foul smoke behind him.

Though Leander's exposed features remained properly uncommunicative, the brow behind his red silk mask rose in wary alarm. My own skill at dual expression was well practiced, yet I did not respond. I didn't trust myself to confine my opinions behind the mask. Mostly I was anxious to judge the weight of the purse. I'd no hope of a luxurious stipend, but my family's future depended on a decent one. At my nod, we reversed course and followed.

Bastien's destination was a low-ceilinged corner chamber, crowded with a writing desk, stools, a scuffed worktable holding a counting board and a wax tablet, and a honeycomb map case filled with rolled parchments. A press gaped open, its shelves neatly ordered with inkhorns, a stack of smaller wax tablets, another of parchment pages, and a few oddments impossible to make out in the dull light.

Leander halted in the doorway. Bastien snapped a loop of keys from his belt and crouched in front of a black iron chest. A snick of the lock, a reach inside, and the coroner sprang to his feet. A gray lump shot across the room toward us.

He barked a laugh when the startled Leander juggled the chinking bag as if it were a burning coal. "Best not spill good coin. We'll have rats coming out the cracks and corners." He widened his eyes and lowered his voice, as if spooking children. "Mayhap dead folk'll come after it, too, hoping to snatch a copper for the Ferryman's fee."

Leander tied the bag to his belt.

My master slammed the iron lid and locked his chest. " 'Tis exactly the price agreed," he added as if he'd never been aught but sober. "I'll not take offense if you count it."

"That will not be necessary, good Bastien," said Leander, admirably recovered. "My superiors have deemed you worthy of a pureblood contract. To doubt your honor would cast doubts on their wisdom. With all respect."

The guardsman swiveled and bowed to me, touching his fingertips to his brow. "*Domé* Remeni-Masson, it has been my honor to initiate your contract with Bastien de Caton, Coroner of the Twelve Districts of Palinur. May your service do honor to your gods and enrich the lives of your master, your family, and the kingdom of Navronne. With your permission, *domé*, I shall deposit your share of the year's fee and your copy of the contract into the safekeeping of your steward."

He glanced up to see my reaction to this last arrangement. The delay in turning over the stipend was irregular, but I'd no family members present to take charge of it, and I'd not like carrying a purse of gold—a well-stuffed purse, to my relieved sight—around here all day. And to transport a year's stipend through the hirudo this evening, when I would be alone and bearing no weapon more serious than my eating knife and some minor defensive spells, would be idiocy.

"Agreed," I said. "And this as well." The same cautions bade me take off my father's ruby ring and pass it to Leander. I hoped the coroner would view it as pureblood custom and not an insult to his honor.

"Servitor Leander, you have executed your duties with exemplary efficiency, deportment, and *wisdom*. You are dismissed. Go in peace and safety." *Most especially safety.*

A pall of melancholy settled over me as I watched the four purebloods march away. The initiation of a contract should be an occasion of pride and satisfaction. My parents should be with me . . . and my grandsire. Yet how could I wish them to be in this ignoble place, breathing the fumes of decay as this coarse ordinary glared at my back, waiting for me to submit?

But I had no choices. The contract was for only one year. I could do anything for a year.

I spun in place and touched my fingertips to my forehead. "Master, you may show me my duties. . . ."

"Ready to work, eh, Servant Remeni?" Bastien tossed the contract scroll onto the worktable and propped his backside beside it. Wide, hairy hands gripped the table edge as his gaze scraped me raw from my mask to my finest leather boots. "You're set to abide by this contract? Obliged to? Every detail?"

"Yes." I would not bow or scrape or address him beyond his rank. Though I would wait for a later time to point out that *servant* was not a permissible form of address.

"You'll do what I ask of you the best you can, without arguing or mincing or weaseling around some point of law to avoid it? Just as if I were the king himself?"

"Yes. As long as the task does not violate the terms of the contract." Registry contracts were very specific about criminal endeavors, excessive risk, or tasks that skirted the bounds of righteous behavior. My stomach shifted uneasily. I wished I'd had the nerve to eat before leaving home.

Bastien settled his back to the wall, gleaming eyes fixed to mine—both of mine. Most ordinaries attended only the naked half of one's face, as if the eye peering through the mask was false or fey. His own features worked oddly, the exact expression unreadable, obscured by his excess hair. "And you're forbid to put a hex on me or use your magic in any way, save what I tell you?"

My gut tied itself in a knot. What was he planning that he had to make these things explicit?

"My magic belongs to you alone for the duration of the contract, and I am strictly bound not to spend it without your permission—whether to my own advantage or that of any other person. The contract contains a clause that exempts reasonable spending of magic in defense of myself or my family." Or it certainly should. That I'd not yet seen the document did naught for my unease. "You've been made aware that a pureblood's reserves of power are not limitless, but must be continually renewed by rest, sleep, food. . . ."

"Oh, aye. I've a notion how it works."

I nodded again. "And, naturally, no . . . hexing . . . of my master is permitted."

Bastien burst into exuberant laughter, slapping his knees and shaking his head side to side. "Mother Samele's tits! When I put in that bid five years ago, I'd have laid gold bricks to coffin nails I'd never see a pureblood sorcerer standing here in his silks and satins, ready to do my will—no matter he's got a broom handle up his ass. Garibald and Constance say you must be the most incompetent spelltwister was ever delivered of woman. But you're not, are you? You've a mot of skill in those hands. I can see that."

"I'm very— Yes. I certainly—" I stopped. Stupid to get flustered. Of course people would assume me of little worth. Sent to this awful place to fill a *five*-year-old bid. *Goddess Mother!*

I sucked in my pride and nodded. "The gods have indeed graced me with a strong bent for portraiture."

"Soon as you started talking of me owning your magic, you tucked those hands behind you. As if to keep them safe. As if to keep their best work for yourself." A frown wiped away his glee. "But you can't do that, neither, can you? No matter that these Registry folk sent you here, where you'd rather not be."

I tried to ignore the speculation in his tone. "You will always receive my best work."

"Good to get that straight." He folded his meaty arms across his chest. "Now *take off* that mask and say it again. I like to see who's I'm having a converse with."

We were alone. I slipped off the bit of silk and tucked it into my belt.

"I am a competent portraitist, Master Bastien. Some judge me better than that." My voice remained cool and empty; gods reward my parents for insisting on constant practice of personal discipline! "My family's honor and my own ensure that my contracted master will ever see the best work I can produce."

"All right, then. Good." He tilted his head, squinting fiercely. "Why wouldn't you before? The mask, I mean. Thought we might have to bust fists about that."

Every day of my life had prepared me to submit to a contracted master, and ninety-nine out of every hundred masters were ordinaries. Even so, pureblood protocols were not common knowledge among them. One could not bristle at every order just because this man was so *very* common. And fierce. And hard. Gods save me from ever needing to *bust fists* with him.

"We were not alone before. We are permitted to remove our masks when in the presence of our contracted masters or mistresses, but not when in the presence of . . . others."

"Other of us ungifted folk, you mean."

I inclined my head. A gesture left the answer less stark. I'd no wish to demean him or his associates.

"Hmmph. And if I was to say you need it off when performing your duties?"

It would likely be a mistake to remind him that my wearing the mask would proclaim to all that he now had a pureblood bound to his service. He was in no way stupid.

"If such an exemption is written into the contract, then of course removing the mask would be permissible. If not, you may apply to the Registry for such a release."

"I'll think on it." He sprang to his feet. "Come. Let's see what you can do."

Bastien rummaged in his book press, then proffered a few worn scraps of parchment and a stick of plummet. "These'll do for now. We needs must find Garibald. Doubt you can do aught with the folks I was examining when you arrived."

Parsing this last comment did naught for my belly. *Dead-pits*, he'd said. *Five-year stew.* Purebloods were laid in family tombs, but ordinaries buried in old cities like Palinur were oft dug up and their burial ground reused. The remains were boiled to clean the bones. . . .

Banishing that vile imagining, I slipped on my mask, clutched the supplies, and trailed after Bastien. The wild hair left his age uncertain, but he moved like a taut spring and his eye displayed the clarity and ambition of younger men. My inner eye—my bent that could create his true image—would judge him perhaps five years my senior—at most five-and-thirty.

We paused on the prometheum steps, while Bastien shaded his eyes and searched the anthill of a courtyard. "Garibald! Over here!"

The bald, grizzled man who had been directing traffic when I arrived waved a hand. He and a tall scrawny girl in leather breeches—none other than the donkey-voiced cloud goddess, shed of her draperies—were shifting a limp form from a cart onto one of the myriad stone tables. Two dozen tables, at the least, were set out in the courtyard, most of them occupied.

"So many dead on one morning . . ." The words slipped from my lips unbidden. The noble dead brought from fine houses would be carried straight to the quiet preparation rooms inside the prometheum. These would be poor folk delivered by their families to be washed, anointed, and buried according to their preferred customs, or those delivered by the dead-haulers that roamed the city streets and refuse heaps, hoping to earn a citré for each load of corpses.

"In truth, 'tis a quiet day, considering yesterday's troubles," said Bastien. "Once this lean winter takes full hold and the wains start rolling in from Prince Perryn's great battle, we'll have 'em piled in every corner."

The bald man and the girl spread a stained sheet over the dead man. As the two headed across the courtyard toward Bastien and me, a snap of the bald man's fingers set a boy to lighting lamps at the man's head and feet, while a jerk of his head fended off a fawning, ruddy-cheeked woman clothed in blue pantaloons who was offering him a tray of bottles and jars.

"Garibald's the sexton," said Bastien, even as I opened my mouth to voice the question. "He sorts out who gets taken inside, who stays out in the yard, who gets washed, who gets burnt, who gets coins on the eyes, who gets dug up and his bones boiled. That sort of thing."

"But I thought you—"

"Nay. I'm the king's law here. I'm needed only if there's a question about the death. Man comes in with a knife hole in his back. Woman comes in with her neck broke. Or maybe someone's dug up that oughtn't be in that burial ground when the sexton's plowing bones. Garibald and Constance see to the common work. I see to the interesting bits."

Garibald and the girl arrived at the steps. The sexton cast a disapproving glare my way. "Bought yerself a pot o' trouble, Coroner."

The girl crowed in bald delight. "You got 'im!" she said in her ear-itching squawk. "Thought sure they'd twink you out of the deal. Near swallowed my eyes when the gate oped to bloods in all their fineries." Her faded blue eyes raked me scalp to boot. "This'n's a prime looker, though his lovely duds'll look a sight first time he takes on splatter or spew. Mayhap his magic can clean him! And mayhap—"

She inhaled sharply and bent over until her nose was scarce a handspan from my chest. She examined the front of my doublet, her bony cheeks taking fire. "Can you set him to magic *us* fine garbs, too, Coroner? Pearls, that's what I'd want. Pearls like what's on his buttons. And ribbons. I do so yarn for red ribbons. And yourself'd look lordly in purple brocady next time you sit a 'quest."

Perhaps she thought the mask left me deaf and blind.

Bastien snorted. "I doubt such gifting would be among his magical skills. Remeni, this would be Master Garibald, Sexton de Caton, and his daughter and chief assistant, Mistress Constance. You will heed their commands as you do my own, save when it comes to pearls or brocades or other such *frivolous babbling*."

The girl didn't seem to mind his ferocious glare. The sexton harrumphed in disgust.

"As you say," I replied, and left it at that. Protocol forbade me offer the two ordinaries honorifics of any kind—even were I so inclined—and discouraged any speech or notice beyond my master's business, even for a girl. Well, Constance was a woman grown, truly, despite her broomstick figure and lack of manners. Close on, it came clear the bloom in her pale cheeks was more windburn than tender years. Her bony hands, stained and peeling in the cold, looked older than her father's knobby face.

Anyway, better fewer words than many, lest these hear some trace of my growing distaste for this place. I didn't like thinking what she meant by *splatter or spew*.

"Have we mysteries this morning?" asked Bastien. "I want to test him right off."

"Constable dumped a fellow last night." Garibald pointed to a corner, well away from the hovering crowds and laborers. "Hard froze. I've set him to thaw."

"Let's take a look."

The taciturn sexton waved a dismissive hand my way. "I'm back to work. Magical foolery won't get these folk out my yard." He stomped away.

Constance elbowed Bastien as we hiked across the bustling yard. "Ye're the right king of our dead-city now, sweeting," she murmured with a giggle. "Da'll be wanting to get 'isself a sorcerer."

"This fellow'd best be useful," grumbled Bastien. "If not, I've set my plans back ten years."

Sweeting? Family confidences? Ordinaries coupled in haphazard ways, as I had learned so hard. Yet, even observing these two so short a time, a match seemed unlikely.

Constance pulled open the door of a weather-worn shed in the corner of the yard beyond the merchant stalls. Smoke and warmth from a small brazier escaped quickly along with a distinct sewer odor as Bastien and the woman carried the body into the daylight.

He'd been a bulky fellow, and no beggar. The cloak that covered the most of him was scuffed and muddy, but of good, thick wool lined with dark fur.

"No blood." Constance hunched over the dead man, examining the back of his head, cloak, and legs, and pawing at his collar. "No rips in 'is clothes. No bumps or blusies."

With naught but a nod between them, Bastien and Constance rolled the man onto his back. They unfastened the cloak and tugged the shirt and scarf away from his neck.

Still no blood or obvious wounding. But someone had tied a linen bandage over his eyes. Most Navrons believed the soul resided in the eyes. The priests of the Elder Gods said the soul could escape this world only through earth or fire, impossible if it was lost to the air before the body was buried or burnt.

I wasn't so sure about souls or their exact location. My own essence seemed scattered in bits and pieces, sometimes floating free, most times bound to other people. For certain a piece of it had died in the fire at Pontia. And another had been stolen by a passionate voice, green eyes, and cool fingers. Some days I couldn't seem to locate much of it at all . . . save when I used magic.

Though most purebloods claimed magic had its source just behind the eyes, my own bent seemed to originate just below my breastbone, flowing upward like hot wine through my chest, around back and shoulders, and down my arms. Magic was surely a part of the soul as well.

"What's his story?" Bastien squatted across from Constance, watching her bony hands skim expertly through the folds of the dead man's cloak, shirt, doublet, and braies. They came up empty.

"Constable said he were found in a nasty little hidey off Doane's Alley in the Stonemasons' District." She yanked off the man's gloves. He wore no rings or bracelets, and his shirt cuffs were worn and filthy. "Wouldn't ha' been found yet if a stonecutter hadn't spied someone live in there with this'n, a body what run off soon as he heard the cutter yell. None knew the dead 'un in the streets roundabout. But 'tis not so likely he just froze dead with such a delectable cloak on him."

"He's lost his weapons," I offered. The empty scabbard and sheath at his belt were old-style and plain, but well oiled. "Dropped or stolen?"

"Aye. His purse, too," said Bastien, fingering a silver cord dangling empty from the man's waist. Cut, certainly. "But he still has cloak and boots. No family blazon, lest he'd one on his purse, sword, or dagger."

The coroner took up the man's hands, examining back and palm, and each thick finger and its fingernail. He yanked open the man's mouth, pulled out his tongue, and sniffed at it. "No signs of poison, though none could say how long he's been dead in this cold. There's recent scrapes on his knuckles, so he'd been in a bit of a fight, but for certain he was no stonemason. Never saw one didn't have calluses or scars on his hands. And he's too well dressed. Hey, Constance! Cloak's too big for you. It'd take a full-size man to fill it up."

Constance jerked her hand away where she'd been fondling the thick fur. "*None* gets the cloak till we find who he is. You know Da's rules. Have you told your sorcerer the rules?"

"Ah, pureblood's got finer than this." Bastien paused his examination long enough to glance up at me, jerking his head at the materials in my hands. "So draw him, servant. I paid five years' living for you. Folk pay well to know how their kinsmen die, who did the deed, and where they're laid. Folk pay to know their enemies are dead, or their neighbor's farm has no man to work it anymore. Nobles pay decent. Merchants pay better. And if they learn the news before rot sets in, they pay more. King pays me, too. A fee to find out who's been murdered, and extra if I point his magistrates at the villain what did it. I've tried sketchers before, but I learned right off that none are good enough that a man could recognize his own mother. But pureblood drawings are said to be the same as truth. Show me truth."

So much about this—their crude handling of the dead man, Bastien's venality—appalled me. Yet the questions, the mystery, were fascinating. I picked up a broken roof tile and sat cross-legged where I wouldn't shadow the dead man's face. Spreading one of Bastien's scraps of parchment on the slate, I laid down a few lines with the gray plummet—appropriate for the gray-blue skin. The fellow was a decade older than Bastien, perhaps five-and-forty. And he was not half so fit. His chin was soft, his nose pitted—swollen and red I'd guess, before death and frost had sapped his color. A sinner's nose, folk called it.

Constance pulled the bandage from the dead man's eyes. Small eyes, close set and slightly askew. I sketched quickly, smudging the plummet to mime the dark patches beneath his eyes, and again to shape the heavy brow. A scribble mimed the old scar on one temple. The image took shape, adequate for common sketching, but for the rest . . .

My hand paused. In the usual way, I would speak with my subject, triggering my inner sight through his voice or some meeting of the eye. Or it might be the way the person laughed or carried herself that sparked my magic. But this man had no voice, no spark, and I had no lifetime's trove of memory to plumb, as when I sketched my dead grandsire. That left only touch.

Goddess Mother, he was cold. My left fore- and middle fingers traced the slack line of his jaw, the thick shelf of his brow, the cheekbone buried deep under frost-hard flesh, the cool, spongy lips. Disgusting.

Swallowing hard, I shoved aside thought and opened that place behind my breastbone where neither reason nor logic, happiness nor horror held sway. Enchantment surged from that dark reservoir in all its glory, infusing the lines, shapes, and textures my left hand explored and creating an image inside me. The erupting fire flowed through bone and sinew into my right hand, building in power until the stick of plummet trembled.

When my chest felt like to burst, I released the pent magic and began to refine my crude sketch. Sound and sensation fell away. There was naught but the image shimmering inside and the enchantment flowing through my hand. . . .

After a time I sat back and assessed the work. Plummet was much too limited. Its marks were faint and its line unvarying. Ink was far more versatile, flowing from brushes or pens of every possible dimension. Yet indeed the man looking back from the page was the man before me. A touch released a bit of magic to plump his lips and reveal the tip of that horrid tongue between them. Another gave a fullness to his cheeks and sagging jowls. Yet another brightened the death-dulled eyes, narrowed the lids, and installed a few fine creases at their corners. He had a habit of squinting. A bit more flare to the sinner's nose. Dissipated.

As I used my bent to ensure the drawing matched the true image in my mind, Bastien knelt watching, hands stilled, attention unwavering. When the work was as complete as I could make it without ink or brush, I passed him the page.

He studied it intently.

Sat back on his heels.

Said nothing. His eyes remained fixed on the scrap a very long time.

"Plummet is convenient, but much too limiting," I said, unable to wait longer. "I can render it more accurately with pen and ink. A thin wash of color works even better. It *is* a likeness. But I can't make it speak, if that's what you want."

His moment's glance near stripped me bare. But he turned away to Constance. "Fetch a runner, girl. I want him to show this to whatever whores ply that alley of a midnight or have a crib nearby, even if they work different streets. Find especially any known for hard play. And send Pleury to fetch the barber. The fellow's mostly thawed. We need to take a look inside before he warms up too much more."

Whores? The barber . . . the *sargery* . . . Great Deunor, a barber-surgeon was going to cut into the dead man's body? My mouth worked in speechless protest.

"Should I bind his eyes back now?" Constance waggled the bandage.

"I'd say yes," said Bastien softly, shaking his head and staring at the portrait, "but I doubt there's need. I think his soul has already been snatched out of him."

CHAPTER 4

His name was Valdo de Seti. We knew it before the midday bells rang. Bastien's runners identified him using the portrait I'd made—and whatever had sparked Bastien's whim to seek out low women.

De Seti was the chief steward of the draymen's guild and, indeed, his favored harlot had a den off Doane's Alley. He himself lived in the Wainwrights' District with a wife and one of three sons—a boy of eleven years. The two elder were off fighting for Prince Perryn.

Chortling in glee as his runners delivered their reports, Bastien issued a summons to both wife and whore, as well as the son, the constable, the stonemason who had discovered the body, four other neighbors, and Valdo's two fellow stewards in the guild. They were to attend him in his judgment chamber no later than fourth hour past midday. The *'quest* Constance had mentioned was an inquest—the coroner's official inquiry into the circumstances of a suspicious death.

As we awaited the witnesses, Constance stripped and washed de Seti in one of the troughs in the courtyard. Then two of Garibald's workmen laid him in a chamber just inside the prometheum doors. It was a barren little cell, its four walls thick with layers of limewash. Easy to see why. The bier, the floor, the small wheeled table, and the pile of wadded linens in the corner were splattered with a disgusting panoply of morbid stains. This was where they cut them.

I pressed my back to the wall beside the door, as far as I could get from the bier.

"You're a putrid shade of green, servant," said Bastien. "You *do* know purebloods shit and die and stink like the rest of us?"

"You can't just slice into a man's body," I said. "The Elder Gods forbid it. How do you know—?"

If the soul could escape through uncovered eyes, how could it not find its way out through an incision? My fist pressed on the tail of my breastbone, where my magic lurked. To be lost in this world, unable to participate in either this life or whatever awaits us beyond, must surely be a horror worse than Magrog's netherworld of fire and ice.

Bastien stepped aside as a scolding Constance and two boys hauled in jars of water and a stack of battered tin basins, setting them beside the table.

"Law gives me the right when there's a question," he said when the storm of noise had passed. "The duty, even. But if it eases your mind, I've had the Mother's high priestess sanctify this room. She laid pureblood magic and temple blessings about it, and said the souls can't escape if we close the door and turn all the vessels upside down before we open it again." He leaned close and dropped his voice. "Besides, I have 'em sewed up after."

He chuckled and laid a genial boot into a slack-jawed boy who was peering in from the atrium to gawk at me.

Bastien had not eased my mind in the least. Nor was I soothed when a slight, unshaven man, carrying a tattered leather case, appeared in the doorway. His dark hair was a greasy tangle, his eyes burnt-out hollows. "Heard you've work for me."

"Ah, Bek! I want this done quick. He's no wounds we can see, but someone's cut off his purse and snatched his weapons. . . ." Bastien reeled off the sum of his observations and all we had learned of Valdo de Seti. "Just need to make sure we're not missing something obvious before the widow arrives. Though she's not pounced on us wailing, as some do. I've a notion this Valdo was not a likable man."

The surgeon's shoulders drooped. "So, the body's claimed, then. Too bad."

His voice was low and surprisingly clear, considering the reek of spirits about him and his unsteady gait as he crossed to the table. He set his case on the wheeled table and opened it. His hands shook as if he suffered a palsy.

Bastien slapped the man's back. "Soon as wounded come in from these quarreling princes' battle, we'll doubtless have a Moriangi or five mixed in by mistake. Mayhap even a Hansker mercenary. You can slice mongrels to pieces as your heart desires. Some folk say Hansker have no balls. Some say they've three balls, but no heart. Do you think that's so?"

"*Some* folk believe burying a live cat at the full moon will cure their crabs." The surgeon picked a short saw blade from his case and set its tip just below de Seti's throat before glancing over his shoulder at Bastien. "You've a good enough mind to know—"

He lowered his blade and fixed his sooty gaze on me. "What have we here?"

Gray threaded the surgeon's hair, and creases seamed a narrow face neither so old as I expected, nor so degenerate. Yet my blood curdled at a man who spent his days cutting flesh—living or dead—much less one who took pleasure in it.

"I've bought me a luck charm," said Bastien, grinning. "Better days coming to Caton."

"If you think a sorcerer can raise the dead to life again or squeeze out where their gold's hid, I've a few bits of anatomical learning to share with you." The surgeon's quiet speech dripped irony.

"Ah, Bek, when you're done here I'll give you a sight of what the fellow can do. Mayhap you'll rethink your tawdry bits of learning. Or pay me to have him redraw that anatomical map you carry about."

They spoke as if I were a dead man or one of the statues in the prometheum rotunda.

It had been the same in Montesard. Pureblood discipline had forbidden me to break silence to exchange ideas with my tutors or fellow students, which sorely hampered my learning. Once the strangeness of my presence wore off, the others talked in just such fashion, which made matters even worse. But one day in our tutorial session, Morgan, she of the green eyes, had wondered aloud whether *those who refused to speak in session* might be required to write out their opinions, arguments, and questions. The tutor could read them aloud so that all might benefit from a new perspective. And so we had done. The others yet spoke as if I weren't there, but they spoke of me by name. *Lucian believes . . . Lucian wonders . . .* It had worked exceedingly well.

Cheating, Investigator Pons had called it. *Compromise of your position in life. Unvirtuous engagement with ordinaries . . .*

"Just don't share your opinions with him, bone-cutter," said Bastien. "Nor your ale nor your vermin nor your secret vices. Don't even look at him. I don't want Registry lackwits finding an excuse to snatch him back. Not only did his little sketch identify our corpse to the folk who knew him, it told me where to look; Valdo de Seti yearned for nasty pleasure."

The surgeon snorted, wiped his brow on his sleeve, and turned back to his morbid work. His hands stopped their trembling as he began. Mine did not.

I bolted. Outside the surgery, I poked the plump youth dozing on the bench—Pleury, Bastien's runner, the lad who'd found the whore. "Clean drinking water?"

Though loath to ingest anything in such a place, my stomach was going to grind itself to pulp if I didn't get something inside it.

"Great lordly sorcerer . . ." The fair-skinned youth with an affliction of pustules on his cheeks dropped to one knee, near yanked his forelock from his scalp, and bent his back until his chin grazed the floor, as if I were some combination of god, noble, and demon gatzé all in one. The dramatic effect was entirely spoiled when he passed wind with the timbre of a royal trumpet.

With a distressed moan, he prostrated himself completely.

A ghostly memory of my younger brothers and certain secret "jousting tournaments" twitched my lips. "Clean water?" I said evenly.

"Fonts, troughs. Comes straight from the wellsprings. So Garibald says."

"Good. All right, then." Relieved, I escaped to the small font I had seen in a bay near the royal preparation room. A tin cup sat on a waist-high shelf beside the little font.

Palinur's wellsprings were a source of wonder. The intricate system of ducts and pipes that brought the highland water into the city had been installed by my clever ancestors, invaders from the Aurellian Empire. Aurellians had overrun the lands of Ardra, Morian, and Evanore centuries past, only to discover that their minor magical talents took fire with power here. They had called Navronne the Heart of the World.

The fonts and ducts had endured far longer than the conquest. Even Aurellian magic could not stave off the crumbling decadence of the empire itself, or hold its expansive territory against the heirs of mighty Caedmon, King of Ardra. Caedmon had united three ever-warring provinces and created Navronne.

Three hundred Aurellian families swore allegiance to Caedmon and his heirs in return for freedom to pursue their magic as they saw best in service to Navronne. They called themselves the Registry. Their negotiations ensured that pureblood contracts, breeding rules, and protocols would be enforced by the Crown. When Caedmon's great-great-grandson

Eodward drove the last Aurellian legions out, the Registry, including my own ancestors, had remained.

The cool water soothed my churning belly. I rinsed the cup, returned it to the little shelf, and sagged against the wall. Both passage and bay were deserted. The prometheum was quiet, the trickle of the font soothing. Sleep had eluded me the previous night. My eyelids drifted shut. . . .

"Still squeamish?"

I startled, whacking my elbow on the protruding shelf. Though a big man, Bastien had crept up on me without a sound.

"I've no skills to aid such activities," I said, wincing as I rubbed my elbow. "I could use the time to reproduce de Seti's portrait in ink. If you have archives . . ."

"There's other tasks more pressing. Anywise, you don't have the original to copy. Come along."

"I don't need it. The true image remains with me for a while."

He paused mid-departure. "You can draw it again exactly, without the face in front of you?"

"Yes."

"As many times as I might want?"

Prideful fool. I oughtn't have mentioned it. Copying was a tedious chore. Pureblood families often requested ten or twenty copies of their son's or daughter's anniversary portraits to pass around to families who might provide suitable marriage partners.

Bastien waited, his brows raised high enough to take flight on their own. He had shown himself most perceptive, and I had pledged my family's honor to this contract. Besides, I'd never been a good liar.

"Yes. But for three days at most. After that, I would need to retrieve the true image by touching the original portrait. I could then copy it or determine if anyone had tampered with it."

"Hmmph. Useful." His not-quite-a-smirk was immensely irritating. "But not now. Constance sent word we've another mystery."

Shuffling off annoyance, I clutched my parchment scraps and plummet and followed him into the courtyard.

Our new mystery was a girl child of eight or ten summers. Her tunic and leggings were little more than sacking. Her dark hair was chopped off short. Though disease and harsh winter hit the poorer ordinaries very hard, she looked neither wasted nor ill. Had it not been for the scrapes and black streaks on cheeks and brow and the mud all over—from tumbling into the ditch where she was found, so Constance surmised—and her unnatural pallor, one might have thought her a healthy child, asleep.

"She were found in the hirudo ditch next the piggery," said Constance, scratching her ear vigorously as if a bug had flown into it, "but none claimed to know her. Demetreo, the headman, swore it so when he had her brought here, with his honorable complinations to the coroner. Not that we'd believe a Ciceron's barbling any more'n a frog's spit. But she don't have the visible of a hirudo kind, no matter her garb."

"Aye, look at her hands," said Bastien, brushing dirt away. "No hirudo child."

Her fingernails were broken, with a thin rime of dirt underneath, but her hands were smooth and plump. And when the coroner pulled the tunic away from her neck, he grunted and spat. "No mystery as to her dying, neither."

Blue-gray bruises around her neck showed the very spread of the fingers that had strangled the life out of her. Bastien glanced up at me. "You've no magic can tell us whose hands made these marks, do you?"

I shook my head. Not even a bent for history, fully practiced instead of a lifeless stump between my eyes, could pull such a revelation out of the air.

"Then bestir yourself, pureblood. We're like to get no bounty from her family, but catching a dastard who's murdered without provocation tots up a decent fee."

Revulsion left me incapable of speech. The slim, pale neck could have been Juli's but a few years ago, or the innocent flesh of my young cousins who died screaming in the fire at Pontia. I already hated this place, this life, this despicable world of ordinaries.

Dispensing with preliminary sketches, my left hand traced her cold cheeks, her violated neck, smooth hands, and ragged hair. Then I reached deep into my bent. . . .

The bawling, clattering business of the city of the dead faded. War and winter vanished. Past horror, present anger, and anxiety about the future fell away. My senses were aflame with magic that seared a river of fire through bone and sinew, engraving the image of the murdered child upon my spirit and pouring through my fingers onto a flimsy scrap of animal skin.

Other images intruded. Bare white bones. Sinuous threads of silver. A heaving grayness streaked with moonlight. Odd. Cursing distraction, I shrugged them off and plunged deeper.

Time lost shape, but at some point well in, an urgency forced its way into my awareness, and a blur swept between my eyes and the page like some great insect.

I growled and shooed it away. I was not yet done. There was so much to convey.

"Remeni!" At the brittle utterance of my name, someone yanked the page from under my hand. The loss of connection doused my frenzy like cold rain down my neck.

"Give it back! It's not done." My right hand shook with pent urgency. I squeezed my eyes shut as if I could hold on to the vanishing lines and curves. But lacking a knot of completion, I could not hold on to the true image even for a few moments. Without touching the page, I was blind to my creation.

"We've guests arriving."

Coroner Bastien crouched beside me, though he sounded as if he were at the bottom of a well. The yard was as quiet as the stone halls of the prometheum. Constance stood on the far side of the bier, holding her cloud-goddess cloak spread wide as a tent, as if to shield Bastien and me from the wind. Her pale eyes had grown to near half her thin face.

I shook my head to clear it. "I should finish it now," I snapped. "Details come sharper on the first connection. What's wrong?"

"Naught, I trust," spat Bastien, mouth twisted into a sneer. "But you're going to work inside the prometheum from now on. You attract far too much interest." He snatched the stick of plummet away. "We'll speak of it later. For now you stay with me."

The portrait wasn't right. But without examining it, I'd no idea why. The image burning inside me would not manifest without my hand in contact with the page. In the main, I was pleased not to be constantly plagued with all the faces I'd drawn, but an unfinished work irritated like grit in a raw wound.

Constance bawled for a yard boy to bring a sheet. As they covered the child and carried her away, Bastien's expression, only half-masked by his unruly hair, was entirely grim.

"Now," he said, once we were alone, "I've a whore to question, and the other witnesses are dribbling in. Best you see how we do things. But don't think you'll escape this contract, no matter how much you dislike it."

Dull and shivering, I followed him across the yard. Never had it taken so long for my senses to clear. But then, I'd been very deep in the work and wasn't used to being interrupted. What had set Bastien off about the contract?

And how long had I worked? The light was failing. Snow drifted from lowering clouds, vanishing into the fire bowls with a quiet hiss. A few of the biers were draped with yellowed sheets, their occupants abandoned, but most were empty. Hours, then. Two, at least.

Something was wrong. I pressed a fist to my forehead. Enchantment smoldered like a snuffed torch behind my eyes.

"If you're dissatisfied"—I matched my stride to the coroner's—"I need to see the portrait to perfect the details." Interrupted while drawing a living subject, I could always insist on a new sitting. But the dead must be burned or buried in a reasonable time, identified or not, and even if held back, I'd no idea how long a dead face would resemble a human person's, much less its living antecedent's.

"Later," snapped Bastien. "And you'd best have answers. That contract gives me remedies if you trick or deceive."

"I've never—" But he was clearly in no mood to listen. What was he talking about?

My steps dragged as I crossed the smoky yard behind Bastien. Gods, how I wished to be home, bathing away the stink of this place!

Most of the vendors had gone. The coffin maker's girl huddled on a stool outside his stall. The purveyor of oils and unguents, pantaloons sagging in the damp, engaged in excited conversation with two of the yard workers. Their attention was fixed on the main gates.

I kept my head down into the sharp north wind, uninterested in any newcomers.

"Coroner!" Garibald's sharp hail halted Bastien. Like an obedient donkey I paused, as well.

The sexton cast a blistering glance my way and shook a dirty finger toward the gates. "Seems your prize has a visitor already—another spell-twister what refuses to step out the gatehouse."

"Damn and blast!" Bastien whirled about, spitting daggers. "Who is it?"

I shrugged, mystified.

"This inquest is a pot boiling up," snapped the coroner. "I must be there to stir it, and I want my expensive pureblood at my side. So be this the First Curator or your revered granny, get rid of him."

CHAPTER 5

Garibald grumbled all the way to the gate. "Someone had best tell the high and mighty that us around here have work to attend. I'm no runner to carry messages."

Speculating wasn't going to soothe the sexton. Perhaps Leander had decided to see me safely home. I couldn't imagine what other pureblood might have followed me to this vile place.

I entered the gatehouse alone. The growing dark revealed only a bulky man in a thick, ankle-length pelisse. But when he turned, recognition shocked me out of mind. "Master Pluvius!"

"Discipline, lad! We do not speak names in a den of ordinaries."

"My sincerest apologies, master. I just—I never expected to see you here."

A Registry curator at Necropolis Caton? No pureblood in the world would expect that. Yet hope struck embarrassment and astonishment aside. *This was all a mistake. He's taking me back.*

"I needed to speak with you privately, Lucian. To express my outrage at . . . this." His gesture at the view beyond the gate completed his thought. "Your talents will be sorely missed in the Archives."

If such words spoken through clenched teeth were not enough to blight my greening hope, the morose head shaking and sympathetic clucks that followed certainly sufficed.

"I'm glad to hear it was not poor work, *domé*." Manners were hard to come by.

"Certainly not. Had Albin allowed, I would gladly have taken on the duties as your negotiator."

"I appreciate that, master." Though it seemed unhelpful that he would say it here, rather than in front of Pons and Albin. "It would be enlightening—Master, why was I dismissed?"

"Curators' deliberations cannot be shared. To come here and imply that our decision was not unanimous is violation enough. But when your grandsire contracted you to the Registry, I took it as a personal contract as well—to see to your development as an artist and as a man."

Pluvius had always been complimentary about my work and supportive as I dealt with our family difficulties, but he had never directed any particular attentions my way beyond suggesting I keep my clothes clean. And though he was forever looking over my shoulder, he'd had little mentoring to provide. He was a historian, not an artist.

"If I just understood—?"

"I will do my best to see this situation remedied. But I have to warn you—"

His hesitation left me teetering on a ledge for a very long while. What could be worse than this shameful fall?

"Warn me, *domé*?" I said at last.

He blew a long displeasure.

"Maintain exemplary discipline and detachment, Lucian, and strict control of your . . . talents. Rumor could cost you everything." His thick-gloved hands squeezed my shoulders. Then he strode toward the gate.

Before I could possibly respond without screaming, he paused and glanced over his shoulder. "Oh yes, did you leave anything behind in the Tower? Access will be difficult with this new contract and all. I'll be happy to have your things sent round."

Confused at the abrupt shift, it took me a moment to think what he meant. Pens, I supposed, brushes, my favored inks that I'd bought for myself.

"No. Nothing." I'd taken everything home.

"All right, then. Be sure we'll find our way through." With a nod, he was gone.

Knowing Bastien's boot was tapping, I'd no leisure to consider this frustrating encounter. It was good to hear I had a sympathetic advocate in the Tower. But as I hurried away, Pluvius's kind reassurances and abortive warnings lodged in my gut like bad meat.

. . .

Constance, adorned in her white robes again, stood beside a bier near the prometheum steps like a divine guardian. A straw-haired girl in a dirty red cloak fidgeted alongside her.

Bastien jerked his head when I joined him, and he pointed to a nearby column, one of a row of them, each topped by a flaming bowl. "Keep close enough to hear, but avoid making a distraction of yourself, if you can tolerate such a state."

I moved into the ring of shadow beneath the fire bowl. Why did I need to be here? These people's business was none of mine. Pluvius's visit was a reminder. Purebloods purposely lived apart from the world. Our lives were not our own.

"First we see if our lady of the night recognizes our corpus." Bastien stepped into the light and twitched a finger at Constance.

A shrouded body lay on the bier. When Constance uncovered the face, the straw-haired girl spat in it. Constance grabbed the girl's hand before she could snatch the copper coins from the dead man's eyes.

The straw-haired girl wrenched her arm away. "A foul day when I told that one where I bedded," she said, sneering at de Seti. "He'd come willy-nilly and run off my other customers. He were a brute, no matter his fine clothes. Favored rough play, though it made him wheeze and sweat like a pig. Praise the Mother he's dead."

"And so you helped yourself to his purse," said Bastien, perched on the corner of the bier, arms folded as if he weren't sharing the seat with a dead man. "Can't blame you for that."

"The scabby prick plunger were alive when he left me three nights ago," the girl snapped. "So you can just stuff that idea. Did I take his purse, I'd not be wallowing in that shitehole where they found me, now, would I? I'd be moved north to the river country, where I've kin."

The girl's coarse manner jolted me. But somehow worse, she was no older than Juli . . . and a harlot. The very idea of a woman who sold her body to strangers was grotesque and appalling, but I'd never imagined one might be so young. Or so damaged; one of her eyes was puffed and livid, her wrists raw, and her lips scabbed. *Rough play . . .*

"Step aside with Garen there," said Bastien. "Soon as all my witnesses have gathered, we'll go inside, and you'll tell us all about the beast."

Garen, the lanky, dark-eyed senior runner, ushered the girl out of the way, as Bastien turned to a burly, bearded man newly arrived in the circle of firelight. "I'm Bastien, the coroner. And who might you be?"

"Ferrand, stonemason," growled the hulking fellow. His arms were the size of the stone pillar and the chest beneath his tool satchel was as wide as the prometheum steps. "Had to leave the mill early to get here, so there'd best be some use in it."

"You found the dead man in Doane's Alley yesternight."

"Aye."

"And is this the man?"

Constance uncovered de Seti's face again, this time far enough to show the black stitches that supposedly held his soul inside his pale flesh.

My throat clogged. The worries of the everyday world had kept me from dwelling overmuch on the next, but no matter the truth of gods or heaven, I believed human folk had souls to hold or lose. Even brutes.

"Aye. The very one."

"How did you happen to be there?"

" 'Tis my usual way 'tween mill and wife."

Bastien yawned and twiddled the corner of the sheeting, as if he were conversing with a taverner about naught more important than a day's brew of ale. "I understand he was tucked in a coal scrape off the alley. Whatever drew you to peek in there of a cold night?"

"A pickthief were trying to cut my tool bag off me. Happens near every night. Just as I laid into him, a second fellow bolted out the scrape. Figured that one were the thief's partner, likely his boy, as he was a squinchy thing. When I walloped the snatch and sent him running after the boy, I poked my head in the coal scrape to see if there were a third. Found this fellow."

Thieves, harlots, coal scrapes . . . Surely a "squinchy thing" hadn't murdered such a big man as de Seti.

Bastien's unblinking gaze remained fixed on the mason. "Would you recognize the pickthief or the runner?"

"I would. Wife says I've eyes like a rat in the dark."

"And did your wife enjoy the contents of this fellow's purse?"

The accusation startled me entire. Had Bastien lost his mind? The mason was clearly an upright man.

Constance hissed as Ferrand yanked a small sledge from his belt and slammed it onto the bier, jarring both corpus and coroner. "I make these tables, you know. Could break this'n if I chose. Man accuses me of stealing from the dead best be ready to lie atop one of 'em."

To his credit, Bastien did not flinch. "Good enough," he said without the least stammer. "Now stand aside for a moment, Goodman Ferrand. I do believe the constable brings the grieving family and the rest of our witnesses."

Indeed an ear-cracking wail echoed from every wall and pillar. I twisted around to see. What now? More *walloping*?

"Valdo! Oh, Valdo!"

A group of men variously dressed shuffled into the firelight, followed by a blowsy woman in black draperies. An old-style pyramid wimple covered her hair and neck. "Where is he? Sky Lord's grace, not here!"

Constance performed her role yet again, flipping the sheet down and back. The woman shrieked and collapsed across the draped body. One might easier believe the violence of her grief if half a day had not passed since she identified him from the portrait.

"Mistress de Seti and all the rest of you, I am Bastien de Caton, Coroner of the Twelve Districts of Palinur, bound by the king's law to investigate suspicious death."

The widow popped her head up and the rest of her body followed. "I understood a trull murdered him and stole his purse. Is that her?" She extended an accusing finger to the straw-haired girl on the steps. "Harlot! Murderer! How dare you stand in his presence? Why is she not hanged already? Where is my silver? *Twenty* lunae in that purse!"

"Where is your son, mistress?" Even as he spoke, Bastien spun in place and lunged toward me. I jerked backward, whacking my elbow yet again, this time on the sheltering column. But the coroner missed . . . or rather . . .

Bastien dragged a squirming body from the other side of the column.

"Young Willem," he said, "why do you lag behind in the shadows? Come, boy, step up and bid farewell to your da."

Bastien shoved the stumbling boy, also draped in black, to the bier and threw back the sheet entirely, so that all could view the dreadful sight—two great seams of black stitches holding the pale flesh together in a V shape from shoulders to groin.

Such a vile cruelty. The boy, slight and wan already, doubled over and retched miserably on his father's bier. I came near doing the same. My appreciation of Bastien's tactics—which had grown without my realizing—plummeted.

"That's the runner!" bellowed Stonemason Ferrand. "Saw him dodging out the coal scrape yesternight!"

"Who is this madman?" demanded the widow. "My son—"

"You're sure, Ferrand?" Bastien had a firm grip on Willem's collar, even as the boy puked.

"Aye. I've eyes like—"

"Like rats in the dark. Yes. Well, boy? Were you in Doane's Alley yesternight?"

A weak head shake. Bastien yanked him up, almost lifting him off the ground. As the Widow de Seti shrieked protests, he posed the question again. The boy just sputtered and moaned as the coroner rummaged inside the lad's cloak.

"Hmmph." With the satisfied grunt, Bastien held something up to the light—a dagger with a ruby in the hilt. "Well, well, what have we here—already a young master of the house? Could this be your da's dagger that went missing? I've a sorcerer nearby, you know. He could magic it and tell me where you got it. Step out, pureblood!"

Sighing, I adjusted my mask and stepped out. The boy wailed and flapped his arms as if he might escape through the air.

"Inside with all of you!"

Surely Bastien could not believe the drivel he spoke. Ordinaries had all sorts of idiotic ideas about what sorcerers could do. Though there had been a time . . . My second bent might have told him a great deal about the dagger, but that part of me was five years dead.

As the odd collection of people moved toward the steps, Bastien jerked his head at me, smirking. I followed the babbling party into the prometheum. Not reluctantly.

The inquest, held in a solemn inner chamber, was quite brief. Bastien sat at the head of a long table of scraped pine. A bronze pendant fashioned in the shape of a hammer hung from his neck—the symbol of his office, I supposed—and a wooden gavel lay in front of him. Everyone else sat on stools around the table. I remained standing near the door.

Bastien went through all the same questions, but in a clear sequence. De Seti's colleagues told of a bitter man whose strength was failing him and who tried to regain it by picking fights with everyone—his wife and sons, his neighbors, his fellow draymen, and his whore.

Bek, the surgeon, his quiet voice steady despite his palsied hands, witnessed that he found no evidence of stabbing, bruising, poison, or any other murderous ending that might evidence itself beneath a man's skin.

"Now you, boy, best tell the truth, else . . ." Bastien's wagging finger led Willem's eyes to me.

His eyes the size of inkwells, the quivering Willem told of his mother sending him to search Doane's Alley when his da failed to come home, as she'd long discovered the location of his harlot. When he returned with the news that his father lay dead in the dark little crawl off the harlot's alley, she sent him back to fetch the purse, the weapons, and his father's cloak and boots.

"I were scairt to touch him, but Ma swore I must before some beggar crawled into the hole and found him. But I couldn't get the cloak, as he were so heavy and hard froze, and before I could get his boots, some 'un yelled at me."

"And then you ran off, Willem." Bastien shook his head like the arbiter of doom. "Left your da lie there. Disobeyed the king's law that says the dead must be collected. What kind of son are you?"

"Ma said, 'Leave the whoring jackleg where you found him.'" The sniveling boy wiped his nose on his sleeve and cast an ugly glance at the straw-haired girl. "Said a slut's cesspool was a proper end."

When all was spoken, Bastien banged his gavel on the table. "It is my judgment that Valdo de Seti of the Wainwrights' District died of an attack of spleen, brought on by his rough whoring. All other matters, such as thieving from the dead and abandoning a corpse, will be reported to the district magistrate. By the authority of the king of Navronne—whoever he might be at present—I judge the Widow de Seti must turn over the purse of twenty lunae and the two weapons as fee for this investigation, which could have been avoided had Willem or his mam reported the death like honorable folk and Willem not sneaked away like a common cutpurse. Constable will retrieve the goods and bring them here to finish this matter. So say I, Coroner of the Twelve Districts of Palinur."

His gavel fell again. And so it was done.

It seemed a reasonable judgment. The witnesses scattered, the widow whining that there had only been *two* lunae in the purse, not twenty, so why didn't someone search the whore. Were I the straw-haired girl, I'd take care to know where my food came from and not to walk in my own dark alley. The evil aspects of the Widow de Seti and her sallow boy would have soured milk while still inside the cow.

As I followed Bastien down the passage to his office, my snarling stomach and soggy knees reminded me how long it had been since I'd eaten anything. Two portraits should not have drained me so, but the second . . . The magic had been extraordinarily intense.

Bastien dropped onto the stool at his writing desk. He did not invite me to sit. I didn't care. Purebloods did not sit down with ordinaries.

Watching the coroner ferret out the truth of the matter had been more interesting than I'd imagined, but I couldn't allow him to assign me another task for today, not even to complete the girl child's portrait. Though the unfinished portrait remained a raw wound, my urgency had drained away with my magic.

"Master Bastien," I said. "What time should I arrive tomorrow?"

"Dawn," he said. "We'll have a full day. But don't think you're leaving until you explain."

Maintaining calm was exceedingly difficult at so late an hour. "Explain what?"

"What were you playing at earlier, *flickering* as you did when drawing the girl?" said Bastien, biting each word as if it were a walnut. His hand waved as if to encompass the necropolis. "A place like this . . . It's taken five years to convince folk we've a mind for truth and reason, not ghosts and ghouls, and in one hour you set us back again. Everyone who saw you will be babbling Caton is demon-haunted."

"Flickering?" Bastien sounded like Constance—using a nonsense word that was close to, but not quite, one that had meaning. Yet, unlike hers, I couldn't interpret this one.

"When you were drawing the girl, you—your whole self—faded, blurred, and then sharpened up again, over and over, as if you were only partly here, partly elsewhere. Half the people in the yard were on their knees, so many palms spread against evil, Magrog's demons couldn't have slid between! Garibald swore it was just snow squalls hiding you. But it was magic, wasn't it? And you're not allowed to use magic I didn't tell you. That's a violation of the contract."

"That's impossible."

I had observed countless pureblood artists, many whose bent was far stronger than mine. None *flickered* or *faded* as they worked. Master Pluvius would hardly have ignored such a manifestation. Gilles and I had worked in the same studio for five years.

"I am *incapable* of working other magic while using my bent. Whatever you saw was exactly as you say—snow or smoking firepots or the foul vapors from your charnel house. It certainly wasn't me." Annoyance, fed by exhaustion and this petty foolery, sharpened my tone more than I liked.

The bells rang out from the city of the living. Bastien glared at me for the full span of their clanging. Nine peals. So late! Juli must be terrified at my absence.

"You swore to obey." He snarled like a wild dog. As if I were one, too.

"So you interrupted my magic and whisked the child away because you thought I was what—trying to get my contract voided by scaring your customers away? That's ridiculous and insulting. I keep my word."

All the awfulness of the day and the previous one boiled out of me—the shame, the awkwardness, the horrors and grief of the past brought so close to mind.

"Indeed, your interruption ensured I could *not* give you my best work. Perhaps *you* are trying to void my contract or work out better terms with the Registry by drumming up false accusations. Perhaps you wish me punished because I was born an Aurellian sorcerer and not a low—"

I snapped my mouth shut. *Fool, idiot, undisciplined wretch, to let him glimpse such emotional weakness.*

"But it wasn't just the magic." Bastien yanked a scrap of parchment from his iron chest and thumped it on the writing table. "You're either inept or scheming. How do you decide what to put in the picture besides the face?"

"What?" My head spun. "I don't *decide.* The magic . . . my bent . . . enables me to make a bond of the senses with my subject . . . to shape a true image of the person. If you're talking about background details, that's just incidental. An artist's instinct, some call it. I draw whatever the image suggests, whatever feels right. I don't think about those things at all."

He turned the page toward me and moved the lamp closer. But divining Bastien's purpose was the issue here, not some imperfection in my art. I gave the portrait a token glance.

But then I blinked and examined it more carefully, squinting in the shifting light. The likeness was good. The round cheeks. The small nose. But the hair . . . How had I got the hair so wrong? It wasn't chopped off ragged, but elaborately curled, pale and shining, caught up in ribbons. Her eyes were light and merry, the color of a winter sky. And her gown and cloak . . . not rough sacking, but the soft folds of satin, edged with beads and elaborate embroidery. And on her bodice . . . Idrium's Gates! Worked in pearls and shining thread in the center of her stiff bodice was a trilliot—the three-petaled lily of Navronne.

My head spun in confusion; words died unspoken. I glanced up at a grim Bastien.

"If you're setting me up to play the fool, Servant Remeni, I swear on Kemen Sky Lord's balls, you'll live to regret it. If not, then you'd best tell me why your drawing shows no dead ragamuffin, but a child wearing the mark of the royal family."

CHAPTER 6

Near an hour I spent convincing Bastien that I had no idea why I'd portrayed the child in such fashion. To explain the mechanisms of my bent as he demanded was impossible. I was baffled. And disturbed. A touch of the page assured me that the image inside and that on the page matched exactly. Of all things, my art was true. Never had any of my portraits shown such a difference in personal details as this one. And such significant ones! Certainly for the coroner to prance around the city, bellowing about strangled royal children, could not be wise. At the least he'd look the fool. At the worst . . .

All I could do was swear up, down, and sidewise that it was neither purposefully misleading nor inept. In truth the drawing was as fine as any I had ever done, no matter that it was scribed in plummet on a scrap of parchment so blotched and worn it would have been burnt in any reputable artist's studio.

"The *face* is true," I said. "Look at it. Look at the child. You'll find no better likeness anywhere. As for the rest . . . perhaps these strange surroundings warped my seeing. Or the noise. I'll start again tomorrow. I'll bring fresh parchment and work in ink." But I *knew* it was true. It was my gift, the magic I brought to my art.

Bastien tossed the drawing into his iron-bound chest and slammed the lid so hard the stack of wax tablets in the book press toppled, clattering, onto the floor. "Be here at six bells of the morning, or I'll report a violation to your Registry. The woman said your people had proper punishments for cheats and violators."

I squeezed out the only words possible without risking another outburst. "I'll be here."

My hurried steps echoed in the prometheum halls, and I burst gratefully through the heavy door into the open air. Once outside the necropolis gate, perhaps I could breathe again. I needed to get home, ease Juli's fears, eat—gods, my belly was about to devour itself—and then try to make sense of the strange portrait. The Registry punishments for contract cheats were severe, for our contracts were the sacred word of *all* purebloods. Violators could be whipped or bound to silence for months or years, or dressed in garishly colored garb and publicly displayed for days on end beside a notation of their crimes.

The fire bowls had been doused, allowing the night's cold to settle into the walled yard. Wind darted hungrily through the gatehouse, setting the torches that flanked the gate to dancing. The yard was deserted, save for Constance. She scrubbed at an empty bier in the erratic light, humming a bouncing, untuneful melody in time with her strokes. Her hands must be freezing.

She glanced up as I passed. Grinned, but did not speak. As I hiked across the snow-dusted paving, I tucked my hands into the thick fur of my pelisse.

Garibald stepped out of a dark hole in the gatehouse wall, a lantern raised high. The wavering light revealed a narrow stair behind him, likely ascending to a watch chamber above the tunnel.

"Guess he wants out." This observation was addressed to the brick wall at my left, though I was the only living person anywhere within hearing.

He unlocked the iron gate, dragged it open, and poked his head out, scanning the sky for a moment as if to assess the weather. As the gate swung shut behind me, another few words tumbled out of him. "Battle was three days north. He'll be busy the morrow. Low, nasty work. Ugly. Better he not come back."

Garibald's annoyance sparked a bitter amusement, certainly not at the thought of wounded soldiers dying in sight of home, but only at his odd interpretation of the law that forbade him speak to me. Would that I dared tell him how deeply I loathed the thought of returning here.

The gate latch clicked behind me, and Garibald's heavy steps retreated. My own feet lingered. All the turmoil of the last hours fled before the daunting prospect of my journey home.

Rarely had I ventured into such inky blackness as lay upon the land outside the walls. A few lights gleamed from the temple heights inside the city, the wind-driven snow leaving them little but blurs. A smudged fire glow wavered in the gusts scouring the field of hummocks, while odd blue flares in the distant trees teased at my eyes.

My mind produced imaginings of fae lights or the wandering Danae of my grandmother's tales. Some of her stories named the Danae tricksters. Some said they danced and mated in the moonlight to keep the earth fertile. All said their naked flesh was limned in shadings of blue. I'd loved drawing Danae as a boy, before my grandsire had declared such myths the province of the ignorant and forbade my grandmother to taint my mind with them. History, he said, must keep its steely eye on firm evidence, logic, and provable truth. The ashes at Pontia had swept away my own faith in mystical benevolence. And if Danae had ever danced to keep the earth healthy, they did so no more.

A rhythmic crunch of metal and ice gave substance to the blockish shadow moving between me and the shifty fire glow of a lantern. A gravedigger I'd seen wheeling a cart through the gates was plying his shovel. Which meant that the hummocks we'd trampled that morning . . .

No wonder the taint of death teased my senses.

Leander had said it took an hour extra to bypass the slot gate and hirudo—surely longer for one who didn't know the route. I'd collapse before arriving home. So I trod carefully between the hummocks—graves—and wished for a lamp.

Quivering shoulders and trembling hands told me how magically depleted I was. I'd not power enough to keep a magelight glowing, unless I could attach the spell to a solid object of reasonable size. The pocket tucked in the waist of my braies held naught but a kerchief. Cloth was too flimsy to hold a steady beam. I'd sent my father's ring home with Leander and wore no other jewels. My eating knife was already wrapped in wards against poisons. And I was certainly in no mind to reverse my steps and beg a torch from the necropolis. My own night sight must serve.

Midway across the burial ground, I regretted that idiocy. Though I believed I was headed for the slot gate in the wall, I couldn't be sure. The snow had petered out. The blustery blackness swallowed the overspill from Caton's torches and reduced the gravedigger's lantern to a pinprick. I trudged on until I tripped on something hard.

Kneeling up on the frozen mound, I searched the turf nervously. A frozen bone would not be so awful. Truly. Though indeed this was old ground . . . a windy height drowned in an ocean of blood. *Raiding parties seeking good vantage. Clashing swords, whining arrows, grunting fighters, and the wild yelling of a charge; roaring magefire and screams of terror, layer upon layer of wounding and death . . .*

I snatched my hands away. I had released no magic; my bent for history was long excised, naught but a charred stub between my eyes. The eerie night had but fired my imagination.

Patting lightly, I resumed the search. No fleshless bone, but a cold curve of iron had tripped me up—a closed half-circle, its diameter wider than my spread fingers. A part of my day's learning: Such cheap artifacts, graven with the deceased one's name, were used to mark poor men's graves. The iron rod would be hammered into a family blazon for those who had such, or the fish-shaped eye of the Mother for a follower of the Elder Gods, or a sunburst symbol for one of the Karish believers. But this, an arché, an empty half circle lacking so much as a name, served for one whose identity and allegiance were unknown, like the girl child whose image burned behind my breastbone.

"Hope you don't mind my borrowing this," I said softly to the mystery who slept here. "I'll bring it back tomorrow."

Using the arché, I gouged a great circle in the mound and left my eating knife in the center of it. The spells on my knife should lead me back to this grave. Now for the light.

To shape the mental pattern of my desire took less time than sketching a tree. Drawing magic to fill it, however, was wretchedly difficult. I was grasping at the dregs of my energies, a sensation much like yanking on the inside of my empty belly.

But eventually, I poured the waiting spell into the chilled iron of the arché and triggered it with my will.

A narrow white beam parted the night, as if a voiding spell had removed a shard of the darkness. Satisfaction warmed my spirit, well beyond the needs of the moment. Touching my forehead to the earth, I vowed a libation to the gods who had graced me with their gift, and renewed my coming-of-age pledge to return them service a thousandfold.

I set out again, amused to imagine what someone at the necropolis might think of the mysterious flaring light in the middle of the burial ground. Only then did I recall my obligation to forgo magic, save at

Bastien's command. If the contract lacked a personal-defense clause, this would be certain violation. But then, Bastien would likely disapprove of my breaking a leg on the descent into the hirudo.

Moving more confidently, I soon reached the wall and the slot gate. The steep descent was slower, as the muddy ruts and rocks were glazed with ice. But cautious steps took me to the pigsty with head and limbs intact.

Coal smoke thick as fog in fen country hung in the ravine. The night itself . . . the frigid air . . . all was heavy, damp, and silent, as if I were the only soul left living in the world.

I rounded the piggery with quiet steps. Perhaps I could slip through unnoticed. Or perhaps the Guard Royale had chosen this day to scour the hirudo as they did from time to time, chasing the cursed Cicerons into the wilderness.

A few quercae forward into the ramshackle warren, and the faint drone of a hurdy-gurdy and the muted rapping of a tabor testified that not all its residents slept. I imagined I heard a trill of piping as well . . . and laughter. . . .

As a fiery lance out of the blackness, grief pierced my breast. Remeni-Masson family gatherings had ever been noisy, joyful celebrations. Games and music and a generous table. Contests of strength, speed, and magic, a rare balance to the strict discipline of our daily life. I had sorely regretted the extra work that kept me away from the last one. Until the Registry messenger had come from Pontia . . .

Keep focused, fool. I muted my light to a deep red and reduced its span to the small circle of a lantern's gleam, just enough to keep me on the muddy path and away from obstacles. The hirudo night opened before me and closed down behind.

The music and merriment swelled as I passed a tarry alleyway, damped quickly as I moved on.

Soft, running steps to my left slowed my feet. I turned slowly as I walked, but glimpsed no movement.

Onward, a little faster. A swish of heavy fabric accompanied a waft of steam bearing the stink of boiling cabbage.

Just as the darker spaces between shacks and sheds grew wider and the path angled upward toward the Elder Wall and the city, my light failed. It didn't fade or dim, but just . . . stopped. I halted, puzzled. A bound spell shouldn't need constant infusion of magic to hold.

"Ye've paid no toll, masked one." The calm, low-pitched challenge came from behind—or perhaps my left.

I held still, squinting into the pitchy night. "You acknowledge my mask. You know better than to hinder me."

"But 'tis the third time this day ye've caused a trespass." He moved as a ghost might, one darker shadow against the rest, ending squarely on the path ahead of me. "Your minions twice and now yourself."

"Yet you waited to interfere until there was one alone," I said, chilling my tone as best I could. "Perhaps you imagine the penalties for interfering with a single pureblood are something less than delaying five or four. That's not at all the case. Step aside."

" 'Tis years since city guards have visited Hirudo Palinur for aught but frighting us. Dangers abound, even for such as you. But I can see to your safe passage."

"I can protect myself." My declaration sounded far braver than my jellied sinews told. I didn't know any magic that could actually hurt a determined fighter. And depleted as I was, I couldn't even confuse them with an illusion.

"Perhaps so. Perhaps no. But then, you are a wealthy man like all your kind. Is not ease of passage worth sharing a small portion of your treasure with those who've so little?"

If I'd had the wherewithal, I'd likely have paid, risking worse extortion the next time I passed. "I carry naught a thief would prize. Certainly nothing worth the trouble he'd reap did he steal it."

"See, now? There you're wrong."

Shadowy movements on every side of me were no fey imaginings. *Magrog's balls!* I invoked the arché's spell binding yet again. Why did it refuse to take fire?

"All we wish is a little magic, *Domé* Remeni, one glimpse of Idrium's glory on our dank verge of Magrog's realm. Naught to violate the law. Naught to hinder one of the gods' chosen on his important business."

Magic? Cicerons were masters at deceit and sleight of hand. Some ordinaries claimed Cicerons could work true magic. History declared that impossible, but tonight I was no better. I couldn't even spark my own light, which meant the only two defensive magics I knew—void holes beneath their feet and spits of true flame—were wholly out of reach. What did he truly want?

I could tell them that constables were on the way to join me to examine the place the dead girl child had been found. But what if they didn't believe me? Because what could a constable learn in the deeps of night? This was hugely, stupidly aggravating. Only one thing left . . .

"You lurk in the dark, refusing me a glimpse of your face." I stepped forward, listening carefully, estimating his position. "How am I to interpret such shyness? I've just spent the day with the dead, and would rather not see more of them, and I am so damnably hungry, I could eat this muck in your street. So, if you wish to take the mortal risk of turning out my pockets or snatching my boots, let's get on with it."

He laughed then. A hearty chuckle, so rich with life and menace that I felt heat beneath my breastbone. Had I pen and parchment, I could sketch him from the sound alone. Instead, I flung the heavy arché directly at that laugh.

His breathless grunt brought a smile to my face as I darted past him, speeding up the hill with a burst of strength drawn from my very marrow.

No one followed. Yet as I gripped the broken pillars at the top of the ascent, relieved and gulping air into my starved breast, robust laughter drifted out of the hirudo, and an unmistakable white fire blazed in the depths of the ravine—my own magic shining undimmed. How was that possible?

The bells pealed eleventh hour by the time I trudged across our inner courtyard, exhausted and wholly confused from the events of day and night, groaning at the thought of retracing my steps not six hours hence. I would have welcomed one of the invisible arrows of my haunted imaginings.

"Luka!" Light streamed around Juli's stark outline in the open doorway. "Where in Magrog's own hells have you been? There were fires in the Oil Merchants' District, but of course, you never deigned to tell me where you were going, and Soflet, the god-cursed wretch, barricaded all the doors when I threatened to go to the Registry to find out. He wouldn't even let me send a message. *'Unseemly,'* he said, which is the most despicable word in any language. If you don't dismiss the vile scarecrow at once, I'll put a knife in his neck while he sleeps. And now Maia's feast is ruined, and I forgot to decant the wine—"

A pause for breath revealed a sob. But when I reached for her, she recoiled. "Aagh! Get away from me! What is that stink?"

"Just let me in, Juli. Move aside."

My head weighed like a cannonball. My feet were frozen. And to think what I must smell like.

"I'm truly sorry I'm late . . . and about the stink . . . about everything. Please, I need wine, then food. Doesn't matter what. And, yes"—in our overheated reception room, everything from my frost-rimed hair to my mud-crusted boots began to drip, and the stench of Necropolis Caton rose from me like the fumes of the netherworld—"a bath first of all. If you could call Giaco and tell Maia. Please . . ."

To keep my eyes open through the wine and the bath was near impossible. At first more nauseated than hungry, and then light-headed with the stout vintage, I could imagine nothing finer than my wide bed and its thick quilts. As ever in cases of magical depletion, I had the shivers.

But I owed Juli an explanation. It had been prideful and selfish of me to leave her in ignorance.

Wrapped in a robe of padded wool and my thickest quilt, I found her in the oriel—once our mother's favorite room and now Juli's refuge. It hung out over our gardens, and its myriad window panes were the best glass in the house—astonishingly clear. Not that there had been so much to see in any garden these past few years. Unfortunately it was also the draftiest room in the house, having so many windows, no fire, and naught but air underneath the floor. A spread of overcooked fowl, a congealed pie of minced rabbit, some straggling green things, and bread—already stale—adorned a low table alongside cheese, olives, and pickled fish.

I poured half my cup of wine into the bronze libation bowl in the middle of the table. Juli did the same. We maintained the custom, though neither of us felt friendly enough with the gods to muster proper prayers.

"Thank you for this," I said, settling on the thick rug beside the table and wrapping the quilt tight enough to suppress my shivers, if not cure them. "It was impossible to eat at my new master's business. Only one of many things I didn't know . . ."

As I savaged the cold, leathery feast, I told her everything. Almost everything. Far more than I would have done if I'd not been half sotted with wine. I told her of my dismissal and my shame and Pluvius's odd visit. I told her of Bastien and Constance, de Seti and the hirudo. Good sense pricked my stupor and prevented me speaking of the strangled child or what act the barber-surgeon actually performed to determine that de Seti had not died of wounding. Everything else escaped me in a septic flood.

"That woman's voice was truly so dreadful? . . . And why did the surgeon's hands shake? Was he afraid of the dead man's spirit? . . . This Garen sounds deliciously handsome. Do you think he has an eye for Constance? . . . You said there were other girls there. What tasks did they do?"

I relished her questions. She'd not shown so much interest in anything since she'd walked up the hill at Pontia and seen our home a burnt-out ruin. Like me, she'd held some hope that the reports of horror were wrong, that someone had surely escaped. The sight had left no fantasies of hope or dream in either of us.

"I'm guessing the surgeon is a drunkard or a twistmind craving his nivat. Or perhaps he's ill. He didn't seem fearful. As for Constance . . ." I had to smile. "She is a strange one. Works very hard and is quite observant. And, well, I suppose a girl would consider Garen a goodly fellow, but he never looks at Constance in the way you mean. He's clever. Diligent. Bastien relies on him."

But Juli's mind had skipped onward. "It's good Pluvius offered to help, though I've ever thought him a fool. This Bastien likes you, doesn't he? Whatever would we do if he reclaimed the stipend? The servitor brought it, you know. Perhaps we should hide it."

The stipend! Mighty Deunor, I'd forgotten. "Where is it? And he left a copy of the contract, yes?"

"He left a scroll with the purse. They're in the counting room."

As if Karish angels lifted me with their spread wings, I was on my feet. "Stay here. I'll fetch them!"

Renewed, I raced down the stair. With even a modest stipend I could hire a bodyguard for my daily walk to the necropolis. Get new boots made that would not leave my feet like clubs of ice on such a day. Recall Juli's tutors. Set aside a marriage portion for her. Summon my old swordmaster; gods knew such skills seemed more and more necessary of late, even for purebloods. And I'd heard of a new kind of brush from the ice lands north of Hansk—made from the fur of a black weasel, wonderfully fine and resilient. They were horribly expensive, as they had to be smuggled through the rugged island routes held by Navronne's perennial foes. I coveted such tools to complete my grandfather's portrait. If the fee was slightly more than modest, we could begin to think about rebuilding the house at Pontia.

I darted across the ground-floor reception room and through the small door at the back. This had once been a wealthy vintner's house. The reception room had held his casks and samples, ready to be brought out to the inner courtyard on fine Ardran days that never seemed to come anymore. In the small room at the back he had counted his gold. And now it held ours.

The fat gray purse sat on a black enamel table, the rolled contract beside it. If the former was sufficient, the latter didn't matter.

The bag was nicely heavy. I closed my eyes, blessed our family's patron, Deunor, and poured out my father's ruby ring and the chinking load . . . of silver.

"No! No! No! Bastien, you scurrilous, vile, wretched cheat!" In no way this side of Kemen Sky Lord's halls could a fistful of lunae be an entire year's stipend. A purse this size should have been packed with gold. I leapt to my feet, ready to head straight back for the necropolis. Had Leander not even looked? Surely he had taken the Registry's tithe. . . .

My heart near seized. Or was this Pons's hand?

"Aperite!" Spitting out the Aurellian word for *open,* I shattered the spelled wax seal and spread the parchment scroll open. The ornate script flowed beautifully. Perfectly. Outlining my perfect and permanent ruin.

. . . for the consideration of One Hundred and Sixty Lunae.

Lunae, not solae. Silver, not gold. Every prospective master looked at previous contracts. And no master in Navronne could look at this contract and believe I could be anything but an undisciplined and untalented idiot.

Juli and I had no treasury to tide us over a thin contract. A hundred and sixty *solae* would have been slim enough. But a solé was worth four hundred coppers, a luné forty. This house alone cost us eighty lunae a year, our servants forty more. That left forty silver pieces for food, clothes, coal, and everything else. For a year.

Not only did this contract preclude rebuilding our home or reinstating the life we knew, not only did it fail to provide the secure foundation that allowed purebloods to concentrate on their duties, but we would not even be able to live as we had. There must be some mistake.

I sank back to the floor, eyes fixed to the document. To the amount.

To the signatures: my own, Pons's, Albin's, Bastien's. I knew pens and ink, lines and curves. There was no irregularity.

At last Pons had given me the future she believed I deserved. But why would she ruin my sister, who had not mortgaged her future for a moment's pleasurable companionship? How could she so dishonor the memory of my family?

"So can your master beat you or can he only make you stink?" Juli appeared in the doorway, wrapped in her own quilt. "I hope you'll not be so stingy with the coal, now we've good coin."

I ground the heels of my hand into my eyes, trying to crush the hammering ache in my head. "Perhaps we need a smaller place to heat. . . ."

"*Domé* Lucian, it's the hour you specified." I didn't break the hand shaking my shoulder. Some god should reward my restraint. "I'm sorry, *domé*. Here's your wool shirt. And Maia's sent up a tisane, fresh brewed and quite hot if you down it right now."

I squeezed my eyes tighter, in hopes the ever-mild Giaco would vanish. He repeated his gentle prodding and gave me his hand as I emerged from the cocoon of quilts and abject stupor—or a sea of mud, as it felt. The wool shirt was a pitiful substitute for the quilts. But the tisane infused a bit of life. Blessed Maia.

The outrage of the previous night came flooding back. How in the name of all gods was I to tell our servants I could no longer pay them?

Sometime after midnight, Juli had laid a charm on me to make me sleep. Livid at the hints of deprivation to come, she had made me beg her for it, as well as insisting I forbid Soflet to barricade the doors to keep her in the house as if she were "a madwoman or a leper." I'd done as she asked. I'd have done anything for sleep.

And now I had to face the wretched day.

Did Pluvius know the disgraceful terms of this contract? I'd certainly need his help. For the Registry to overturn a signed contract was rare in the most compelling of circumstances. We would have to plead Pons's bias, my awkward family situation, my grandfather's memory, Juli's needs, even if it brought a Registry minder into our house. But I would see it done. Yet it couldn't happen immediately. I would not disobey my master's command to attend him before dawn, violating the contract even as I demanded to have it voided.

"The tisane and the shirt are most welcome, Giaco. My boots?"

"They're as dry as I could get them, *domé*. I've had them next the fire all night." With his quiet competence, he had me shaved, dressed, fed—I was no such fool as I had been the previous day to let nerves hinder reason—masked, and out the door before I could blink. I would miss him—all of them—and not just for the comforts and care they provided. They had come from our house at Pontia. My parents had trained them. Their memories and good service were our inheritance. I'd need to contact acquaintances, find them good positions, while I found us a new place to live.

The inner turmoil was a blessing in a way. No phantom archers or windswept voices plagued my nerves as I traipsed through the waking city. I had no difficulty ignoring the cold seeping through my boots, the filth and debris piling up on boulevards that had once been pleasant, or the pent violence in the crowd gathering in the *pocardon*. No one bothered me. The contract did indeed include a clause permitting defensive magic. I'd need to learn some this winter; no sword training was in my future.

When I reached the broken brick arch and the descent to the hirudo, I did not hesitate. If the laughing thief knew my name, he likely knew about my bent, as well. Perhaps he thought a portraitist an easy mark. Even with my limited skills, I'd show him elsewise.

Though the night had not yet begun to fade, the hirudo was already stirring. Torches and cook fires pushed back the shadows. A woman fried dough balls over a dirty fire pit. An emaciated dog nosed through a pile of indeterminate filth beside a collapsed shed. An ebony-eyed Ciceron with a mottled beard and thick mustache played a wild farandole on a syrinx. At any moment I expected a chain of drunken men and women to dance through the forest of hanging laundry in frenzied answer to his piping.

Watchers were everywhere. A bony young Ciceron with hooped earrings. A graying, hard-faced woman in leather jaque and breeches, idly twirling a well-used sling. Two ragged men dicing in the light of a barrel fire, one observing the tumbling dice, one watching the lane.

Some halfway along the ravine path, I halted. Pointing my finger, I pivoted just fast enough to billow my cloak, waiting until every watcher's eyes were on me—even those I couldn't see.

When the syrinx fell silent, I raised a pen in one hand and a small knife with a broken hilt in the other. With a spark of will—drawing full upon my seething anger—I released magic into the two implements and the shaped inflation spell waiting on each. Then I tossed them onto the frozen muck. In a hiss and flash of light, they grew until each was a forearm's length. None could mistake their shape.

"I am an artist," I said, pointing to the pen. "*This* is my chosen weapon."

The knife shriveled, while the pen flew upward and sketched a silver tree that shone bright against the lingering night above my head.

"I am also pureblood, as you see. The law of Navronne declares I pass unhindered wherever I choose." As I spoke, I moved around a broken cask left to rot alongside the path, my footsteps marking a circle in the snow. "Some who dwell here may not be aware of the king's law, and I dislike having to prove my right again and again."

The tree collapsed in a shower of sparks. With a quick second infusion of magic, I triggered a voiding spell, the only serious enchantment I knew outside my bent. The earth inside my circle collapsed inward; the cask toppled and crashed to the bottom of the hole.

Gasps sounded here and there, quickly muted.

"Whichever of you is Demetreo the Ciceron, hear this. It is your responsibility to see that the arché, the grave sign I carelessly lost here when passing last night, is left where I'm now standing before I pass here again."

No one in such a place would have challenged a pureblood without the headman's permission.

With that, I unraveled the inflation illusion and the void spell in one move. The pen and the gouge in the earth vanished. Tossing pen and knife alongside the splintered cask, I continued on my way, ears pricked for any movement at my back. The only person I passed was a crone in a bone necklace, stroking a dog's back. Her black eyes followed me onward.

As I passed through Caedmon's Wall and the slot gate, I traded one anxiety for another.

Frosted mist hung over the world like a curtain of grace to hide its ugliness. It also left me the familiar sense of a presence just beyond the range of seeing.

Trying to ignore it, I hiked across the burial ground to the nameless grave where the snow had buried my eating knife. The taint of death seemed multiplied a hundredfold on this morn. Perhaps because I had touched the field or simply because I now knew what kind of place it was.

"Forgive my faithless promise," I said, pressing a hand to the mound. "I'll return your marker tomorrow."

As I trudged onward toward the gates, a bright blue gleam flashed at the corner of my eye, as if the sun had sent a stray beam ahead of its rising and found a bit of lapis on a woman's wrist or a sapphire ring on a man's finger. The second time it happened, certain that I felt a person hidden in the mist, I called out, "Halloo. Who's there?"

No one answered, of course. Giaco had likely sprinkled my clothes chest with herbs, accounting for the hint of rosemary intruding on the stink of death.

Another hundred paces and I halted. Blinked. Squinted. Two tall, slender shapes strolled down the cart road away from the necropolis. Human shapes. They carried some strange lamp that illuminated the intricate designs of their garb in hues of cerulean, lapis, and sapphire. Or perhaps a merchant had formulated some kind of luminous ink that could be transferred to his fabric . . . or directly to . . .

I blinked again, this time holding my eyelids closed for long enough to ensure I controlled my own seeing. But it was not simple weariness or living dream.

Truly the work at Caton must have drained me past reason. My mother's family had portrayed mythic beings—gryphons, dragons, angels—in artworks for generations, but my historian kin had never found evidence of them. Only a madman or a fae-struck child would believe two Danae walked naked on the Caton plateau on a winter's morn, their bare skin etched with exquisite line drawings that shimmered with indescribable enchantment.

A gust of wind-driven snow obscured the sight, and when it had passed they had vanished.

My long-held breath released. I needed to get on, yet my feet would not move. I stared into that pocket of night until my eyeballs near froze. But by the time the temple bells pealed, I was no more enlightened and shivering uncontrollably.

Feeling entirely foolish, I hurried my steps through the last hummocks. The sixth bell chimed as I rushed breathless through the open gates to find the courtyard awash in torchlight and corpses.

CHAPTER 7

In a dawn grayness brightened by a ring of torches, Constance and Garibald had marshaled their troop of laborers to deal with the savaged remnants of the royal brothers' war. Broken bodies lay everywhere, lifted from five half-emptied wagons.

I had studied the history of war. My grandsire had taught me to examine a battlefield, to hear the clamor and feel the horror of brutal death, to taste blood on the air, to see images of ruin, and use these things to make sense of the past. But never had I seen the actual carnage laid out before me. And these were only a few, the wounded who had died along the way home.

Kings and emperors had always sent their ducs and barons home from war to heal or be buried. Common battle dead were buried where they fell. Most of the wounded were left behind, as well, to heal if they could or die at the enemy's hand. But King Caedmon had believed that every man should have a chance to die on his home ground. Thus he had brought every one of his wounded home, despite the risks of pursuit and thin-spread lines. As ever, many—most—had died along the way, but his soldiers adored him for it. As in most things, all Navron kings had followed Caedmon's example when it served them. Prince Perryn must have won a decisive victory in the north or be a truly courageous man in the mold of his great-great-grandsire.

Uncertainty paralyzed me. If anything was to be done about the contract—my future, my sister's future—it needed to be addressed right away. And I longed to contemplate what I'd just glimpsed outside the walls. Danae—myth become real? Who else could they be? And yet a man could not encounter such a display as lay in this courtyard and turn away to private grievance or even his soul's wonder.

Constance waved a hand and hurried over, dodging laborers with litters and shooing the coffin maker's girl away like a pesky fly.

"Coroner's off to the Council District, arranging with lardships about their kin-dead. Da rathers Bastien do it." She brushed away dull strings of hair that had escaped her skimpy braids and eyed me with a gleam of avarice. "But he's left tha orders. See those six rowed nearest the steps off rightmost? *Mysteries worth solving*, he says of 'em. Ye must have a drawn of each by midmorn. And he's set an inside for the doing."

Her grin spread ear to ear. "Coroner said ye must do as Da or I bid."

Indeed he had, and, for now, I was bound to his word. Yet neither the onerous contract nor personal discipline nor any threatened consequence induced my obedience. In that busy courtyard were overwhelming pain and sorrow made visible. A few sketches were simple enough.

I would redo the girl child's portrait today, as well, as much for my own peace of mind as Bastien's. I didn't plan to return here another day.

"When the coroner returns, tell him I must speak with him."

Constance dipped her knee and pranced away.

Once I retrieved two sticks of plummet and a stack of parchment scraps from Bastien's book press, and a dusty folio of a size and stiffness to use for a lap desk, I headed for the victims Constance had indicated. They were laid out like pens in a writing case, their death pain writ as clear as their blue-gray flesh or their filthy garments.

Why were these six singled out? Out of scores of new arrivals, surely half could not be named, and it wasn't as if any of the deaths were suspicious. The battle woundings were dreadful—no simple stabs or slashes, but brutal hacking and mutilation, most around the head and face, far beyond what would bring down an enemy.

A stroll down the row spoke the distasteful answer to my curiosity. None of the six had weapons remaining, but one wore a sword belt of excellent quality, another a single fine boot I would have been happy to own. An intricately embroidered silk shirt was tucked under layers of another man's shredded leathers. Two bore a crest or insignia on their garb—a sure sign of a family or lord who might claim them—though the badges were damaged beyond easy recognition. One had pinned a wealthy woman's lacework kerchief inside his shirt. Each displayed evidence that someone would pay well to learn who he was.

Swallowing disgust, I waved at two of the laborers and told them to carry the man with the boot to whatever chamber the coroner had set aside for me to work. An inside room, I guessed. Constance's contorted verbiage recalled Bastien's stricture and the idiotic accusation that had prompted it. Solid bodies—even those of sorcerers—did not *flicker.*

They led me to an upper chamber at the rear of the promethium. A clean room, thank all gods. Waiting in quiet dignity were a stone bier, a washing trough, and a beautifully carved laver protruding from the wall. A shelf held a variety of jars and oil flasks. A preparation room, then. For nobility, I guessed, from the privacy and the quality. Perhaps for purebloods.

The best furnishings were the two windows, one north, one east. Opening the shutters left the room frigid; neither glass nor even horn or oiled parchment served as panes. But the extra light was well worth the cold.

Settled on the stool next the bier, I pushed aside every concern save the gift I had been born to share. I touched the soldier's cold face, and opened myself to magic. . . .

"Damn and blast! Well done! You see them without their wounds. Never imagined that."

Bastien found me seated on the floor beside the prometheum font. Sometime in the past hour, I had staggered out of the preparation room and down the stair. After washing my hands, I had slid to the floor and forced down a cupful of water and the cheese Maia had sent with me that morning. My head rested on my knees.

"May it p-profit you," I said, teeth rattling with my shivers. "And if you have more work for me, it will have to wait."

"A bit testy today, are we, pureblood? Have I worked you too hard? Constance said you had ants up your backbone when you first came in. So, what is it?"

Parchment rustled above my head.

Oh, aye . . . the contract. I needed to be out of here. Merciful gods, my true life seemed a thousand quellae distant.

Many times I'd done six or more portraits at a sitting, but never had I emerged so drained. And never had I experienced *pain* as I worked. So strange . . . with each drawing the discomfort had grown worse than the last. By the time I finished the sixth, my jaw radiated torment throughout my skull, and my right leg felt as if it had been ground in a mill wheel. Which made no sense at all, save that an axe had cleaved the soldier's jaw clean through his cheek, and that his right leg was yet bandaged in rusty linen.

I'd never heard of any such manifestation of an artistic bent. But with all those horrid wounds waiting in the yard . . . Truth be told, my shivering was not solely from magical depletion.

"Did you have something to say to me?" Bastien's enthusiasm had vanished. Surely his humors were as variable as the colors of sunlight.

The future . . . Juli . . . our family's place in the world . . . I needed to direct my attention to what was immediately important. Even the chimera of the Danae must wait. "I must speak with you about the c-contract."

"The contract is settled," he snapped.

A glance upward registered the stack of new portraits in his hand and a somewhat startling change in appearance. The coroner's sand-colored hair had been oiled and tamed with a green brow band, his exuberant tangle of a beard trimmed close around his mouth, and the rest of his jaw shaved. A spruce green velvet tunic, trimmed with black embroidery and buttoned from just under his chin all the way to his knees, was bursting at its threadbare seams. The garment, no doubt quite fashionable when my grandsire was a boy, displayed Bastien's chest as wide as his book press.

But it was one of the portraits that seemed to have frozen his satisfaction as solid as Valdo de Seti's heart. And my scrutiny only soured his face the more.

"It's just"—now I'd come to it, I wasn't sure how to couch my inquiry—"a curiosity. I understood the year's stipend was left open in your initial bid. I wished to know . . . the negotiation. You must be extraordinarily p-persuasive."

I bundled my cloak tighter, despising my stammering weakness.

Bastien snorted. "Here's how it went, my fine gentleman, so's you'll not bother whining at me again." He squatted beside me, a cloying perfume clogging my nostrils. "You'd best figure out what you did to stir that woman's bile. She asked what you were worth to me. I told her a price, starting with half what I thought I could muster. She wrote it down and had me sign. There weren't a cat's whisker of *negotiation*. You could have stole my teeth."

No negotiation? Was it exhaustion or sheerest disbelief set the world spinning? Everything—the foundation of the pureblood compact with the Crown, with the gods, with ourselves, our independence paid for with obedience and strict discipline that forbade us friends and choices, even the choice to marry, love, or have children—all of it rested on the sacred nature of our contracts. Otherwise, what were we?

The coroner continued his crowing. "Best deal I ever made. Already sent a purse to take up your contract for a second year. She's offered three for the price. And from what she tells me, you've naught to say about it. Four years. I'll have my due."

If Bastien spoke true, Pons had sold me like a slave for a year, now stretched to four, when at last I would be old enough to negotiate for myself. Yet my elevation to Head of Family at thirty required Registry consent as well. Surely Pons was not so powerful as to override that? Surely . . .

Bastien stood up again, his glare scalding my head. "Now, what's *wrong* with you? It's not so frosty as all that in here, and you've a cloak a man would sell one of his brats for. By Iero's holy balls, if you've brought a fever to Caton, I'll bury you with these fellows."

Dizzy and nauseated, I squeezed my eyes shut. Surely Pons had already buried me.

But discipline, unthinking habit, forced breath in and out of my chest. This Bastien was an ordinary, a clever, despicable, volatile pickthief, who used the law and families' grief to line his purse. Yet he was merely the beneficiary of my downfall, not the cause. Rebellion would certainly make matters worse.

"I'm quite well," I said. "Show me the girl child. I can redo her portrait before I leave for the day."

"Then come along." Bastien led me through the vaulted colonnade where I had first encountered him, behind the prometheum. "We've put her in the Hallow Ground."

Moving made it less tempting to plow my hand into a marble wall. It gave me time to summon self-control, to remind myself that the life I knew, that I believed in, was worthy. *Pons* was the betrayer. Not this greedy man.

Halfway down the colonnade, the coroner unlatched a low iron gate. As so many things in Necropolis Caton, the place beyond the gate was wholly unexpected.

The snow lay deep, shielded on all sides as it was by high walls, imbuing the enclosure with a deep and peaceful quiet. It recalled the pureblood necropolis in Pontia, though instead of grand marble monuments bearing storied family names, the crowded headstones that peeked from the snow were modest, adorned with carved images of birds or gods or nothing at all—the Hallow Ground, not the Hollow Ground as Constance named it.

Our boots crunched on a well-trod path. In the corner farthest from the gate, they had piled snow and ice as high as my head, packed and shaped it, and cut a door through the side. Sheltered from the sun as it was, such a frozen barrow could last well into our weak summer.

"We've a few special cases we keep here," said Bastien. " 'Tis a luxury of a rotten winter. When you deem your fine self in the mood to work, tell Constance, and she'll have someone pull the girl out. No tricks, or you'll regret the day you ever heard the name Bastien de Caton."

The pleasure of telling him the current extent of my *regret* was not worth the dregs of my pride. Perhaps a little while alone in such a peaceful surround and I could regain some sort of balance. "Give me half an hour."

But Bastien didn't leave. Instead, he folded his velvet-sleeved arms and stared grimly at the mound, as if his vision might penetrate its walls and the mystery inside. To escape his company I'd have to plod around him through thigh-deep snow. So I waited, seething, surprised when he spoke up again.

"On my visits in the Council District this morning, I let slip a few mentions of the king-to-be and his heirs." His bellicose basso had yielded to a quieter tone. None but I and the sleeping dead could have heard him. "Perryn's acknowledged five children of his wife, three boys, two girls, all aged under seven years. None's counted his by-blow, of which, gossip says, there are many. That seems likely, with a wife producing five live brats in eight years."

His silence extended a goodly while, his thick fingers tapping their opposite elbows. I cared naught for the royal family or its breeding habits, and tried to focus inward and rebuild my power. Breathing deep, I forced mind and body to let go of the day's annoyance. Closed my eyes. Closed my ears.

But Bastien mumbled on. "Prince Bayard has two strapping boys of ten and twelve. No girls. And he's spent the most of his days since age fifteen on his warships, chasing Hansker raiders, keeping Navronne's coastal cities safe and his wife lone. None knows of Osriel the Bastard's couplings any more than they know whether he's yet a human person or has truly forfeited his balls to Magrog in return for sorcery. But he's no marriage nor heirs recorded and, as far as anyone knows, hasn't left Evanore's mountains since he was a boy. I doubt this girl is his. For certain none but a child in the direct line could wear the tri-part lily. Thus she's likely Perryn's."

"You believe what my drawing showed!" My every sense flared alert. He'd been so certain of my scheming. I wasn't even sure that *I* believed the dead girl had royal blood.

"Didn't say that. I deem you a pompous pureblood twit who believes he's been ill-used because he's got to smell shite. I believe you'd do just about anything short of cutting off your hands to weasel out of this contract. But none's ever said Bastien de Caton fails to take advantage of what it might profit him to know, and it's not every day I earn favors from those who can tell me of princes and their get. And now these"—he shifted his gaze to the stack of portraits in his hand—"are shown without their woundings."

Was that all? I had purposely used the undamaged parts of the men's faces to rebuild the dreadful gaps, just as I could fill in a full head of hair for a woman who had lost hers or make a man's rheumy eye clear.

"Any skillful portraitist can do the same. Magic simply makes it easier to get it accurate."

"So, you truly don't know . . ."

Control yourself, Lucian. "Know *what*?"

"This one." He held out the face on top. "I know this man."

A narrow face with prominent cheekbones and a wide, straight nose—the one whose dreadful jaw wound yet throbbed in my skull. Instead of hair glued to his skull with blood, I'd given him a thick, waving mane to match the beard on his intact cheek, a logical extension of what I saw. And over his bloody hauberk, I'd sketched a clean, well-cut surcoat instead of the filthy remnants of his own.

"*You* chose him from the deadcarts, not I," I said. "He wore decent mail and an expensive swordbelt."

"But it's not from the yard I know him. And I never met him in the flesh. But whole like this, he's the very image of the chief magistrate of Wroling, and of proper age to be old Maslin's son. And that"—he pointed to a badge on the man's surcoat, an intricate device of a wolf devouring a falcon—"is the badge of the Edane of Wroling. Perhaps you knew that already. Or did you hear some gatzi-fed slander and think you'd put it there for a jest?"

He bit off his last phrases as he might snap the neck of a stray chicken. Though I had no idea what *slander* he might mean, that was surely the source of his current annoyance, not my skills or lack of them. That relieved me. Complaints about my skills would only complicate matters.

The portrait glared at me as if daring me to solve its mystery. This soldier was not one of the two wearing torn badges. This man had worn no device. Which meant . . . what? Why had I interpreted his prosperity with a particular badge . . . as if I knew him?

Bastien's fingers tapped, his impatience feeding my own.

"Nothing in that courtyard would put me in mind of a *jest*, Master Bastien, even if I knew what you were talking about. And by the time I did this portrait—"

No. If I told him about the pain, he'd just think me whining again. And I certainly couldn't explain it. So I held to plain truth. "I've never been to Wroling nor met its lord or its magistrate nor heard any stories of them. I've no knowledge of Ardran noblemen's badges. You're certain of its design?"

"Aye. And I'm as certain of his parentage as I can be without showing him to his da. Seems uncanny two men would be birthed so like and not be kin. If I didn't trust your art so far as a decent likeness, I'd have had you up before your Registry witch already."

My shivers had waned, thanks to the food and drink and passing time, but my temper was as threadbare as Bastien's velvet. "Hear me, Coroner, for the first and last time. I will not, not *ever*, deliberately falsify a drawing. My magic, my art, is the only thing—"

Again, no. I would not admit him to my privacy. But I had to convince him.

My fingers raked my hair. "I cannot explain the badge or the portrait's likeness to someone you know. I cannot explain the girl child's lily. But I swear upon my dead sire's name and upon my dead mother's heart, they arose from no artifice, only from magic . . . or instinct . . . or some blending—"

My breath caught. Was it possible that reaching for the life behind death's mask had roused some fading ember of my second bent? My grandsire had discovered many marvels with his magic—new meanings for glyphs and symbols, legends that he could confirm only later, ideas that meshed with other discoveries to reveal a story unexpected. And he had often warned that pursuing our shared bent was fraught with the agonies of war, but, stars of night, I'd never imagined that meant *physical* pain. Yet it made much more sense that I could inherit a dead man's pain by way of a bent for history than from drawing his portrait. And on the night just past when touching the frozen graveyard, I had glimpsed . . . threads . . . threads of vision that mimed the investigations of history.

My face heated under Bastien's glare. "I gather that's a strong oath for a pureblood," he said. "I'll take it for now."

Compared to the storm rising inside me, his words pattered like raindrops. In the days when I practiced both bents, I'd felt the streams of magic entirely distinct—history deriving from the mind and art from the soul, or so I had explained it to my family. Never had I been able to merge them for any task, no matter how useful. When I was twenty and a fool, such a skill would have elated me. The blending would be a marvel, an unprecedented extension of the divine gift. But now? All I could see was the most cursed, wretched consequence.

It had taken my grandsire months of persuasion to delay my Declaration of Bent when I turned sixteen and to secure the Registry's approval for me to continue exploring both gifts. And even *his* tolerance had collapsed at my first hint of undisciplined behavior. Now I was so clearly in trouble; if I were to plead my case to the Registry, try to bring Pons to account for her betrayal, any hint of a dual bent would undercut everything I said. History said that those with two strong bents inevitably went mad. Great Deunor preserve, they might try to excise it again! The memory of that pain made the echoes of wounding no more than the brush of a gnat's wing.

Bastien thrust the page into my hand. "Copy this, and I'll send it to Magistrate Maslin in Wroling. We'll see what he says. Then, perhaps, we'll both know something new."

The coroner rejoined me in the preparation room, where I was standing beside the window, wiping my hands with a damp kerchief. The aches in my thigh and jaw were fading, for which I was profoundly thankful. It had taken me less than an hour to reproduce the soldier's portrait, as if the throbbing in my own jaw had kept the lines and curves of the soldier's face ready in my fingertips.

"I suppose you're quit for the day," snapped Bastien.

I could not summon the strength to challenge his insolence. "The light's going. I do better—"

"Yes, yes. You can redo the girl's portrait tomorrow. And I've a number of new subjects for you to work on."

No point in broaching the subject of the contract. My flimsy hope of getting the cursed agreement voided lay in some Registry curator—Pluvius, I supposed—who could see what Pons's betrayal meant to pure-blood honor. And that was beginning to seem a very flimsy hope indeed.

I stuffed my kerchief in my waist pocket. "Master Bastien . . ."

He halted on his way out the door. "What?"

I'd thought to mention my need for new lodgings, but the wretched words wouldn't shape themselves. He was an ordinary. He owned me. "At the same hour tomorrow?"

"Every day the same. And wear more of your furs if you're so thin blooded as to get the shakes. Wouldn't want a Registry inspector to think I'm mistreating you."

Wordless, numb, I touched fingertips to forehead.

CHAPTER 8

Profound night awaited me outside the walls. Half-hopeful, half-terrified, I peered into the sable winter of the burial ground. No blue threads teased my eyes. The wind gusts whispered no words. Living myth . . . Surely the morning's vision had been but imagining.

Pride had vetoed such a violation of custom as bringing my own lantern from home; purebloods did not march about the city dangling lanterns or waving torches like linkboys. My fury over the contract had fueled my stubbornness. Laughable, now, that I had thought the penurious stipend the worst part of it. I had vowed to reserve enough magic to see me safely home. The long day's work might well have undone that vow; without question identity portraits of the dead consumed more of my capacity than anniversary portraits at the Registry. But at the least I'd had sense enough to wear silver bracelets about my upper sleeves—ideal for supporting a spelled light.

As on the previous night, I shaped my desire and filled it with magic. Then I crimped the thin silver band around my left wrist and triggered the spell.

The ivory light guided me across the burial ground to the gap in the wall. Praying that my demonstration of the morning had sufficed to keep the Ciceron rogues at bay, I descended into the hirudo.

A bone-clawing chill had settled in the ravine. A number of folk huddled about small smoky cook fires. They'd bundled themselves head to toe in so many layers of rags and sacking, hats and shawls, one could scarce tell men from women from children.

Nattering, arguments, the clatter of dice, and drunken laughter died as I passed. No one looked at me. No one approached.

Feet and spirit longed to race through the lane, to distance myself as quickly as possible from Necropolis Caton and this, its wretched appendage. But running from a predator only set the beast's juices flowing, so I kept my pace measured, eyes forward, ears alert, and fingers ready to snatch the dagger from my boot. The clearest answer to my morning's work would lie ahead, before the path turned upward toward the city.

The arché was waiting for me, as I had commanded, though it remained secure in the grasp of a short, sinewy Ciceron. Red ribbons wove his black hair into five plaits, and the false gold of his dangling earrings glinted in the wavering torchlight. His gray-mottled black beard and heavy mustache identified him as the syrinx-player of the morning. His confident stance named him the headman of Hirudo Palinur.

"Demetreo, is it not?" I extended my right hand for the arché. The left, the wrist with the silver band, I raised just enough that those I sensed closing up behind me could see the light flare in silver spikes.

The Ciceron's dark face blazed with more than my enchanted light. No sign of deference graced his posture. His gaze slid to the iron grave marker, then flicked back to me.

"So ye grant us the taste of glory we begged, *Domé* Remeni. I am most impressed. And more so that no soldiers or Registry inquisitors have invaded our homely swamp to beat proper manners into us. Though I must say"—he grimaced and rubbed a spot near his breastbone—"I'm like to wear the mark of this sturdy item until Voudras Day."

So he was also my challenger of the previous day. My pleasure at his bruising was choked by dread that he would not yield. My hand remained outstretched.

He proffered the grave marker, hesitating half a quat before it touched my fingers. "Rumor says Caton's new pureblood turns his magic to the murdered child was found here. Ill fortune to have such a discovery in one's own district. The estimable coroner is dogged in his mission and, for certain, no friend of the hirudo. But perhaps you, one of the gods' chosen, could say him again: She was not one of our own." Sly humor and brassy posturing vanished like ice in fire. "Child strangling is more trouble than any here would invite. I see to that."

No one with eyes or ears could doubt the headman's sincerity . . . or his ability to enforce such a rule. And it was no mystery that he would be concerned. A constable or city guard captain given a hint of a noble child—much less a *royal* child—found dead in the hirudo would not bother listening to explanations. Blood and fire would bloom in the night, and every one of these people would be reduced to severed necks, charred bones, and ash.

But then why had he turned her body over to the necropolis in the first place? Unless he hadn't known . . . *With complinations* to the coroner, Constance had said of the headman's sending the child's body to Caton—*compliments*, perhaps. He'd been seeking to curry favor with Bastien, and only then heard gossip about me and the portrait.

A fair humor rippled through my skin. Demetreo had likely cursed Serena Fortuna's whim to the depths of his being when he learned what the portrait showed. Perhaps an opportunity lay here to learn something. The child deserved the truth. And the wound of her unfinished portrait yet stung.

"I could report such a statement to the coroner, as you ask," I said. "Yet its verity would surely be strengthened by a demonstration of goodwill. For example, if you relinquish this grave marker I so carelessly dropped . . ."

He laid the arché in my hand.

". . . and if you showed me the place where the girl child was found."

"Easily done."

Demetreo motioned to one of his watchers, an elderly woman wearing a bone necklace. She grabbed a smoky torch and led us up the lane.

As if the settlement breathed a sigh, the other Cicerons went back to their business.

My daily route to the slot gate and Caton's plateau climbed up from the north side of the piggery, where the rocky slope of the ravine supported Palinur's outer wall. Demetreo, the old woman, and I veered to the other side of the wallow, where a soggy drainage channeled all the moisture from between the two ramparts, including the city's seeps and sewage, down through the hirudo. We slogged across the stew of snow, ice, muck, and lifeless vegetation to a low embankment thick with leaf-bare willows.

"A boy was out skinning bark for his mam yestermorn," said Demetreo, pushing through the willow thicket. "He found the dead child caught in the tangle."

Wrenching hair, collar, and sleeves free of willow snags, I emerged from the thicket to an open hillside of patchy snow and dead grass. Impossibly steep, the ground rose all the way to the base of the inner wall—the Elder Wall. Not that we could see much beyond our ring of torch- and magelight.

The Ciceron pointed out a clump of disturbed willow withes a few steps away. "There."

The unrelenting slope offered no easy access for anyone thinking to hide a body. My boots insisted on sliding back down toward the line of densely packed willows. One could have more easily and safely buried the girl in the pigsty or even the muck of the channel. A week's warm weather would have her rotted beyond identification. Why stow her behind the thicket?

Something whitish caught my eyes near the spot Demetreo had indicated. I slipped and slid across the muddy slope and crouched to see it better. Bark shavings, half-buried in the frozen mud. The boy's tale was true. . . .

Fruitlessly, I scanned the ground for anything else that might have fallen from the child or her murderer. *Faugh!* Surely such a heinous act must leave traces.

My fingers picked again at the strips of bark, then moved hesitantly into the crescent of trampled grass beside the willows. People, especially those in heightened states of fear, anxiety, or other passions, left traces that were not solid artifacts. The gift to discover and interpret those traces had once lived in me. It might again. *If* my grandsire's excision had not worked completely. *If* I dared violate his stricture and the most solemn oath I had ever sworn.

Yet what meaning had youthful swearings in the face of true wickedness? If I could use my maimed bent to expose a child murderer, would that not be a virtue to counter any violation? Why had I been given such a gift, only to have it ripped away because I'd been young and foolish, overheated by my body's urges? Perhaps that punishment had run its course, and the strange effects of my bent in this place were the gods' sign that I must begin again and use what I was given.

"Is a great sorcerer like you as flummoxed as ordinary folk?"

The Ciceron's taunt propelled me forward onto my knees. Laying my hands on the cold ground, I offered a swift prayer that I was not wrong and a swifter apology to my grandsire. Then I plunged deep into the cold, dark space between my eyes.

A flash of vermillion flared in the dark . . . an ember, hot and bright. *Blessed Deunor, Lord of Light and Magic, let this be your sign. Empower me.*

I sparked the ember with my will, and a storm of magic raced through my neck, shoulders, and arms and into my waiting fingers. And when my hands felt swollen with it, I released the flood into the earth.

Impressions assaulted my senses like a stampede of wild boars. *Leash the threads—bind them!* The memory of my grandsire's teaching rang out above the thunder. *Tame the avalanche! Parse out your magic slowly, else you'll have no time to think, to make linkages, to see truth.*

I grasped wildly at the fleeting sensations—noises, images, ideas, scents, emotions, people and beasts, sun and wind—and tried to bind them into patterns that made sense. It had been so long.

There! Hunters . . . generations had tracked the beasts that came here to the springs . . . tall grass . . . bare feet . . . spears and crude arrows. Enmity and death had permeated all endeavors here, a swirling cyclone threatening to obscure the rest.

Grasp a thread of substance and collect the stragglers that cluster around it.

The massive walls. Pride, pain, and elation swelled as the stones rose; devastation ruled when they broke or failed. Magics so large as to crumble cities had been expended hereabouts, only to be quenched by more blood and stone. Anger had been trapped between the elder and newer walls, furies soaked deep as the storm floods that raged through the channel.

But I was not interested in the distant past. I would be here for days if I could not sort out the recent from the ancient, small from large. How did one find the pebble in the raging river, the grain of sand fallen into the ground wheat?

Seek a precise emotion and then trace its source.

The boy, of course, startled by his discovery. He knew death; all in the hirudo knew death. But this one would have surprised him, made him curious and a bit fearful. Perhaps the victim was not so different from him in age.

Another lesson. *We all believe we are immortal, no matter the death around us.*

I almost didn't grasp it. The scents fooled me—incense, moonflowers, oils of rose and ephrain, the latter a pungent rarity found in bathhouses. But the exotic threads entwined the curious boy and a pattern formed around willow bark and a stained white bundle tumbling downward. . . .

Before I could form a conclusion, the tide of visions receded. What dregs of power I had brought to this enterprise had dissipated quickly and cold seeped into my bones.

"I'm finished here," I said, rising on unsteady legs. "I need to go." The wavering light from my bracelet would not see me home.

"As you wish." The old woman's torch lit our way through the dark thicket. Arms like lead, eyes watering from the icy air, I could scarce push through the thicket. As willow branches scraped my face and frozen hands,

I clung to the last image: the spinning bundle of white . . . falling. What did it mean?

We reached the channel and the path through the settlement. I trudged through the mud behind Demetreo's determined back. Almost crashed into him when he halted at the spot where I'd met him. Then, like a latch snapping into place, two clear questions emerged from the turmoil in my skull.

"I detected naught to contradict your story," I said. "Clearly the child's death was not accomplished here. I shall report your insistence to Coroner Bastien. But I need to know what happened to her wrapping."

"Her wrapping?" Demetreo hesitated just long enough to tell me I'd made him curious.

"At some time before her body was deposited beside the willows, the child was draped in a white cloth, yet she was not wrapped when she was delivered to the necropolis. Coroner Bastien will need the cloth. There may have been other garments underneath, different from the ones she was wearing."

The Ciceron jerked his chin to the old woman. She hobbled away.

Unlikely that the lily dress was here. Demetreo would never have delivered the girl to Bastien if he'd seen it. And the girl had been strangled, yet the white cloth in my vision had been stained with blood.

A spindly man returned instead of the crone and whispered in the headman's ear.

"There was no winding cloth," said Demetreo, firmly. "No garments but those you saw."

I believed him. What I had seen was truth, but not necessarily the truth of the moment the child came to rest beside the willows. Rolling down the steep slope had abraded her skin and torn her poor garments. Perhaps the winding cloth had been ripped off her partway down, the scraps blown away in the wind or buried in snow or mud. Or perhaps it was removed before she was dressed in rags, so none could identify its origin. For I saw no conclusion but that she had been delivered to the willows from above.

All of which led to my second question. One I could not ask of this man, for the asking itself was a certain risk. But I would discover its answer: What house scented with moonflowers lay just inside the Elder Wall of Palinur, so high above the hirudo piggery?

CHAPTER 9

Shivering until my bones near rattled, I dragged myself uphill, wondering if every day was to be so draining as these first two. Yet I could not but feel a joyous awe that soothed long grievance. My second bent was not entirely dead. No matter the complications if the Registry found out, the fullness of the gods' gift lived in me. Using both had never felt wrong or aberrant. And my grandsire had encouraged that belief—until my fall from his grace.

The mystery of the child murderer must await the morning. The Temple heights lay just above the hirudo. Nobles, members of the Sinduri Council, Karish hierarchs, and other people of wealth and influence made their homes in the district. But even if I could find the exact street on a starless, moonless night with snow threatening, what excuse would allow me to barge in and ask who lived there? The villain would likely have *me* dead before I could muster an accusation. Observing Bastien had given me a useful lesson in subtlety when pursuing a murderer. It would certainly help if I could handle a sword.

Palinur's streets were deserted. Cold seemed to have driven every honest man and beast under cover, and I kept my eyes open for the dishonest. Taking lodgings nearer the necropolis could be helpful for many reasons.

Every day we remained in our town house ate into our pitiful treasury. Tonight, without fail, I must give Soflet and the others notice. And though the thought of asking galled beyond words, perhaps our faithful steward would know where I might find cheaper lodgings. No pureblood acquaintance would.

Despite my weariness, I took a short detour through the Clothmakers' District. Nowhere close to riots or burnings, it might be a respectable place to seek a house we could afford. Juli's safety was paramount.

My magelight revealed a dreadfully grim prospect. Dark, cramped tenements overhung the dye shops and merchant stalls, almost touching above the rivers of slop that served for lanes. Stretched ropes crisscrossed the narrow space between, hung with lengths of new-dyed cloth or displays of some weaver's art.

I could not imagine life in such a place. Even at summer's height no sun would reach the ground. No leaf or blade of green would sprout, nor could a breath of fresher air ever sweep the acrid reek of dye pots and wool finishers from between the close-packed buildings. I'd never considered how our house in the Vintners' District was so well positioned to catch Ardra's golden sun and fairest breezes . . . did those ever come again.

Even as I mourned summer, the scent of honey clover wafted round me on a tendril of warmth. My skin prickled oddly of something that was not frost, more the sensation of balmy nights than any familiar magic. Glancing round, I glimpsed a slight movement a few quercae behind me. Probably someone late home to supper, as I was.

I quickened my pace. Encounters with smirking Cicerons and corpses frozen in ditches and coal scrapes had done no good for my already fractured nerves. It was likely a fox or a cat I'd seen. Who could traverse these tarry districts without cursing when his boots filled with icy muck or slipped on frozen ruts?

The lane opened onto a small cobbled square, where all the district's streets and alleys came together. Here one would find a font fed by one of Palinur's twelve wells and graced by some sculpted figure from Aurellian myth. One would also find a pillory and flogging post. Ever-practical King Caedmon had believed justice should be administered within sight of a man's home. He'd said it required fewer strokes to properly chastise a villain when his neighbors' wives and children could witness it.

I hesitated. If some rogue was indeed following me, I might lose him easier in the darker edges of the square. But instead I struck out across the cobbles as fast as I could manage, straight through the center, using my last whimpers of magelight to avoid crashing into the posts and pillory. When I reached the far side, my light was dead.

From the shelter of a drying frame I peered back across the square, squinting. Wind gusts sucked fat snowflakes from the heavy sky and set them dancing, thicker by the moment. And yet . . . My stomach lurched.

Two tall slender shapes stood beside the font—I'd swear the same two I'd glimpsed that morning, naked, one male, one female, their exquisite markings gleaming bright against the pitchy night.

I squeezed my eyes shut. Surely this was but imagining wrought by exhaustion and nerves and a craving for beauty that seemed lost from the world. When I looked again, the two were vanishing into a dark alley.

I charged after them.

Three strides into the alley and a rope across my shins sent me face-first onto hard-frozen muck. Air escaped my chest in a great burning whoosh. As I fought to reclaim it, someone sat on my hind end. Firm hands—warm—dragged my wrists behind and pressed them to my back at the waist.

My feet scrabbled for purchase. The pressure was not so great. If I could just get my knees under me, maybe I could lunge forward . . . throw him off.

Only I couldn't.

Angry and humiliated, I growled. "Who are you? What do you want?"

I didn't believe in Danae any more than I believed in angels or water sprites. This was someone's trick, an elaborate illusion.

"Thou'rt dull as mudstone, human." His words slid into my hearing like warmed oil. "Spirit bound by walls of iron. Ears plugged with tree sap. Blind, too, art thou, save with thy hands and feathers, so I am told. So we must descend to brutish grappling to force thy attention."

The scent of rosemary filled my nostrils as he leaned closer, hot breath on my neck and ear.

"Heed my word, Remeni-son. Delve not so deep. Some boundaries are not meant for human trespass. Is the world not broken enough that thou must seek out dangers beyond thy understanding?"

"I've no idea what you mean." *Feathers* . . . my quills? "Do you speak of my drawings?"

He sighed, breathing the scent of honey on my cheek, then shifted his weight. "How can we warn one who refuses to see? Thou shouldst destroy him and be done." He was not speaking to me this time.

"Prideful are those humans who touch the heart of the Everlasting." A woman's voice, scarce more than a whisper. Why did it set my every nerve aflame? "But they learn. Adapt. This one will. Thus, I choose not. Not this day."

"Tell me," I said, trying to lift and turn my head to see. "What are you talking about?"

The one on my back shoved my head to the cold ground. Blue markings gleamed from his long fingers like twined strands of sapphires embedded in his skin, yet I could sense no magic.

"We say this only," said the male. "Heed thy workings; learn of the true world. Trespass the boundary again, and thy wit is forfeit. We have forged a weapon apurpose to chastise thee."

A different finger touched my cheek, gently this time. The markings were coiled patterns of azure and indigo, and the scent—*her* scent, for I knew this was the female—was meadowsweet and sun-warmed grass.

"Gentle Lucian . . ."

A sweet, piercing ache near stopped heart and breath, no matter years, no matter disgrace and punishment and grieving. She sounded so like—*Impossible.*

By the time I groaned and named myself an idiot, a man celibate so long he knew only one name to call a woman, my hands were free, the weight gone from my back. I scrabbled up, but I was alone in the deepening snow.

The storm worsened as I walked home. The wind howled, driving the snow before it like wild dogs. Feet and hands grew numb. Had I encountered living Danae? Every word the two had spoken was burnt into my spirit, yet even ten times over I could make no sense of it. A *weapon* readied to destroy my wits. But for what crime? *Trespass. Delving too deep.* What *boundaries* could they mean? Certainly if I told anyone of the warmth that lingered on one cheek or of naked bodies scribed with blue markings that spoke naught of magic, I would be judged mad.

And yet . . . the power of childhood memory was astonishing. My grandmother's stories had told that the trickster Danae relished pureblood children born with two bents and would steal them from their families, bind them with stems of meadowsweet, and carry them off to the kingdoms of the night to be their slaves. For years the scent of meadowsweet had left me anxious.

Every few steps I spun around. At every turning I peered behind as far as the blizzard would let me see. Were they yet following me? Surely they were proof that my sensations of being watched were true. Unless I was already witless.

I refused to believe that. The two of them, at least, were real. My hand clutched a finger-length bit of woven rope that smelled of green vine, rosemary, and meadowsweet, of sun-warmed grass . . . and Morgan.

"She's gone, *Domé* Lucian!" Soflet's panic dragged me out of my frozen, half-blind stupor the moment I stumbled into the house.

"*Gone?* Goddess Mother! Not—" The word slammed into me like a mountain of midnight, threatening to split head and heart. After a day submerged in corpses, I could not think of any other meaning. "My sister? *Dead?*"

"Vanished." He could not have spoken *dead* in any more hopeless a tenor. "We cannot find her anywhere."

Vanished, lost, run away? In this city on such a night? Holy, blessed gods!

"Maia set out her supper tray, but the young mistress threw it on the floor. When we came with mops and rags to clean up the mess, *Doma* Juliana was gone. We mustered everyone and searched house and gardens, even the street. I sent Filip to other houses on the street, inquiring about a lost hound, thinking she would hear him and make herself known."

"No sign of her? No word?" Light of Deunor, if she'd run away . . . Anger, horror, and fear rose in tandem, indistinguishable. Images of the strangled girl child threatened to choke me.

"None. We didn't know what else to do. Without your permission we did not presume to approach the three blood families, but every other house . . ."

"Yes, good." I fought away visions of Juli wandering the dark, filthy lanes in such villainous weather. I needed my wits. "Well done."

Three pureblood families kept houses in the nearby streets. I didn't know them, only touched a finger to brow as protocol demanded when we passed in the street. But whether Juli had merely gone out unchaperoned or something worse, we could not allow the Registry to catch a whisper of it until we had exhausted every other remedy.

Simple indiscipline would complicate our lives beyond bearing, compounding our already wretched family reputation. But if Juli had truly run away and the Registry discovered it, her life was ruined. They would name her *recondeur*—renegade. When they found her—and only the infamous Cartamandua *recondeur*, still running or dead, had ever eluded capture for more than a few months—she would be subject to unrestricted contracts. Contracts without protections—enslavement. She would never be permitted to marry or have children, nor would I, like as not. It would be the end of our bloodlines. And I'd likely never see her again.

My lungs would scarce pump at the thought, the massive hurt that had existed in me since Pontia risen again to squeeze life's breath from my chest. To lose Juli, the last of us, was a grief unimaginable, even after our hard tutelage in grieving. I had to find her without involving the Registry. *Think, Lucian!*

The storm raged with a malevolent fury, rattling the glass windows and banging the shutters as if the Harrowers had roused the blade-keen wind to raze all human works. Even if Juli's perversities drove her to such mad rebellion, she would never pick such a night to run. A fall, an injury—gods save us, an assault that left her lost or hurt—and she would die before morning. She, a girl who constantly named me miser for rationing her fire, would know that. She could not have left voluntarily.

"No one came here? Invited her to visit? Could someone have breached the house wards and abducted her?"

"The wards did not trip, *domé*. And no one came. None she would speak to, certainly, or—" Soflet's broad brow, so rarely anything but smooth, drew into tight furrows, and a crimson flood washed his age-mottled cheeks. "I saw no one."

"But you suspect someone."

"Last winterset, a linkboy started coming round to light the gate torches at dusk. Filip's always run to the market for Maia about that time, and my rheumatics have been fitful—"

"She's spoken to a *linkboy*?" *Oh, great gods,* serena*! Didn't my stupidity teach you anything?*

Soflet released a deep sigh, as if expelling a demon. "I warned her not, *Domé* Lucian. Locked the doors when he was about. Sent him off and told him I'd have the constable on him did he show his face here again. But I've suspected he's come back since."

More than *suspected*, from the rue that wreathed the old man's face. "And you didn't tell me? Soflet, I trusted you. My parents trusted you. You know the consequences for her if she's seen flouting such discipline."

But he couldn't know, really. Soflet wasn't pureblood, though he had served in pureblood houses since well before my father's birth. And I knew exactly what he was going to say.

"She was so very lone, *domé.* And the boy was mannerly and respectful always. Sometimes I pretended not to see. When your trouble came down, day before this, I told him *no more* . . . and warned her, too."

And she had been livid. Last night she had bartered a sleep charm for my promise to forbid Soflet from locking her inside. Which I had done.

I sagged against the wall. "Where did they go on these visits?"

Please all gods, let it not have been to his bed. Not even a month past, I had tried to warn her about low men. But bound up in my own embarrassment, I'd stammered like an idiot and left her mystified. I'd gone promptly to Maia and asked her to see that Juli knew whatever was seemly for a maiden—whatever my mother would have wanted her to know—but I'd never asked what had actually transpired.

"They never went beyond the gardens, *domé,*" said Soflet, earnest and apologetic. "I'll swear to that. And I never saw him lay a paw on her. Never would I permit such. They played the peg game from time to time. Talked mostly. Laughed a bit, as children do. That's all."

"How long has she been gone? And what do you know about him?"

"'Twas half seventh hour when we found her missing. I think his name is Elgin or Edan or some like, but I've not a notion where he bides."

Footsteps hammered on the stair. "Soflet! The sneakers are—" Filip, our excitable footman, burst into the atrium from the cellar stair. "*Domé* Remeni!"

Pale as alabaster from hair to fingertips and deceptively slight for a youth who could lift a wagon bed while Soflet installed a new wheel, Filip halted, whipping his glance between the steward and me.

"My sister?" I said, praying he brought good news.

"Two bodies are creeping through the south hedge, *domé.* By size, one could be the mistress."

My blood surged. "You two keep them talking. I'll see he doesn't get away until we have some answers. And beware. Her magic . . ." They both knew the sting of Juli's ire. Though she'd never truly hurt anyone . . . or so I would have said that morning. Did I know her at all?

I raced through the kitchen and into the garden. The icy blast scoured my face as I sped across the frozen ground, over the low wall in a single leap, and out to the lane. Silencing breath and footsteps, I slipped through a side gate so as to creep up behind them. The two of them had reached the inner gate, a wild-haired boy in snow-crusted slops, gripping Juli's arm. She wore no pureblood cloak and no mask. No matter that my magic was depleted, I'd have him dead if he'd touched her ill.

". . . brother is off searching, near out of his head with worry, *doma.*" Soflet blocked the gateway, arms folded across his breast. "Though 'tis not my place to speak, I take it anyway. I've known you since you were birthed, as I have your good brother and all those lost to us. You've betrayed their trust in you and in him, in me and the rest of the staff, and I know not how—"

I clamped my arms around the youth's thin shoulders and, with no gentle force, dragged him away from my sister.

"Luka! Wait—"

"I'll break your scrawny neck do you so much as twitch, vermin!" I could do it. He was almost as slight as she was.

After a brief resistance, he went limp.

"Are you all right, Juli? Has he hurt you, touched you? If he's laid a hand . . ."

"Certainly not! Luka, let him go."

"No. Have you the least idea—? Go inside. I'll speak with you after I speak with this person." With every word I squeezed harder, but he refused to so much as squeak.

"*Ancieno,* listen to me. This is Egan. He's my friend. *Only* my friend."

"He is *ordinary.* You know—"

"I know he laughs and eats and works hard and cares for his mother. I know he's clever at games and has taught himself to read. Let him go and I'll tell you the rest. If you fear for my virtue, you can be easy. But if you hurt one hair on his head, I'll give you such a case of boils, everyone you meet, including your new master, will believe you have the plague."

I could not allow her to distract me. "Where did he take you?"

"He took me to his home, *ancieno.* Showed me how he lives . . ."

My heart sank. *Oh, gods,* serena, *have you no idea what comprises your virtue?* "Juli!"

". . . and introduced me to his mother and his landlord. Luka, I found us a new place to live."

"We cannot," I said, holding patience as well as I could. "Not in the same house as an ordinary you've companioned so freely. I will believe you that he is all innocence. He may be respectful and clever, but we must live by certain rules."

It was the same stanza I had repeated for the hour since Egan—indeed a mannerly boy of Juli's age—had gone. My sister and I were both wrapped in heavy quilts, seated by our hall fire and drinking a thick posset that had at last begun to thaw our bones.

"But you said we'd need new lodgings, and I knew you'd not wish me left alone all day. I'd surely go mad and give you all sorts of trouble. Egan's mam is so like Maia, you'd believe them sisters. She said she'd even cook for us if we paid for our own food. Certainly *I've* no idea how to do such a thing, and even if you did, I'd never stomach it when you came home smelling like a rotting carcass. The house is ugly and vile, but unless you've found better . . ."

Which, of course, I hadn't. Juli's plan was eminently sensible, if we were ordinaries. But we were not.

"I'm not stupid enough to believe we can maintain full Registry protocols on a hundred and sixty silver pieces a year, *serena*. But we must try, else—"

"*They* broke the rules first." She sparked and snapped like embers in the hearth. "Ask those dried-up sticks at the Registry who else had a contract accelerated two days ago. I'll lay you Matronn's thickest quilt against this luscious one of yours that you were the only one. Just listen to your story of the *non*-negotiation! Pew-Pons wants you punished. Perhaps she wants you to beg her mercy so she can force you into her bed, since no man could bear to look at the old cow. Or perhaps she's one who takes her womanly pleasures seeing beautiful young men whipped!"

"Juli!" Great gods, how did she know of such things?

Something strange was happening to my sister—a twisting, twitching, squinting struggle that resolved itself only when she shook loose of her cocoon, flung her arms wide, collapsed flat on her back, and burst into great whoops. "Oh, Luka, you should see your face! Are you not the most priggish, solemn, dearest *ancieno* in this miserable world?"

Such was the measure of my weariness that it took me a seeming lifetime to comprehend that the noise was cascading laughter. Then I grabbed hold of her arms, raised her again, and wrapped her quilt so tight about her it near squeezed her into hiccoughs. I was bereft of words. . . .

Until she began pestering me again. In self-defense, I agreed to look at the house in the Bakers' District where Egan and his mother had a room. No promises beyond that. No assurances. And *no* permission for her to visit it again.

". . . and you will wear your mask and cloak *every* time you stick a toe outside our door. Promise me. No! Hush your excuses. Swear it on all we hold in our hearts. Promise."

She promised. And then said Egan had shown her a shop where one could sell unwanted goods. Perhaps she could go there and take things we didn't need and would have no room to keep, adding a few coins to our box.

I hated that it made good sense. I'd never imagined visiting a pawner's shop. "Filip can go. Not you. No, not *ever.* Pick a few things, but only things Matronn sent here from Pontia. These furnishings, the plate, the bedclothes, the hangings—all go with the house and we'd have to replace them when we turn it back to Tessati." Whom I needed to notify very soon. "And keep your best clothes and jewels. We'll still be summoned to sittings, to entertainments, to Registry feasts, and we must make a respectable appearance. This is your year for an anniversary portrait. Yes, gossip will spread about our situation. Many will expect us to crumble, but we won't. We'll not dishonor our family." Even if some in the Registry did so.

It was not the time to mention that as soon as she turned sixteen in the summer, families would begin inviting her to visit. Though we had naught for a marriage portion and our influence was ash, Juli carried powerful bloodlines. Eligible families would be foolish not to consider a match . . . as long as she behaved. My own marriage negotiation was supposed to begin at the end of my first contract. Now that rested, as did my entire life, in the hands of the Registry. Not that I could imagine any pureblood family matching their daughter with an artist who worked in a graveyard.

"And *serena pauli*, please, about this Egan, you cannot—"

"Oh, to be rid of that ivory nymph Camatronn sent me for my birthday. It looks like the hind end of a goat. Some half-blind crone will adore it!" Juli crushed my face into her quilt wrapping, smothering my command. Then she planted a kiss on the top of my head and danced away, giggling as I'd not heard in forever.

As I drained my posset and gathered my quilt, she poked her head back through the doorway. "*This Egan* will be waiting in the inner court. I'll let *you* tell him when we're coming to see our new house."

She grinned and vanished.

An entirely unwarranted laugh rose from somewhere not related to good sense. I wished I could share her enthusiasm. It was certainly understandable. After so many months of grief and boredom, such a change promised adventure, as the prospect of the university had done for me. If I could just cushion the worst consequences, it would be a blessing indeed. Perhaps Master Pluvius could advise me on that as well as the contract. He had both a daughter and a granddaughter. I had to visit the Registry Tower on the morrow, whether Bastien liked it or not.

But first I needed sleep. And before either I had to speak with the boy in the courtyard. Egan was likely an icicle by now.

Soflet had called the boy respectful and indeed he was. He kept his eyes down and waited for me to speak. To begin I draped one of my old cloaks over his shoulders. His teeth were clattering a galliard, his legs shaking, and it was impossible to miss the dirty strips of rag tied round his hands and bird-thin legs for warmth.

"I'll visit your house tomorrow midday," I said. "But it is highly unlikely to suit. My sister's position in life—her gifts granted by the very gods you worship—make demands of her that you cannot comprehend. Nor does she fully, young as she is. She cannot be your friend. Not that you are unworthy of friends, only that the course laid for you is different. We must all attend the work we are given. Do you see that?"

He drew the cloak tight around with a sigh, as if it were his mother's arms. Then he shrugged it off and pushed it back into my hands. "Didn't come here to take nothing from you nor the lady. I'll show you the house midday. It's hard to find. Where shall I meet you?"

"In the Temple District, at the point where the Elder Wall juts out over the west end of the hirudo." Over the pigsty. I'd make the errand count for two.

Tomorrow morning, I'd tell Bastien of my discoveries in the hirudo, insisting I needed daylight to discover the exact house where the girl's murder had taken place. It would provide the excuse to leave the necropolis.

"Do you know the place?"

"Aye, lord. I light divine Arrosa's cauldrons every even, though her priestesses are squinch on the pay."

"Arrosa . . . that's where Arrosa's Temple sits?"

Revelation exploded in my soggy mind. Of course! It explained my vision—the moonflowers, the ephrain, the baths. The Goddess of Love saw cleansing of the body as a prayer; thus, her temple housed the finest baths in Palinur. Or so I'd heard. Three days ago, someone had defiled those sacred precincts with child murder.

"Aye, lord. And if I may speak . . ."

"Yes?" I forced my thoughts back to the youth.

Fourteen, I'd guess his age. His light brown hair draggled on his brow. His bony, unfinished face was pinched with cold and raw with windburn, but his clear gaze met my own through my mask, fearless.

"Mam prays to the Mother, but I don't count nothin' in it. She bakes when she can afford the makings for bread. We hunger when she can't. So I've lit torches and lamps for them as have oil to burn since I was big enough to climb, and candles for those who can afford such. Wouldn't like to see a gentle young lady sit in the dark when I could show her what's a rushlight. Mayhap your gods gave me the *task* to show her." He shrugged. "Or not, as you may see it."

A bold youth. And honorable to give back the cloak. Foolish, perhaps, but honorable.

"I'll think on that," I said, considering gods and chance in a most favorable light just then. "And no matter what, I'll see you tomorrow midday on the steps of Arrosa's Temple."

He let himself out the gate. I followed him to lock it and stood peering into the snow-whipped night for a while, but no streaks of sapphire light intruded on the storm. Nor could I detect any scent of meadowsweet or sun-warmed grass.

Great gods, Lucian, get you to bed. Next you'll be seeing Karish angels hovering over Necropolis Caton, ready to transport believers to Iero's Heaven.

Though I could come no nearer to understanding what my two assailants had said, the encounter in the alley was not imagined. I had evidence. My hand sought the length of rope in the inner pocket of my pelisse. But I drew out only a handful of dry litter—grass or straw with no scent at all.

Shivering, I locked the gate. The bells pealed half midnight. Only four hours until time to rise and start a new day.

CHAPTER 10

The wind packed snow into Palinur's every crack and crevice through the night, then fled like a thief. When I left the house before dawn, the sky crackled with stars and the cold was deep enough to freeze the marrow. The *pocardon* bustled with grim-faced women stripping the food stalls like geese at gleaning time. I hoped Filip had stocked our shelves the previous day.

Humming a nonsense tune under my breath and pressing my hand to my nose, I raced past alleys and side lanes without a glance. I didn't want to hear warning voices or smell meadowsweet or glimpse blue-limned figures out of myth walking the streets. I dared not acknowledge the encounter as truth. Pureblood sorcerers of healthy mind did not see Danae.

In a firelit doorway of a hirudo shack, Demetreo the Ciceron played a haunting melody on his syrinx—one that spoke of mysteries and happier times. He didn't look up as I hurried past. Someone had told him my name and what my portrait of the dead girl had revealed. I needed to squelch such dangerous talk. Only a few in the necropolis would have known.

Once through the slot gate, my spelled eating knife guided me to the proper burial mound and I returned the arché to its owner. I'd brought a flask of wine, as well, one of the few that remained from the Remeni-Masson vineyards. I poured half onto the grave.

"Sleep well, brother or sister. May the Ferryman deliver you to blessed Idrium, where all will know your name. Let this small gift refresh your time of waiting and serve as thanks for your help in time of need."

I poured out the remaining wine as a libation to the gods and renewed my pledge of service. My sleep had been restless as I wrestled with the guilt of venturing my forbidden bent. Things weren't so clear in the deeps of the night. Did my portraits actually show truth—the girl's dress, the soldier's badge? What if they were no sign of the gods' favor renewing my second bent, but falsehoods fed by my own pride? Worse, what if they signaled the very madness dual bents could cause? How would I know? And these other things—visions of myth I had been ready to accept as truth . . .

"Help me know," I whispered. "Help me recognize the truth and bring honor to my blood-kin as they feast in your halls: Vincente, Artur, Elaine, Germaine, Emil . . ." So very long it took to name them all.

Though the sun had not yet risen when I arrived at Necropolis Caton, Bastien had already left word with Constance about five more prospects for my pen and his purse. I rifled his book press for parchment and sought out Constance again.

"We need a new supply of parchment," I said, waving the few bits I'd salvaged. "Beyond this there's naught left worth using. I could as easily draw a smooth curve out there on the wagon road. And I've brought my own pens and ink so I can do better work, but I'll need a brazier to keep the ink from freezing. You seem the one to get things done."

Her thin cheeks burned—pleased, I thought. "Oh, aye, I can see to it. Coroner's confounded in his investigationing. Da's burthened with burnings. Some just won't wait for the Mother to take their kin, but must send 'em off in smoke. 'Specially these so ruint already."

"You burn corpses here!" Some Navrons believed fire was the cleanest way to send their kin on to Idrium, but to smell burning flesh, to raise the imagining of those I so loved screaming as the flames raged all around them—the very thought scalded my throat. "When?"

"Sunset mostly, so's it makes a better show. For sure I'll see to your pages and a bit of fire. Just holler for Garen or Pleury when you need a new corpus brought."

Constance hefted a load of cheap tunics she used to replace fouled clothing and set off toward the prometheum. Her awkward gait set her earrings to swaying. Long, dangling earrings of orangey gold—false gold. She'd not worn them before.

"One more thing, Constance!"

She halted and looked round as I caught up with her. I wished to speak without the entire population of Necropolis Caton hearing us.

"Demetreo the Ciceron knows things he should not, Mistress Constance. The law forbids any to spread gossip of a pureblood, and I'm sure you abide by it faithfully. But beyond the details of my person and my family, that restriction must include my name and the drawings I do. The portraits are the magic I provide as the gods' instrument. Not only are they private matters between the gods, my contracted master, and me, but revealing aught of their nature—especially the wondrous bits that recommend themselves to a lively imagination such as yours—could compromise the coroner's work, which I'm sure you've no intent to do."

"But I never—" Her protest died quickly and she wrinkled her long nose into a rueful grimace. "Ah, you've the right of it. I might have barbled to the Ciceron about the girlie's drawn. But you are such a *tale*! And bits of gossip do help pay for a girl's necessaries." She shook her head vigorously, setting her earrings glittering in the torchlight. "Now on I'll keep my tongue more privacy where you come in. You'll not tattle to Bastien?"

I shook my head. Bastien clearly trusted her. "I'll keep my tongue private as well," I said. I didn't blame an impoverished ordinary for wanting trinkets, but I couldn't allow her to compromise my safety or Juli's.

She hurried off again and I headed after, slower, considering the day to come. I wouldn't begin with the soldiers, but with the girl child, no matter what Bastien had preferred the previous day. I had to know if the first portrait I'd done was true.

Garen, the lean, dark-eyed runner, was lounging on the steps, waiting for a mission. I beckoned, and we set out for the Hallow Ground.

The child's features hadn't altered much as yet—a little darker, a little drier and less plump. Constance had replaced her muddy rags with one of the white tunics, which I doubted was the usual practice for unknown beggars. But then, who knew who might come to fetch this one, if Bastien discovered her name.

Arrosa's priestesses taught that the goddess made mortal love divine—as her own birth had made holy the mating of her mother, divine Samele, and a mortal man. Did the Temple of Arrosa take initiates so young? Is that what one did with a royal bastard? But who would have killed her and why?

Once we had the girl laid out, I spread a sheet of fresh parchment I'd brought for her, sharpened a pen, and filled an ink cup from the horn I'd brought. While the sun rose and gave me better light, I attempted to clear my mind of the past three days' upheaval. I centered my thoughts on the banked fire behind my breastbone. As for the dark place between my eyes . . . If my second bent was involved in these portraits, it was because somehow it had become entwined with my art, not because I'd called it up apurpose. For now I'd do only as I'd done before.

By the time a diffuse sunlight illuminated the child's face, the exercise had yielded calm and focus. Only then did I dip my pen in the cup. With a whispered apology to the girl for intruding on her yet again, I stroked her brow and jaw and reached deep for magic. The divine fire rushed through me, filling the simple lines and shapes with truth, and as my fingers transferred the image to the page, my body ached with bruising and quivered with terror, shame, and sickness so vile it repeatedly darkened my inner sight.

"Why isn't it the same? You've drawn naught but what we see here, and not so accurate at that. So which is truth, or is this yet another lie?"

I had known Bastien wasn't going to like the new portrait. But his goading was not going to rattle me this morning. This time I was prepared. For the hour since I'd completed the portrait, I had been puzzling over the identical questions. The dregs of terror and phantom bruises had taught me the answer.

"Both drawings are true. This one just depicts a different time. Though her hair is black, it's long and not chopped off ragged. What if the black streaks we saw on her face and tunic weren't just dirt? What if someone *colored* her hair black, as some women do, perhaps to change her enough she'd not be recognized? The day she died wouldn't have been the first time they did it. Look at her eyes . . ."

No merriment. No spark. Though the shape of her face remained unchanged from the other drawing, her eyes were no longer those of a child. The child's pain explained it all.

". . . and notice that the garment in the drawing is not this plain tunic from Constance, but good fabric and finely embroidered. These stains are her blood." Just as my vision in the hirudo had shown.

Bastien growled like a dog sensing its prey. "Someone was swyving her."

Never could I have stated such foulness so bluntly.

"What if you drew her a third time?"

"I doubt anything would change. Since the last, I've learned more of where she died. . . ." Without mention of a revived bent for history, I told him about Demetreo and the willow brake. "As the thicket is so tangled, and Constance said the girl had likely tumbled down an embankment, it seemed logical that she'd been let go from the walls, deliberately left to roll down into the ravine."

Thrown away like refuse. They'd never imagined anyone might look beyond her garb. And then I told him that it was a goddess's house abutted the wall so high above the piggery.

"Demon scat!" he said, jumping up from my stool. "I've no love for noble brats, no matter which side of the blanket they're born to. Most grow up scum, male and female alike. But them that priss and preach of gods, then turn round and debauch babies . . . that I cannot abide."

Corruption had always existed among the gods' human servants, but this? I could not abide it, either.

"So, how does a prince's ladylove get her babe into the temple?" mumbled Bastien. "She might have been a temple girl herself. A priestess or an initiate. Maybe a bath girl. I suppose they'd keep the babe and raise her to the goddess's service. Or it could be the child's mam was just a servant or a court lady with a devotion to Arrosa, and she chose to stow the mite in the temple to hide her. Or just to get her out of the way."

"I doubt she was born to a servant." I scanned the portrait for any detail that might have escaped me. "The first portrait showed her in court dress, so I'm thinking she lived for a while according to her station. Perhaps she was even known to the prince. She didn't age much between the depictions, which suggests this nasty business has all happened recently. It might be you could turn over this much information to Prince Perryn. Even if he hasn't acknowledged his bastards, he couldn't take well to one of his own blood brutalized. And surely someone at Arrosa's Temple has noticed she's missing. They might know who saw her that day or who might have reason to hurt her. Surely the child's *mother* couldn't know what was being done to her."

When I glanced up to see why he'd not responded, Bastien was scrutinizing me as carefully as if I were a knife wound on one of his corpses. "You've lost your doubts," he said. "What's changed? Tell me why you can draw things you've no way to know."

My skin heated. He seemed able to read me right through my mask. I averted my eyes, vowing to be more cautious. "I'm not certain."

"Come, come, Servant Remeni. You've arrived at some thought about it. I am your contracted master, and I've the right to understand. I bought you."

Perhaps it was this evidence of corruption in a place that should be holy. Perhaps it was my fears for Juli and my inability to protect her from danger, poverty, or humiliation. Perhaps it was simply because this crude, venal, clever ordinary had reminded me that I was his slave in all but name. Whatever the reason, my anger erupted like the volcano Aesteo that had burst from the earth in a single ferocious moment.

"You have the right to my best work. That I will give. You have the right to control my magic, save what I use to defend myself and my family. That I will give. But understanding? My thoughts? The inner workings of my power—of my *soul*? You have no right, and you could not pay enough. *Master.*"

I touched shaking fingers to forehead as I was required and walked out. Wrapping arms around my throbbing head, I invoked every mental discipline I knew, determined to forget every single happening in my life since I had left home for the university.

Bastien found me seated on the prometheum steps in welcome sunlight. He made a great show of dusting off the steps to preserve his threadbare velvet. More wealthy cows to milk today, I supposed. When he sat, I ignored him. Once in sufficient control, I would return to my erstwhile studio, do a portrait of one of the dead soldiers, and then leave to visit the linkboy and his vile lodging, where I must house my virgin sister.

"Wondered when you were going to stop hiding behind the mask, show a spine, convince me."

Was he trying to goad me into another outburst? "Command me as you will, Coroner, but soon, if you please. I'm going out at midday on family business. If you disapprove, complain to the Registry."

"We've two strikes already from yesterday's six portraits," he said, matter-of-factly. "One was a palace understeward's only son. One was an edane's heir. The lowly understeward offered a grateful twenty coppers; the mighty edane a grudging ten. Did I not tell you how it goes?"

I tried to imagine warmth emanating from the pale sun.

He waited for a bit, then heaved a dramatic sigh. Perhaps he was disappointed I expressed no amazement at his accurate prediction of relative generosity. Did he wish me to beg for a share of his tainted earnings?

He pulled a sliver of wood from his sleeve and picked at his teeth. "Good work on the child. I think we partner well."

"We are not partners." Even if I was stuck in this contract forever, even if Juli and I were reduced to eating raw wheat, I would not sell the dead's secrets for money.

"Humph." The grunt sounded more resigned than angry. He tucked away the toothpick, rose, and dusted off his backside. "See to your family business as you like. Just make sure you get those five done before tomorrow morning."

He didn't wait for my agreement. He recognized that honoring the contract mattered to me. I hated that he knew me even that much.

Once a frosted haze obscured the sun's brief visit, I signaled Garen to carry in the first of this day's corpses, while I returned the child to her ice barrow. I offered a brief prayer for her soul's peace to whomever might be listening, then returned to my studio, touched a man's brutally cloven brow, and reached for magic.

"'Tain't a palace," said Egan the linkboy, understating the obvious, as we descended the decrepit stair into the Bakers' District alley, scattering a collegium of bony cats. "But we're below, and Mam's fierce about vermin. She lays traps and ratsbane, and sets out alder leaves and glue for the fleas. You'll never see none of either. . . ."

House was too generous a term for the ungraceful stack of soot-blackened stone. From its shape, the lay of the land, and other hints scattered through the street, I'd guess a grand Aurellian villa had once stood in this place, destroyed in the war that expelled the last remnants of the empire. Egan's residence was likely built around the hearth of the main residence. Stones from the ruin would have provided the extra walls, as well as accounting for the baking ovens that gave the district its name.

". . . and when we've a fire, the heat'll warm your floor. Last lodger said his toes were never chilled. I won't lie, there's rough in the street, but Ju—the lady says she's got ways that I know I'm not supposed to speak of. Nor will Mam, though she'll have to know such if she's to companion the lady. Got to say, it feels anxious, knowing such persons as yourself suffer the hard times." Egan's verbiage had never slowed since I met him on the broad steps of Arrosa's Temple.

I had already visited the dank corner where the temple precincts abutted Palinur's inner rampart. A stair had taken me to the walk atop the hoary Elder wall. The view was most enlightening. Had someone dropped the child from the top of the wall her body would have been much more damaged than it was. But at a place where the Elder Wall bounded the temple's gardens, a drainage grate opened from the bottom of the wall. Seeps had carved channels down the earthen rampart toward the dark tangle of the hirudo willow thicket far below. The murderer had rolled the child downslope with the sewage. *Despicable.*

"How much?" I said, interrupting Egan's description of his mother's bread. "What must we give for it?" For two rooms, one approximately the size of Juli's clothes chest, the other perhaps twice that.

"Uh, four citrae the day, one more for coal. Another copper for each extra shovelful. But it's a clean house, and to have its own fire grate is a rarity, even in the Bakers' District."

Great gods, he was apologizing for the amount. I'd spent more than the year's tally on my last order of ink and parchment. That wouldn't be the case this year.

"And your mam's cooking, we would pay."

"She'll not take—"

"We will *not* be obligated to you. If a stranger asked her to cook the food he supplied, what would she charge for the doing?"

He pondered this as if it were the fate of the world, scuffing his boot in the alley filth, while the frost wind billowed my cloak. "Can't say exactly, but her bread's a citré the loaf, as it's promised no weevils nor droppings in it. She'd surely think a citré for the day's cooking was fair, as she cooks for me and her anyways. If she had to cook aught that was strange, maybe two?"

"We eat normal food." Perhaps he thought sorcerers might require delicate birds' livers poached in nectar, no weevils or droppings preferred. "A citré a day seems fair, along with an extra shovel of coal from time to time, perhaps." A charm against vermin would be more valuable, but Bastien would have to consent and I could not imagine asking such a boon. Yet my imaginings had certainly fallen short already. Here I was negotiating with a linkboy.

"Aye, that should do it."

A quick calculation told me the story of our future. We could allow ourselves approximately fifteen citrae a day. The rooms, the cooking, and two loaves accounted for half of that. Other food, wine, ink, parchment, Juli's lessons, and our clothes . . . everything else must come out of the remainder.

"Come to our courtyard tonight and I'll give you an answer." Perhaps the sky would turn a summer's blue in between or the warm breezes blow in from the west bringing us a better alternative. "To see the house was useful."

A few other squat houses along the street were stone built, similar to Egan's. The rest were the usual ramshackle sheds with tenements above. The lane itself was a wallow, little better than the hirudo piggery, and the district was poorer than the Clothmakers' District, but in truth, not as awful as it could be. The air was certainly fresher and fragrant with yeast and baking bread. Blackened ruins here and there, overgrown with winter-matted weeds, testified to local fires, but naught suggested riots. Yet what might happen in a bread makers' street when famine ground tighter in the spring? Indeed, where in the city would be safe?

Here at midday, the street was jammed with people hurrying on their business; loading or unloading carts; hauling grain sacks, water pails, or children. Elders sat on barrels or benches minding children or playing dice or pegs. Activity had stilled and voices had fallen silent when Egan and I arrived. As we stepped from the alley, it happened again; every eye gawked. I didn't want people noticing . . . gossiping.

"Do you need me to lead you back to the temple?" Egan's gaze darted between me and a clot of neighbors.

I beckoned him close where we could not be overheard. "I can find my own way. But, Egan, you clearly know the law forbids discussing purebloods or their business. That includes *any* mention of their families, their circumstances, or even their names." Juli would hear my opinion of her revealing our straits to this boy. "You must and will adhere to the law strictly, no matter what's asked of you—even by your mam."

"For certain. Always have. Always will." No flush of guilt or embarrassment tainted his cheeks. "The lady swore me. Though she worried more about you hearing how I was coming round."

My sister's surprises seemed never ending. But I could not have anyone know we lived in such a place. Purebloods would never walk here unless it was on the business of their contracts; and they'd never imagine one of our kind might come here voluntarily. Fortunately, purebloods rarely heeded ordinaries' gossip, either.

"Not a word to anyone. The Crown's penalties for violation are severe, but mine will be worse. You'll regret the hour your tongue flaps."

Indeed now all color left him, leaving cheeks bone pale and eyes huge. "Aye, lord. I swear on my mam's head. Honest, truly, I'll be silent. Like a tree. Like a rock. Like a—"

"Yes, yes." No need to have him choke on his heart. "And should we meet again, the proper term of address is *domé.*"

I hurried away, my own cheeks hot, wishing for a thousandth time there existed some spell that could blot people's memories. *Obscurés,* spells that could divert people's attention, were terribly difficult. I'd never learned how to work one. Until I did so, Juli and I would forever make a show in such a street, as noticeable as jongleurs with monkeys on their shoulders.

It was a relief to see the Registry Tower rising above the Council District like a god's finger pointing the way to Idrium. Even after such a brief foray into the lower city, it seemed a sanctuary. I raced up the steps, my heart lighter already. Pons was not the only curator here. My grandsire had been one of the most respected men of any pureblood generation. My father's chronicle of the music of the Middle Kingdoms was considered the finest work ever conceived on the subject, and my mother's murals graced temples, cathedrals, and grand houses of living and dead all over Navronne. Their reputations had not died with them. Pons's failure to negotiate my contract was a serious breach of pureblood protocols. Someone would listen to me.

CHAPTER 11

The guards at the outer door of the Registry Tower nodded crisply as I passed. Trained to sense the magical deadness of ordinaries, they knew who belonged inside and who did not.

Across the atrium at the grand stair, two more liveried guards held blackwood staves wrapped so tightly in spellwork, they made my lips itch. Somewhat surprisingly, the guards crossed the staves at my approach, barring my entry to the stair. "Your business, *Eqastré* Remeni-Masson?"

"I'm to see Master Pluvius, *servitor*," I said coolly, unaccustomed to being challenged, and even less so to being addressed as a guardsman's equal.

"Master Pluvius is not in the Tower today," said the servitor.

"The Overseer of Contracts, then."

"Curator Albin is unavailable to outside visitors." Not the least hint of apology or accommodation. My gut tightened.

"First Curator Gramphier himself, then," I said. "He promised to consult with me about my Registry position."

My grandsire's longtime colleague now held the highest rank of any pureblood. Though I'd met Gramphier often in the company of my grandsire, I'd spoken to the man only once in five years, when he sat for his official portrait. But this was more of a test than a true request. In truth, his offhand *promise* had been made to my grandsire when I began work here.

"Surely you cannot expect curators to abandon their business to see just anyone at a whim." A lean, balding man with the sinewed grace of a racing hound had joined us from the guardroom. Fortieri's iron hand had commanded the Tower Guard for a generation. "I suggest you apply in writing for an appointment before returning to the Tower."

Containing my rising anger required all the self-discipline I'd squandered at Necropolis Caton that morning. "Master Pluvius has never required me to apply in writing," I said. "He has been my contract master and my mentor for five years. He declared his door open to me always."

Fortieri's hard gaze traveled my length, head to boots and back again. He sniffed, nostrils flaring in distaste. Great gods . . . the graveyard stink. Had I already sunk so low as not to notice?

"The Master of Archives no longer holds your contract, Remeni. Perhaps if your current master applied on your behalf for his counsel or tutelage, Curator Pluvius might have time to see you. Until then, it is our duty to ensure the serenity of these halls. As you well know, *eqastré*."

Such insolence! I did not trust myself to respond. Cheeks aflame, anything but serene, I spun to go, only then glimpsing a host of curious observers on the gallery above the atrium. The humiliation I had felt when leaving the Registry chambers in Montesard in disgrace had been naught to this. And this time I had done *nothing* to deserve it.

Holding dignity, I maintained a steady, unhurried pace as I left the Tower and crossed the courtyard to the outer gate. But I had no intention of giving up so easily. I knew one person who would speak to me.

Touching my brow to the single guard at the gate, I hurried into the steeply descending street. I turned left into the first alley and sped past a series of painted doors: a copyist's, a glover's, a parfumerie. Halfway along the alley, I slipped into a niche scarce wider than a coal scrape. A narrow stone stair, so ancient as to predate almost every other structure in Palinur, climbed back toward the Registry Tower.

I sped up the shallow steps. The dark stone was treacherous, skimmed with ice where the drips from adjacent roofs had pooled and puddled in scoops left by centuries of boots.

Long before King Caedmon gave the Tower to the Registry as part of their accommodation, the kings of Ardra had brought secret prisoners through a low iron door in the foundation of the Tower. Much more recently, the Royal Historian, Vincente de Remeni, had used the entry to teach his eager grandson the marvels of reading thresholds. Thresholds held the threads and knots of history in the same way crossroads and mountain passes did. We had spent hours here.

The black iron door remained exactly as it was the last time we'd come—and every time I'd used it since. Plain and smooth, its handles, locks, and latches long removed. Its hidden hinges were impervious to bars or levers. And I had no need to work magic.

"Aperite porte mordé!"

The door swung open silently at the incantation and closed softly behind me.

Magelight led me through dank, windowless iron chambers the Registry didn't see fit to use for anything. I bypassed the twisting iron stair that led up to a guardroom on the fifth level of the tower. Just behind the stair, a seam in the wall housed a latch that would respond to a small infusion of my magic. Mine alone.

My grandsire had said that a man who visited the Archives at odd hours as often as he did tired of guards asking what was his business so late. And the iron stair was steep and tiresome. This particular door, cleverly hidden on both sides, opened onto the Registry's back stair—the servants' stair. The back stair also served as a highroad for junior portraitists and other low-ranked employees arriving late of a morning, but I was likely the only person living who knew about the secret access through the cellar.

Three turnings and a wrought-iron gate took me into the fourth level of the Tower. Were I blind I could recognize the Registry Archives. The scents of parchment and leather and the reek of sour vitriol and acrid tannin used to mix inks made the air a fragrant brew. I'd never noticed how pleasurable it was before donning the perfumes of the necropolis.

It was early afternoon—not the hours for portrait sittings, thus easy to slip unseen through the Archives and around the corner into the junior portraitists' studio. The unruly black hair and broad, meaty back roused a grin. Gilles was working at his easel, retouching a drawing of a wrinkled dowager. I was only three days gone, and he already had the place a jumble.

I closed the door carefully, slipped across the floor, and perched in the window seat, waiting for his pen to lift from the parchment.

After a while he sighed and yawned noisily, as he always did when he released his magic.

"Grace of the Mother, Gilles," I said softly.

He poked his head around his easel.

"Lucian! What the devil—? Great gods, I've missed you! I'm buried!" Hapless, he extended his arms to include the stacks of portrait folios, as well as his usual litter of discarded pages, blotted rags, emptied ink horns, broken pens, and the remnants of half a dozen meals.

"Shhh. I had to sneak up the back stair." I tried to maintain some tone of levity. "Don't think I'm supposed to be here."

His broad brow creased. "I didn't expect to see you for ages yet. Truly I've not known what to think—all the stories going round. On that last day you were standing by the open window, so I told myself you'd taken some sort of fever instead of . . . anything else. Earth's Mother, you *do* smell like a sickroom."

"Sorry about the stink. It's my new master's business—smoke and such. I've certainly not been ill. That would have been better in a way. No one told you I had a new contract?" He hadn't been here when I picked up my things that day, but I had assumed he'd learn soon enough. His own uncle Albin had announced my dismissal.

"Not ill? But everyone says it." Puzzlement creased his brow. "We've heard you needed a change of scene for now, else—"

"Else?"

"You'd do something awful. Hurt yourself or someone else. Run away. Rebel."

"*Hurt* someone? *Run*? Why ever—?" Juli's taunt echoed in my thick skull. "Gilles, has no one else had a contract terminated early these past few days?"

"Certainly not. Who's ever heard of such a thing?"

"Three days ago your uncle Albin told me that all contracts scheduled to expire next year were accelerated, to be renegotiated—or not—immediately. They didn't renew mine. Booted me out that same day."

"Perhaps"—flooding sympathy erased his disbelief—"that's just what they told you. To make it easier."

"Easier?" I exhaled disgust. "I am neither ill nor violent nor rebellious, but I am assuredly an idiot. This is all Pons. The witch has stuck me in a contract you couldn't imagine in your nightmares. And no curator will see me so I can protest it."

And the witch's revenge was worse than I knew. To put it about that I was on the verge of rebellion . . . a *recondeur* . . . driven to violence or, great heavens, self-murder! No wonder I wasn't allowed into the Tower.

Even if I found someone to listen to my complaints about the lack of negotiation or Pons's five years of spite, who would believe them? Without funds to maintain our station, rumors of my disintegration would seem to be true. At best Juli and I would fade out of sight; at worst . . . Lord of Fire. Mad sorcerers were extremely dangerous.

Gilles shook his head vigorously, then plowed his inky fingers into his hair and yanked on the unruly mop, holding his locks stretched out until it seemed his scalp must be torn off—his customary reaction when details of a portrait refused to come together. "I'll say the rumors threw me. You've always been so well disciplined. You're saying the other curators let Pons dismiss you—the finest portraitist in the Registry—because of that matter at the university?"

At one of our late suppers I'd told him why Pons was always looking over my shoulder.

"They didn't give me any better reason."

Gilles shoved his easel aside and leaned forward, forearms planted on his formidable thighs, ink-stained fingers clasped. Unaccustomed sobriety stilled his face and lowered his voice. "The rumors say you went out of your head with what happened to your family. That it's been getting worse for a while and was affecting your work. Reports—I can't even say whose, as it seemed to be common knowledge all at once—said you were on leave and that everyone should keep away from you."

"Why would anyone think that?" It was true that rumor held disproportionate sway in pureblood life. Families were closed, insular, the six Registry curators worst of all. No pureblood was intimate enough with any other to counter widespread gossip. "Did your uncle tell you this?"

"You know Uncle Guilian doesn't talk to me about serious matters. But he did remind me that I should be exceptionally discreet because we worked together, you and I. Investigators plagued me right after you left. I swear I told them I'd not seen evidence"—his complexion colored a bit—"well, not anything so dire as all that. I mean, you were grieving, that was clear, and angry, but who wouldn't be? As for the rest . . . perhaps someone is just seeing you've got some time to settle matters, financial things, your sister. Pons would never spread false rumors over an old discipline matter."

"She's done more than you know. She was appointed my negotiator, and she failed to—"

Caution halted me. Pons's betrayal of every principle we lived by was very serious and should be reported only to her superior Gramphier, the First Curator of the Registry. But first I needed to understand who was circulating these reports. If Pons's influence was so sweeping, I didn't want Gilles left in her bad graces.

I sagged against the casement, letting the cold draft chill my anger. "Well, it's no matter. I'll get to the bottom of it. Pons pawned me off on an old bid from outside the city. Perhaps the curators truly believed the change would do me good."

Perhaps someone had got wind of Pons's malfeasance and was trying to hush it up. Lay it all at my feet somehow.

"Sometimes our superiors do things for our own good that make no sense at the time." Gilles's black eyes shone like those of a proud uncle, relieved, it seemed, that I'd thrown sand on my fire.

"Perhaps you did need a change of scene," he said. "No matter the stink, you're a deal more lively. Honestly, Lucian, a runaway chariot heading straight for you wouldn't have roused you three days ago, nor any of these past few months. Unless it had six new sable brushes on it."

Laughter belched up from somewhere, a decent good humor that seemed to cleanse the clotted fury from my veins. Gilles had always been able to get it out of me.

"I'm still drawing portraits," I said. "But the subjects aren't very lively, so I've had to use some new methods. Which reminds me: Has anyone in your family ever shown"—it sounded so ridiculous, but Gilles came from an even longer line of artists than I did—"an obscured presence when he worked, as if the magic created a fog or curtain that veiled him? Someone said—Of course, we were outdoors at the time, so I'm sure it was snow and mist."

"Never heard of such a thing." He scratched his head vigorously, as if trying to put it all to rights. Then his chin lifted and he grinned. "Though there have always been strange manifestations of talent. Patronn was telling stories of Janus de Cartamandua, the cartographer, the other night, when we were speaking of—Well, old Janus has long gone loony, you know. But it was said that when he was making his maps, he could walk right out of this world."

"Ah yes, into the *realm of angels*." According to some, good King Eodward was actually Caedmon's son, instead of his great-great-great grandson. Supposedly the boy prince had lived with the angels for a hundred and forty-seven years before claiming his throne and becoming the greatest king in the history of the Middle Kingdoms. "Earth's Mother, Gilles, did you really think I'd gone mad like old Cartamandua?"

"Certainly not." His cheeks could have roasted a goose. "I was just worried and asked Uncle Guilian if they'd heard any news of you."

"I've got all my wits for the moment," I said. "Truly I'm doing some of the best work I've ever done. Though it's odd—"

"Oh!" His head popped up. "Speaking of your best work. Perhaps it was not quite your best. Master Pluvius is having the curators' portraits completed for you. They want them hung for, well, I can't quite remember what occasion. It's too bad you can't do it yourself."

"But the portraits were completed months ago. You know I can't leave a portrait unfinished."

Pluvius had never explained the delay in unveiling the results of my first senior commission, but neither had he mentioned any need for modification. And for one pureblood artist to alter the work of another risked compromising the image's truth. The disharmony was instantly detectable to anyone who took the trouble to look.

"You must come to the ceremony, then, and see. Wash off the stink, but come."

All of this was profoundly disturbing. Curators telling people I was ill and unstable, and then sending me packing—burying me in a contract that would keep me away from everyone I knew. Claiming that grief for my family was affecting my work, and then altering my best efforts. Master Pluvius had praised his own portrait and told me he'd never been so proud to show one of his portraitist's works to their subjects.

My recent experience with the child and the soldier glared at me like noonday sun in summer. What if my magic had included something odd, something secret? I'd never paid much attention to the backgrounds of the portraits. I had chosen the setting for some relevance to the person. The Archives for Pluvius, vineyards for Albin, and so forth. After that, as long as they were well crafted and harmonious with the subject's appearance, I paid little attention. The truth of the *person* was my focus. Had this prompted Pluvius's vague warning on my first morning at the necropolis?

"How many were deemed incomplete?" I said. "And whose?"

"Two or three, so I heard, but I've no clue as to which." He shrugged an apology and picked up his pen. "I'd best get back to work."

"Could you find out? And also when the unveiling is to be. I'll be working late tonight, but perhaps tomorrow evening you could meet me at the Star. We could have supper as we used to. But, Gilles"—unnamable urgency swelled in my chest, compressing my lungs and squeezing my heart—"don't tell anyone I've been here. I'd like to surprise the curators with how quickly I've . . . recovered."

Gilles grinned. "An exceptional plan! Tomorrow night, eighth hour. I have to work late every night since you've gone. Now you're better, you'll be back here and get me caught up."

I doubted that. More so by the moment.

"Leave off this one," said Bastien, barging into the studio as I dipped my pen to begin the fourth portrait of the afternoon. "We've other matters to look into."

It had been foolish to promise five more portraits after traipsing over half the city. I'd not returned until two hours past midday. Now the daylight was long gone. Though Constance had installed torches in the preparation room, firelight never yielded as good a result. Before magic, before grace, my own eyes must comprehend the lines, planes, and textures of the physical being before me. No enchantment could compensate for poor observation.

"I'll begin with him tomorrow," I said, already calculating all Juli and I must do to prepare for our change of residence. "My business took longer than I expected this morning."

He waved off my explanation, poked his head outside the door, and bellowed for Garen to retrieve my current subject. ". . . and tell Constance to keep him good and cold. He's a ripe belly wound."

My unused parchment went back on the stack.

"The blowflies will have already settled in his gut when he died," said Bastien at a more conversational volume, as if I'd asked him to expound on his morbid pronouncement. "They're tucked in there, warm and working despite the outside cold. He's going to cave in any time now."

Shuddering, I averted my eyes as Garen and Pleury carried the corpse away. Something to anticipate overnight. My head, back, and right leg yet throbbed with pain from the portraits I'd done this afternoon, as if axe and spear had violated my own flesh. Had Pluvius or any of the other portraitists heard of such a thing? Better I had asked Gilles about that than the "flickering" idiocy. Though either topic could feed rumors of madness. And if I'd been stupid enough to mention a Danae encounter . . . Did madmen believe they were sane even when raving?

Trying to shake off the worry, I wiped my pens and installed each in the leather pen case my mother's brother had given me at my sealing feast. Erich had created exquisite catalogues of bird drawings for an eccentric ducessa in Morian. Now that would be a pleasant study. Outdoors in fine weather. Inside when the snow flew, coloring the illustrations. Clean. Innocent. Highly unlikely to involve dangerous talents, phantom pain, Cicerons, corpses, or murderers.

Having dispatched Garen on some other mission, Bastien planted himself in the doorway.

I needed to be home. The conversation with Gilles unnerved me more by the hour. Purebloods who went mad vanished. Their families locked them away and laid heavy bindings on them, so their skewed magic couldn't harm anyone. And if one had no family, who took on that responsibility? It was difficult to believe a simple error of personal discipline and an investigator's frustration could carry such dread implications. Were the rumors the work of Pons alone? If not, then who else and why? I needed time to think. Time to prepare.

The coroner's boot tapped a quiet rhythm on the cracked floor.

"What *matters* have we to look into?" I said, crushing my own impatience as I placed the last pen in the case. I had best learn to accommodate Bastien. I doubted I'd be leaving his service any time soon.

"You hold to the Elder Gods it seems, and in a prayerful manner, not just mouthing. Am I right in that?"

I wrenched the buckle on the writing case and snatched my cloak from where it lay across the dry laver. Would the damnable ordinary never stop prying? "I believed I made clear—"

"Now don't get all prune-faced again. In the ordinary way, I'd not care if you sacrificed beetles to a lizard god or held that men turn into tree stumps and women to barley when we die. But we've a matter needs investigating in a goddess's temple, and I need to know if you're on good terms with divine Arrosa."

This was about the dead girl child. Despite all, curiosity pricked. "My father's kin were ever devoted to the Lord of Fire; my mother's to the Lord of Vines."

Neither family had been strict in observance, taking more stock in our gods' celebrations of magic and life than in sacrifice or arcane practices or overreliance on mythic signs and omens. Since the ravaging at Pontia, I'd lived as if no gods existed . . . save when I touched magic and knew better. Perhaps our easy relations with the divine had been presumptuous.

I tugged my mask from my belt and fingered the cool silk. "I've naught but passing familiarity with the Goddess of Love and her practices."

Bastien grimaced and scratched his jaw, where bristles left from his shaving had already sprouted into a hearty thatch. "No point in my going up there to ask questions. Commoner folk aren't invited into the presence of Arrosa's priestesses. The Writ forbids even those of us with the force of law in hand, unless we've sure evidence of their involvement in a crime. Most inconvenient."

Caedmon's Writ of Balance had codified a truce between the priests and priestesses of the Elder Gods, the Karish hierarchs, purebloods, and the Crown law, preventing any one of them from interfering with the inner workings of the other. Only the king could overrule the Writ in any matter. Inconvenient, indeed.

"But surely there are more than priestesses to summon to an inquest." Even as I tossed out this sop, I knew it was foolish. "Though I suppose without knowing the child's mother or how such a child had come to be at the temple, you'd have to fetch in half the city. And you're not looking for just one villain. One pair of hands strangled the girl, but I'd vow there were more who put her in the way of it. Some who just turned a blind eye." Her mother, the priestesses?

"Aye. She's three days dead and none's raised a hue and cry. And 'tis a fool's exercise to summon any to witness to murder when we've naught but a gutter child and a sketch too outlandish to believe. Aaghh!" He growled and spat. " 'Tisn't even the crowd of testy witnesses would be the worst problem, but the danger to my living past the morrow if it becomes known I'm investigating a *royal* murder. Powerful people take offense at the suggesting of crimes that could remove their heads."

Now I was paying attention, it took no skill of logic to catch his aim. "You want *me* to act as your runner—to visit the temple and ask questions without raising a possible murderer's suspicions." A task that had naught to do with portraits or my bent, and thus skirted the terms of the contract. And yet the prospect of learning more . . . of exposing that murderer . . .

His eyes sparked and his thicket brows lifted. That he found it unnecessary to speak, much less persuade or command me, was wholly annoying. But of course, my magical investigation in the hirudo had already taken me well outside my duties.

"Purebloods do not bathe in public. . . ."

My feeble play bounced off him like a soap bubble. He said nothing.

". . . though if a pureblood is an adherent of Arrosa, I suppose they make some arrangement for private baths. But how ever would I introduce the topic of the girl?"

"Surely you've some kin whose contract might involve Ardra's royal household." So casual he was, leaning against the doorpost as if discussing the price of fish. "You could say a kinsman had done a portrait of the girl, heard she was living at the temple, and sent you a trinket he'd promised her, or something like."

"But I'm a wretched liar . . . and to a priestess . . . gods!"

"A ruse. For justice's sake. No one will ask which relative it might be."

"Hardly difficult when I've exactly one living kins—"

My blurted confession popped Bastien's head up. But to stop was to give the fact weight. Personal information provided handles for manipulation, the very reason pureblood discipline demanded strict privacy. So I babbled on.

"But my sister visited Palinur a year ago to study the buttressed vault in the Karish cathedral. It's believable she might have sketched the child on the same visit."

"A pureblood with no family," said Bastien, thoughtfully. "I'd wondered."

Naturally, he would have noted my slip. The man was like a hook trap.

"My *family* is not your—"

"Not my business. I know. But it explains a few things." He straightened, enlivened like a hound catching a scent. "So, you'll do this? 'Twould be a coup to bring down a child strangler."

"And profitable, if the child has royal blood," I snapped.

Bastien's broad, ruddy features hardened. Then he shook his head slowly, flaring his nostrils and pressing his wide lips together for a few moments, as if holding his words until they had mellowed.

"Easy for you to judge me from your lofty perch, pureblood," he said, soft and intense. "And easy for a rich man to scorn my pay. But think on this: There's a number of these dead soldiers would bring more certain coin than this strangled girl, and with far less risk. I do decent work here and see no shame to get paid for it. If catching this devil brings a benison that jingles, all to the good. But such a devil deserves to get caught."

No matter that my perch was no longer lofty nor my treasury replete, his point was undeniable. Even after so short a time, it was clear that those in Necropolis Caton did decent work. Likely far more valuable than bird catalogues. My future lay with Bastien for now. In the girl child's case, even if our reasons differed, our goal was the same.

I dipped my head and spread my hands to acknowledge his point. "Do I have your permission to use magic in this business?"

He nodded. "Aye. To pursue this felon, whatever you need."

I held out my pen case. "Then, if you would keep this in your chamber . . ." I'd hate to lose it, and there was no use to carrying it back and forth every day. And, too, it bore my family crest. The fewer who noted that the better.

Bastien's slow, smug grin blossomed in a way I was coming to detest.

"Knew it," he said, as he took the pen case. "Saw it in you from the first. We suit."

"We are not partners." I slipped on my mask and strode down the stair and into the night.

CHAPTER 12

"How may I introduce you to the high priestess, *domé*?" asked the young woman standing in the doorway of the perfumed salon. Her gown of summer blue and white drifted in the rising heat of the braziers set about the floor.

Though I'd just sat on the silk-cushioned banquette, my head was already swimming with the excessive heat, the hot wine offered on my arrival, and the certainty that I had no idea what I was doing. Should I question this woman? Would she know the children here or would she tattle to her superiors that the pureblood visitor was strangely inquisitive?

Surely my brow flushed as deep a scarlet as her own smooth complexion. "Are you a priestess of the goddess?" I said, falling back on the customs of rank. "I cannot reveal myself or my business to one of lesser status."

Lowering her eyes, the young woman pointed a long finger at a white ribbon around her slender neck. "I am but an initiate of the temple, but I am privileged to serve Sinduria Irinyi as her handmaiden. Please forgive me, *domé*, but even one of the gods' chosen must have urgent business to intrude upon the Sinduria's evening prayers."

"You may tell her—" On my walk from the necropolis I'd decided that using Juli as a ruse to obtain an interview was purest idiocy. If someone in this place had truly conspired in murder, it would be dangerous to involve my sister in any way. Yet now I was here, the story I had concocted instead—wishing to do a set of portraits of temple residents—seemed as insubstantial as smoke. Surely something closer to truth would be easier to manage. "Tell her I seek guidance on a private matter of the heart and conscience."

The girl bowed and retreated, and I settled back against silk cushions. The perfumed smoke tempted me to close my watering eyes, to relax, to surrender. Deep in the sprawling temple precincts, someone picked at a lute in an ancient mode. The music floated on the overheated air, insinuating itself into my flesh, hinting at sacred mysteries and fragrant nights under the goddess's moon.

I wished I could shed my pelisse and perhaps the brocade doublet as well. If this priestess took too long, I'd end up a soggy dumpling floating in a puddle. A stinking puddle. The stench of the necropolis rose from my garments in rancid waves.

Blinking away my weariness, I forced attention to my surroundings. I was here to uncover evidence of corruption and murder.

Arrosa's Temple had been in decline for decades. Women's mysteries centered ever on Samele, the Goddess Mother. And my grandsire had postulated that although men's thoughts would ever turn to physical love, King Eodward's skill at war and just governance had directed men's devotions to Kemen Sky Lord or the Karish god, Iero.

Certainly the temple's artworks were uninspired. Low, heavy ceilings were hung with ornate lamps that smoked worse than torches. Every hall and vault was painted with flat, smoke-dulled renderings of humans and beasts engaged in elaborate feasting or processions through indistinguishable fields and vineyards.

This room was no different. Every table and shelf was burdened with heavy ornaments—alabaster eggs, lifeless bronze birds, thick-walled cups. The painted panels were separated by pilasters in the mode of barley sheaves, and the doorway framed by a painted brick arch, as if one might walk right through into another part of the scene.

But a stone frieze, far more distinctive than the murals, drew me across the chamber. Just above my eye level, it bisected the walls into upper panels and lower. Against an intricate background of forest and ponds, worked in such low relief they seemed but an imagining, the sculptor had imposed well-defined, lifelike human forms. In the smoky lamplight, the figures took on a lovely semblance of truth. The subject matter, though . . . The naked revelers lounging in these ethereal glades were twined in ways that did naught to cool my overheated blood. Overseeing these activities hovered divine Arrosa herself, the crescent moon above her head. If I closed my eyes, the impression of that moon shimmered silver in the darkness . . . magic.

"The frieze is evocative, is it not? Created by one of your own kind."

I pivoted sharply. A tall, handsome woman, robed in silks the hues of lavender, violet, and plum, had stepped through an open panel in the wall. Blue paint made her gray eyes deep and huge; her full lips were stained crimson. Though her skin appeared smooth as a child's, she was not young; the cloud of wheat-colored hair that framed her refined features was mottled with gray. A wide collar of intricate beadwork, gold and lapis and amethyst, marked her as a Sinduria, a high priestess of the Elder Gods.

The painted panel closed softly behind her.

I touched fingertips to forehead and inclined my back slightly. "Sinduria."

She crossed her arms, touching each opposite shoulder, and closed her painted eyes—a portrait of serenity. "Welcome, chosen of the gods. I am indeed Irinyi, but for this hour I surrender my name and person and become the Lady Arrosa's vessel. All spoken between us is prayer between you and She Who Loves."

Nothing for it but to plunge ahead. "That would be very nice to believe."

Irinyi's eyes flew open, sharp and startled.

"Understand I intend no insult to the goddess or her vessel. But my life is in turmoil. I dare not even reveal my name. If so much as a hint of my story travels beyond this room, I face ruin on a scale one who is not pureblood cannot possibly comprehend. I have been told that my kind, even those pledged to other gods, may find clarity under the goddess Arrosa's roof."

Naught of lies so far. *Ruin* and *turmoil* properly named these past three days.

She motioned me to the banquette. She sat next to me, close enough I could have touched the bony fingers cupped in her lap. My own fingers itched for a pen. Would her portrait show the serene vessel of a goddess or a child murderer? Unfortunate that I could not draw a portrait from simple memory and ensure its truth.

"My temple offers many paths to clarity," she said in an elevated timbre, as if her goddess had indeed possessed her. "Trust in me, Seeker. Let me cleanse this trouble from thy spirit."

Fist clenched on my breast, I offered a fervent prayer to Deunor and Erdru that I was no lunatic, and begged them to intercede with their sister-cousin on my behalf if questioning her servants offended.

"Perhaps this *is* a summoning," I said. "One I should have heeded years ago. Are you familiar—? My people believe strict social constraints necessary with regard to those we call *ordinaries*—those who do not share our gifts."

"Yes."

"Then hear the dilemma of one who failed in obedience and has only now reaped the full measure of his sin."

Fingers ringed with pearls and amethysts motioned me to continue.

"Six years ago, I lived in the house of a kinsman, apprenticing in his work—work that required me to move amongst ordinaries in a distant city."

All true in its fashion.

The Sinduria sat quiet as I steeled my nerve to go on. I had never told this story aloud. And I needed to remove or recast any piece that might identify me or my family. Fortunately, neither my garments nor my appearance bore anything to distinguish me from five hundred other pure-blood men of an age between twenty and thirty.

"The association with so many good minds distracted me from my responsibility to maintain appropriate detachment from those I encountered. One day, a young woman arrived . . ."

Unable to stay seated, I paced the small chamber and without names or specifics told her about the most fascinating person I had ever known. About her intelligence and easy laughter. About how my eyes refused to leave her or my mind to dismiss her. About our first furtive words, our walks in the city, the longer excursions in the wood, in the hills, anywhere we could meet without being seen.

". . . an unfamiliar elation had taken possession of me, flesh and bone, mind and spirit. Though not a devotee of your goddess, I named it love. Yet always I knew it was built on lies and impossibility, and that a single word could bring scandal upon my family. But like a twistmind bound to the cruel seduction of his nivat seeds, I was enslaved to her presence. Every moment away from her grew my need. . . ."

The priestess closed her eyes and pressed her folded hands to her mouth as I spoke of the day I first kissed my friend, and about the day she asked me to work magic for her.

Memory came flooding over and through me, building an image of color and emotion entirely unlike the empty story I spoke aloud. It had been a glorious summer afternoon in a forested glade very like those portrayed in the frieze. Morgan had asked me to draw her portrait.

Emboldened by a passion that made the very air between us tremble, I told her that one who bore so much vibrant life should be portrayed as part and portion of the earth itself. With trembling hands I removed her clothes and laid her naked on a grassy hillock. Kneeling beside her, I traced my fingers over every line of her bones, over eyelids and rosy lips, along the perfect line of hip and thigh, over the low mounds of her sweet breasts and her long, powerful legs, every quat of her from brow to toe. Then, with such an ecstasy of magic as I had never felt, I began to draw. I felt transported to a world apart—sharper, clearer, the sounds of bird and water chiming sharp like silver, the thick grass green as emerald and soft as goose down. By the time my magic was spent, I was naked, too, and the jeweled sun could not compete with the heat of our coupling.

Sated, we slept. And when I woke she was gone, along with the sunlight, the clarity, and the drawing. I'd never even looked at it.

My colorless narrative of these events did not disclose the nature of my magic. And from that divergence, I plunged wholly into deception.

". . . and when I woke, she was gone, along with my jewels, my boots, the substantial contents of my purse, everything of value. My ravishing lover was naught but a thief. Before I could find her again, someone informed the Registry that I had seduced an ordinary and trafficked in my magic. My family recalled me from that city and properly chastised me, and I was glad of it, as such sweet obsession had turned so bitter. I believed the whole affair but a hard lesson until yesterday. That's when I learned a child was born of our coupling. . . ."

The lies flowed easy as the currents of heat and memory drove me onward. For if a girl child *had* come of that precious day, and such horror had come down on her as happened to the one who lay in Bastien's ice barrow, I would invade Idrium itself and lie to the assembled gods to expose those who had done her such evil.

"You're certain the mother is dead?" Irinyi's question washed over my back as I gazed again on the sculpted goddess, begging her continued indulgence. It was time to fix the cold ending to my heated tale.

"Just yesterday. The stink of the graveyard yet clings. The child remains tonight with this taverner who searched me out. But the woman is hard, and says that on the morrow she'll sell the girl to a dyer who values small hands for scrubbing his pots and boilers. The seductress had no family, and neither I nor my family have any interest in the spawn of a thief. Yet a fate of hard labor for a child so young seems cruel. I've nowhere to turn for advising, save to the goddess who rules the divine madness of the heart."

"A halfblood child," said the priestess. "A rarity, indeed. Would your family truly refuse to train her in whatever magic she may inherit?"

"We are not permitted to nurture halfbloods. They are abominations to the gods, and their talents minimal at best. She's more likely to inherit a skill for thieving."

No matter my current playacting, the words stung my soul bitterly. After that glorious afternoon, I'd seen Morgan only once, when the consequences—and possible consequences—of my folly had already begun to constrict me like a shroud. On my last day at the university, she had met me in our favored bower. Amid my hurried professions of love undying, she had assured me, without my asking, that she was incapable of conceiving a child. While expressing sorrow for her incapacity, I had, most cowardly, thanked Serena Fortuna at the news.

Shamed, even in memory, I averted my eyes as Sinduria Irinyi contemplated my story.

In truth I wasn't sure what happened to halfblood children, save that their own children were born entirely lacking the gift of magic. That simple fact was the foundation of pureblood life and discipline. It had built the Registry, focused on preserving and defending our divine gift. Aurellians were not the most fertile of races, and we dared not squander our seed on ordinaries. Even when I became our Head of Family, I would marry only a person the Registry permitted me to marry. As would Juli. As did we all. Love or passion had naught to with it.

"Would you be willing to surrender all claim and interest in the girl," the priestess said, at last, "leaving her to the disposition of the goddess from this day until the end of her life and yours?"

The stark question drove out the distractions of memory and guilt.

"Surrender? Disposition?" Crimes had taken place in this house, with or without this woman's connivance. I wanted her to think I would allow such wickedness or at least look away, yet yielding too easily might raise suspicions. "Are you speaking of . . . blood sacrifice?"

"Sweet goddess, no! The temple shelters unwanted children from time to time—those we determine to be somehow especial gifts of the goddess. The low history of this mother speaks against acceptance. But then, the deep obsession that possessed you at the child's conception—the very model of divine frenzy—suggests that this indeed could be our lady's divine hand at work. I am willing to give the girl a home in the temple. It's easiest for the child if the parents relinquish all claim and interest in her future. She would never know you, your family, or the story of her birth."

So now we had come to it. Had a prince's bastard been deemed an *especial gift* of the goddess, too?

I feigned a puzzled curiosity. "I assumed you might know some upright family to take her. What would she do here?"

"We would feed and care for her. Teach her of the goddess and her mysteries. She might come to be an initiate, destined for the mystic functions of a priestess. Or she might serve as a bath attendant, assisting those who seek cleansing here. Her mother's blood might win out and take her to the scullery. There are many ways to serve the goddess. It would not be your concern."

"I don't know. . . ."

Her facile talk stung like salt on raw flesh. I wanted to ask if whoring was a proper service for a pureblood's bastard, as it had been for a prince's. Or if child whoring in a god's house was somehow holier than child whoring in a dyer's alley. It was this woman's responsibility to know what went on here.

The high priestess laid a hand on my shoulder. "Let this telling rid you of false love and useless guilt, Seeker. Dedicate yourself to Arrosa's service, not forsaking the gods of your house, but rather opening yourself to her care. Release the boundaries of your will, so that from this day she may guide you in the proper ways to fulfill the needs of body and heart."

Sincere piety wreathed her voice and posture. Yet was it solely imagination that I felt her life pulse racing? Did she think a halfblood child might fetch higher fees? Bile stung my throat.

"I'll prepare an agreement as I've outlined," she said, as if replacing her silken mantle with a shopkeeper's apron. "We shall nurture the child to the goddess's service; you will relinquish all right and interest in her. Would you prefer to wait here or to take advantage of the goddess's cleansing rite? We've private rooms and baths for the gods' chosen, and attendants especially trained in pureblood customs."

The baths had brought me here—the scent of ephrain revealed by my bent. I should follow that thread as my grandsire would pursue a clue unearthed by his.

"The baths sound most excellent. What better than to rid myself of the stink of this whole affair?"

"My handmaid will guide you." She rang a bell hung at her belt. "When your devotions are concluded, she'll return you here to seal our bargain. An offering of gold to acknowledge our service in this matter is not necessary, but would be most welcome in such difficult times."

I touched my forehead in respect. I would have preferred to see the woman pilloried. To speak of children as if they were hounds to sell and train should itself be a crime.

The sylphlike handmaiden led me into a hive of warm, moist halls that reeked of ephrain and moonflowers. Her filmy gown clung to her body in the damp. It was impossible to look away.

Was it my own guilt or the aura of this house that made me feel more unclean? As with marriage, pureblood customs in the matter of casual mating were, of necessity, stricter than those of ordinaries. I understood that and accepted it—and with it the guilt of my own sin. Even so, to think that under the aegis of a goddess any man might be offered the same pleasures he could buy in the streets—even the most debauched . . . I doubted any amount of water or prayer could wash away the reek.

"Through there, *domé*." The young woman pointed me through a narrow, foggy passage. "A bath attendant will meet you in the changing room and accompany you to the private pools. May you find healing and joy in the divine lady's hand."

Answers. That's what I wanted.

Moisture beaded the stone walls and dripped from the barreled vault. Jeweled lamps cast colored beams through the eddies of steam, guiding me to a small chamber.

As I entered a small room, a slender young man wearing a white loincloth crossed his arms over his breast and bowed. "Welcome to divine Arrosa's baths, *domé*. I am Leo, and will attend you through the cleansing rite."

Behind him, a lattice wall woven with flowering vines separated the small chamber from some larger space. Heat rose from the tiled floor as if the fires of Magrog burned just beneath.

With silken grace, the attendant slipped around behind and removed my pelisse. A simple gesture toward my face and I passed him my mask. He laid both in a carved chest.

The scent of sandalwood and flowers mingled with the aroma of a strong vintage as Leo took a pitcher from a shelf and filled a bronze cup. When he passed the cup to me, I inhaled its aroma. Wine, yes, but something more pungent, too, that carried a searing pleasure straight to every one of my joints.

Between the heat and the heady scents, I was near panting. Fearing to lose my head completely, I took only a sip.

"Though I am ever Lord Deunor's servant," I said, "the goddess Arrosa has summoned me here this night. I am unfamiliar with her customs."

"Be easy, *domé*. Our purpose is to soothe the cares and urgencies of common life that Lady Arrosa may touch your soul." Leo gestured to the cup in my hand. "The wine contains a tincture prepared from herbs grown in temple gardens. Drink deep that you may hear the songs of the goddess. If you will permit me to remove your garments, I'll guide you first to the tepidarium to cleanse and anoint you, and then to the hot pool, the caldarium, where the goddess shall make known her will. Command me as you desire. I am accomplished in all ways of soothing a body's needs."

He extended a hand toward my buttons and laces. "May I?"

"Yes, certainly . . ." In no time at all, everything but my shirt and underdrawers lay in the sandalwood chest. Leo motioned me to the stone bench. His breath was soft on my thighs as he knelt in front of me, unfastening the wrist bands of my sleeves. His pale hair smelled of moonflowers. The pungent wine boiled in my blood.

All ways of soothing a body's needs. Had he answered my first question already? He seemed entirely unembarrassed. I felt a bumpkin; how was I to learn what he meant? I needed to understand what was done with female children and if the child I had drawn was familiar to any here.

"You're quite skilled, Leo," I said, grasping his wrist. "But in my house a woman does such tasks as these."

His head popped up, his brow creased in concern. "The temple provides male bath attendants for purebloods, *domé*, out of respect for your strict customs. But of course, if you prefer, I can fetch a female attendant."

"My head . . . I get terrible headaches. Female voices . . . and hands . . . are more soothing." One of my uncles had forever claimed his wife's was the only voice he could tolerate. "A female will . . . enter the bath with me? Soothe me? She wouldn't mind?"

"We rejoice to answer divine Arrosa's call to service." Was it the heat that caused the slight flush across his back? Or inflamed my own fiery cheeks? I hated this.

The youth bowed and withdrew.

I had taken only a few calming breaths when someone stepped from behind the lattice—not a child, but a woman near my own age. She was lovely—dark, liquid eyes and thick black hair shorn close to her head as some men wore it, though there was no mistaking her sex. A sleeveless white tunic set off perfect skin the hue of hazelnuts.

She bowed. "*Domé*. Leo says you prefer a female attendant." Her voice flowed deep and thick like dark honey. "I am Eliana. Command me."

Unseemly thoughts sent urgent messages to every part of me, threatening to obliterate reason. *Command* her? I dared not even consider her removing the rest of my garments or—Great Deunor give me strength—bathing alongside me. I dared not even stand up just now. Rather my eyes fixed on the floor tiles in front of my bare feet . . . which helped not in the least, as the tiles' designs glorified Arrosa's works in every possible variety.

"I—" The next word refused to come out. How did I ask?

"Leo also said you were new to our lady's baths, and, perhaps—please take no offense, *domé*—*unsure* what to expect?"

I took another desperate sip of wine.

"True." My croak would label me as approximately fourteen.

"I attend men every day—mostly ordinaries, as you would refer to them, but also others of the gods' chosen—and I am neither shocked nor offended by men's bodies as they respond to the songs of the goddess. Nor do I consider such responses as an invitation to step beyond the boundaries of your comfort or my own. . . ."

Though delivered in cool sobriety, her reassurance contained some essence beyond pious business. Enough to encourage a glance upward.

She had clasped her hands behind her back. Her gaze was fixed on the wall above my head, but a portrait artist learns early to notice nuances of expression. Those dark eyes sparked like summer lightning, and her well-proportioned lips hovered on the verge of a smile, as a kestrel hovers above its prey.

". . . though, naturally, the Goddess of Love moves in ways beyond understanding to heal and nurture those who seek her cleansing. Her service is a joy and a devotion to me. Ask what you will. *Whatever* you will."

And there was my first answer. Whatever I wished was available from a bath girl. And she was neither afraid nor repulsed.

In my current state, even such a loveless act would have been quite easy. Save for discipline. Save for the pervasive odor of debauchery. A child of eight or ten would find no joy in serving men. Had they plied *her* with tinctured wine?

Arrosa's rites made good sense. To wash away pent anger and frustration, to empty out one's surfeit of grief or the stench of failure and replace it with bodily abandon must surely rank with the holiest of experiences. But I could not. Certainly not here. But she had to think I could.

"The goddess already moves in me, I think." My eyes explored Eliana's womanly body with deliberate thoroughness. "Proceed."

CHAPTER 13

Stretching out my arms, I stood cold and unembarrassed as the woman Eliana removed my shirt and underdrawers. She closed the chest and led me around the vine-covered lattice.

A mantle of mist drifted over a rectangular bathing pool designed for one or two, not a public throng. The tepidarium chamber was grand, though, ringed with a variety of ugly statues, both male and female. Across from the lattice wall, an open arch and a few steps down led into a smaller chamber filled with billowing steam—the caldarium, the hot pool.

Eliana poured water into a bowl and mingled in droplets from several flasks along with rose petals from a basket. Dipping a linen square into the bowl, she invited me to recline on a cushioned bench beside the pool. I stretched out on my left side, and she began to wash my back. *Goddess Mother . . .*

Questions, Lucian. The lily child. "Have you grown up here?" I said, propping my head on one fist.

"Nay. My mam was a tap girl at a sop-house outside Avenus. Serving the Goddess of Love kept us from starving after my da was killed soldiering." Her firm circular scrubbing moved lower and her voice was low and throaty and inviting. "Mam taught me *all* her prayers and rites."

She dipped the cloth again and worked down my right leg from buttock to foot. My fist clenched stone hard as I fought to keep my mind on business. I must remain this unpleasant pureblood who had come here to discard his inconvenient bastard.

"Then how did you come here?"

Her strong, sure hands rolled me to the other side. Then she began again. "Mam believed the goddess would grant me a better life than hers. She held off till I was fourteen. I hated waiting."

"Only fourteen," I said, as she stretched my arm toward her and began washing at my shoulder. "So young?"

"We've several much younger here in the household. The goddess takes us when she will."

Would they truly send a child to a grown man? I needed answers before I fell into my old sin. Despite my disgust, her closeness, her touch, the damp heat of her as she bent over me, was entirely distracting.

"Do all of them come from taverns and sop-houses?"

She sat back on her heels and met my glare, puzzled. "Certainly not. Yet what does it matter, *domé*? Divine Arrosa purifies us. Sanctifies our work. Makes holy our giving."

My left hand clenched, recalling the cold, dead flesh my fingers had traced. The bruises. The stillness. Eye sockets that housed no spark. The shift stained with blood. Blood entirely *un*holy.

I yanked my arm from her grasp, shoved her away, and shot to my feet. I towered over her. "I am one of the gods' chosen," I bellowed, echoing every arrogant pureblood rant I'd ever heard. "How dare this temple provide me a tavern whore's daughter old enough to birth brats of her own? You are all the same! You'll lure me to take my pleasure with you, then try to steal my magic. Send me an innocent. And young; the younger the better. I prefer smoother, cleaner hands."

Eliana rose, all dignity, eyes lowered. "*Domé*, we have strict rules. Our youngest cannot participate—"

"The goddess brought me here to seek solace after a broken love. You've all convinced me of the necessity, assured me of your service. I must be *free* of this!" I clamped my hands to my skull. "Do as you are bound by your goddess. Bring me the solace I require."

Eliana retreated without turning her back on me or meeting my gaze. Indeed, my blood was pounding, my discipline near fractured by wine and lust and horror. Until these three days past, I had never truly comprehended the depravity of the world. I felt tainted. Filthy.

I snatched up one of the damp linen squares and scoured my face.

The distant music had stopped. Faint drips and seeps punctuated a heavy stillness. Had my ruse worked? With every moment that passed, new doubts crept in. The woman had appeared so quickly, but now . . . What if they had summoned the Registry?

No. The Registry would never heed a complaint from an ordinary, not even Irinyi, unless it was a matter of her own contracted pureblood. Did she even have one?

More likely they were fetching a child . . . preparing her. Holy gods. And here I was, naked as a plucked goose.

Hoping the goddess would forgive yet another violation, I slipped into her pool only half cleansed. The pleasantly warm water closed over my head, tickling and teasing my skin as if filled with constantly bursting bubbles.

I stayed under as long as breath allowed, scrubbing at my hair and every bit of flesh I could reach. If refreshment was a sign of Arrosa's favor, then I had done her no wrong.

Shaking my head like a wet hound, I surfaced for breath and inhaled for a second plunge. A quiet sneeze arrested my movement.

Without rippling the water, I turned, peering into the shifting lamplight. No one was there, unless . . .

I rubbed droplets from my eyes. Behind one of the statues a shapeless lump of gray moved ever so slightly, resolving itself into a slight girl in a gray tunic and bare feet.

My outrage near burst its bounds. Horrid and depraved to send a child to a naked man for his pleasure. But how much more cruel to send her alone.

"Come out," I said softly, propping my arms on the edge of the pool, determined not to frighten her. "Come into the light. I promise I won't hurt you. Whatever you think. Whatever anyone's told you."

She edged out from behind the statue but kept her back pressed to the wall. Her hair was dark and short, her pale face all eyes. She clutched a bundle of some kind—linen, perhaps, very like the cushions on the bench.

"Come, sit on the bench. I'll stay in the pool if that pleases you better."

Still not a word, and still she moved sidewise. Deliberately. Toward the caldarium arch.

I lunged from the pool just as she broke into a run. Long strides took me across the chamber, through the caldarium arch, and down the steps. I caught her just as she reached a stair beyond a second archway. Clamping a hand over her mouth, I hauled her back to the tepidarium. No one beyond this chamber must hear us. Fortunately the tepidarium itself had no hiding places and no detectable magics.

When I sat her on the bench—harder than I intended—and transferred my hands to her upper arms, she bit off a whimper and averted her eyes. Her flat chest heaved like a bellows beneath her ungraceful garment. She could not have reached her womanhood as yet.

Suppressing fury, I squatted in front of her and kept my voice low. "I'm not going to hurt you. Honestly. I just want to talk a little. Stay still and I'll let go."

"Didn't mean no harm. No offense. Didn't know there was a Seeker." Her murmur was soft, as if meant for herself alone. Her eyes were squeezed shut. "Sorry, sorry, sorry. Didn't mean no harm . . ."

"We'll just talk. I won't hurt you. . . ."

Both of us continued our litanies, as if creating some new musical counterpoint spoken in whispers. When at last I felt her muscles stop straining, I loosed my grip, finally removing my hands and opening my palms as if to show her she was free. But I didn't remove them so far as to prevent my grabbing her again did she take advantage.

She was no sacred bath attendant sent to pleasure a man, but a servant. Her gray tunic and leggings were the coarsest kersey, her face smudged. The small hands that clutched her bundle of dirty linen were cracked and reddened, though she could be little older than the dead girl child. Ten at most. Her dark hair was cut short and ragged. . . .

"They made her look like you," I said softly. "Like a scrub girl. Dressed her in rags. Blacked her hair; chopped it off."

Her eyes popped open so wide I thought they might swallow me. "Please, lord, please. Just wanted to see a bit of magic. Please don't—"

I grasped her arms again, careful not to pinch, and I shook her gently. "Hush. Look at my face. I'll not tell. I'd never hurt you. I've a little sister not much older. I'll take my hands away and not touch you again, if you just stay still and answer me. Tell me your name, and I'll work a bit of magic for you."

"Name's Gab," she said, flinching so violently, my chest near cracked.

"Good. That's good. Forgive me for hauling you over here so roughly, Gab, but I can't let anyone hear us. I need to know about the little girl. You know exactly who I mean, don't you?"

She shook her head briskly.

"The truth, Gab, and I swear I'll tell no one you were here watching. We must be quick."

Whoever was coming to supervise my devotions, it was not this child. Guilt nagged at me for detaining her, but I was sure she knew the dead girl. This might be my only opportunity to learn more.

"Now, again. What was the girl child's name, the one who was so hurt, the one they dressed up to look like you?"

"Priestesses called her Fleure, but she said that weren't her true name."

Flower . . . Gods, the lily.

"Do you know the man who hurt Fleure? I want to make sure he can never do that again. Not ever. May Deunor, Lord of Fire and Magic, be my witness, all I want of you is a few answers."

"Don't know his name. She were so scairt of him, she daren't speak it, nor even her own. She called him the devil lord, and said if he ever come to fetch her, she was done for."

A lord. That was something. "All right, Gab. That's good. When he'd come to visit her, did you ever see his face?"

She shook her head and clutched her bundle tighter. "He didn't never visit her, not since he brung her. She said he'd come to the temple sometimes, but always chose men to bath him, so I wasn't allowed near. But on that night I was scrubbing the front steps, and he marched right past me and I knew who it was right off. He were dark and hairy, as she always told me, and he yelled at Hostler to cool his horse and rub it down good, or he'd whip him. And his boots were shined like a black mirror glass. I called him the Bear Lord with Shiny Boots."

Damn, damn, damn! If only I knew something of court nobles. Perhaps Bastien did.

Gab was shivering. "I tried to get to her to warn her, but it took me so long, she was already fetched. Her pretty dress was left lie, and her fine shift and her gold hair." She swallowed a sob. "She said he'd ever swore to rip out her hair. She were so pretty. So kind. Why would he do that?"

"I don't know." The answer lay in words like soul-dead savagery and demonic cruelty—dry concepts that had taken on their terrible life for me only after my family's slaughter.

"Just one more question," I said, glancing at the lattice wall and the caldarium archway. I wanted much, much more, but could not allow Gab to get caught. "Who among the priestesses and others in the temple helped him? Did you see?"

Her smudged brow crinkled. "Didn't see nobody. By the time I got down here and saw what he was about with her—" She heaved a great, wet sob.

"Here? He brought Fleure here to the pureblood baths and was . . . lying . . . with her? Hurting her?"

"Had her head dangling over the pool. Not swyving, but blacking her poor cut-off hair, so's it was ugly like mine—as you said. He'd his other great hand on her neck, choking so she couldn't cry. Weren't no one else with 'em." Gab's lips thinned into a line much too hard for a child. "But 'twas sure Motre Varouna would have took him to her. She tends all the young ones, pretties them, and chooses which go to Seekers what ask for their sort. And she's the one knows about hair blacking or soaking the color right out, as a Seeker might want it. She—"

Gab inhaled sharply and twisted her neck toward the lattice wall. She stayed sitting, but quivered like a trapped rabbit. "Please, please let me go, lord," she whispered. "I'm whipped if I'm caught here with a Seeker, less'n they've asked for one like me special."

Multiple footsteps approached from behind the vines. But I had to know. "Is there a drain here? That's where he took her, isn't it? The drain?"

"Down the stair." Her throat was so constricted the words scarce made it through, but she stayed put and pointed to the caldarium.

"Good. Now run," I said, waving her away, "but peek back this way when you're well hid." As she scurried off, I snatched one of the jeweled lamps and quickly bound it to the inflation spell I'd worked in the hirudo. With a word and an infusion of magic, fountains of brilliant light—ruby, emerald, and sapphire—filled the chamber between the pool and the lattice wall, as if the goddess herself had arrived from Idrium.

Under cover of the light beams and gasps from the direction of the lattice wall, I slipped into the pool again. And I opened my palms in thanks toward the caldarium arch, where two great dark eyes reflected my paltry bit of magic.

I knew Motre Varouna instantly. Not from her soft young body or the dimples that framed her all-encompassing smile. Indeed I had expected anyone called *motre* or "second mother" to be a crone or at least of the maturity of the high priestess, not a woman younger than I.

No, it was the woman's fingers gave her away. Her knuckles were white as ivory, as the tips gouged the slim shoulder of a girl in her early teens. When the woman said, *"Domé,"* and bowed so gracefully, those fingers slid subtly up the child's neck and into her shining, unbound hair. A telltale yank and the girl winced and slipped gracefully to her knees, her sleeveless silk shift floating about pale, trembling limbs. The child wore nothing else.

The woman's plump fingers, rigid as a stone spider, settled atop the girl's bowed head in a mockery of affection. It made me want to vomit.

"I am Varouna, servant of Arrosa, mistress of the temple's younger charges," said the woman in a voice like cream. "I have prepared one of Arrosa's newest servants to assist you in your distress, Seeker. She yearns for the goddess's mysteries and will do anything required to aid your devotions. She trembles, as do I, at this glory we viewed as we arrived! Was it an offering of magic to the goddess or her bounteous response to your devotion?"

"My particular devotions are none of your concern."

I climbed out of the pool, sorry if my looming nakedness terrorized the girl further—I doubted there was much help for that—but I wanted to get these two out of the chamber and have some time alone. I had more work to do before leaving the temple.

"If I frightened you, servant"—interesting that she was no priestess—"then that is unfortunate, but I begin to think the goddess has already answered me through her divine cousin, the Lord of Fire. Only a fool would accept her most bountiful gift before going penitent to Lord Deunor's Temple. So take your charge away and leave me to my closing devotions."

Disappointment soured Varouna's round face. "But surely you need service . . . to dress if naught else. This maiden's hands are soft, her manners exquisite, her blood rare and entirely worthy to grace the presence of the gods' chosen. She is well trained."

Her fingers riffled the girl's silken hair and traced the soft line of her neck and shoulder. No alleyway procurer in Montesard had spoken in tones so ripe with allurement—and avarice.

I memorized the gatzé woman's face. "In the humility of the gods' chastisement, I shall tend to my own dressing. But later. I must experience the scouring of the caldarium first."

The woman's simpering hardened like plaster. "Then do please recall that the Sinduria has a document for you to sign before you depart the temple. Her handmaiden will await where she left you."

Varouna's plump fingers snaked into the girl's hair and dragged her toward the lattice wall.

I released a beam of ruby magelight to strike the wall in front of Varouna. When she yelped and spun round, I splayed my fingers, smearing the light beam as if taking a brush to a line of wet ink until rosy light wreathed the wondering child.

Varouna jerked her hand away from the girl so fast, I thought she might fall backward.

"Be sure, servant, that the goddess intends no rebuke of this maid," I said, laying my fist to my breast and ordering my features in pious ardor as if I'd naught to do with the display. " 'Tis a part of the great revelation of this rite. From this day, I shall become divine Arrosa's devoted worshipper, striving to be worthy of such tender service on a future visit. I anticipate such devotions with the greatest delight."

As she bowed, wordless, and they vanished behind the lattice, I bared my teeth like a wolf. I would enjoy seeing Bastien turn this vile woman over to a magistrate.

Now quickly, before Irinyi's handmaid came looking for me.

I turned slowly, examining the pool chamber, trying to put myself in the mind of the villain. Gab's testimony had changed everything. Fleure's death was not the result of some lustful temple encounter devolved into guilt or frenzy. Child and man knew each other. He'd brought her here. Threatened to rip out her hair . . . why? He'd bent her over the pool as he blacked her hair, silencing her with his great paw, disguising her as the lowest of servants while she yet lived. Deliberate. Purposeful.

Had her death been an accident of the silencing? I didn't believe that. Didn't want it. I wanted him to hang.

So, where had she died? Would he have killed her here apurpose? Not likely. Someone could have intruded while he manhandled her. Witnesses like Leo or Eliana. More likely, once her hair was darkened to his liking, he would have walked her to the drain and killed her there.

I gambled my short time on it.

The caldarium chamber was a few steps lower, steamy and hot. Dipping a finger told me that entering the murky water would be no trifling devotion. The chamber appeared barren, save for the small pool and the archway to the stair.

The downward steps were much older than the ascending stair. No surprise. The baths and their system of flues and furnaces were likely built by my Aurellian ancestors when they laid the pipes and drains for the city wells. I padded quietly down the tight twists into the cellar—into Magrog's fiery hells, so it felt. If I needed any reminder that I was naked, the least brush of the stone walls served. The hot floor, skimmed with drips and seeps, kept my bare feet moving down a gentle slope. The drainage channel would be down.

Hoarding power, I chose to forgo magelight. The torch mounted at the bottom of the stair would serve me partway down. Beyond that, I'd go by feel until I found the grate at the end of the channel.

Sturdy, well finished, graceful, and efficient, as with every Aurellian structure, the drainage channel could have been the passage to another bath, save for the slimed floor and musty stench. No perfumes here. No sensual music. As the torchlight faded behind me, so did the killing heat.

Something brushed my bare foot. Recoiling, I pressed to the wall. There was movement everywhere, a faint clicking . . . and harsh scritches and shrieks from ahead of me; more from behind. My sweat chilled all at once. Rats.

If a man could walk without touching ground, then I would have done. Ridiculous that the threat of vermin could so trump the fear of discovery as to speed me even faster.

Soon the heat of the caldarium was but a savored memory. A breath of icy air promised an ending to the dreadful passage.

When naught but shivering, I risked a single beam of magelight. The iron grate stood ten paces ahead, its rusted latch broken and dangling free.

Once beside the grate, I held my blazing fingers behind me, setting off a vile, shrieking stampede. I didn't look. Didn't want to see. Kneeling in the ankle-deep sludge, I let the light die and prayed both rats and priestesses to stay away. Then I set foolish fears aside and closed my eyes.

Lord of Fire and Magic, grant me your grace. Goddess of Love, help me erase this defilement of your house. No smoldering embers but white-hot coals waited between my eyes. No need to let the power build. The merest touch of will sent magic rushing to my hands, scouring vein and sinew, until I near cried out with the glory of it.

One touch of my hands on the slimed floor and I was already sorting the threads. Generations of warriors posted on Palinur's ramparts. Hot, dusty summers and chiseled stone. Clever, dark-haired builders and sweating slaves as the bathhouse rose. Odors of perfumes, oils, excrement, and sacrifice, the songs of ecstatic devotions and the grunts of mindless rutting.

Seek the precise emotion . . . A child who knew she was going to die. Resigned to it. Brutalized, the bruises on her neck aching, warning her. Find the scent of ephrain . . . the heat and smells of the pools . . . the horror of this ending place. The shriek of rats. And her murderer, dragging her barefoot through this slime. She knew him. He wasn't the Prince of Ardra, not if he was dark and hairy; Perryn was wholly Ardran like his royal father, tall and fair.

"Fleure," I whispered. The lily had led me here. She took her blood from Caedmon and Eodward—two of the mightiest kings the world had ever known.

And there she was, facing her fear and certainty, not a being of breathless terror, but of timeless courage. *Blood under her nails.* So brave, clawing, scratching, even here in the dark when she knew it was hopeless. Biting the fingers that dragged her. And even as the beast roared and shoved her down, she spat in his face. She, the descendant of kings.

But he was so big. Her hands dropped. Limp . . .

My arms began to quiver. *Tell me, child. Tell me something. Who was he? Turn around, devil, and show me your face!*

But the image was awash in blood, its threads erased before I could follow them to any discovery. A stabbing pain between my eyes warned that my well of power was running dry.

I sat back on my heels, shivering, heaving, trying to sort through the impressions of the seeing for some gleam of enlightenment before I opened my eyes to failure. Nothing . . . nothing . . .

A sting on one of my feet brought me back to full awareness. I'd thought the winter beyond the grate had frozen my limbs. Another fiery peck on my ankle and more brushing movements. Shrieking. Chittering.

"Aagh!" I jumped up and reached for magelight, but the knife in my skull twisted, leaving me dizzy and nauseated. Flailing, retching, blind, I retreated. The rats seemed emboldened by their success. I stumbled up the passage, kicking at them, slipping on the disgusting sludge. Though the broiling stink of the filth on and around me had me near delirious with sickness, I welcomed the hypocaust fire for the grace of its light.

Up the stair. Around the never-ending spiral, panting in the heat. At last the scented steam warned I neared the caldarium landing.

Somewhere voices murmured. But where? No murderer must discover I'd been poking around a place I'd no reason to be. Purebloods could die, too.

I crept to the arch and peered through. Steam curled and billowed over the hot pool.

"Seeker? Are you here?" Irinyi's handmaiden called hesitantly from the tepidarium.

"He's not up here in the latrine." A male voice—Leo—called out from the stair above my head. "Eliana says he's not on the roof, either. He must have gone." The youth, descending, was almost on me.

No time to think or doubt. No power for magic, even if I knew anything that might help hide me. I darted from the stair and slipped soundlessly into the scalding pool.

Gods in all heavens! Perhaps my sins would be boiled away, for it seemed certain my flesh would be.

I held still underwater as long as I could, the span of twenty heartbeats, perhaps, or the striking of the bells at midnight. Then I launched myself into the air with the booming groan of a sonnivar—the mountain horn. "Mighty goddess!"

Astonishing how much easier lies become, once you've told a few with some success. As Leo dressed me, I let slip the awe-filled revelation that Arrosa had bound me at the bottom of her hot pool far longer than nature would permit. And when he remarked on the bleeding pricks about my ankles, I let flow some nonsense about the goddess reminding me of an illicit romance that required me to escape bootless from a lover's bed through her rose garden.

"Clearly she wished to chastise me for all my transgressions and itched my ankle until I clawed my own skin. I am a new man!"

Though words of apology and appreciation were rare in a pureblood conversation with an ordinary, once returned to her chamber I smothered Sinduria Irinyi with so many, her cool serenity withered. Smile fixed like an aingerou carved into a parapet to frighten children from its edge, she dipped the pen and shoved it into my hand. "Just sign the document, *domé*, and tell me the name of the tavern where the child bides, and the last vestige of your sin shall rest in the goddess's hand. Divine Arrosa has clearly favored you for bringing your trouble here."

I feigned hesitation. "Others have signed such documents? My family . . . Perhaps you have other arrangements for those whose families cannot allow scandal." Had Gab's Bear Lord signed *his* name? Bastien would like that.

"The goddess requires all to commit their intentions by name, *domé*. Pureblood, noble, the king himself, should he petition her."

"All right, then." I scribbled an unreadable signature on the document that described my forfeiture of all interest in the five-year-old child of my youthful lust and again on a paper that ordered a tavern keeper named Drysi—the name of my father's favorite bitch—under pain of law to turn over the girl to a representative of Arrosa's Temple. "On my woolly head, Sinduria, I cannot recall the name of the tavern. I scribed it in my journal and will send it, and a generous fee, as soon as I return home."

I cut off her annoyed response with my palms in the air. "Nay, no need to send your man. I've visits to make on my way home—to my Lord Deunor's Temple foremost. By morning you'll have her and I shall face the new day cleansed and living in the favor of the gods."

"Very well. We shall await your messenger." Lips thinned to the point of vanishing, she rolled and tied the documents into a scroll scarce larger than a reed. With a sharp pivot, she shoved them into a scroll case that spanned half the wall behind her. The force of her insertion could have bored a hole in the dark wood case.

Despite my frustration, I left the temple eager. Perhaps Irinyi and the others here had not laid hands on Fleure's throat; perhaps fear of the lord who had last visited the child had prevented their reporting her missing. But they had placed her naked in the hands of a beast—and they were willing to do the same with a child of mine. I could not wait to pass what I'd learned to Bastien.

The stars glinted like frost shards as I trudged through the deserted streets. No matter the lack of lamps or fires so late; the starshine itself created hard-edged shadows and allowed me to see my way. No phantom Danae, no voices, no creeping footsteps shadowed me.

A strange elation gave a spring to my step despite the long and exhausting day. Such pleasurable satisfaction seemed wholly odd after investigating so vile a crime. I had violated a goddess's tainted temple; practiced lies and deceit that would have shocked me a mere four days past; used my forbidden bent a second time without a smat of hesitation; and put my personal, and thus my family's, reputation at risk to come up with—I had to be honest—very little solid information. Yet it might give Bastien a place to start his investigation.

As I began the last climb to the Vintners' District, the bitter cold at last seemed to penetrate my bones, and the concerns of true life pushed away the phantom hopes of justice and redress for a murdered child. Tonight, without fail, I had to tell our servants we could no longer pay them, and send a notice to Tessati that we no longer required his house. Egan would be waiting in our courtyard; I had to tell him we would take the rooms. How long would it require to pack up the little we could take with us, clean and furnish the new rooms, and see to our servants' new positions and the move itself?

As I turned into our lane, a red-orange aurora sheened the sky above the trees, dimming the stars. Unintelligible shouts pierced the quiet. My feet understood before my churning mind did and began to run. And then the window of my soul was torn open and darkness flooded in.

Fire!

CHAPTER 14

"Juli!"

The portico had collapsed, blocking the front doors. Hacking and coughing in the billowing smoke, I tried again to shift the burning timbers. "Please, someone help me. My sister's in there . . . my steward . . . servants."

The lower floors were entirely engulfed. The winter-bare trees of the garden smoldered, the vines and trellises already ash. The courtyard walls wept ice melt.

Strong arms grabbed me from behind, dragging me away from the thundering horror.

"Do not touch me!" Snarling, I fought to break the arms restraining my own. "I've got to find them!" All but Soflet would be abed so late, and he moved so slowly. . . .

A black-draped arm wrapped about my neck and yanked me close, crushing my back to the man's chest. "None's coming out that goes in there. And well you know it." Bony, maggot-pale fingers ringed in copper gripped my chin like a vise, holding my head immobile as their owner spat the words in my ear. "A masterful job. We heard them screaming."

Incomprehensible words, terrible words.

I wrestled free, shoved the man aside, and reached for magic . . . water spells . . . quenching spells . . . damping spells . . . anything I could think of. I shaped images of Juli, laughing, singing, driving me to exasperation.

Her scent, her terrible silences, her brilliantly honed spellwork. Surely I could shape a summoning and she would come to the upper windows. She could jump and I could catch her.

My skull drummed. My body shook and spasmed. But I had practiced no such spells and could not conjure a dewdrop.

A burst of fire from the kitchen building drew curses and shouts from the onlookers. None from inside the house. Maybe they'd gotten out before I arrived. *Please, Holy Deunor!* Wild with fear, I turned to the crowd.

Buckets and pots dangled empty from shoulders and elbows. Water casks lay abandoned on the flagstones. *No, no, no!*

Fifty or a hundred dirty, sweating faces gleamed like holy icons in the demonic light. Some shook their heads, some gawked, some chatted, pointing for their children as if mortal horror were a solstice-night bonfire. Strangers. All of them strangers. Five years I'd lived here and deliberately stayed apart. What use was our holy discipline in this case?

"Has anyone seen a young girl . . . only fifteen? Please, did she come out? There would have been an old woman with her . . . others. Where did they go?"

They dropped their eyes and shifted backward, uneasy and murmuring, "None's come out . . . Saw no one . . . Heard them screaming . . ."

"Quench the flames, Godling Remeni! You're the one who knows how. You brought this judgment down on your own!" The husky voice came from a tall man, cloaked and hooded in somber black wool, an orange scarf tied around his neck. Long pale fingers banded in copper poked from his sleeves—my rescuer.

His words held no more meaning than the rush of the fire wind. I could think of naught but those who had screamed, but did so no longer.

A noisy blast, a blaze of new heat, and a rain of shattering glass wrenched me around again. Gouts of flame spewed skyward through the upper windows. The front wall bulged and sagged, driving the crowd backward through the gates. My eyes watered. My skin blistered. But I could not retreat. To leave without them . . .

"Juli!" Again I reached for magic and found nothing.

"Help me, Patronn. We can't watch him burn, too." Hands grasped my arms, no pale fingers, but fine, thick gloves worn by two men in wine-colored cloaks and half masks.

They hauled me back as far as the gate just as the whole structure quivered and collapsed in roaring thunder. The impact raised a hurricane of rabid fireflies that swirled and bit my flesh. Shattered roof tiles and flaming timbers lay where I'd stood just moments earlier.

Juli . . . serena . . . *beloved* . . . Despair welled up to blind and strangle, to obliterate reason. My rescuers' faces blurred. My knees buckled. I clutched my hollow breast and bellowed.

"Go quickly, son," said a man behind me. "Send Zircus to the Registry. I'd no idea Remeni lived so near us."

"The madman?"

"Indeed. Now look what he's done. Several of us saw it all. I'll hold him."

The pureblood touched my shoulder, murmuring.

A weight of iron settled over me . . . a shroud of ice . . . of death. I curled forward and wrapped my arms about my head as if I could hide the unbearable. "Please don't be dead, *serena*. Noble Soflet, dear Maia . . ."

"Should have thought of that before you set the fire." The pureblood's annoyance drifted over my back like ash. "At least you were considerate enough to confine the destruction to your own house."

Warning pricked like a rat's bite through the thickening shell of paralysis. But it was too late and the darkness was too deep for me to comprehend.

Cold. Enveloping, boundless dark. My head ached, dull as lead. Time to get up . . . to eat. Knew better than to set out for the necropolis hungry. Perhaps it was too early yet. Giaco would wake me.

Teeth chattering, I curled up and reached for my quilts. Only they weren't there. And the bed . . .

No bed. Just iron.

I scrambled to my feet, fumbling in the tarry blackness. Iron everywhere. Walls, floor. Great gods, an iron ceiling but an arm's length above my head. Where in Deunor's mighty name—?

Truth slammed into my chest like a boulder, crushing me against the iron wall. I slid to the floor, scarce breathing under the weight. Dead. All of them were dead. And I? *A masterful job . . . summon the Registry . . . before you set the fire. Madman.*

Naked and shivering, I scrambled into a barren corner and groped for memory, for words—the right words to defend myself. Anger, indignation, or accusations would not convince anyone that I was sane, that I had not set my own house afire, that I had not killed my own sister and our servants. Great Mother of All . . . Juli!

Reason was impossible. A gaping void in soul and spirit swallowed my every thought and question. Juli had been so slight a body, yet her spirit so much larger than I had ever suspected. I'd hardly known her. The world had never known her. Never would. *Impossible.*

Perhaps this place was just the world transformed. What more proper ending than empty darkness, than silence, than unremitting cold and nakedness, when the whole of my family was dead? When every new artwork; every writing; every bit of beauty, laughter, insight, and understanding their magic might bring to this world was destroyed unborn?

A cry rose in my chest, so huge, so powerful my ribs ached to contain it. But contain it I must, for if I once let it out, this horror would be real. I propped my elbows on my drawn-up knees, folded my hands over my head, and kept silent.

A very long time passed until a metallic scrape heralded a change.

"Remeni? Lucian de Remeni? Speak up. Where are you? Do you see him, Virit?"

Words would not come.

"By the Mother, lad, fetch me a light. Why didn't they summon me right off? *Domé* Pasquinale's binding has likely worn off and we dare not impose another before the prisoner's judged. Muzzy heads can't hear what's spoke."

A thread of yellow light wavered for a moment, offering blurred glimpses of two figures in gray tunics. Of dry, aged hands clutching a spool of thin cord. When the full onslaught of a torch's light poured through the door, I buried my head in my arms once again.

"There in the corner, Master Nelek."

"Ah, you see, he's already waked. Have your knife at the ready."

"Aye, master."

"Well, now, *Domé* Remeni, we need to get you dressed proper for your judgment. 'Tisn't respectful to greet curators without a stitch, now is it?"

One elder man, one younger. Their talk peppered the silence like the pecking of birds. Yet the nagging discipline of six-and-twenty years insisted I heed. No matter how devoutly I wished to drown grief and guilt in the dark, I could not allow it to mask a danger that had swelled to monstrous proportion. For of course, Juli had not been the last of the Remeni-Masson bloodlines and the magic they were meant to bring the world. I was.

"Why am I unclothed?" My voice rasped like grit underfoot. My throat felt clogged with ash. "And why does it require a knife to dress me again?"

"Mere precautions, *domé*," said the elder, the one called Nelek. "We were told to take precautions, as you were . . . excitable . . . and might misunderstand our duties."

The danger had a name, of course. "I am not mad."

"Virit and I are not here to judge. We just see to your dressing."

Nelek, standing over me now, smelled of garlic and had a habit of sucking his teeth. "We're going to slip a nice shirt over your head, first off. Need to raise it up."

He tapped on the back of my head. I obeyed, though my eyelids refused to open. I didn't want to see the box of iron where they'd stuck me.

A cascade of soft linen fell over my hair and settled on my shoulders.

"Now your hands into the sleeves, if you please. Virit, help with the left and keep hold as I taught you."

They guided my hands through long sleeves—not tight sleeves, thank the gods, as the backs of my hands were scorched and every touch arrowed straight to my gut. Once through, each man gripped a wrist. The younger man's hands were cold . . . and trembling.

"I'm too tired to fight you," I said, tugging gently.

They didn't let go.

"I'm magically depleted, else I might have saved my sister's life." Grief squeezed my lungs like a fist of iron.

"Well and good," said the elder, "but we must do this anyways. Now, Virit . . . and quick." With firm grips they twisted my arms and pressed my hands together, back to stinging back. A deft hand interlaced my fingers. Then they folded my hands around my locked fingers until the heels of my palms touched.

Before I could understand the purpose of this beyond tormenting my raw wounds, they began wrapping cord briskly about my bundled hands.

"What the devil are you doing?" I tried to wriggle away from them, but sitting in the corner with the two bodies pressed close, I had no space and no leverage.

"Just precaution, *domé*." Nelek's iron digits ensured my fingers were tucked away tight, as the younger, Virit, wrapped the cord. "Can't have you working magic, now can we?"

Silkbinding. That's what they did for undisciplined children . . . for *recondeurs* . . . for madmen. The fingers were the conduit of magic.

"Now for your britches. Want no dangling bits to scandalize the curators. Let's have you up. . . ."

They pulled up baggy slops and shod me with soft velvet slippers. The shirt gaped at the neck and wrists. Shirt, slops, slippers—the garb of a pureblood prisoner. Fine linen and wool as our heritage demanded, but neither button, clasp, chain, nor bit of leather that might carry a spell. Loose fitting; no layers, no pockets. They didn't want me hiding things. Shapeless and unadorned, unfit for the gods' chosen to wear outdoors or among ordinaries. They weren't planning to let me go.

"One more little item, laddie, and then we'll be done," said the old man, a gray sinewy fellow. More and more he sounded like an elder addressing a balky infant. "But first, perhaps, as you've been well behaved. Fetch him a drink, Virit."

Virit was a blotch-faced, twitchier replica of his master. Either one could likely break my neck at will.

With my hands bound, young Virit had to pour the water down my throat, dribbling more on my shirt than in my mouth. I did not refuse it, though. I had to be able to speak. Calmly. Rationally. With impeccable manners.

I inclined my back. "Thank you both for your assistance."

"Let's have you kneel, lad, as we finish up here."

I did as he said. Perhaps they were going to comb my hair. Wet from Arrosa's pool, tangled by wind and sweat and ash—I aborted the thought, lest calm escape me.

The old man stepped behind me and slipped something over my head. Hard leather drooped over my face, blocking one eye. I shook my head to get it off. Tried to push it up with my bound hands. But quick movements settled it lower, covering the left half of my face. A mask. Protrusions of stiff leather cupped my chin, crossed my brow, extended down my nose like a soldier's helm. "What in the name of—?"

The old man yanked a leather strap through my mouth and around my head, latching it to the back side of the mask. I tried to protest, with no effect but to set myself gagging. The devilish strap had a stiff flap, shaped to still my tongue.

"Now, now, don't panic. Just swallow easy." Young Virit pressed down on my shoulders while the elder stroked my throat. "You'll get accustomed. Would have been easier had we done all this while you were nogged. Your body would have worked it out on its own, and you'd have been right with it already."

Bright shards of fear pierced discipline's dull armor. *Right* with it? *Accustomed?* Surely they weren't going to keep me in this dreadful device. Surely they would let me speak.

A growl of fury rose from my depths.

The gray man met my one-eyed glare. His watery eyes were brown and yellow, and he tilted his head, smiling sadly. "Can't hide it no more, can you? Can't keep up the show of manners." He bent over me solicitously, dropping his voice. "I've been taking care of your kind since I was Virit's age. I've seen every kind of ruse to hide the breakage inside. But eventually the truth comes out."

My *kind*? I shook my head. I knew what he was intimating. "Not mad," I said, but the words came out like the panicked grunt of a beast.

"We'd best go ahead with the rest, Virit. He's mightily upset with us. Loosening up, you see."

The rest was shackles. *Magrog's hells*. What did they think I was going to do? I could not run. My life was over if I ran.

Virit grabbed the torch. The iron-fingered Nelek grabbed my arm and guided my awkward progress out of the cell and through a series of musty corridors lined with empty rooms. Only when we arrived at the twisted iron stair did it strike my tangled wits that I had traversed these same passages on my visit to Gilles. They'd stowed me in the bowels of the Registry Tower. No one ever came down here.

My breath pumped hard and fast. I could not swallow. The vile bit in my mouth had me drooling and gagging. If I retched, I would drown.

"Calm yourself. 'Tis just precaution. The judgment will tell all."

But if I was not allowed to speak, any *judgment* was a farce. Like my contract negotiation.

Nelek shoved me up the narrow, twisting column of iron—a laborious ascent, hobbled as I was. The chains clanked on the iron steps. "All the way up, *plebeiu*."

Plebeiu. Nelek believed I was already fallen to the lowest of pureblood ranks.

Discipline, Lucian. The Registry had been the foundation of pureblood life for centuries. My sire, my grandsire, all my kin had taught me that our way was worthy and honorable. Purebloods didn't vanish into cellars. Purebloods didn't get declared mad because their family died or their house burned. This was wartime, for the gods' sake. The Harrowers despised purebloods as much as they despised the Sinduri or the Karish monks and hierarchs, as much as they despised nobles and magistrates.

Like a kick to the head, the implication struck me. Was that it? Were the Harrowers finishing what they had begun at Pontia? The man who had pulled me back from the fire and accused me of setting it myself—the *first* man, before the pureblood—had worn an orange scarf, the Harrowers' token. Here in the heart of Palinur . . . a Harrower raid? Someone should know that!

I halted and pressed the old man to the rail. "Harrowers! Harrowers set the fire!" But it came out gibberish. The younger man hauled me off him and pushed me up the next step.

At the top of the steps, Nelek unlocked a heavy door.

"Move along, boy." All pretense of respect fell away as the elder shoved me staggering through the door and the guardroom, and around a corner to the servants' stair. Surprisingly, he directed me down. All the way back to the ground level. By the time we reached the bottom, I was near exhaustion.

Sunbeams—afternoon sunbeams—stretched long across the patterned floor of the Tower rotunda, dizzying me with brightness and a confusion of lost time. I'd come from the temple before midnight.

"Now we go up." Up the grand stair I had tried to breach all those hours ago.

The guards who had blocked my passage stood aside, unable to hide their appalled curiosity. I dared not look up to see how many gawkers stared from the gallery. My skin was ablaze.

Every step was more awkward than the last. My legs ached from the unaccustomed weight of the shackles. Worse, with one eye blocked by the mask, I could not judge depth or distance. Stumbling like a drunkard through the Tower rotunda in shirt, slops, chains, and a madman's mask, I might as well have been naked. Not a pureblood in Navronne would fail to hear of it. The ascent seemed endless; the shame, boundless.

. . .

The Curators' Chamber was the topmost in the tower. Only twice before had I been admitted there. All pureblood children were brought before the curators at the age of seven to be acknowledged as pureblood sorcerers of proven bloodlines, ready to begin their formal schooling in magic. And all pureblood young people were brought there to declare their bent—most at sixteen, I at one-and-twenty, after my grandsire had stripped me of one bent and left me the other.

Elegant and austere, the chamber overlooked the city from a height that had seemed close on divine Idrium itself. After such a climb in shackles and the mask I'd already come to regard as Magrog's foulest torment, it was all I could do to breathe and keep upright before the six who held my future—my life—in their hands.

The six curators, unmasked in their private domain, were seated at their horseshoe table, conversing quietly among themselves. It jangled my nerves that they took no notice, yet I was grateful to have a chance to gather my wits.

First Curator Gramphier, a spare, flat-faced, inexpressive man, held the center chair. Cold-eyed Gramphier could have sat under the table and any stranger would have picked him as the master of this room. When I had expressed surprise that my grandsire had considered him as a brother, Capatronn had told me, "Gramphier is a man of great intellect and the deepest passions. His actions reflect what his features do not." My hope might rest in that, because the others . . .

First Registrar Damon sat at Gramphier's right hand, second only to Gramphier in rank. Short, tidy, black haired, with a long nose and complexion the hue of olives, Damon could have stepped straight off any centuries-old pot or fresco from the Aurellian Empire. My uncle Eurus, who had shared Damon's bent for languages, named him ruthless in the practice of personal discipline—his own and everyone else's—and said his favor was hard won. Rumor named Damon forever loyal to those who earned it, yet no gossip addressed what *earning it* entailed. I did not anticipate his favor.

As Second Registrar, Pons sat at Damon's right hand. Her broad shoulders and heavy presence cast a blight on the room. If hate could burn flesh, the flames would burst the Tower roof above us and be seen as far as Syanar. These rumors of madness were surely her doing.

Dapper Curator Scrutari-Consil, wearing his sunburst pendant of the Karish god, sat next to Pons, already sneering. A petulant man with a large family, Scrutari gave Gilles and me endless trouble every time he brought one of his annoying brood in for anniversary portraits.

Gilles's uncle Albin, the Overseer of Contracts, sat on Gramphier's left, his squat, thick body that of a blacksmith and his garb that of a prince. The Albins owned such an expanse of vineyards, pastures, woodland ranges, and manors as to comprise their own kingdom. I had been surprised to find an Albin in so humble a contract as a Registry portraitist. But then, Gilles expressed surprise that a Remeni was contracted to work alongside him. Reportedly Albin, not Damon, was favored to succeed Gramphier when the First Curator's term was done. Adamantly devoted to tradition, Albin would offer no leniency.

White-bearded Pluvius, the lowest ranked of the curators, sat at the far left, elbows propped on the polished table, mouth resting on his folded hands, staring at the floor. Disheveled and loose, his robes looked as if they belonged to an even larger brother. His demeanor left a void in my belly. He, of all the six, failed to look up when my shepherd shoved me into the center of the horseshoe and snapped, "Manners, *plebeiu*."

I hated that any of them heard the command, as if I were too stupid or rebellious or crazed to recall proper protocol. Indeed my spirit churned in a most rebellious fashion. But I touched my bound hands to my forehead and bowed to each curator as deeply and gracefully as my restraints allowed.

Only then did I notice three others standing off to my blind side—two men, an elder and a younger, their features so mirrored as to name them father and son, dressed in such elegance of gold jewelry and scarlet brocade as to make me feel a floor mop. A third man stood behind them, indistinguishable in the shadowed corner.

"Thank you, Nelek," said Gramphier. Young Virit had remained outside the chamber. "You are efficient as always. Perhaps you would escort these witnesses back to the rotunda."

Wait! I wanted to scream it. Was I not even to hear them? This was a Registry hearing, not some Evanori warlord's mockery of judgment. The Registry was founded on respect and reason. Even at Pons's inquiry in Montesard, I had been allowed to speak. And I needed to warn them about the Harrowers.

The well-dressed pair paused and bowed to each of the curators. Were these my neighbors, the purebloods who'd summoned the Registry?

Their delay slowed the third man, tall and spider limbed, dressed in a sober, common black wool cloak that scarce reached his knees. Pale, long-fingered hands and wrists dangled from sleeves cut too short. My frantic breath caught and chills shivered my spine. This was the acid-tongued rescuer who had yanked me from the fire. No orange scarf today. But the daylight revealed his face, exceptionally long, with huge protruding bones in cheeks and brow, and eyes so deep one could not spy the color.

His un-Aurellian features and his common, ill-fitting attire named him an ordinary, yet the curators remained unmasked in his presence. Who was he? Surely they didn't know of his Harrower sympathies.

As he turned to go, he smiled at me, a grimace shocking in its malice. No curator could see it.

I pointed my bound hands at him and bobbed my head, trying to signal he should stay. Gramphier averted his eyes, as if shamed at my antics. Pompous little Scrutari blew a disgusted exhale. Pons and Albin leaned forward and whispered to each other. Damon, the curator I knew least, stared with such cold, unblinking interest, I stepped backward.

The heavy door closed solidly behind the strangers. I breathed deep and forced calm.

Gramphier struck the table with a gavel that seemed to add cannonball weights to my chains. "Lucian de Remeni-Masson, it is with utmost sorrow that I gather this council and certain witnesses to examine your behavior. Your grandsire and I lived in mutual respect from our youth until his dreadful end, and to see the future of his bloodline in such peril adds a solemnity to this proceeding that words cannot convey. Despite the insistence of some amongst us, we are not here to address your notable failure in discipline of five years past, but only your erratic behavior since the tragedy of three months ago. Moved to indulge your natural grief and inexperience, we chose—wrongly, I fear—to let those incidents pass without mention, ignoring history that warns of aberrant tendencies in certain of our kind. When it was decided that your skills and temperament no longer fit the requirements of the Registry Archives, we debated amongst ourselves: Would you fare better under some kind of benign confinement or in an undemanding contract away from the exigencies of the Registry? To our everlasting guilt, it appears we made the wrong decision."

The First Curator's chilly words froze my bones, as if the gods themselves spoke my doom.

What incidents? What erratic behavior? My protests died unspoken. Animal grunting would get me nowhere.

"The terrible events of yestereve have forced us to confront our failure. We've a witness to the time you left your current master's place of business. Not long after nightfall, you were seen walking the perimeter of Vintner Tessati's town house—your residence. Both purebloods and ordinaries saw you raising magefire in the center courtyard. It was assumed you were honoring divine Deunor, as was your family's practice. But then you vanished, only to reappear when the blaze was on the verge of consuming the residence. Not a single spark traveled beyond the perimeters of Tessati's property—a sure sign of deliberation. Did you truly not recall that you had kindled those first sparks and set a boundary for their reach? Or was your frenzy at your return a murderous pretense?"

I shook my head, attempting to make some noise that expressed dismay and negation, not brutish fury. It was all lies! I'd been at Arrosa's Temple just after nightfall. But then, no one knew that, not even Bastien. Would the coroner admit he'd sent a pureblood to spy on Arrosa's high priestess? And if they'd not let me speak . . .

No one heeded my display, save Damon. His gaze had not wavered since my arrival.

"In the end, I fear, it does not matter which," said Gramphier. "Either answer signifies a deviant mind. We have confirmed that your young sister, a gods-gifted sorceress not yet come into her full power, was found dead in the ruins of the house. Five ordinaries in your service likewise. We cannot let this pass."

The words, spoken aloud, arrested breath and heart and pulsing blood. Juli dead. Like the dull-eyed shells piled one upon the other at Necropolis Caton. A frenzy of denial stormed behind the mask. My teeth near severed the sodden, choking leather, wanting more than anything in the world to scream it so all could hear.

Discipline, Lucian. You must hear what's said.

Gramphier struck his gavel again and rose from his chair to his imposing height. "Curators of the Pureblood Registry, we are charged with administering the gods' holiest gift to humankind. We have heard damning testimony. We have heard the advocacy of Curator Pluvius and the recommendations of Curator Pons, who has observed him even longer. The time has come to render judgment. I determine that the man before us is responsible for the death of one of the gods' chosen and five ordinaries, this crime explained, though not excused, by reason of a broken mind. Say, each of you, *yea* if you agree, *nay* if you dissent."

"Yea." Pons settled back in her chair, arms crossed, after pronouncing her resounding verdict. Was she satisfied at last?

Damon looked inscrutable. And voted yea.

Master Pluvius looked aggrieved. And voted yea. I glared at him, horrified. My advocate.

Yea. Yea. Each cold-eyed affirmation drove a nail into my coffin lid, and I could do naught but stand and hear it.

Gramphier struck his gavel again. "It is our unanimous judgment that Lucian de Remeni-Masson is broken and must be held in close confinement so that his magic cannot be used to serve his madness. Until we find a suitable house and a guardian who will enforce the strictures of close confinement in more comfortable and dignified circumstances, he will be kept here in the Tower in conditions to ensure his health, his personal safety, and the safety of all. He is hereby forbidden to speak to any person without my personal consent, to marry, to sire children, to teach, to walk free, or to show his face to any person, pureblood or ordinary, unmasked, save those we set in custody over him. He shall pursue no activity, magical or other, save with my consent. . . ."

I did not faint. Did not rage. Did not die, save inside where all was ash and ruin anyway. As one dire stricture after another fell from Gramphier's thin lips, this tableau came to feel like an ancient play put on in a crumbling theater, where everyone knew the outcome before the first *scena* had even begun. There was no justice or right judgment here, not when the condemned was given no right to speak. Instinct . . . the study of history . . . years of observing faces and extracting their truth with my ink and my bent suggested that everyone here was an actor, and that no word of mine could have changed the course laid out for me since three days ago. Or was it five years past? Had my grandsire, too, believed me deviant? Mad? Was that why he had contracted me to the Registry, where I could be watched every moment of every day?

Somewhere behind raging disbelief and heartsick certainty, First Curator Gramphier yet droned. ". . . swear to you upon your grandsire's name that we shall help you overcome this illness that has riven you from our kind. Our hope is that with time, work, and proper care, you will heal and reclaim the gift the gods have granted you."

He nodded to someone behind me. I wrenched my arm from Nelek's iron grip long enough to touch my forehead and bow to each of the six. With each rising my uncovered eye caught and locked a curator's glance before I moved on to the next. Gramphier, Albin, Scrutari, and Pluvius dropped the gaze before I did. Only Damon's stare of chilly curiosity held. And Pons's, which spoke nothing at all.

I would likely have many empty hours to contemplate that, along with the rest of my questions. These curators would be in no great hurry to find me a *comfortable confinement*; the idea of *healing* was laughable when there was no illness. But through whatever came, I must hold to the truth: I had not murdered my sister or our servants. I had done nothing to warrant this punishment. For the honor of all my beloved dead, I would endure.

Part II

The Killing Season

CHAPTER 15

YEAR 1292 OF THE ARDRAN PRINCIPALITY

YEAR 215 FROM THE UNIFICATION OF ARDRA, MORIAN, AND EVANORE AS THE KINGDOM OF NAVRONNE

YEAR 2, INTERREGNUM, MOURNING THE DEATH OF GOOD KING EODWARD

LATE WINTER

The door scraped and I squeezed my eyes shut. I no longer looked up when the light came. It pained my head too much and delayed every new accommodation to the dark. Eyes closed, I took my proper place, while my jailers inspected me for vermin or disease.

It was always Nelek who inspected me or hacked off any growth of hair on my head or chin, while poor Virit had to shovel my foul mess from the corner and replace the litter with clean. Occasionally they replaced my bedding, too, in the corner opposite.

Straw would have been more satisfactory for both uses, but straw was considered too solid, too easy for a mad sorcerer to infuse with spellwork. So they gave me a litter of dead grass and dry leaves to sleep on. It lasted three sleeps on average before crumbling entirely to dust.

Dust and light. They prescribed the rhythm of my hours in close confinement. The count of the days themselves had eluded me from the first night after my judgment, when Nelek had led me back to the iron cell and stripped off my clothes. The hateful mask, shackles, and hand bindings had remained in place. He said he would remove them when he was convinced I would obey his commands absolutely whenever he opened the iron door. I was not to speak so much as a word, nor touch either him or Virit, nor touch the food or drink or other things they might bring until he said. To any question, I was to respond *appropriately*. To submit, I assumed. To confess to madness and murder.

I had howled that first night. Not in madness or despair, though I felt very near both, but in a determination to purge fear, hate, and anguish so as to make room for reason. I howled in mourning for Juli, for Soflet, Giaco, and the rest, for all of my dead, for the hurt of such loss as could never, ever be eased. I howled for the world, too, missing its noblest king, suffering an evil war that broke men's bodies so cruelly and a disastrous winter that could cause humans to don orange scarves and descend into most *in*human savagery. I howled for the blight on men's and women's souls that could lead them to debauch and murder children. If such crazed corruption had somehow penetrated the Registry, too, then how would any of us survive this accursed season?

Discipline, so my family had taught me. Reasoned behavior derived from custom, clarity, and conviction. I was six-and-twenty. I had a powerful bent for magic. I was not entirely stupid. As long as blood pulsed within me, and as long as reason guided my actions, there was a chance I would be free again to discover the truth of these horrors.

So I howled. Hour upon hour upon hour until my soul felt empty, my throat felt like broken glass, and the cold and the hateful bindings, and even the lurking terror that there might be rats in this cellar, could not stave off sleep.

When next I woke, when the door scraped and the light appeared for the first time of my close confinement, emptiness enabled me to do exactly as Nelek had prescribed. I stood in the center of the room with my back to the door and did not move. He inspected me, unfastened my mouth strap, and set out a bread bowl filled with ale. It had made for a hurried meal, and an awkward one when I had naught but bundled hands to manage it. When I was done they fastened the mouth strap again.

"Have you any ills to confess, *plebeiu*?"

I shook my head and they left. And so it had been every waking since.

On the present occasion, as ever when they left me alone again, I tried to thread together the happenings of the days leading to my fall. Someone had been seen setting the fire apurpose, even preventing its spread beyond our house. A Harrower, perhaps. A skilled arsonist could limit a fire's reach, especially in the snow and wet. Yet fanatics ran in frenzied packs and did not mime purebloods in cloaks and masks. To believe a *pureblood* had set out to murder my sister or me left me teetering at the brink of an abyss.

My thoughts chased one another in widening circles, seeking some motive for such a crime. What could anyone hope to gain by our deaths? Our treasury was minuscule, our family properties blighted or burnt. Our influence had died at Pontia, and to think that Juli had somehow brought this down on us was ludicrous. Personal grievance led me nowhere but back to Pons. Her stone-gray eyes stared at me through the cold dark, but told me nothing. Panic nibbled at my spirit. What was I missing?

There was the matter of the altered portraits. Gilles had said two or three were being *completed*, when I knew very well they were already complete. Unfortunately it had been so long I could not call up the true images. And I knew none of the curators well enough to speculate about any flaw in character my portraits might have revealed. But it seemed unlikely that the petty offense of two or three could condemn me to this.

They believed I was mad. In his judgment, Gramphier had mentioned *aberrant* behavior of *certain purebloods*. I hadn't caught it at the time. Had he meant my dual bents?

I dismissed the thought. Gramphier, at least, knew my second bent had been excised. I had shown no aberrant tendencies. I was not mad.

But of course, I also knew the excision had not worked, which left a lingering uneasiness in my soul—a simple blot, like the bruise on a leper's finger that left her with no hands, or the freckle on a man's forehead that consumed his eye and cheekbone and, eventually, the rest of him from the inside out.

The next time my jailers came—I had no way to judge the span of hours between their visits, but only that I was hungry—they brought a fresh pile of litter for my waste and a bread bowl filled with stewed parsnips. I hated parsnips, but I ate every morsel. As ever, I moved the litter to the corner where I could find it easily in the dark.

Never facile at pure abstraction, I was accustomed to developing ideas with pen in hand. Without that aid, I had to grasp random threads of memory and follow where they led, hoping to discern the moment when something felt awry. But magical ball games with my lost brothers, exuberant family dinners, and history tutorials were much clearer than any hints of grievance or conspiracy. Five years working in the Tower and I could scarce recall any difference from one day to another. Had I been asleep the whole time? Enchanted?

Frustration set my bound hands to pounding my half-leather skull. My restraints seemed particularly crafted to inhibit clear thinking. If I tried to pace, the shackles rubbed my ankles raw. My burns seeped and stung beneath the hand bindings. And the leather mask forced me to consider every swallow, every cough, every sneeze, lest I choke or drown. Its weight and stiffness left my neck aching, the corners of my mouth bleeding, and sleep unsatisfying.

Persistent dreams had me chained while wearing the mask, unable to run or cry out as flames consumed me, and a man with an orange scarf and long pale fingers banded in copper laughed and watched. I bit my lips in my sleep and clawed at the sores in my mouth until they bled. Someday I would know that man's name, and why a man who had worn a Harrower's colors in my burning courtyard was allowed to see the unmasked faces of the Registry curators.

A few more visits and Nelek removed the shackles. Eventually my hands were unbound. The burn on the back of my right hand had grown septic, and my jailers fetched ointments. Over the next span of endless inspections, eating, and sleeping, the wound healed—bless the gods—with no damage to my favored hand. Sitting in the dark, I felt shamed that I fretted so about that possibility, when Juli would never use her gifts at all. The image of her took shape in my head, sharp and sudden, as if someone had sliced open the walls of Idrium to taunt those of us left behind. Her dark eyes sparked; her agile body spun in exuberance; her fingers, laden with magic, touched a block of marble, ready to waken it to good use.

Forgive me, serena. The knife twisted in my heart. *I should have taken better care. . . .* And I told her how empty was a world where no one recalled our mother's weakness for lavender or our brother Germaine's for sour plums, where none could sit admiring the Cartamandua map hanging in our library for the sheer beauty of its illumination, or where no sister shared one's scorn of women who thought lisping made them alluring. Small things. Trivial things. But important because they spoke of family. How would I remember it all without her to help? Already details were slipping away into the dark.

I apologized to the dead girl child, Fleure, as well. What had Bastien been told of my disappearance? His luck charm, he'd called me. My brief career at the necropolis already seemed so remote as to blend with tales of myth. *Please, gods, let no one at Caton be dead because of me.*

Tales of myth . . . For one brief moment, I thought back to that night of the blizzard—of naked forms etched with exquisite fire, of warnings that made no sense and a voice that roused forbidden memory when speaking my name. It was the voice that convinced me the incident must have been the result of exhaustion and magical depletion. I had seen Morgan naked, and she was no Dané.

Of course, the contrast of the sharp-edged memory and the certainty of its impossibility fed the uneasy blot on my soul. I had to push it all away. I was not mad. I was not.

Never did Nelek and Virit take me out of the cell. Never did they speak to me of my crimes. I could not fathom why the curators kept me alive. If this was supposed to heal my madness, I had no idea how. Truly, I feared the reverse. The more I tried to think, the more I slipped into confusion. Soon I could no longer put two ideas together in a logical sequence, each one scarce a whisper in the dark, flitting away on silent wings.

A longer span of repeated warnings that I must never speak, and Nelek removed the vile mask. I wept that night. It was the first time since my howling night. My sobs made no sound at all.

The hours blurred until I could not judge one from the next. Worsening headaches kept my thoughts muddled. My eyes began playing tricks on me, as well. How could shadows exist where there was no light? Human-sized shadows. Hovering. Watching. Vapors, no more than that, yet their pervasive malevolence terrified me.

I brushed at them. Turned away. Hid my eyes. Lay naked in the cold, praying the pain in my head would ease, praying I was not going mad.

No god answered my prayers. The shadows commanded me to draw a corpus sitting in a chair. But when I touched the pale, still face to spark my magic, the flesh was warm, and thready breath tickled my hand.

No! I would not. Someone had once said my art could steal a man's soul. To snatch a soul from a living being would be a crime beyond redemption.

Again and again the dream shadows presented me corpses. One and all their chests rose and fell like shallow, quiet seas. Dream or waking, I fought the shadows' will until my head felt as if they drove nails into it. Magic was an act of will. No one could force a sorcerer to work magic.

The dreams persisted. Came an hour I considered yielding. Perhaps if I did what the shadows wanted, they would stop. Nelek's braying arrival woke me. I stumbled to my feet, weeping. Tears came more often now.

The degrading inspection. Yet another inexpert scraping of head and chin. Boiled fish, olives, and bread, spread with pasty beans that tasted of wormwood. As I ate, I smelled ink on my hands. Madness.

When they left me alone again, the blackness within me was as profound as that without. I dared not sleep.

You need occupation, Lucian. To despair was to repudiate the gods' grace. *Magic* . . . Everything purebloods did, everything we were, centered on the gift we held in trust. If I could just work something small . . .

No one knew a sure way to prevent a skilled sorcerer from conjuring, save to silkbind his hands and allow him nothing for his spellmaking to affect. Sheets of iron, as enclosed my cell, did not preclude magic, but had a way of causing spells to work erratically, dangerously so. To touch the walls or door with magic would risk mind-destroying backlash, thus escape by brute force was impossibly risky. But if the spellwork was wholly contained inside the walls and sufficiently small, no harm should come of it.

The first enchantment my mother had taught me was an aerogen—a simple wind spell, scarce a ripple in the sea of life and magic. It should leave little or no residue for Nelek to find.

I sat cross-legged in the approximate center of my cell and began.

Difficult. Extraordinarily difficult to consider structure, magnitude, and effects in the formless dark. My brow broke out in sweat. My fingernails dug into my palms. But with care and labor I created the pattern to reflect my desire—little more than the promise of movement—and bound it with my will. Fingers spread, I let the magic flow into the air.

Ah, glory . . . the essence of all that was beautiful in the wide world filled both the great emptiness inside me and the waiting pattern. Little more than a puff stirred the fetid air, but it was magic, it was new, and it was my own.

Starving, greedy, I wanted more. I gathered a handful of dust left from the repeated deterioration of my litter bed. Dust, like smoke, ash, and fog, existed on that borderline between the physical and the ephemeral. If I could make air move, why not dust? And though the individual particles were too insubstantial to support a full-blown light spell, something smaller for each might yield an interesting result.

The task would be tedious and time-consuming, but it wasn't as if I had something more important to do. Thinking . . . solving unsolvable mysteries . . . was impossibly difficult locked in the dark with a head like a smith's forge. But magic was muscle and bone. Exciting, ever and always.

First, I worked at modifying the aerogen to move the dust, not at random, but in very particular directions. When my spread fingers at last felt the spinning dust cloud above my head, the resulting shower set me sneezing . . . and laughing. Unnerving that I couldn't stop either one for a very long while.

I reduced the spell pattern for magelight to a pinpoint. Then I made four more patterns exactly the same and bound them together. I replicated that construct and bound the two together. Ten such pinpoint spells. Thus and so until I had built thousands of constructs, each holding thousands of pinpoint spells.

Already, I felt stronger of mind, more lucid, more in control of myself.

Eventually, my great pattern was ready. Holding it carefully in mind, I gathered a handful of dust, bound my enchantment with will, and filled it with magic.

The cascading power set my spirit soaring. And when I threw the particles of dust into the air and they spun in a cyclone of sparkling scarlet, lapis, and canary yellow, I fell to my knees and crowed in wordless delight until my sides ached, until the dust drifted to the floor in showers of fading color.

Clutching my fists to my breast, I tried to hold on to joy and wonder. But as the light faded, abject terror sent me scrambling to a corner. How could I be so stupid?

Hours I spent quivering, waiting for the door to crash open, waiting for the leather mask, for the shackles, for worse. No one came. And when I at last believed that magic so deep in the underbelly of the Registry Tower could go undetected, I sprawled on my back in the dust, flapping my arms and cackling. Perhaps I was not quite sane just then.

Another cycle. And another. I considered new magic. But some affliction of bad meat or soured milk blighted an endless succession of hours and shredded my reason. Virit could scarce bring enough dry litter to soak up the vile mess. The pain in my head threatened to crack my skull, and sometime in my thrashing, my fingernails clawed long, deep scratches on my arm. The cold was especially bitter in that time, and I came very close to begging for a blanket. But I could not, would not speak. The punishment for speaking would be dreadful.

Like the burns, the illness passed and the lacerations on my arm healed. Nelek granted me a pail of lukewarm water and a rag to clean myself. Trembling with weakness, grateful for the indulgence, I could no more have conjured an escape by way of bucket and rag than I could have climbed to Idrium by way of the dust on the floor.

"Take no satisfaction from this grace, *plebeiu*," said Nelek. "We're charged to keep you healthy. But you've shown no remorse as yet. I've reported that to the curators."

But I would not confess to murder, not even in pretense.

My stomach returned to its more common unease. My eyes played tricks in the dark. The headaches grew worse, leaving thought . . . and magic . . . impossible. I was hungry all the time. Either Nelek was bringing food more often or I was sleeping longer as time passed. That worried me. What if I fell asleep here and never woke? What if they stopped coming?

Gods, don't think of that.

"Lucian?"

A faint pinpoint of magelight creased the midnight of my cell, enough to illuminate the dusty iron floor and the hem of a scarlet robe. I drew back into the corner and clutched my knees. More ghost dreams? I knew better than to speak.

"Ah, lad, this is so dreadful, so wrong." The voice was quiet. Furtive. "They've kept you healthy, at least."

Mad, though. Surely that. His voice was so clear, the robe's scarlet so vivid.

A warm bulk crouched beside me. The soft light came from a twisted ring worn on thick, ink-stained fingers . . . so familiar. But I could not remember.

Before my mind knotted irretrievably, his hand rose just enough to illuminate his worried face. *Pluvius!*

My spirit scrambled from the depths. I rolled to my knees before him, clenched my fist to my breast as a beggar might, and motioned toward the iron door. *Take me out of here!* My mind yelled this at such volume, he must surely hear. *I killed no one. I am not mad.* I yearned to bellow these things aloud, but this could all be illusion—a cruel trick. If I spoke, they would know.

"I cannot set you free. Not yet"—his denial pierced my soul like a poignard—"but if I'm to help, you must tell me the truth." He raised my sagging chin. I would have told him anything.

"You took something from the Archives after your grandsire died. I'm not sure in what form—scrolls, tablets, artwork? Vincente told me that he had stored his greatest discovery in the Archives—something of extraordinary significance, something most secret and most dangerous because it propounded a great and terrible historical lie. He made me promise to destroy it if anything ever happened to you. Yet no work of such significance is there now. I've looked everywhere. So you must have taken it."

I opened my palms in confusion and shook my head. I'd no idea what he meant.

He crouched in front of me, all urgency. "You *must* tell me, boy. If I can convince the others that no such thing exists, they'd have no reason to keep you. So I must know where you hid it. You could not have removed it from the Tower without my knowing, which means you've stored it somewhere here. Tell me, lad. I'll help you every way I can."

Perhaps I'd forgotten. The past was so murky. What did a scroll or tablet have to do with my captivity? Yet one thing . . . one thing I knew. Everything Capatronn stored in the Registry Archives—whether journal, document, or crumbling potsherd—was a part of the history of magic. King Eodward himself had agreed that everything relating to the divine gift belonged in the Tower, where it could be studied and preserved, rather than the Royal Antiquities Repository amid shields and spears, jeweled combs and ancient coins. Magic, and the power it took on in the lands of Navronne, was the greatest mystery of our kingdom's history. To abscond with any piece of the puzzle would have been unthinkable. And why would I? If Pluvius said . . . then I must have done . . . but I couldn't remember.

Tears pricked my eyes. I cupped my hands at my breast and shook my head yet again, until Pluvius laid a cool palm on my brow to stop it. Care flowed from his fingers, calming my frenzy, deepening my despair.

"By the spirits, what have we done to you? I'm so very sorry, Lucian." He bent close. "You must not tell anyone I've come. The consequences would be terrible for both of us."

My folded hands flew to my lips to vow silence. Telling would mean speaking. Telling would mean all this was real and no dream. Already the edges of the world blurred, the light playing tricks as if the dust had risen from the floor to hide us.

As I curled up in the dust to sleep, murmuring shadows closed in around me. I wasn't quite sure if the Master of Archives had walked out or vanished, or if he had ever been there at all.

CHAPTER 16

The door clanged shut behind Nelek and Virit. They'd shaved, trimmed, and blotted me with a damp towel, and soothed my ravening hunger with a bread bowl of milk. Now I could return to the contemplation they had interrupted.

Sitting in a meditative posture, I blessed Master Pluvius and prayed fervently for his good health. His presence had borne such a different quality than the usual ghost dreams—the lines so sharp, the color so vibrant, his concern so real, that my mind had begun to function as it had not since my sickness.

Certainly his visit *had* been a dream. Waking logic—how fine it felt to hold two thoughts in tandem!—demonstrated that truth. My grandsire had pursued no historical investigations since his retirement five years before his death. The curators could easily have consulted him about any questionable discovery. And if they believed I had removed something dangerous from the Registry Archives, they'd had ample opportunity to question me about it before stowing me in Magrog's bunghole.

I pinched my arms and scrubbed at my bristly head and chin. I was not mad. No madman could have come up with such excellent reasoning. And if I was not mad, then I had not murdered my sister and our servants.

Hot tears rolled down my cheeks. Not frantic tears. Just relief and simple sorrow. When it seemed enough, I was able to stop—another small victory—and return my mind to the great question the dream of Pluvius had raised: Why?

My captivity was not solely Pons's doing. Her initial argument with me—a breach of discipline insufficiently punished—had naught to do with madness or violence. Even for the Hound of Correctness, it could, in no wise, merit the horror of my confinement. There must be something more.

Besides, all six of the Registry curators had sent me here. Pons. Pluvius, my sole advocate, though not so effective an advocate. Gramphier, my grandsire's colleague, who had made no move to *heal* me. Damon, the inscrutable, whose eyes had bored into me during the judgment, who prized discipline and loyalty, but evidently not truth. Had I insulted Scrutari's annoying family? Or Gilles? Albin had been vicious and decisive in his condemnation; had he planned for *Gilles* to do the curators' portraits?

The six portraits. Gilles might have been wrong about only two or three having been altered. Yet even if I could recall the images, I might not recognize what my strange combination of bents had revealed. I needed to know more about their subjects. And in the Tower cellar—deprived of speech and human contact—only my bent could teach me anything. Perhaps if I sought out the faces of people I knew, like the curators . . . like my grandsire . . . I could discover something of their secrets. Each of them had walked, taught, and spoken in the Registry Tower over the course of decades.

To invoke my bent was riskier than working light spells or aerogens. A pureblood's intrinsic gift was to other magic as Ocean to a rain puddle, more easily detectable while it was active, a more distinct residue after. Better to risk the consequences for useful purpose than mere occupation. And better to attempt this while I had some clarity. If the ghost dreams returned . . .

I rolled to my knees and touched the iron floor in front of me, brushing away the layered dust and a fear that investigation might reveal only what happened to prisoners confined here too long.

Emptying my mind's canvas was easy. *Lord of Fire and Magic, grant me your grace, if grace be left in this world. Allow me to see truth.*

My bent responded to my desire with bounteous glory. The power risen between my eyes set blood and bone afire. And when my fingers released the cascading magic into the resistant iron, I focused all my strength of will to draw the history from the earth below. Images of ancient warriors, sentries, and wild-haired marauders held me rapt.

This place was very, very old. The marauders' curved swords were bronze, not steel. The settlement surrounding the tower—Palinur—was but a cluster of sod-roofed huts, housing a few herders, pigs, and goats. No vineyards had yet shaped the green hillsides into a patchwork. On every horizon thick forests loomed dark like invading armies.

In a sensory barrage I witnessed the coming of sheep, the coming of kings, the fall and rebuilding of the stone surrounding me. But I had a purpose. The anchor I sought for my seeing was a man of strength whose mind had ranged Navronne's past with the vigor of those marauders, whose insights and intelligence had shaped the stories of the past into truth. My grandsire had shared his gift with me, forming my hand and mind, infusing them with his delight in creating order from tangles like these.

From the chaotic stream I snagged an image of black-haired strangers—Aurellians, so unlike the fairer Navrons we found here. A thread of magic led me to caskets of gold and jewels hidden in these iron vaults, which led me, somewhat surprisingly, to Cicerons in gold armbands and dangling earrings, wearing braids wound with gold thread, mail shirts, and black tabards marked with a white hand. Though curious—who ever thought of Cicerons as warriors?—I abandoned that image. I wanted sorcerers—purebloods—not magical cheats.

Amid threads of wine-colored cloaks, silk masks, and wondrous magics that would take a lifetime to explore, I sought my grandsire. Truly *history* was a difficult concept to pursue, in the same way that pursuing *words* or *talespinning* would be, for each concept encompassed everything of humankind's experience. But the scroll, quill, and mask symbol of the Registry Archives took me right where I wanted.

Images showered like falling leaves. One: Pen in hand, Vincente de Remeni scribbled in one of his journals opened on a slope-topped writing desk that, even now, found use in the archive chambers far above my head. Years ago, this was, as his queue of thick hair was not entirely grayed.

Holding tight to his thread, I sought others of the curators.

My belly lurched when I came upon myself, seated in a wooden chair in a candlelit cell, chest and wrists strapped to the chair to keep me from toppling forward. The scent of beeswax from the wall sconces seared my nose, and the taste of ash near choked me. My grandsire stood behind, hands gripping my head. I was screaming.

Magic boiled through my fingers into the dusty iron floor and brought the fading vision into clear focus. Never would I forget that dreadful day.

Capatronn had brought me to the Tower, prepared to ensure my dual bent would never lead me to disgrace our family.

To my surprise, two others kept us company in the delicately named Procedure Chamber. First Curator Gramphier stood beside my grandsire, his hands spread as if invoking the blessing of the gods on the rite. And behind them both, scarce visible in the doorway, was Pluvius. At first I thought Pluvius was preparing to attack the other two. His arms were raised high as well, holding a staff and a long dagger crossed above his head. But the dense magic swirling about the weapons merely flowed into the larger magic of the excision.

More unsettling than unexpected witnesses to my breaking was my grandsire himself. Unlike on that day, when agony had kept me blind and deaf, the vision revealed my grandfather's face as he reived my soul. His jaw was resolute as I remembered, but neither grief nor anger scarred his face. Only fear.

None of them spoke when the magic was done. Pluvius vanished. My grandsire unbuckled the straps and walked out with Gramphier, leaving me spewing my previous day's meals into a waiting bucket.

After Montesard, my indulgent grandsire had entirely reversed his character. He had done this horror to me before we knew for certain what the gods intended or whether I might be an exception to the belief that two strong bents indicated a deviant mind. Why had he taken a youthful indiscretion so seriously? He had forced me into a contract with the Registry, where he knew Gramphier and Pons would note my smallest lapse. He had refused to speak to me, as if my childish assignations and a single glorious afternoon of love were some personal assault upon him. It had never, ever made sense. Unless my grandsire, too, believed me deviant, broken, mad.

No. No. No.

I was *not* mad. Gods save me, I was not, unless this place had driven me to it.

I released the thread into grayness and grasped the next that slid into the range of my seeking. Capatronn's thick gray hair was cut off short, as he'd preferred it after retiring from court. A solitary lamp set on the floor illuminated the near side of his face with a soft glow. He knelt beside a painted chest, pulling out artifacts and piling them on the floor: potsherds and rusted daggers, linen scrolls, gold earrings, elaborate necklaces displaying the finest artistry of silverwork, goldwork, and gems, stone-carved cats and fat-bellied images of the Mother. From an ivory box he lifted an intricate gold armring, beautifully wrought in the mode of a curling vine.

Inside the box lid was engraved a five-branched tree, the mark of the lost city of Xancheira. Xancheira and the massacre that erased it from the earth had been my grandsire's last historical investigation, pursued while I frittered away our honor at the university.

Someone stood in the murk across the open chest from him. Silver gleamed from a woman's thick-fingered hands waving in earnest argument—the very hands that signed my contract on the day my life collapsed. Pons! Capatronn gestured in dismissal, but she persisted, not angry but urgent. I'd no idea they'd had dealings beyond Montesard.

With every scrap of my strength and power, I reached deeper, determined to draw that thread close and hear what they said. But my body spasmed as happens in that sliver of time between sleep and waking, when the world seems to drop out from under. In the matter of a heartbeat, darkness swallowed every image, scent, and sound of my magical vision. Power yet flowed in my veins, but not through my fingers, for they no longer touched the iron floor, as if that, too, had been devoured by the dark.

A gust of icy wind sent shivers through my skin. Naked still, dream or waking. Sharp, clean air scraped my nostrils, its faint scent redolent of the river country.

A flutter of great wings and the screech of a hunting bird drew my gaze upward. I blinked once, twice, as my heart swelled. Surely I had fallen asleep or been enspelled, for above my head was such an array of stars as if Kemen Sky Lord had crushed all the gems in his treasury and scattered them across the sky.

Unlike the usual progress of dreaming, movement seemed my own choice. Wondering, I spun in place.

Narrow spikes of spruce and pine stood black against the glittered sky. On other sides rolled the larger silhouettes of soft hills. A pool might have been a splash of stars fallen to the grass—dry grass that tickled my bare feet and ankles. So strange, so . . . sensual . . . to be naked outdoors at night.

Never had I been a participant in any vision drawn from my bent for history. Yet never had any dream exhibited such a sense of life.

My breath caught. At the edge of the shadowed trees appeared a woman wearing only a draping of spidersilk that left no significant mystery to her womanly form. On her bare arms gleamed the most exquisite line drawings of full-leafed vines, though worked in traces of silver and not the vivid blues I'd seen or imagined those uncounted nights ago. A graceful eagle scribed on her cheek wrapped one wing about her left eye and across her brow, and the other down her long neck. And across a shoulder and the low mound of a breast, a second bird took flight.

But it was her thick, unruly curls that drew my gaze to her eyes—so large and angled ever so slightly and as luminous as the Wolf Moon of winter's end. Though she was too far away for me to discover their hue, I would have wagered my soul they were green.

Morgan? Even the unspoken name witnessed to dream . . . or madness.

The woman raised her chin and shrilled a piercing call. The nearest I could identify it was a falcon's yip, though longer and so loud it must strip the bark from the trees at her side.

Before the cry faded, she stepped from the shadows, the cold wind rippling her hair and filmy draperies. She might have been a creature of the wind and starlight, so light was her step. My soul longed for pen and ink to capture her wildness.

She halted just out of arm's reach. Paralyzed, chilled to the marrow, I could not drag my eyes from her. Alas, though very like beneath the strange markings, only in wishing was she Morgan. But if ever myth had borne a shred of truth, she was Danae.

"The beacon holds! Thou'rt crossed at last." Clear, fluid words, like a brook below its sheath of ice. She tilted her head, a sidelong smile blossoming on her elegant features. "I did not expect thee unclothed. Dost thou pretend to be one of the long-lived?"

"Beauteous lady." Wonder loosed my tongue, but it was the ragged hoarseness of a stranger that grated on my ear. I hadn't heard my voice in so long. "What is this place? Who are you?"

A crackling in the undergrowth behind brought dark shapes to the edge of the trees. A red fox trotted from the shadowed wood to her side.

"I could ask thee the same," she said. "Long have we seen this day rising, as thy makings twist and strain the boundaries of the world. Tyr Archon bade us sentinels watch, that we might prevent damage from thy clumsy trampling. Divided are we about what to do with thee. Lead astray . . . or grant sanctuary?"

She ignored the fox that, catlike, rubbed its fur on her bare ankles. "For my part—"

"Remeni! Lucian de Remeni! What are you playing at?"

The world shook, rattling my teeth as the harsh call enveloped me in blackness.

"Praying, are you? Beginning to feel the burden of your crimes?" Iron fingers gripped my shoulder. "Or have you possibly been trying to escape?"

Grief welled from my breast in a monstrous wave, curling my back until my forehead touched dusty iron. It required every scrap of will inside me to keep from crying out the loss of so marvelous a dream. The glory of the night, of the Dané. The lightning power of her voice that had charged my flesh with heat and light akin to magic. No moment of my prisoning had been so cruel as this waking.

"For a moment I thought you'd slipped your cage, *plebeiu*. Virit said you weren't in here when he brought your ale. More fool, I, to send the birdwit alone."

Heart dull as lead, I moved to stand as was required. But Nelek's firm hand kept me on my aching knees. "No matter this time. We've brought a gift for you."

Quick as a bird snatches a ripe cherry, hard leather cupped half my face, and before I could claim my wits, my mouth opened in protest and the evil strap compressed my tongue.

The magic . . . Gods save me, they had detected my magic. Why did I not just die in my dreams?

From there all proceeded as before, save they left my shackled feet bare. It seemed more hurry than intentional shaming, though Nelek did not spare insults as he led me through the open door.

I was near gibbering. My disjointed eyes could not decide what they looked on—visions of the past, dreams of the impossible, the glaring torchlight and iron of present horror, or the mask's unrelenting blindness. Heart and loins ached with the memory of the dream, while magical depletion left my knees like porridge and my hands shaking so violently that Nelek threatened to drag me. Anyone hunting evidence of lunacy would not have far to look.

The climb up the iron stair was harder going than before. My shackles weighed like the doom of the world. Once onto the back stair, we didn't go all the way down and back up again. Rather we climbed straight to the top of the Tower. It was full night. Not a glimmer of light came through the arrow loops to aid Virit's torch. *Holy Mother, let them just throw me off. . . .*

When we arrived at the Curators' Chamber, I was near collapse, concentrating so hard on standing, breathing, and not choking on the vile mouth strap that I could not have said who was present. Some of the six seats were filled, some not. Someone breathed on my blind side. I could not say if it was one or ten, male, female, goose, or gander.

"We require that you maintain his close confinement when he is not working, until a Registry investigator judges his mind repaired. A locked room or restrained as you see him here. In the presence of anyone other than you, he must be masked. He is not permitted to speak with anyone—"

"—save those I direct, and only in my presence." This from a man standing at my shoulder. A new jailer? Dull and sick, I could care naught about that.

"Save those you direct, and only in your presence. Of course." The speaker sounded like a most annoyed Gramphier, but he looked odd. The lamplight was weak. My exposed eye blinked and squinted. The curators—four of them present—wore masks. My dull wits could not sort out what that meant.

"Aye, honorable Lord *Domé*. You've made your conditions clear three times over and writ them down for my perusal. I'll see he behaves, you can be sure. He's ever been a stiff-necked prick. And he is clearly a risk. But I've paid well, and I'll have no more interference with my rights. Caedmon's Writ is clear."

The words whipped me alert.

Speak no name . . . breathe no prayer . . . see no hope. I clamped a hold on mind and soul, squeezing them still until I could be sure.

"So if you'll hand over his clothes and boots and remove these shackles—your jailers must be the truest lunatics in Palinur—I'll take my peevish, prideful mule of a servant and go."

I leaned my head back, and if I could have managed it, I would have crowed in joy and vengeance and gratitude eternal. Bastien.

CHAPTER 17

"Can't you go any faster, pureblood? The sooner we're away from that den of sorcerous snakes and back with nice friendly corpses, the better I'll like it. These damnable princes and their bickering— Shite! Out of sight!"

Shouts and running feet burst into the deserted *pocardon*. I dove behind a fishmonger's cart, as the coroner drew his battered sword for the third time in our race through the snow-drenched midnight. As I gasped for breath, he kicked the tail of my cloak over our lantern, dropped the hefty rucksack that held my shackles into my lap, and took up a wary stance between the cart and a shuttered stall.

Bless all gods, Bastien had convinced the curators that leaving me shackled on this night was a death sentence. I had thought it a useful exaggeration, but clearly not. The festering wounds of war, winter, and famine spewed violence into every corner of the royal city.

Gangs of men and women tore apart market stalls and abandoned carts—anything that would burn. Before we'd even left the Council District, Bastien had driven a band of rapacious beggars back into an alley, hamstringing two of them. Not a quarter hour later, he'd yanked me to his side by the mouth strap, threatening to unleash me—his mad sorcerer—on two drunken soldiers who had blocked each end of a short lane with us in between. I didn't know whether it was my grotesque mask, Bastien's more than competent sword display, or his inspired maledictions that frightened them more. But they gave up quickly and let us pass. Still exhilarated by freedom and open air, I had roared in my best bestial fashion. They left the stink of fresh piss in their wake.

My chest heaved. The mountain of fish entrails half melted into the muck just beside me did naught for the turmoil in my gut.

Heavy boots—two pair—stumbled past, their owners panting as hard as I was. Shouts and savage whoops heralded their pursuers. "Make it level! Make it smooth! Purify the servants of privilege!"

Harrowers.

I hissed at Bastien, frantic to warn him. *Don't let them see you, Coroner. Don't tell them who you are.* Harrowers believed any who served crown or temple were abominations to their wrathful Gehoum.

The coroner raised his sword.

I twisted round and swung my bound hands at Bastien's knees. He fell backward, landing silently on my legs, sword jolted from his hand. As he flailed to get up, I looped my arms around his and shook my head vigorously. He glared and shoved me away.

"Set hand to the Harrow! Take them; rend them! Strip flesh from them as serve worldly masters and pretender gods!"

Bastien stiffened as cascades of voices from all sides shrilled and hooted their approval. Silently he hefted his sword again and drew his dagger, but he remained crouched beside me as the mob surged past, his broad back a rampart between me and the stampeding madmen. For the thousandth time in an hour, I blessed his stubborn spine. How many ordinaries in this world had balls enough to challenge the Pureblood Registry?

Two men bellowed and screeched. Savage howling erupted into wolfish triumph as the men's agonized shrieks became less and less human.

"Shite, shite, shite." The coroner's quiet litany reflected my own helpless horror.

I pressed my locked and useless fingers to my head. Someday, if Serena Fortuna was kind, I would strike a blow again these lunatics and the woman who led them.

As blood-drunk songs of victory faded, Bastien dragged me up. "Come along. Your damnable curators refused to transfer you in the daylight. Mayhap they wanted us to die out here."

We sped through the dark city as fast as I could stumble. I could spare no glance for anything but the spot of lantern light before my feet, though my fevered imaginings had Danae marked in both silver and blue, luring unfriendly pursuers into midnight byways. If I could only breathe . . .

By the time we reached the brick arch that would take us downslope into the hirudo, my shivers were so violent and my nose and throat so clogged, I had to stop. I sagged against the broken bricks and grunted a plea that halted Bastien as he headed down the narrow lane. He sighed and came back, holding his lantern high to expose my misery.

"Damn and blast, you look like you've just spent a century in Magrog's realm."

I nodded assent and leaned my head back against the broken bricks, swallowing repeatedly, telling myself I would not die of shivering and a gatzé's idea of a pureblood mask.

Resting wasn't going to help all that much, either. A summer-weight cloak, thin shirt, slops, and bare legs were wholly inadequate for a snowy night. Nelek had put my boots on me in the Tower, and a mantle of claret-hued silk, but Bastien hadn't been willing to wait for the jailer to locate my *misplaced* pelisse or even to dress me better, with all the accompanying removal and replacement of my restraints. I had not disputed his choice. I couldn't get away from the Tower soon enough.

"Let me unclip that damnable mouth strap," mumbled Bastien. "Maybe if you could get a whole breath, you could hurry your feet a bit."

I shook my head with all the vigor I could muster. Someone could be watching.

"The rules, eh? Even out here where none can see but rats and beggars. Never thought they had you all so cowed."

I gathered myself together and pointed my bound hands down the slope. I'd no way to tell him that right discipline was not a matter of being cowed, especially when your ill behavior endangers the very ones who've helped you. It was one thing for me to chance punishment for myself by working magic in my cell, entirely another for me to let Bastien wager his own safety just to make me more comfortable. Interfering with pureblood discipline was against the law. Violation could see him dead. My legs weren't going to move faster anyway.

We trudged on, the coroner holding his lantern in one hand, my arm in the other, guiding my stumbling steps when the path grew steep.

"These curators must think they're the lords of divine Idrium incarnate," grumbled Bastien, assisting me around a swale of ice and gravel.

"Took me a month just to get through the first door. When I accused them of stealing my property, I thought the pompous ass biters were going to squash me like a cockroach. But I know the law. That woman that didn't negotiate your price also didn't bother to write up terms for a man like me that might differ from those writ for a noble." He elbowed my ribs. "I can whip you if I want! More important: My contract for your service stands as long as you're breathing, no matter what else you've done or what the Registry might want with you."

The cold fuddled my thinking. None of this made sense.

"They likely wouldn't have acknowledged my rights even yet," he continued, "save that we had a lucky charm, you and me. Recall that dead boy I said was the image of the Wroling magistrate?"

As we plowed through a wallow of ankle-deep ice and mud, I recalled a young soldier with a cloven jaw. My portrait had shown him with a whole face and the crest of Wroling's lord on his surcoat.

I grunted.

"Not long after I had a Registry secretary tell me to go drown myself, Magistrate Maslin showed up himself to claim his boy, grateful, and said to name a price. We've had dealings, Maslin and me, and not always good ones, but he knows the law, and if there's a palace, temple, house, or shop in this kingdom, he likely knows a way into it. So I asked if he knew anyone could get me inside the Tower to press a contract dispute with the Registry. He mentioned a fellow, name of Collium, the chancellor of Navronne's first secretary. Happens this Collium is the very person charged with enforcing Caedmon's Writ, and he's not overfond of purebloods. Well, here we are. . . ."

Bastien halted and passed the hem of his cloak over the lantern three times quickly and then once more. From the murk below came an answering pattern. Curious.

With a satisfied grunt, he took my quivering arm again. "Samele's tits, pureblood, are you entirely frozen?"

My bundled hands waved him onward. Both blood and brain felt like slush, but his talk, and every step away from the Tower, warmed me.

He shrugged, dimmed the lantern just enough to guide us one or two steps at a time, and led me onward. Downward. But he didn't take up his story. Fresh snow muffled our steps and laid a pall of quiet over the hirudo. Not even a dog barked.

As we passed through the dark, cramped lane, I sensed watchers on either side, but none hindered us. A pulsing glow and the weedy scent of pipe smoke hinted at more of them lurking beyond the piggery. Once past, we climbed.

Bastien paused at the top of the steep ascent to uncover his lantern again. I gulped air and swallowed spittle. "The Harrower who steps into Demetreo's demesne had best bring himself a surgeon alongside," he said. "He'll end up with enough holes in his back to need a year's sewing. We've seen a few who've tried it of late. But our restraint in the matter of the dead child has won us safe passage. Can you go on now?"

The shivering was uncontrollable. The world spun slowly like thick porridge in a pot. But the gates of Necropolis Caton rose gray and solid from the murk. Who would have thought they could be so welcome a sight?

Again I waved my hands forward—and almost toppled onto a grave.

Bastien steadied me. "So, this First Secretary Collium knew your grandsire, as it happens. Said Vincente de Remeni was King Eodward's Royal Historian and one fine man out of a shiteload."

He glanced at me. Impossible to tell him it was none of his business—even if I'd a tongue to use. He grinned through his tangled beard as if he knew exactly what I was thinking.

I dipped my head.

"Secretary Collium was most disturbed to hear that the Registry had breached a Remeni's valid contract with a servant of the Crown, albeit a lowly servant he'd never heard of. He wrote up a document and sent it to the Registry, declaring that the First Curator must meet with me and work out the terms, else they'd stand in violation of the Writ. Guess that curdled their bones, what with a new king like to be named soon. And so they let me present my case. Ho, Bek!"

My foot chose that mystifying moment to get tangled in the mud. I pitched forward. From my blind side, hands reached out for my flapping clothes.

"You must have a gatzé in your pocket, Coroner," said Bek, the hollow-eyed surgeon, as he hauled me to my feet. "Never in this world did I believe they'd let you have him back."

"Touch and go," said Bastien. "He came nearer hanging—or whatever purebloods do to their own—than he will enjoy thinking about when his brain's not froze. Though I'm not so sure hanging wouldn't be a preference. They gave me *lessons* in how to bind his hands properly."

The two of them mostly dragged me across the mounded graves. A roaring in my ears muted their talk, and I was doing well to breathe. But as the city bells struck first hour of the morning watch, the gates of Necropolis Caton swung open and welcomed me home.

"Are you sure it's him?" The booming voice interrupted the general confusion. "Best get that devil thing off his face and see if you've hauled back a ringer."

Bastien and the surgeon hefted me onto the blood-stained slab where Bek cut corpses, which in fact didn't bother me in the least on this night. Bone saws wouldn't cut ice.

"Can't take it off around you lot," said Bastien. "Only when I'm alone with him. Registry gave me strict rules or they'll take him back. And you can be sure they'll be sending inquisitors. For now, he needs food and ale. Lucian, can you hear us? You need food and drink to repair your magic, yes?"

I'd no way to give answer. All I could do was shake.

"Warmth first," said Bek. "Blankets, more clothes. Something hot to drink. A tisane, broth, milk . . . Boiled water if naught else. What were you thinking, dragging him across the city half-naked?"

"Pssht. He'll thaw. We were lucky to make it here without spilling our guts to the Gehoum, and he'd have liked that far less. Do what you need, bonecracker. But I know he needs food, drink, and sleep to replenish his magic, and I need him working as soon as may be. Come another thaw, we'll lose the four."

The meaning of their bickering was unintelligible; the sound of it, somehow soothing. My lonely eyelid closed.

"No, no, no, not until you drink, sorcerer. Coroner, get this hellish thing out of his mouth so we can feed him."

Darkness swallowed me. Dreams beckoned. I had been dreaming of Danae. My grandmother had been wrong. They didn't steal children with two bents and carry them off to the sea. They stole moments of our lives, infected our souls with wonder and beauty, and then abandoned us to this dismal world. I groaned with longing. It came out the braying of an animal.

Fingers fumbled at my mouth. "Heed me, Lucian de Remeni! It is my duty to remind you that you may not speak."

The command was a lightning bolt writ in bone and sinew. My head bowed of itself. *Must be standing, back to the door, else they'll keep you in this leather horror forever.* But my limbs were lead. Something held me down.

Dust . . . a thousand years of dust, and these scraps of clothing . . . Panic tangled my thoughts. *Must be naked for the inspection. It's disobedient to die before inspection. How else can they find the vermin? They must see the rat bites, so they'll keep the beasts away.*

I clawed at the layers, choking on the dust, gasping for air, but everything was dust and leather and I was retching, drowning in bile, and I'd no hands . . . only blunt clubs . . .

"Get it off him! Where are those blankets?"

Someone hammered at my head. Nelek must be bolting the mask to my skull. *Sweet Mother, please, no!* I writhed and flailed with handless arms, battering whatever flesh was in my way. *Without hands, I've no magic.*

Hands crushed my limbs, pressing me onto bare stone. Maybe they would fix me in stone, wall me up in a statue, without voice, without hands, without magic. Registry curators were the most powerful of sorcerers. Despairing, I fought and bellowed like a brutish beast.

The choking leather came out of my mouth and I coughed so hard and so long, it seemed my lungs must rip. Until the world turned black . . .

". . . Not been starved or beaten. Just frozen and worn thin. Keep him warm. Keep him drinking. Let him sleep. And get that infernal mask off him."

"Can't just yet. He is who he is. And I've got to have him working."

Bek stood on one side of me. Bastien on the other. I was bundled in magnificent warmth. I cracked open one eye—no surprise the vile leather yet covered the other—and noted that my cozy nest comprised Constance's entire stock of sheets for covering corpses. My hands ached . . . unbound. A beautiful, blessed ache as I wriggled my fingers and drew them to my breast.

"If he's to be keeped in here, I could see to him of a morn. That he's fed and got his necessaries while you're off with your investigationing." Even a whisper identified Constance unmistakably.

A smile curved my lips—gods, what a pleasure—and some kind soul had wiped the crusted drool, blood, and vomit from the corners of my mouth. My eye drifted shut again.

"I think our sorcerer's back with us, Coroner," said Bek, quietly, "though I suppose I'm not allowed to acknowledge his existence. Isn't that the rule?"

Someone harrumphed and spat.

"What's doing here, girl?" No whispering from Sexton Garibald. "We've two new dead out the yard. Garen, Pleury, we've bones need hauling. Some can gawk at god-cursed spelltwisters of a morn. Others got work."

They were all here, the mainstays of Caton. Honor required an act of importance.

With my blessedly free hands, I pushed up to sitting and squinted into the yellow light until I spotted a broad man with a thatch of wiry, sand-colored hair. I pulled my legs around and slid from the table, lowering myself to one knee. Pressing my fingertips to my half-leather forehead, I inclined my back toward him as if he were a king. I wanted all to see. The Registry had no rule about *not* kneeling to an ordinary, as what pureblood would ever imagine doing so? Unless he had been liberated from the netherworld.

No one spoke after, and my unobscured eye refused to stay open long enough to note their reactions. I just climbed back on the stone table and buried myself in grave windings. Everything else had to wait for a while . . . magic, grief, understanding. Perhaps I could recapture that glorious dream of stars and Danae . . . Sanctuary sounded marvelous.

I didn't wake in the surgery, but on a hard palliasse in a corner of the pureblood preparation room—my makeshift studio up the short stair. Constance had reclaimed some of her sheets, but a small brazier sat nearby, giving off warmth in a circle about one pace wide. It felt magnificent. Even better, the leather mask sat on the stone bier instead of my head, and gray daylight peeked around the closed shutters. I breathed deep, sat up, and then stood on wobbly legs.

Thought had been given to my situation. An earthenware jug and a folded rag sat in the empty laver. A soft wad that looked like chewed gristle and smelled the same was evidently someone's idea of soap. Bread and cheese sat atop the bier alongside a mug that I prayed was full of any drinkable liquid. And one of the covered urns, such as they used for holding human ashes or bodily organs, sat under the stone table, inviting me to relieve myself. Very practical. I took advantage. From my prodigious output and the vast cavern where my stomach ought to be, I estimated I'd slept more than a day.

Interesting that a wooden plank blocked the doorway, though it didn't seem to be attached as yet and was wholly out of keeping with the faded sanctity of the prometheum décor. A laugh bubbled through my chest.

The rules said I was to be kept in close confinement. This was likely the best they could do on short notice. Bastien knew I wouldn't run. Every road led back to the Tower cellar. Necropolis Caton was my sanctuary.

Thoughts fell into a quiet emptiness. I felt scraped clean. Newborn. Not in some exhilaration of sanctity or purification, but because the life that had encompassed and defined my every thought and action was ended, and I had no idea what to do. For the moment, I existed, grateful for the small amenities.

Shivering, I scrubbed face, hands, and every part of me within reach with the oily soap and cold water from the jug. The bread, cheese, and sour ale vanished in one great inhalation. Then I moved on to arm myself against the cold. I layered my own clothes over the prisoner's garb, silk shirt over the linen one, woolen braies over the slops, and then, quite inexpert, set about doublet, hose, buttons, lacings, and boots.

The velvet doublet smelled of smoke and sandalwood. I needed to tell Bastien about Gab and High Priestess Irinyi and Fleure and the big, hairy Bear Lord with Shiny Boots who'd killed her . . . so many things; so distant they seemed, as if my true life lay elsewhere.

When I was dressed, I flung open the shutters and rested my elbows on the sill. Down below, Garibald's legion pushed barrows of bones toward the charnel house—not a structure of horror, as I'd once imagined, but a tidy stone building with a pillared portico and a nicely proportioned dome. The laborers didn't just dump their loads. The sexton stood close by, making sure they took time and care to place the bones in some arcane order. Carved angels, beasts, and impish aingerou flanked the wood doors and guarded every corner, drainpipe, and seam to prevent Magrog's gatzi from creating *fengrash*—soulless human simulacra—from the resting bones. Old-woman stories. Myths. Like the Danae.

Questions swirled in my head like windblown dust. Was it possible they were real? They'd certainly felt vivid, especially those who had attacked me in the alley. Both those limned in blue and the woman in silver had spoken of boundaries—of trespass or twisting. With my magic, I thought. But the former—those in the alley—had issued a warning. They'd known my name, vowed to drive me witless, while the woman in silver seemed more . . . welcoming.

The door scraped open. Actually, it scraped, shifted, and toppled backward into the passage with a great thud.

"Constance!" bellowed Bastien. "Need these hinges done first off."

He clambered over the door into the chamber, muttering, "It'd be just like those arrogant sons of Magrog to send an inquisitor this first morning."

Bastien eyed me at the open window, then stuck his head back through the doorway. "Constance! Need to install locks on these shutters, too. And none's to come near this chamber without my say, or I'll throw 'em in the lime pits!"

He drew my tall stool to the window and sat. I straightened, touched my forehead, and bowed, raising my eyes to meet his ever-penetrating gaze. My life was here, not in myth.

"So, my very expensive and troublesome servant, are you mad?"

I shook my head.

"Speak. You're out of the damnable mask."

"I am not mad." Astonishing . . . gratifying . . . to hear words emerge. And to believe what I said. "Nor am I a murderer. I did not set the fire that killed my sister and our servants." Harsh, unforgiving words, twisting the spike that would forever be lodged in my chest.

"Didn't think so. 'Twas only three days you worked among us, but I've never been so wrong about anybody as all that. Well, save one other young fellow, once." His natural ruddy flesh darkened to the color of bricks. On one side of his forehead, a great bruise glared in its first purple-and-green glory.

Bastien hooked his bootheels on the top rung of the stool, leaned forward, and rested his elbows on his knees, his fingers twiddling the ties of his jaque. "For what it's worth to you, the Registry does not want you dead. Secretary Collium's document forced them to decide the matter. It said that if you were being detained for a matter entirely of civil law, then they must turn you and all their evidence over to a royal magistrate for prosecution—which would likely have your carcass swinging in the wind, from what I know of the matter. If the offense was a simple violation of pureblood rules or even a tangle of both civil law and pureblood rules, then the Registry could punish you according to their own lights—even execute you. But as long as you are breathing, they must ensure you are available to me for the duties as outlined in the contract."

He scratched his beard. I believed he was grinning. "Took 'em so long to decide, I thought I might have got you dead after all. But then they summoned me back to the Tower and agreed I could make you work. I told 'em they could lock you up at night if they wished, as long as they delivered you safely by sunrise every morning and fetched you when your day's work was done, which might be any hour twixt dusk and midnight. That's when they laid out the rules for me keeping you here. Guess they've the right to do that . . ."

His pause invited an answer.

"Yes." I flexed and folded my sore fingers. "And I'll abide by them. I swear it. Last night . . . if I did that"—I touched my own forehead and then pointed at his bruise, before uttering words that would have scalded my mouth in my former life—"I apologize. I was . . . confused."

"You're stronger than you look. Bek claimed it was the cold unhinged you."

My panicked lunacy on my arrival disturbed me. How long had I been confined? Though I had lost count of the days so early, I could not shake this notion that it had been little more than a few tendays . . . a month . . . maybe two.

"I was dreaming. Thought I was back in the Tower. Coroner, I would know how long—"

The rules I'd just sworn to obey halted my query. Bastien was not supposed to speak to me of matters beyond business of the contract. "Honestly, I am not mad."

His scowl was not reassuring. "So, you claim the fire was happenstance? Witnesses saw a pureblood setting it. And the flames seemed designed to burn only your residence and no one else's."

Custom demanded I refuse to speak of these matters, as they were personal and not my duties. Yet my sanity or lack of it was very much my master's business.

"I don't even know how to set such a fire as that, confined to boundaries."

"It was fire killed the whole rest of your family—the very circumstance they said left you most of a lunatic."

"Grieving did not drive me to murder." I needed him to believe me.

"Perhaps it was not grief, but failure to complete the job."

"How dare you suggest—!" I glanced up sharply, leashing the burst of outrage in the instant of its birth. This was Bastien the coroner. The questioner. His head was tilted, his eyes alight with curiosity, not accusation. But very determined curiosity. He had laid his neck on a knife edge to get me back. He wasn't going to let me hide anymore.

"My family—including every person who died last year, my young sister newly deceased, and the servants who lived with us and saw us unmasked—was more precious to me than the crown of Navronne to its princes. They and the magic they nurtured in me were my world, my *life*. I did not arrange for their deaths. And yet . . ."

My arms wrapped my chest and my eyes squeezed shut, as if the act might redeem my coming treachery.

"My every bone tells me that my sister's death was no happenstance. As for the rest of my family, Harrowers slaughtered them all in a raid on the town of Pontia last autumn. It was merest chance that my sister and I weren't with them. Was Pontia selected for a raid that night because the entirety of the Remeni-Masson family was gathered there? Harrowers loathe all purebloods and want us all dead. And I know of no reason my family would be singled out . . ."

Though my voice shook, I pushed on.

". . . and yet speaking of it aloud this way, it seems obvious. If none of these recent events was random, how could that one be so?"

Bastien's fingers paused in their idle occupation. "Are *they* responsible, then? The Registry? And if not you and not the Registry, then who? You would like to tell me it's none of my business. But it strikes me that a sorcerer who has such a grievance with you might not stop, and 'twould behoove your master—and jailer—to pay attention, you see."

I scrubbed my shorn scalp. So casually he suggested that the unshakable foundations of pureblood life were as flimsy as a bridge of feathers—hinting at calculated murder and unimaginable corruption. Yet bringing such questions into the light, speaking the words aloud, made them take on the shape of reality . . . of horror . . . of truth.

Chest and gut had tightened, so I could scarce squeeze out speech. "I've no idea who or why. They didn't question me. . . ."

Not that I knew of. Yet it would have been so easy to touch me with enchantment or slip a potion into my food. The persistent hunger; perhaps I had truly lost hours. How would I know? I had been sleeping so much near the end. Those ghostly shapes . . . the malevolent whispers just beyond hearing . . . the headaches and nausea and the cut on my arm. Yet I would surely remember their faces, their questions; rumor said certain powerful sorcerers could erase memories, just as rumor said some sorcerers could fly or walk in dreams. But no one I knew had ever witnessed such magic for himself. Such a short time ago, even on that morning I'd been told the Registry no longer needed my service, I would have indignantly denied such possibilities.

". . . but yes, I believe not the Registry itself, but someone *at* the Registry is behind the fire at my town house, at the least, and certainly the rumors of madness. Families of mad sorcerers have to lock them away."

"And as you've no family, the Registry must tend to mad Lucian de Remeni, just as they negotiated for you. It gives them freedom to do as they want with you. And ensures that no one will believe a word you say. But to what purpose?"

Bastien was a hound straining at the leash. "Only one possibility has occurred to me. It might be nothing. Last year I painted portraits of the six curators."

He was right. Those who had murdered Juli and our servants to gain control of me certainly weren't going to flinch at destroying Bastien and the others here, if they chose to try again. And whether they truly thought I was mad or wanted me burnt or buried alive, they wouldn't leave me here forever. Someone should know these things.

"This matter of my magic revealing things unexpected . . . I never noticed it before coming here. But I'm thinking some of those portraits might have disclosed something their subjects wanted hidden. And, gods have mercy . . ."

The man who wore Harrower orange in my courtyard had stood in the Registry Tower. Harrowers had sworn to kill all purebloods. My hands gripped the casement with such ferocity as could keep the vault of the heavens from collapsing on the sorry earth.

". . . it wasn't a tenday after I finished the portraits that Harrowers slaughtered my family."

"You've no idea which portraits? You've no magic can tell you?"

"Be sure if I could redraw the cursed things, I'd do it this moment." I scraped my fingers through my scruff of hair, struggling to keep my thoughts straight. "But I would have to see them." Which couldn't happen any time soon. But it would. Somehow, sometime, I would learn the truth. "Touching them would tell me exactly what's been altered."

"Could you undo what was done—make them look as they did at the beginning? *That* would be a weapon to use."

"No." Privacies poured out of me as if the days in the cellar had rotted the barriers I'd spent my life building. "Magic can't just strip away the changes. I can do that with my own work, to make it match the true image I carry. But if a different artist makes the changes, I'd have to correct it with paint or ink."

Shaking his head, Bastien relinquished the stool. "Well, you're befouled good and proper. And whoever they are, they've got me stuck keeping you quiet for them. So, as I'm unlikely to get admitted to the Tower again without a new king bearing me on his shoulder, I'd best get all the work out of you I can. And I'm off on other business in the city this morning."

"Work will be very good," I said, feeling a bit desperate. If I kept thinking, my head would fracture. "Magic—using it for good purpose—is important to me. Necessary. After I left here that night, I went to the temple as you wanted . . ."

A gesture dismissed my opening. "We've gone ahead and buried the lily child. But I've other interesting cases stacked up in the barrow, waiting for you. Once they're done, we'll talk about what you learned at the temple."

It surprised me he wasn't more interested. He'd seemed intent on solving the girl's murder—Fleure's murder.

"Your inks, pens, and pages are up there on the shelf," he said, moving quickly to the door. "A bell, too. Take what time you need. Then ring it when you're ready to have one brought. I'll tell Constance what order I want them done. As they carry your subjects in and out, you stand facing the wall. I'd rather not have to put that mask on and off you all day. Clear?"

"Yes."

"Until we've bars on the windows, the shutters will be locked save when you're drawing. I understand you need the light to work. Behave yourself."

The conversation was at an end. I touched my forehead and bowed.

He paused at the doorway and looked around. "A hundred and fifty-eight days. That's how long they had you." He jerked his head and vanished.

A hundred and fifty-eight days. Almost half a year. Lord of Fire and Magic . . . what did they want of me?

CHAPTER 18

To immerse myself in magic and art once again was blessing immeasurable. I began with a quiet hour sketching, limbering my fingers and the linkage between eye and hand. I purposely refrained from any subjects that might influence the work to come, keeping to birds, dogs, horses, anonymous faces, and hands—one of the most expressive parts of the human body. Perched on my stool beside the window, I worked at capturing the bustling energies of the cart road below. Runners, diggers, Constance flying hither and yon, slow and steady Garibald. One deadcart after another rolled through the east gate.

A hundred and fifty-eight days. Despite intermittent showers of snow, sleet, and rain, it was spring . . . the season of promise and planting . . . famine time. Bastien likely had a hundred starvelings for me to draw. What did it feel like to starve? No pureblood ever thought to know. This dread new aspect of my bent—to feel a subject's death pain—could teach me a thousand things I never thought to know.

Shaking my head, I focused on line and shape and movement. Distractions, especially of the life-afflicting kind, must not interfere with my power to probe the truth of my subjects.

When my fingers felt an extension of my eyes, I laid down my pens and sat cross-legged on my palliasse. My tutors had taught me mental exercises useful to smooth the pathways between art and magic. Now I had this notion that my two bents had begun to work in harmony, I wondered if it might be possible to forge a more certain joining than passing chance. My duty, as a holder of the divine gift, was to explore its nature and improve it.

With the breath of my will, I blew upon the two centers of my magic and brought both banked fires to life, keeping them in balance as they grew to flame. Then I focused my eyes inward and began to release magic, not to flow through my fingers—not yet—but to invest the ephemeral energies with solidity so I could manipulate them.

Easy. Astonishing. Between twin ingots of gleaming silver—one between my eyes, one behind my breastbone—stretched a spiderweb ribbon of light. Perhaps the connection would strengthen on its own, but with my future so uncertain, I wanted to be sure.

I wove molten magic through the connecting web, twisting and shaping as a silversmith draws his heated filaments into the straights and curves he desires, until the two centers were joined with a solid strength. From this gleaming bridge, I forged new channels to guide my magic from both centers at one. Once all felt stable and secure, my will released the image.

My eyes opened. Lungs filled and emptied. And still I felt the power inside, spanning heart and head—a strength as real and available for my use as if the width of my thighs had somehow doubled or the brawn of my shoulders could now hold up the sky.

The desire to share the wonder of it with one who might understand wrenched my heart. I offered a petition to Mother Samele that she might embrace my little sister and reunite her with the rest of our kin, and I tried to envision them all together in some grand feasting hall in Idrium. But every effort rang false. Only magic would speak truth.

Whispering an invocation to the Lord of Fire and Magic, I rang the bell and took my place facing the wall.

When the shuffling footsteps and nervous whispers died away, an elderly woman awaited me on the stone table. Her face was not deeply wrinkled but creased with tiny lines like old linen. Capable hands, not coarse or scarred, but accustomed to work, suggested a shopkeeper or housekeeper. Her limbs were straight, her cheekbones quite prominent, though without suggestion of starvation. In truth she looked quite healthy, save for the gaping gash across the great vein in her neck.

Magic answered my summons swiftly and in glorious abundance, flowing through my new-wrought channels as cleanly as Palinur's springs flowed through its pipes and fountains. Before I knew it, a fire-eyed, thin-lipped harridan had taken her place on the parchment, a well-filled purse in one hand, a sturdy cane in the other.

My fingers rubbed my neck, where the sensation of a fiery knife cut yet stung. Someone would know her. Identifying the *particular* person who had slit her throat might not be so easy, however. Her pitiless visage suggested that those who had grievances with her outnumbered the graves at Necropolis Caton. Heart and bone, eye and spirit, swore the likeness was true.

A brief, grateful interlude with a mug of ale and a withered plum that had been left in the dry laver, and I rang the bell again. As the echoes faded, I took my place facing the wall.

My second subject was an ancient Ciceron, so lean I could count his knobby bones. His few teeth were stained dark by pipe weeds, his sagging earlobes riddled with punctures. Naught suggested how he'd died, save only the expiration of age. And the portrait bore that out, though it showed him standing straight and tall, his ears bearing a hundredweight of brass and silver earrings, and his tattered black vest clean, new, and blazoned with a white hand.

A handful of old figs had been left for me. Though hard and chewy, their sweetness was invigorating. I finished them off and closed my eyes for a short while, then rang the bell again. On this day at least, Bastien would get full measure from me.

The new subject was entirely bald, like the barbarians from the lands south of Evanore's mountains. Unlike the squat Kafru, however, this young man was tall and slim. Or . . . I examined him more closely. Not a man, but a youth, despite the lack of hair. Not so much tall as gangle-limbed like a colt, still out of proportion. He'd been dead for a while. His cold flesh had begun to darken and shrink as Fleure's had.

Many would deem an accurate portrait impossible now the body had begun its final change. Bastien believed I could do it. And I? I wasn't sure what my limits were. I laid out a fresh parchment and began to trace my left hand over the youth's cold, leathery features.

Constance had clad him in one of her white tunics, likely because his clothes had been shredded. Near every quat of the boy's flesh was abraded, crushed, or battered—unhealed. Death wounds, then. The scars and calluses of his undamaged hand testified to a childhood and youth of unremitting labor. A hard life and a hard death.

I reached deep, accepting the pain sure to come. If my art touched the youth's spirit, as Bastien claimed, then perhaps he could experience my magic's glory, as I experienced his hurt. Again the surge of enchantment was swift and enormous, filling me with warmth, life, and purpose. When it set my right hand trembling, I released it to spill upon the page before me and began to draw. . . .

A stiff, cold breeze brushed my short hair, flapped my shirt, and teased my eyes and nose, redolent of damp and fish and a tang those in the river country ever named Ocean.

"What—?"

Astonished, I spun round. Light bathed gentle hills, scattered with clumps of slender pine and spruce. Though snow yet nestled in the shadowed clefts between the hills, slips of green peered from the matted gold of the year before. And beyond the rolling landscape a strip of blue sparkled like diamonds in the morning sunlight.

Rising urgency spurred me through the wakening grass, stepping tuft to tuft through a spongy gully until I reached a rib of rock that would lead me upward. I climbed, sweating in the damp chill. Halfway up, I paused and turned to look. The vista took my breath. A vast, heaving water stretched all the way to meet the gray-blue sky. Was this Ocean?

What was this place?

I clambered upward again, using both hands and feet when the way became too steep. Something waited for me at the top . . . an answer . . .

I shuddered and blinked. The fingers of my left hand rested on the dead youth's brow. My right had paused after lying in the curve of a soft hat that wrapped that brow. Had I fallen asleep in the midst of magic working? Inexcusable weakness, if so, but I wondered. Pushing distraction aside, I summoned power. . . .

The city bells rang the first hour of afternoon as the footsteps faded down the prometheum stair. Body aching as if I had tumbled down Monte Cleone in a rockslide, I faced the wall, awaiting whomever Constance would bring to replace the battered youth—not the hairless, withering remnant of life who had lain on my table, but the sun-browned, gangle-limbed boy who now looked out boldly at the world from the portrait laid beside the earlier two.

Easy, confident, graceful, the youth sat astride a sleek stallion that would be found only in a wealthy man's stable. His threadbare tunic, slops, and padded jaque were those of a common laborer, his cheap boots clotted with muck and hay. His hands were bundled in dirty linen, and an old-style liripipe sat atop his head, the long tail wrapped about his neck for warmth.

Most would name the boy a common stable lad, exercising a noble master's favored horse. Yet I wondered. Like the horse, the youth's bones were fine, elegant, and strong, and the spark in his eye spoke of intelligence and ready humor. And his head was not bald. Shining curls the color of sunlight peeped out from under his poor man's hat, and his mount's saddle skirt bore the lily of Navronne.

Doubt nagged at me. Visions . . . lapses . . . impossibilities . . .

I abandoned the wall and snatched up the portrait. It would take them a while to bring the next, and I wanted to test the truth of the image. With a few strokes of the pen and dollops of magic, I transformed the lily into scrollwork, darkened the boy's hair, and thickened the legs of his horse. I tossed the pen aside. The drawing screamed falsity.

Eyes closed, I touched the page and called up the true image, summoning will and power and a spell I had learned in the earliest years of my training. The *quadreo* was a massive enchantment, designed to strip away all conflicts between the true image and the actual. It used inordinate reserves of power, hastening depletion, and my masters had insisted that using it too often risked dissolving the very pathways of magic in one's body. Having tested my work several times in the course of my training, I could believe that. But of all times, I needed certainty. A rush of magic scoured my sinews in arm and hand, blurring my vision as the world shifted. Taking deep breaths to settle my racing heart and spinning head, I opened my eyes.

The lily was back. The youth's curls gleamed like summer noonday. The horse would be a worthy mount for Kemen Sky Lord himself. The drawing spoke truth.

Satisfied for the moment, I moved back to the wall. When Bastien's work was done I'd give more thought to the strangely vivid dream—vision? distracted imagining?

The new subject brought in was the most challenging so far—a small child, little more than a babe, whose head had met with a wooden beam or a stone wall at some time not so recent. Swallowing my gorge, I touched a withered limb and reached for magic and justice and a touch of the gods' grace.

This time the portrait showed not a child of royal origins, but a dull-eyed starveling Syan boy, his wrists scarce bigger than my thumb. No royal lily anywhere.

Three more children followed.

A filthy waif of similar age to the hostler's boy, her body clotted and stained with sticky black muck, became a pouting girl in a ruffled silk bedgown. The three-petaled lily was carved into her bedstead. Not even the few spoonfuls of mead left in my cup could soothe a burning in my throat.

Another ragged child had black, chopped hair very like Fleure's. I'd no expertise and no physical sensation to explain why she had died, but her portrait showed naught but a ragged, dark-haired child in striped skirt and dangling necklaces, armrings, and hair braided with cheap ribbons. A Ciceron child. She wore no royal lily, but interestingly, a tiny ball of fire hovered above her cupped hand. Some claimed that Ciceron sleight of hand mimed true magic.

The last was a small swollen body, scarce identifiable as human. My art deemed him an infant, swaddled in lace and satin. The pattern of the lace was Navronne's lily.

Despite the nourishment left for me with each subject, my strength had reached its limits. For the drowned infant, I'd had to dig deep into my reserves.

I covered the babe with one of Constance's sheets, sat beside him, and mourned the short, cruel life he'd known. And then I waited. Bastien had not given me a signal to tell them no more.

Clouds and night devoured the light. Rain pattered on the flat roof outside the smaller window and dribbled into the cistern. A profoundly melancholy night—how could it be other after spending the day with dead children?—but so very blessed to hear and smell the rain. The splat of each droplet etched shapes in my fallow mind—curved roof tiles, stone walls, leafless shrubberies, the carved aingerous at the end of the drainpipes spewing the collected rivulets onto the road from their long noses or pouted lips.

The contrast with the Tower cellar seemed to grant me an intense sensual clarity. The scent of damp wood evoked the shutters; that of hard-packed mud bespoke the cart road. The must of old stone conjured the flat roof and its round cistern.

Which took me back to my visions. Several more times during the day,

I had lost focus. Twice the world had simply plunged into darkness as if I'd dropped off asleep. But once . . . Great gods, these happenings were so strange. I had been kneeling atop a bald, rocky prominence, the highest point of the very hills I had dreamed before. The same urgency had driven me there. Yet I could see naught but beauty. Steep-angled light of afternoon gold sculpted a greening land of hills and vales that jutted into the embrace of Ocean like a great hand, its five fingers spread, a slender wrist joining it to a dark continent to the south. Scarps of white stone ridged the five fingers of the land like exposed bone. The smell of the sea borne on soft wind gusts, the warmth of the angled light bathing my face, the certainty of the stone under my knees had insisted on the truth of my existence in that place.

At each lapse I had pulled myself back, dizzy and disoriented, until I could grasp the stream of magic and purpose. Astonishing that I'd produced aught but scribbling.

What else could I call them but visions? Yet I had been shivering from the cooling wind when I blinked away this second experience of land and Ocean, and even now, sitting in my studio, I caught the lingering scent of the sea as if it were imprinted on my clothes.

Perhaps my bent for history had deposited some impression of the hairless youth's history in my senses, like the lingering taste of garlic. For certain, the landscape had been nothing from my own experience.

If the cause was magic—perhaps some strange effect from the joining of my bents—it wasn't my conscious work of the morning that had done it. The vision that had interrupted my use of the bent in the Tower had borne the same sensual clarity. The cold wind had raked my naked body as I walked through dry grass under the stars and met a Dané. A Dané who spoke with Morgan's odd archaic lilt . . . *thee* and *thou* . . . an untouchable memory that could summon the fire in me as if she stood at my side. The incident in the blizzard, though not triggered by magic working, was very like. Intensely vivid, and the two limned in blue had spoken in the same patois.

What could such odd lapses signify? A mind's weakness, perhaps, affirming what the curators said of me. How could they be truth? Morgan was no mythic creature, but as real and human as anyone I'd ever known. Ah, gods, her mind had been bright and keen as a blade; her body as lush as the summers of my childhood; her skin rose-brown, kissed with sunlight, not marked in blue or silver fire. Was she so deeply embedded in my spirit that visions took on her voice?

The pattering rain began to puddle on the floor. Reluctantly, I closed the shutters. As I fastened the latch, torchlight flickered behind me.

"So, you've declared an end to the day's work?" Bastien clambered over the fallen door, torch in hand, bringing the real world with him.

I nodded.

"Presumptuous of you."

My empty hands spread helplessly. My truer retort—asking how he expected me to draw in the dark—remained unspoken. He wasn't stupid. Like a mosquito, he just enjoyed pricking at people. Depleted by work and memory, curiosity and wonderment, I doubted a lion's bite could rouse me to anger just now.

"From now on, ring twice when you're done and they'll carry the last corpus away without bringing another. Where are the drawings? And speak aloud, for the gods' sake."

But before I could say, he spotted the row of pages spread on the floor well away from the windows. He crossed the room with the speed of a spider toward warm blood.

"Never expected seven portraits on your first day back." He squatted beside the row.

"The sleep helped, and the food." I rang the bell twice and moved to face the wall. "It was an interesting selection. Sad. So many children."

"Children of ordinaries die all the time. From many causes." He snatched up one drawing, his nose almost touching it. "Horns of the goat, I knew it!"

I couldn't see which portrait drew his exclamation, but it told me what had become obvious as the day wore on. He had suspected what some of the portraits would show.

Footsteps on the stair held me silent. "So, he's done with all, is he?" Constance's whisper bleated from the doorway. "About 'is supper: I've naught extra but a bit of olive paste and old bread. Garen says he knows a man gots a cartload of pignuts to sell morrow dawn. I'm sending—"

"Whatever you can spare," snapped Bastien. "He needs it to keep working. We'll arrange better for tomorrow. But later. I've business here until *ninth hour.* Do as I instructed."

"Oh, aye. I'll see to it. Da says locks and hinges will have to come after that if you want 'em today. 'Twar a busy—"

"Yes, yes, *after* is fine." Bastien sounded as if he might kick her. Once all was quiet again, he sighed deeply. "That woman is the gods' retribution for every sin I ever contemplated, much less every one I committed."

"She's the foundation of Necropolis Caton."

"Aye. She is. Were it not for her, the dead would lie unwashed and unburied and the rest of us fly into giblets. Garibald bellows, but even he does the squawking goose's bidding."

I joined him alongside the row of portraits. "A plank to spread them on would be useful," I said. "With props under it, if we're to see a rainy spring."

"Mmm." His thick finger tapped the boy on the horse. "Witness said a black charger went wild and trampled this boy in the *pocardon* one night. None knew him. None saw where the horse went or if anyone was even riding it. 'Twas not four days after our lily girl was found in the hirudo."

I rubbed one aching shoulder, ready to vouch for the witness's story. The wretched sensations of battering and crushing had not yet faded, despite the four other portraits in between.

"That bald head had me curious. The older girl was found in a midden up in the Council District. Bek suspects poison. Her mouth and gullet were blistered unlike any disease he knows. A half month since, we had a thaw week, and this babe bobbed up from a pond inside the walls of Palinur's royal palace. The gardener who found it is a Karish believer. He brought it here, as he knew we would bury it proper."

"Infants die all the time," I said, echoing his caution.

"For certain, and more than a few with a rag stuffed in its gullet. But this . . ." He pulled the infant's portrait close. "Bek spends all his time thinking about dead folk and studying their nastiest parts. He believes these five young ones died within a few days of each other. And within a few days of the lily girl."

"But that could happen for many reasons."

"Mmm. But you've shown me the lily girl and these three others with possible royal connections, all between age three and twelve, all dead within a few days." He dropped his voice as if a gossipy ghost might be listening behind the shutters. "None of 'em were starved like these others. None showed signs of sickness. The lily girl and the horse boy had their hair color hidden, one was an infant with no hair to hide, and that midden happened to have a vat of tar thrown in, so we don't know what color was the bed girl's hair. And what is the one thing everyone knows of Perryn, even those have never come near royalty?"

"He's fair."

"Aye. The Prince of Ardra has his mother's hair—fine curling hair the color of gold thread. I do believe someone's been cleaning up *all* Perryn's leavings. Certain there's someone inside his own household in on it. Who else would know where to find them all?"

"Killing children," I said. "What place has that in honorable warfare?" The callous brutality appalled me. So brazen. So contemptuous of the law and everything righteous. "If Bayard had won the war, I might see it. But with the matter settled, it makes no sense at all."

"Naught's so new about killing children or holding 'em hostage," said Bastien. "But you've likely not heard much news of late. The war's not over, as we thought might be. Perryn's not won his kingdom as yet. Seems his elder brother took offense at the outcome of their battle in the north and used the break in the weather to chase him westward. That fight didn't go so well, and Perryn had to dig in for the winter. Now we've a thaw, Perryn's racing homeward, hoping to make a stand here in Palinur. He'll need support from every noble, cleric, and pureblood he can rally."

I'd certainly given no thought to politics. "Such weakness isn't promising."

"Aye," he said. "There's alehouse talk of a brokered succession. Even if Bayard drums Perryn into the ground, he wouldn't like anyone proposing we find some other offshoot of Eodward's bloodline to raise up instead of him. Perryn seems to have left enough spawn about the countryside that every noble in Navronne could have his own little kinglet or queenlet. Perryn's rightful get could be next for the knife."

Cold, deliberate murder. Bastien needed to know what I could tell.

"I don't have a name, but the murderer's a nobleman. And he's big and hairy and wears polished black boots." I gave him the tale of my venture to Arrosa's Temple.

"Blood and thunder!" He slapped his hands on the bier when I reached the conclusion. "It fits. It would have to be someone close to Perryn, likely suborned by one of the brother princes. Curious that he delivered the child to the temple in the first place. But documents, you say . . . if he signed documents and I could get hold of them . . . You'll be worth the trouble yet, pureblood."

His optimism eluded me. Certainly it would be gratifying to identify a man who would slaughter children. But spring would melt Bastien's ice barrow. By the time he could learn the murderer's name, no one would be able to identify the small bodies. Purebloods were considered unimpeachable witnesses in matters of their magic, but a Ciceron would be believed sooner than a madman. And from whom would Bastien collect his pay?

Weariness weighted arms and eyelids. "If I'm to do decent work tomorrow, I should sleep. Perhaps you could tell Constance that, with all sincere gratitude, I've no need of her food tonight."

Bastien wrenched his attention from the portrait. "Nay, we've business yet tonight!"

My spirit groaned. "As you wish, naturally, but my magic—"

"Won't require any. In fact"—he jumped up and strode over to the shelf and took up the leather mask and spool of silk cord—"as we're keeping to the rules, we needs must do this."

Though my spirit recoiled, I dipped my head. The universe had not changed since morning.

I dropped to my knees. "Easier to get it on this way. I'm not allowed to do it myself."

He stared for a moment, then shook his head. "You are the damnedest."

Once he'd latched the mask in place, he detached the mouth strap and tossed it back onto the shelf. "Won't need this. You've permission. But the rest . . ."

Silkbindings—inexpert, but effective. Shackles. Gods! Trust came hard, but I allowed him to do as he was required. I would give no one an excuse to bury my gift.

He snatched the torch from the bracket and led me down the stair and through the colonnade behind the prometheum. Our destination was the Hallow Ground.

The grave markers seemed to have doubled in number and grown larger since I'd last been here, but it was only that the snow had shrunk to less than half its former depth. What were we were doing here in the frigid night? Ice pellets shot through the lamplight. At least it had stopped raining.

We halted deep in the center of the burial ground. And then we waited, unspeaking.

As the city bells rang ninth hour of the evening, Constance, in her finest cloud goddess costume, glided through the colonnade, guiding a hooded figure wearing a wine-colored cloak—a pureblood cloak.

My heart froze. An investigator already? Bastien likely didn't want him to see the unlocked shutters and—

The visitor's hood fell backward, erasing every thought from my head.

"Oh, Luka, what have they done to you?" Juli raced across the snow and flung her arms around me.

CHAPTER 19

"Juli! How—? I was sure— They said none—"

Juli ducked under my bound hands and into the loop of my arms.

"Gods, *serena.* Holy, mighty gods. Forgive me . . . wasn't there . . . couldn't get inside . . ." Joy, confusion, apology, grief tore at my wits.

Bending my elbows, I used my forearms to lift her up and crush her to my breast. Her hair was fragrant against my cheek. "Where have you been?"

The need to know and to tell her everything I wanted before she evaporated shoved words out of me so fast no human could possibly respond.

"The others—Soflet, Giaco, Maia. They aren't—?" One miracle might imply more.

"Put me down. And let me loose." She wriggled and squirmed. "Luka, I can't breathe, and I can't understand your mumbling."

Even without the strap, the cursed mask prevented my mouth opening more than a finger's breadth. I let her go, but only a little.

"Oh, *ancieno.* You look awful. Your poor hair. Filthy clothes. And this dreadful thing . . ." Her finger brushed the hard leather band across my brow. "How can you bear it? I've been so afraid for you. That night . . . I heard what those horrid people were saying."

"Truly I'm all right. It's just believing that you and the others . . . Holy Mother. Lord of Fire." My knees jellied. The resolve that had held me together all day was crumbling rapidly.

"Here, sit down and I'll tell you everything." She ducked out of my embrace and dragged me in the direction of a mourners' bench just emerged from the snow. I hobbled after, chains chinking and dragging snow into my boots. I was not dreaming. Was not.

"He said I could stay only a little time." She dropped her voice and jerked her head toward Bastien, who strolled along the path to the colonnade as if on a courtier's meander. "He is dreadfully stubborn. I knew you would yell at me for speaking to him, but I had to find out what became of you."

Even the astonishment of Juli naming someone more stubborn than herself had to yield to the deeper truth. "You came *here* on your own? Approached *Bastien*?"

"How else was I to find you? It had been a whole day already. I was afraid to go to the Registry, which sounds stupid, I know—though it seems not, now he's told me—but I knew your master wasn't going to be happy if you'd not come in to work." Behind her mask, she widened her eye. "He wasn't. He growled and yelled at me. Only when I threatened to conjure his manhood into a turnip did he stop. Once he heard me out, he started bellowing again. Said he'd see his contract fulfilled, if it took him until the last day of the world. It certainly seemed that long, as it was only last night he sent me the message that he'd gotten you back. I think he's the one who's craz—"

I pressed my bundled hands to her mouth. "Mind your tongue, *serena*." Joy and gratitude threatened to burst my skin, but I could not shake off caution.

Bastien had sat himself on a grave marker not so far away, elbows propped on his knees as if he were contemplating the particular arrangement of the memorials.

"My master hears everything we say. As is necessary just now. The Registry's given us strict rules, and I would very much prefer not to go back to the Tower. But just to see you . . . by the Mother's heart . . ." I touched my naked cheek to her hair again, just to make sure. "The curators told me they'd found a girl dead in the ruins."

Juli wilted like a blooming rose doused with hot water. "Kila stayed late to help me sort my clothes for the move. I'd promised to give her things that she could use or sell—for her pay. As it was so late, I ordered her to stay and sleep in my room." The lamplight glittered in my sister's dark eyes, awash with tears that did not fall. "I killed her, Luka."

"No, no. You did not. Not at all. But six—" They'd said six and we had only the five servants. "Ah, *serena*, not your friend."

"He was so brave, Luka. And Kila, too. If the warning had only come a bit earlier! Egan brought it inside, asking if the message was from you, as he had been waiting for you so long and needed to get to his work. I didn't even know he was waiting. When we read it, he insisted on getting me away immediately and promised to see the others safe. Kila refused to come, but went off to wake Soflet and the others."

"Warning message?"

"It said we had to get out immediately or die like our kinsmen. No signature, no seal; I believed it came from you. I was so frightened. We could already smell the smoke. I tried a water spell . . . three of them. Usually I can draw water from anywhere, but they didn't work." Her voice rose . . . tremulous. "*Nothing* worked. I felt like an ordinary. What use is magic if you can't use it when you're afraid?"

"Not your fault," I murmured, touching my forehead to hers. "Not your fault."

"I ran away."

Heartsick at Egan's and Kila's sacrifice, at the terrible deaths, at Juli's anguish, I wanted to crush my sister to my heart until we were inseparable, to draw her tears away with a touch of magic and ease the terrible burden of this new grief, to cry out sorrow and loss and injustice like some ordinary mourner come to the necropolis. But my silk-bound hands could neither touch her nor work magic. All I could offer was words. "You did right. It's all you could do."

"Egan left me at the Vintner's Well." She pulled away, but not too far, keeping my wrist in her grasp. "I waited an aeon, but no one came. I'd brought Kila's black cloak so she'd have it when she got out. I pulled it over mine and went back. The fire was everywhere already. Some in the mob said you had set the fire yourself and likely meant to fire the whole district. I knew that was lies. But the talk spread through the crowd and people were so very angry. Coward that I was, I hid and kept silent, even when you came. I saw *Eqastré* Pasquinale enspell you and send for the Registry. Then the Registry servitors bound you and took you away. Oh, Luka, knowing you believed me dead near drove me mad! If I'd spoken up . . ."

"No! You did exactly right. They *would* have taken you."

"But why? Why would they believe that rabble instead of you? No one could ever believe you mad. Me, yes. But never you."

"I don't know why." I'd never had a chance to tell her about the rumors Gilles had spoken of. "But none of this was about truth—not from the day they terminated my contract. I *will* find out, but it can't be yet. For now I must obey the rules of my confinement. But what of you? Where did you sleep that night and all these months?"

"I went to Egan's mam. I told her of how brave he was and how good a friend. I was in an awful state. I'd no idea what to do. She insisted I stay until I could think clearly. I'm able to pay for my keep, of course."

Her brow lifted and her eye glared, which mystified me until I understood what she was telling me. She had saved my stipend purse.

"As is proper." I kissed her hair, in awe at her forethought and relieved that she had some resources at least.

"You mustn't worry about me." She laid her hand on my exposed cheek. "Trust me, *ancieno.* Now I know you're here, I can get on with things. It's actually quite useful being dead. I'm free to try things and to learn and no one yells if I make mistakes. Ulfina, Egan's mam, is so sad, and yet so brave and strong just like he was. She's taught me so many things. Did you know . . . ?"

She prattled of rushlights and cooking, of buying and selling in the *pocardon.* But certain words stuck, scalding like hot tar. *Being dead.* Of course the Registry believed Juli dead. And they wouldn't go looking for her unless someone caught sight of her. But, gods, the risk.

". . . and now you're out of the Tower and safe here, perhaps I can discover what this is about. I could sneak into the Tower by the back door Capatronn showed you—"

"No! You mustn't! Let me think." It was all I could do not to snare her in my arms again.

"Oh, be easy. I'm just teasing. I'll stay with Ulfina like a good girl until you're able to find us new lodgings. Trust me!" But the grin playing around her mouth told me otherwise.

She had to understand that my freedom was impossible now and unlikely in any near future. In a kingdom engulfed in war and famine, she needed pureblood protection. And if she stayed dead, she would have to remain dead forever, unable to use her magic, lest it be detected and traced to her. If the Registry discovered she had knowingly maintained such a deception even for a few months, they would name her *recondeur*—with all its dread consequences. No marriage. No children. Unrestricted contracts. And that was the *best* we could hope. Yet neither would I have her dragged to the Tower cellar. Not ever. Neither dread nor denial could obscure the only way to protect her. A risky, terrible, painful way.

"Juliana de Remeni-Masson, listen carefully to me." I used my severest tone, even through the mask. "I am your eldest brother, your Head of Family in all save age and Registry blessing."

"Luka, what—?"

"Bend your knee before me and acknowledge my claim." No softness or lack of clarity must give her ideas of escaping my command.

All the bright animation of hope erased, she nodded. With dignity, wariness, and a smothered fire that near broke me, she left my side and sank to one knee in the snow. She did not bow her head, though. "I acknowledge your claim. Of course I—"

"On this day, you are the only hope of our bloodlines, and your first duty is to our family and the gifts we are charged to bring to the world. Yes?"

She shrugged.

"Answer me! Confess it!"

"Yes."

"You must give yourself to the Registry. Tonight. Straightaway as you leave here."

"What? But you just said—"

"I know what I said. But now I speak with the authority of my position that you have just acknowledged. You will tell them a story: that you were so stricken with horror and grief to see someone you believed was me set fire to our house that you collapsed and lost all memory. Say nothing of the warning message, but rather that someone in the crowd dragged you away, thinking to have a pureblood at her beck, and you've only now come to your senses and escaped. Make them believe, Juli. I know you can. Your life, your future, the lives of the children you are destined to bring into this world depend on it. My life may depend on it, as well. Repudiate me. Tell them how cruel a brother I was, always scolding you. Tell them of my erratic behavior since Pontia, of my devastating grief and my everlasting fury at our grandsire's chastisement for my disgrace. Tell them that I have no bent worth the air I breathe. Think of every grievance you've ever had with me. Tell them whatever—and I mean *whatever*—it takes to convince them that you have not spoken with me, that you despise me, that you want nothing to do with me, that you believe I am a madman who could burn down his own house and kill—"

"I could never speak such lies!"

"Yes, you can. You must. *Think*, Juli. If you stay away, you are dead *forever,* your magic forsworn. You are already a *recondeur* at *best*. And they *will* find you and execute anyone who has sheltered or helped you—Egan's mam, Bastien, everyone. That is the law. Believe me, if you want to help me discover the truth of all this, you must live safely among purebloods, develop your magic, learn what is in you to learn, but always, always with care. If I had the skill, I would erase your memory of these months and plant this story in your head, even if it meant you would despise me forever. I will *not* have you dead. And I will not have them make you a slave or a prisoner or whatever these villains have in mind. But I must let them have you."

She sank back on her heels, gaping at me as if I were indeed a madman.

"Swear to me, Juli. On everything we deem holy. On our beloved dead. There is no other way." I believed that with a certainty I could apply to nothing else in the world.

Her eyes widened. "Luka . . ."

"Swear it."

Without shifting her furious, frightened gaze from mine, she swore. "On our name and blood, on our holy gifts, on the lines of magic unbroken, I vow all that my Head of Family has asked of me. Witness my oath, great Deunor, Lord of Fire and Magic. Witness my truth, mighty Erdru, Lord of Vines. Witness, too, that I will not rest until the need for this posturing is undone."

Her speaking was bitter, her body rigid. If someone told me I had worked the very magic I had wished for, I would have believed it.

She broke off her glare and rose, cold and pale as one of the stone grave markers. "To whom shall I surrender, *ancieno*?"

And this was near the hardest part of all. "Pons. I think it must be her. She will believe the worst you say of me. But she is hard and very intelligent. Convince her, and you convince them all."

I wanted to beg her to be careful, to suggest she get herself filthy and torn before going to the Tower, to remind her that she was everything in the world to me and that only the lack of any alternative could force me to send her into such danger. But her back was already turned.

"Whip him if you need, Coroner Bastien, and keep him shackled," she said as she rejoined my master, "for he is assuredly a raving lunatic. You and your woman must forget me."

"We shall forget everything we've seen or heard, *Doma* Remeni. I warrant my life on it."

He exchanged a few insistent words with Constance. Juli did not look back as she waited. Only a moment and the two women vanished into the vaulted passage.

Bastien near yanked me from the bench. "Mother save me, Remeni, you are the hardest bastard I ever hope to meet."

He left me silk bound and shackled that night, the chain linked to a new bolt in the floor. And he installed the mouth strap so I could speak no words of magic. Perhaps he thought I would regret my decision and run or set his prometheum afire. Yet it was not second thoughts that kept me awake until dawn, nor was it Garibald's hammers and chisels installing locks and hinges, but only the sick certainty that I should have frightened Juli more.

CHAPTER 20

By the time dawn sneaked through the cracks in the shutters, my studio in the necropolis resembled a prison cell. Both the solid wood door, now hinged, and the thick shutters sported new brass locks, soundly fastened. Yet the very same light proved the cell's vulnerability. No such petty prison could confine me. Every pureblood youth was taught spellwork enough to burn wooden barriers and break mundane locks.

In the Tower cellar, the possibility of backlash from the iron enclosure sufficed to keep a sensible prisoner well behaved. What of a wildly angry, terrified young girl, though?

For the hundredth time in the long hours, fear and anger curled me into a knot. Fear for Juli. Fury at those who had driven us to such circumstances. I near bit through the sodden leather strap, growling through a blizzard of impossible schemes. Lock the curators in their judgment room and demand answers. Stalk Pons to her residence and hold a knife to her throat until she explained herself.

Every alternative crumbled. I could not run. I could not fight openly. If my sister and I were ever to be reunited, if we were ever to use our gifts as the gods intended, then I had to learn what had happened to our family and why. There was no learning to be had in the Tower cellar, nor did I imagine there would be any escape did they find cause to lock me in there again.

Bless the Mother, Bastien arrived early with instructions for the day. Discipline reared its weary head. I stumbled to my feet.

"I've decided that you're to draw every corpus brought in that's not already rotted." New keys jangled from the coroner's belt as he slipped the silk knots on my hand bindings. "As we've seen, there's no guessing whether the unlikeliest mess might be a person of interest."

I dipped my head. Work would be good.

He unbuckled the leather mask and threw it on the shelf. He did not invite me to speak aloud. Indeed, I had naught to say.

In a blur of leather, he was gone. To my chagrin, the shackles remained in place.

A cupful of beechnuts—pignuts, many called them—waited in the dry trough. Bitter and annoyingly small, they were scarce more edible than an acorn. But someone—Constance?—had taken time to roast them so they were less likely to cause a rebellion in the gut. I downed them and the cup of robust ale. Then I rang the bell, hobbled to the wall, and awaited the dead.

Presented with a never-ending stream of corpses, I worked each day until dusk. Determined to keep these drawings true—and to prove myself sane—I allowed no extraneous thought to interrupt the work. I saw no visions, felt no sensation of falling and glimpsed no scenes of other places. I was not mad. I was not. But my denials had an increasingly false ring to them.

Each night, once the last corpse had been removed, I hobbled to my palliasse, knees flaccid, magic depleted, cramped, blackened fingers silk bound, determined to untangle the mysteries of my life. Each night, despite my best intents, exhaustion took me to sleep before it was full dark.

Though Bastien kept me in shackles and bound my hands at night, he never put me back in the mask. He offered no conversation, entering the studio only to bind or unbind me or collect the day's portraits. A bowl of water greeted me each morning, too little and too cold to do aught but splash on face and hands. For the first time since manhood, my beard sprouted untended. I didn't care.

A month, more or less, we continued in this fashion. On the night Garibald finished installing iron gratings in my windows and replacing the wooden door with one of solid iron, Bastien removed my shackles. When he did not bind my hands, either, I nodded my understanding and acquiescence. He had complied with the Registry rules and I would as well.

Without a word, Bastien took the chains, the silk cord, and the light away.

Outside my shuttered window, a steady drizzle whispered across the city of the dead. Did the corpses I drew lie in their pits, listening to the rain they could not touch, contemplating those they would never see again or a life that had once held meaning? Silence and detachment in a house of death certainly gave one a bit of objectivity. And clarity.

For the first time in a month, I dared contemplate what I had done to Juli. The consideration that I might never know her fate hurt like a bruise on the heart itself, but no longer did it drive me wild. My decision had been the only one possible.

Men could rightly judge me a lunatic that I should approve my own confinement and the possibility of hers. Yet I'd ever heard tales of the Cartamandua *recondeur*, old, mad Janus's drunkard grandson who had run while just a boy. Ten or fifteen years and the Registry had never found him—the only renegade who had never been reclaimed. Pureblood magic flared like a beacon in the ordinary world, and Registry investigators were always on the watch for it in places where no sorcerers should be. Which meant he used no magic. One might as well say he no longer breathed or had cut off his own hands. More likely he was dead. Juli and I had matters to attend before we died.

Freed by that surety, other truths unfolded before me like a parade of compliant servants.

They—the ones who spoke rumors and set fires—wanted *me*, not Juli. My comings and goings had been watched; they knew I'd not yet come home on the night of the fire. Had it not been for the boy Egan and the warning he had delivered—how stupid I'd been not to ask Juli the exact words—my sister would have been sleeping and died with the others. No crime could have been planned more perfectly to convince the pureblood population that I should be locked away.

So why me and not Juli—or one of my brothers or cousins or uncles? I could no longer avoid the possibility that my family had died as a result of this same savage conspiracy. We were of the same blood, the same upbringing. Our family's gifts had ever displayed strong. If one discounted sex and age, only one thing marked me different enough to choose over the others: my dual bents.

Why were dual bents so feared? Rumors. Old women's tales. My family had ever celebrated the varied manifestations of magic, whether amongst our own or in other pureblood families. They were part of the beauty of the gift—of our lives. Which brought me back to my grandsire.

Always I had assumed that it was my failure had sealed my grandsire's lips and heart. But it seemed so clear now that the severity of his reaction had been entirely out of proportion to my offense.

Capatronn had instilled in our family his belief that our magic was not our own. Grumbling at Registry intransigence, he had vehemently defended his decision allowing me to pursue both bents for a few years. "My colleagues are wrong about this, Lucian," he'd said after postponing my declaration of bent when I turned sixteen. "How are we to judge the will of the divine Givers, whether they be gods or angels or nature itself? Study and strive and you will find the harmony inside yourself. Every step you take toward your future is a joy to me."

And indeed as I grew older and expressed my longing to pursue my bent for history beyond our household tutors, my grandsire had agreed, despite Registry disapproval of a pureblood youth mingling with ordinaries. He would take a house in Montesard, he'd said, as it was situated near a region he had wanted to explore for many years. While he pursued his own work, I could study as I wished, yet live securely within the discipline of family—a circumstance that should mollify the Registry. By the age of three-and-twenty, I could declare a single bent or prove the Registry's hidebound tradition wrong. It seemed a perfect solution.

Three short years later, over a passing indiscretion, this same wise, generous grandsire had tried to obliterate half of my soul. What had changed?

As a rising wind rattled my locked shutters, I drew up my blanket and rifled through my memories of those years. All my efforts served up no disagreement, no reprimand, no incident or encounter that could explain his change.

In spring of the year I turned eighteen, once the roads were free of snow, we had traveled through northern Ardra and into the eastern reaches of the province of Morian. Vigorous and eager, Capatronn seemed to feed on my excitement at the adventure. Once we were settled, Capatronn took up his work.

Xancheira was a small duchy squeezed somewhere between Navronne's northernmost province and the Aurellian Empire. Xancheira's culture, law, and beauty were common bywords for elegance—whether in art, fashion, or judicious governance. Yet no scroll, painting, building, or artifact remained to support our use of the terms. Supposedly, the duchy—a single great city and its outlying villages, their grazing lands and fields—had been obliterated in one savage day during Aurellia's prolonged retreat from Navronne. The city had been razed and the population slaughtered. Every source gave a different date for the Xancheiran Massacre, somewhere between a hundred and two hundred years previous. King Eodward had charged his Royal Historian to discover the truth of Xancheira's end, as well as what he could of its laws.

That first summer in Montesard, I had accompanied my grandsire on his search. We found no ruins, artifacts, or even a town site, much less evidence of the massacre. When the university term began in the autumn, I became wholly immersed in my studies. In early spring, my grandsire took his investigating to a new site, one promising enough to keep him in the field for many months. He'd sent one exuberant letter, saying he had found clues to his hunt and looked forward to telling me more when he returned.

But by the time he returned to Montesard the following autumn, I had met Morgan. Guilty, afraid he might discover my transgressions, I had kept my distance, displaying no curiosity about his findings. I'd thought myself skillful and clever. And then someone had reported my dalliance to the Registry.

I sat up, drew my blanket around my shoulders, and summoned everything I knew of Vincente de Remeni. His presence was yet so vivid—I could smell the oil he used on his ancient leather boots, the soap his manservant used to wash his hair, and the fennel seeds he chewed while he read or wrote. His deceptively long gait had me doubling my steps to keep up until the year I reached my full height. When he joined and guided my boyhood magic in the way of experienced tutors, his hands were dry and cool.

Never had I seen him afraid . . . not until my vision of him as he excised my second bent. Would Gramphier know why? Or Pluvius? I'd never suspected anyone had watched.

Attempting his portrait again might give me answers. Bastien would have to approve. . . .

As if his name had conjured his presence, the iron door flew open and Bastien's torchlight flooded the studio. "Up, sorcerer. Quickly. Serena Fortuna shows her spite yet again."

It was not yet midnight.

"Feet first. Then the hands. Remain silent."

His urgency declared this was no petty jousting. Mumbling curses under his breath, he sped through the binding and locking. Even the leather mask came off the shelf.

I did not resist. Only one eventuality could spur such tight-lipped preparations. The Registry.

When done, he jerked his head to the pallet and raced out again, securing the iron door behind.

My gut scarce had time to tie itself into a knot when the door clanged open a second time. I raised up on my elbow and shielded my exposed eye against glaring magelight. Two of them.

"On your feet, *plebeiu*." Even with so few words, I recognized Pons's contralto, as warm and cheery as one of the headstones in the Hallow Ground. How could I have sent Juli to her? A month it had been. *Holy Mother, forgive me.*

The two swept in, garbed in full display of brocades and jewels, silk masks, and fur-lined cloaks. Behind them two servitors held magelight lamps on poles. I stumbled up, raised my bundled hands to my chest, and bowed, suddenly conscious of my filthy clothes, my unwashed body, and the scraggle of beard that itched so sorely under the mask.

A murmur between the two, and Pons moved briskly to examine the shuttered windows and their locks. Her companion tested my hand bindings and the locks on the mask and shackles. The man's modest height, his hair cut straight at ear length, and the twist of his spine that caused his head to appear forever cocked to one side named him Curator Scrutari-Consil.

Scrutari was a prickly sort of man, always finding fault, meticulous in his grooming despite his distaste for any hint of color. My family had scorned Scrutari as a bit too involved in the politics of ordinaries for a curator. Purebloods did not consider ambition unvirtuous, of course, unless it was so very obvious. Scrutari had contracted himself as an advisor to the most prominent clergyman in Navronne—the Karish hierarch Eligius of Ardra—and he bustled in and out of the Tower as if his dual positions ranked him as exceptional in both divine and human realms.

Arrogant and condescending, Scrutari had not exchanged ten words with me as I painted his portrait. It was easy to imagine that *his* might be one of the suspect portraits—a highly unjust supposition. Most purebloods were excessively prideful, myself not excepted. Gods, how low I had fallen this month past. Scrutari had certainly noticed. He held a kerchief across his nose as he stepped around me.

Shame heated my cheeks, not for how my state reflected on me, but for the disrespect to my family and Bastien.

"These bars are inadequate, Coroner." Pons cut through the oppressive silence. "Plates of iron over the windows would be more secure."

Bastien, little but a shadow in the doorway, bowed. "Unfortunately, excellency, my requirements—supported by our contract—mandate that my servant create identification portraits. But drawings done in firelight are unreliable, costing us money and speed. As we deal with bodies in varying stages of corruption . . . I'm sure you understand. And, of course, this chamber—the only one at the necropolis suitably isolated—has no provision for breathing save the windows. If you wish the pureblood smothered, you might as well take him back and do it yourself."

"Watch your tongue, ordinary!" snapped Scrutari. "We can do exactly that."

"Indeed," said Bastien, far more relaxed at this exchange than I. "So First Secretary Collium informed me. Thus I am scrupulous in obedience to the rules I was given. Test my truth in it: The pureblood's neither left this chamber nor spoke to any living person in more than a month. 'Tis a great deal of trouble. As I said before, if you wish to house him while still making him available to serve his contract, you're welcome to it."

"Insolent—"

"We shall continue to monitor your compliance, Coroner Bastien," said Pons, interrupting her fellow. "And the First Curator wishes me to inform you that we intend to fetch Remeni to the Tower from time to time. He must be tested to better judge the state of his reason."

It was all I could do to keep from shaking my head *no*. If they took me again, I'd never come back.

"Certain, you're welcome to take him for a visit," said Bastien, "as long as his work is caught up, which I judge might be in whatever year this god-cursed weather eases. He's required to draw every corpus we receive. More every day, and I'll not have his time wasted. Nor mine. You might consider turning your magics to the weather. Excellency."

Scrutari's visage near melted, as if the gold sunburst pendant gleaming at his neck—the symbol of his Karish loyalties—had captured the sun's heat. Pons's face mimed an ice-sheathed torrent. A fine thing the mask pinched my mouth, else I might have found myself grinning in a wholly inappropriate fashion. Indeed, wild-haired, leather-clad Bastien could have been a master hound, prancing back and forth, guarding his yard against a pair of mountain lions twelve times his size. I'd never known anyone at once so perceptive and so foolish.

"Show us these portraits," said Scrutari, snarling. "I'll not have a murdering madman coddled."

"If you like. I've a few in my chambers—a pair of soldiers, a starveling or two. Not every drawing is useful. Though just today we've turned over a murderer to the magistrates—a vintner's steward who had borrowed too heavily from a hard-fisted pawner. The fellow thought cutting the crone's throat would ease his troubles."

So my portrait of the old woman had been true. Satisfaction stirred my blood, spawning gratitude that Bastien had allowed me to know. And his choice of sketches to show did not include impossible portraits of royal bastards that might feed the Registry's belief in my madness.

"No. I wish to watch him work," said Pons, eyes glittering in the harsh white light. "Have a corpus brought in, Coroner. Unbind his hands and command him to draw."

What did they think to see? Did they think I summoned gatzi to fill in unexpected details in my portraits? Lord of Fire, if I could only see the curators' portraits.

Bastien puffed his cheeks and sighed in dejection. "I'd be most pleased for you to witness my servant's diligence, excellencies. But with all respect, it's nigh on midnight. Our laborers are home and bedded. Unless you're willing to roust them or conjure a dead man through our halls and onto this table yourselves, whilst at the same time making the sun to rise and give my servant proper light to work, you'll have to wait till day for that enjoyment."

"I told you he'd have an excuse," spat Scrutari.

"We'll come back for our observations, Coroner," said Pons, unruffled. "Be sure of it."

Magelight burst from a ring on her finger, spreading into a glowing ball. She stepped close, raising her hand until the light was contained between us, illuminating eyes of gray marble set in a body of stone. The features behind her gray half mask revealed no more than those exposed, neither glee, vengeance, triumph, curiosity, nor righteous sorrow, nothing to reveal her purposes, and nothing at all to hint at what she had done with Juli.

"You are a deviant soul, Lucian de Remeni-Masson," she said, "one who has been too long shielded from the understanding of his aberrant nature. You have no place in this world."

Her pronouncement slammed me in the gut like a fist, its mortal weight forcing a bellow of denial into my throat. I had done *nothing* wrong. My portraits were *true*, my magic holy and right, no matter that it stemmed from two sources. How could one bent be divine gift and two be deserving of death?

To keep silent and bow as was required near broke my back. Foolish even to attempt control of my posture. My indignation, anger, and loathing must be clearly visible to one with the skills of an investigator.

"Come, *eqastré*," she said, hurrying to the door. "We'll examine those samples of his drawings before we go."

They threw the latch and left me in the dark. The shackles prevented my pacing, so I sat in the corner, elbows on knees, bound arms crushing my skull in an attempt to silence useless anger.

Later, when the door latch clattered again, I could not make myself rise or look. Let them think me asleep. Let them drag me if they wanted me up or elsewhere.

But it was only one heavy body that shuffled across the room and sagged onto the pallet just beyond my feet. He stank of old leather and death. Bastien.

"That went well, I think," he said, yawning. "What a pair of arrogant gatzi spawn. How did you ever put up with folk like that? Good thing you had that muzzle, eh? Likely I should have had one, too."

He shifted his position, reached around, and unlatched the mask. Dislodging my hands, he dragged it off me and tossed it across the chamber. As I coughed and swabbed the spittle from my mouth, he unwound the silk hand bindings.

"So, you've got to tell me one thing, pureblood. Do they know about the flickering? The only rise I got out of them was when I said I had a way to watch you as you worked without you knowing it. The woman snapped her head around so fast I thought she might break her neck . . . something like you've just done."

No light was needed to know he was grinning in his smug fashion.

"There was no flickering," I croaked. "That was only snow . . . mist."

"Not so! I've watched you careful. Before your prisoning, it was like a cloud came between you and my eye. But when you drew the horse boy, you vanished entire. Might have thought I just blinked . . . save it was four or five blinks until you showed up again in exactly the same position you were when you vanished. You weren't here, and then you were. Happened again with every one of those dead children. Most times only an instant, but once even longer than the first. Damnedest thing I ever saw. Since that day it's gone back to like before. You fade from time to time, neither exactly here nor exactly gone. What's the difference? And where in all hells do you go?"

Impossible to see his face in the dark, but his voice demanded sober answer—of which I had none.

"I don't—I never believed you about it."

How could I believe such idiocy now? Save that something *had* been different since the Tower. The lapses. The visions. The insistence of both physical senses and instinct that I existed somewhere else entirely for those few moments. And in the Tower cellar itself, Nelek's young assistant had reported me vanished from the iron room as I invoked my bent . . . when I'd dreamed of starlight and silver-marked Danae.

"I've never heard of anything like," I said. "But . . ."

I had to tell Bastien the truth; he had rescued me, defended me. Yes, for his own interest, but for mine, as well. He had kept Juli's secret. And he had been wise enough to see that freeing me from the Tower was not enough. He had allowed me a fallow time, with naught but a steady stream of work, time for me to regain balance. Clarity.

". . . a few times I've felt as if I've dropped off asleep as I work. I lose focus and slip into dreams, see places and people that make no sense, though they feel *true*. The smell, the sensations, they linger when I open my eyes here—like a true experience, not dream. It sounds mad, I know."

Was that what the Registry was looking for? Evidence of madness? Such a phenomenon would surely be considered aberrant magic. Unless they knew more about it than I did. "Earth's Mother, you didn't mention this to Pons?"

"Give such a delicious tidbit to those who are rabid to take you away from here?" Bastien's satisfaction near blazed a hole in the dark. "Not in any age of the world! I said that as long as your pen was moving, I was happy, and that, otherwise, watching you draw was about as exciting as watching the leaves turn color in the autumn and drop off the trees."

"Holy, blessed gods." My fingers scraped through my greasy mat of hair. Words were insufficient to express my astonishment . . . or my fear . . . or my guilt, as the cascading implications battered me like hailstones.

"So, you truly didn't know?" said Bastien, muting his excitement. "You weren't just being pigheaded?"

"No. On the day I visited the city, I mentioned the possibility of such a phenomenon to another portraitist I worked with. He'd never heard of such a thing, either—" My throat constricted.

"And on that same night your house burned and six people died." As if our minds worked as one, Bastien voiced my own hideous conclusion.

Who had Gilles consulted? Master Pluvius? Or his uncle, Curator Albin—more rigidly traditional than Gramphier himself? Or some other curator whose portrait had been altered? My teeth ground. "Stupid, ignorant, blind!"

All these events were linked in a chain of lies and fire and murder. Answers so near, yet so unreachable. Rage and curses spilled from my lips until I could no longer come up with new ones.

Bastien ignored my bellowing fit and settled his back to the wall and fumbled in his jerkin. After much unseeable business involving flapping leather, taps, scrapes, and strange mouth noises, a pulsing glow appeared in the region of his beard. A few breaths and a curl of highly aromatic smoke teased at my nostrils. A Ciceron smoking pipe.

"I'm thinking," he said between leisurely sighs that enveloped us in a weedy fog, "now you're more settled in your mind and we've got their first little visit out of the way, it's time to unravel a few mysteries. The way I see matters is we've got to find out who's this hairy, black-booted devil been killing off royal bastards. He could be Prince Bayard's man or Osriel the Bastard's. He could be one of Perryn's own nobles, ready to betray the best hope Navronne's got. We need his name, so's you've got to get back to Arrosa's Temple and find the document he signed when he left the child there . . ."

He left me no pause to name him lunatic. *Settled* in my mind?

". . . and then we've got to discover who's trying to bury you, else your testimony won't be worth a barrel of squirming slugs when we get the goods on the villain."

"You'd help me?" Astonishment prevented any more purposeful answer. "It would violate the contract."

"Now just stopple that annoying conscience. According to this holy contract, whatever I deem my business is my business, no matter that it doesn't exactly involve ink and paper and corpses. So it's no violation of your beloved rules. You can thank your empty-headed vixen of a negotiator for that; she likely thought I'd set you to stripping bones. Besides, when I show you things like this"—he wagged a pale blur in front of my face—"it's going to distract you from your drawing work anywise, so we might as well get the matter untangled."

"And *this* is what?" The light of his pipe was hardly sufficient to reveal what he held.

"The message sent to warn you and yours about the fire. That nameless person who informed me that my prickly servant had been hauled off to the Registry Tower left it with me. She thought we might have more use for it than she would."

Oh, brave and clever Juli. "What does it say?"

"It says: *Leave. Now. Else suffer your blood-kin's fate.* Unsigned, as you might guess. Addressed to you, not your sister. Naught else about it tells me anything."

"It speaks several things," I said. "The writer knew the rest of my family had died in a fire. He believed I would be at home, so it couldn't have been the same person who spied on my movements for the Registry. A friend, one might say . . . but not friend enough or powerful enough to stop it." Pluvius, perhaps. Kind and cowardly, and not so skilled at his craft as his curator's rank would imply. He had professed sympathy and intent to help, and then left me hostage to Pons and the other curators.

"And what shall we do with this other thing was left alongside the message?" He stuffed a small heavy object into my hand. A heavy ring. Inner fires of vermillion and yellow glinted from a modest but perfect ruby—a sign of the small enchantments it held.

"My father's ring," I said softly. My finger traced the gem's sharp edges and the cold curve of the gold ring. "It was the only item we retrieved from Pontia. I think . . . if you would keep it safe for me . . . for her . . ." I forced my fingers to let it go. Such a treasure had no place in this life.

Bastien harrumphed. "The person who gave me these things said I should make you tell about Montesard, as that's when things went wrong for you and your grandsire and that Registry female. She was sure all this was connected. And she said she didn't really mean it about the whipping, unless your stubborn righteous self locked everything all up inside you, as you had a bad habit of doing. I mentioned how I'd noted for myself how your ass was tight as a practor's conscience."

"She was right about everything," I said, my throat graveled with anger and grieving. "More than she knew. The curators . . . they didn't mention . . ."

"No. Not even when the other fellow was going on about how your lunatic self might murder all of us here in our beds. Which I said would be difficult, as mostly the folk here were already dead."

He drew on his pipe, the glow swelling, and blew out long and slow.

"I did nick other gossip of interest, though. I had babbled summat about all the work we've had, as the Guard Royale wants no corpses on the streets when Prince Perryn returns to the city. And then the devil woman says I am to make sure you are chained and locked away on the day *the Prince of Ardra comes calling to honor Remeni's kinsman.*"

"My kinsman?"

"I fussed a bit and asked what Prince Perryn had to do with you and said I understood you had no kinsmen alive. The witch said it was naught to concern you nor me, neither one. But I persisted. She said the prince is set to honor the anniversary of Caedmon's Writ and all the politeness between the Crown and the Registry it signifies shortly after he returns to the city—a tenday from now, more or less. Perryn's to come to the Tower to honor his father's late Royal Historian."

"My grandsire." It seemed so odd.

"Seems to me it might be an interesting occasion. On a night when there will be comings and goings and hullaballoo and strangers in the Tower, even ordinaries, even princes, so all the purebloods will be in masks, yes? And an intruder might have a chance to look at certain portraits hung there out of common sight, don't you think?"

My head popped up. "It would be a terrible risk." My fingers rubbed my sprouted chin. A beard might change my appearance just enough. "For you, too, if I'm caught, which would be more likely than not. You'd allow me?"

The glow of his pipe pulsed again and the smoke surrounded me before he answered. "Told you, pureblood, I solve one mystery, I get a witness for the other—the biggest has ever fallen in my lap, a mystery that could affect the future of this kingdom. I'm good at what I do, just as you are. But I've needed the right partner. Unfortunate that he's brought me a pot load of trouble, but then, Serena Fortuna and I've had a testy relationship nigh on forty years now. And I'll not deny, you've got me blasted curious about matters beyond imagining—this vanishing business, and portraits that show things you couldn't know. Yes, indeed, I believe you must do both. Visit Arrosa's Temple to learn of our murderer and attend this lordly celebration in your grandsire's honor."

We sat in silence for a while. Partner with an ordinary? Risk my freedom to discover an ordinary child's murderer? My ancestors must surely turn their backs on me in shame. Yet the pride and certainty that had given shape to my life lay in ruins. Perhaps the foundations I clung to remained intact beneath the dust and rubble; perhaps they didn't. But Bastien offered me purpose and a chance to find answers. All I could do was scratch my head in amazement and relish the opportunity.

"I'll need clothes for both Temple and Tower. Fine ones. A heavier pureblood cloak than that ridiculous thing they left me. If my boots were cleaned, they'd do, and I presume these damnable shackles will come off. Most important, I'll need a new silk mask, different from my old one. An ordinary tailor can make it and I can apply the enchantments. . . ."

He didn't interrupt. The next pulse of fire from his pipe revealed the pale gleam of his teeth. He was enjoying this.

"You gamble my life quite easily, Coroner, considering I'm the best coin you've ever had."

He broke into bellowing laughter and slapped my shoulder. "You play the game hard, my prickly servant. Exactly as I do. But we'll do better together, eh? We, the lowly, shall bring our arrogant adversaries to their knees."

Part III
The Waking Storm

CHAPTER 21

"Scarce a shadow." Bastien stuck his head through the door of my prison studio. "I thought now you knew, you might manage it every time. Vanishing could be a most useful skill."

"It would," I said, examining the portrait of my latest subject, my third of the day.

The bony, gray-skinned young woman lay peaceably on the bier. It was difficult to resist pulling up my shirt to ensure no one had slashed open my gut. The portrait explained the truth of her . . . her emaciated hand laid over a belly swollen with child. Someone had cut the babe out of her. Murder? Necessity? My magic couldn't tell us—nor whether the child lived.

The coroner took the drawing from my hand. "Requiring a corpse at hand whenever you wanted to vanish could be an inconvenience, though."

"Whatever makes it happen, it's not sketching the dead." I dragged the sheet over the woman's lifeless features. "In the Tower cellar, I was using only my bent for history. Today, I've called on each bent alone and both together."

"I've one more interesting subject for you; then we'd best figure out how to burgle the temple." Bastien didn't wait for my agreement before the door slammed shut behind him.

We had decided to learn what we could of my vanishings and the child murderer in these few days before Prince Perryn visited the Registry. We both knew my chances of returning from a venture into the Tower portrait gallery were tenuous at best. Perhaps I could learn to vanish from in front of a captor—and not return to the same place.

I hobbled over to the window, chewing the dates Constance had left in the laver. Rain again today. Spring had arrived and Caton was awash in mud. A full-loaded deadcart had bogged down in the east gate, blocking the road all morning. Constance was screeching at her laborers to empty it. My windows displayed a distant sliver of hillside free of snow. Unfortunately it wasn't green, either. Mud meant no planting.

Juli detested rain. "Snow is perfection," she'd once said. "It hides ugliness. Rain just turns the world to muck."

How I would love to tell Juli of the Danae. My little sister's dark eyes had ever gleamed huge in the candlelight as our grandmother spun tales of naked dancers in the moonlight, of blue-flame bog lights ready to lure the unwary traveler to his death, of the beautiful young man enamored of a Dané, dissolving as he followed her to her lair in the Western sea, nevermore to walk the earth. Were the guardians of the earth real? Every time I considered what I'd seen, my breath caught in wonder. Perhaps Juli's sharp mind could help me learn what all this meant.

What have they done with you, serena*? I should have been able to protect you. Instead I sent you into the lion's mouth.*

The scrap of parchment sent to save us from the fire lay on the plank alongside my drawings of the morning. I had examined it at first light—before we'd begun this futile experiment. The words were as Bastien had stated: *Leave. Now. Else suffer your blood-kin's fate.*

One thing Bastien had not been able to tell me, however. Turning my bent to the scrap's history revealed exactly nothing. Nothing of the page or the ink or their provenance, and not the least hint of the writer. Someone had left the page magically sterile—astonishingly worthless.

Manipulation of anything that touched learning or memory was a monumental skill. Perhaps one of the curators could do such things. Certainly not Pluvius, who was the logical sender. My grandsire said it was Pluvius's skill for organization, not exceptional talent, that allowed him to take charge of the Archives and gain a curator's rank. Had another curator sent it? Was a curator the murdering arsonist? At one time I'd have assumed no curator could countenance murder. Now I wondered. . . .

The heels of my hands gouged my eye sockets. My eyes were grainy with lack of sleep. Bastien and I had talked late into the night. Somehow the darkness had made it easier to speak of Capatronn and his indulgence of my dual bents, of the hurt when he broke with me, and all that had happened since. I'd told Bastien everything I could recall of my visions, and he confirmed that the occasions he saw me vanish entire were the very ones when I had climbed the heights of the fingered peninsula at the verge of the unknown sea. He had pelted me with questions, as if I were his chief witness at an inquest—as I suppose I was.

I rubbed my ankles, chafing under their iron bands. What business partners ever agreed that one had best stay in shackles? I wished he would send in the next corpse.

Bastien had a keen facility for pursuing his threads of inquiry to their end. Some of his questions I could answer. Some sat in my gut like undigested food. *Was it your grandsire reported your philandering to the Registry in the first place? What if this Pluvius* did *visit you in the Tower?* And, *What are you wearing in these visions?*

To consider the first fueled instant denial. To *instigate* the inquiry, to offer me up for such punishment as the Registry might require for my indiscretion, relying solely on his influence to mitigate it, meant my grandsire had put every person of his own bloodline at risk of dishonor, and those of my mother's blood as well. Whyever would he do that? Indeed, now they were all dead, Juli lost, and I in shackles, with a madman's mask waiting on the shelf nearby. Our name was ruin. Had he damned us all apurpose? Had I done something far worse than I knew? Did he think me mad? What was he afraid of?

As for Pluvius's visit, the perfect logic that had named his visit a dream did seem thin in the daylight. I had seen and heard him clearly, felt his hand on my head. But to imagine what my grandsire might consider his "most significant discovery," something that propounded a "terrible historical lie" that he had sworn Pluvius to destroy? I couldn't even begin. Much of accepted history was lies.

The question about clothing was far simpler, and yet its implications stretched beyond my petty circumstances. In the Tower vision, I'd been naked, as I was when I worked the magic. In the two visions raised here at the necropolis, I had been clothed as I was here: in layered slops and breeches, prison tunic, my own filthy shirt, anything to keep me warm. That circumstance testified to the reality of my experiences. It was curious that no chains or silkbindings had hindered me. And yet . . .

I fingered the iron links joining my ankles. Had I been wearing any?

When I'd pursued my grandfather's history in the Tower cellar, I was no longer required to wear restraints. And on my first day back here, when I experienced the displacement, Bastien had not yet replaced the mask or shackles. Mighty gods . . .

The door flew open. I stepped quickly to face the wall as the runners carried in my new subject. Yet I was near bursting with the need to speak.

Two sets of footsteps retreated—Garen's brisk trot and Pleury's shuffle. A heavy tread followed. The door creaked.

I spun around and yelled, "Bastien! Get these shackles off me."

The door paused halfway and his face appeared in the gap. "Told you, if your friends from the Registry pull another inspection—"

"The magic *does* take me somewhere else!" Impossibility could no longer mask the truth. "My senses told me so, yet I couldn't believe. But your question about the clothes: In the Tower vision, I wore none; in the visions here, the exact layers I was wearing that day. I could see the garments, feel them, smell them. How could some random dream be so exact? But in none of the incidents was I shackled or restrained in any way. Nor was I in truth. Perhaps it's the chains make the difference; iron and steel interfere with magic. Or perhaps it's just me, unable to bring my magic to fullness when I'm restrained. We need to try it with my feet unchained."

Without a word, he unlocked the shackles. Then he closed the door and left me alone. I'd not yet guessed where his spyhole was.

My new subject was near a skeleton already. A tall man, he was missing one arm and one leg, but from old injuries. The stumps were ugly, but showed no signs of recent sepsis or other disease. A soldier, perhaps.

I closed my eyes and breathed deep. Offered a prayer for skill and guidance to whatever divinities might care. Wriggled my lightened ankles. And this time, I invoked both centers of magic equally—forehead and breastbone, history and art—for surely every part of this mystery stemmed from their duality. Only then did my one hand begin its passage around the dead man's cold, scarred flesh and the other touch pen to parchment, and when the glory was grown in me and the world trembled, I did not resist the breathtaking fall. . . .

Rain drenched me to the skin in moments. Shivering as much from excitement as cold, I spun around on a rocky outcrop, hunting, needing . . . what? Sea, sky, and the land below had become one turbulent grayness, seamed by the bony ridges of white stone. A cluster of pines on a shelf of hillside above me swayed wildly, lashed by the wind. My sodden garments flapped.

"Lady Dané!" I yelled into the storm. "Are you here? Tell me what I'm searching for."

Now I had accepted the truth of this place, I could give credence to the words she had spoken to me in the Tower vision. *The beacon holds!* she'd said, as if some signal fire were responsible for my arrival. And then she had remarked how my *makings*—my magic, surely—had twisted and strained the substance of the world. And she had said that *they*—the Danae?—were *divided* about what to do with me: *lead astray or grant sanctuary?*

Those who had met me on the streets of Palinur had warned of dangers, too, of my need to learn and to heed my workings because certain boundaries were not meant for human trespass.

"Tell me what you want!" I called. "Tell me where I am! Is this where humans are abandoned when you steal them from their beds? Is this a sanctuary for mad sorcerers in prison cells? Tell me why I'm here."

"As I suspected, thou hast no knowledge of the world, though thy makings draw upon its essence." The voice, low and rich as sun-warmed honey, came from behind me. "Thou'rt like a youngling dancing with flame."

The silver-limned Dané woman perched in a rocky niche, long arms wrapped about her drawn-up knees, head tilted to one side. Two breaths ago, the niche had been empty. All my bold words fell away.

She smiled. Knowing. "Thou dost walk the true lands of the Everlasting. Clothed this time, I see!"

The Everlasting. The blue-marked Danae had spoken of it, too.

"This is Idrium?" I croaked softly. "The gods' own home? Yet I am not dead. Mad, perhaps, but not dead."

Her long sigh wove with the wind. "Exactly as I have spoken: Thou hast no knowledge of the world. That's why thou canst not remain here as yet or hear all I might tell thee."

"The others told me the same. Warned me of dangers beyond my understanding."

"Others?"

"In Palinur—the city where I live—two of you, male and female, came to me."

She stretched out her arm, turning it so the silver markings gleamed. "And they were like to me? Or perhaps they were my excitable kin whose gards shine the color of day sky."

"Blue, yes, but like you in grace and beauty. They, too, said I needed to learn. They gave me no answers, either, and threatened to steal my wits. I *want* to learn."

"Learning must come as it will. My kin know that, too, though their view of human usefulness differs from mine own. Ever more generous than they, I grant thee a second question. One only."

So many questions. Did the Danae truly dance at season's turn to renew the earth? Were they wingless angels, a bridge between a god and humankind, as the Karish claimed, or were they living aingerou—impish sprites entirely of this world? Would she know what caused Navronne's disastrous weather? Her blue kin had called the world broken. Was this Everlasting even a part of Navronne, for if enchantment could snatch me out of the Tower prison or the necropolis, why would my destination be limited to our land? A thousand things. How could I choose?

She brushed aside her wet, tangled curls and widened her eyes, spreading the eagle's wing so delicately drawn across her brow. "Ask or I shall choose for thee."

"Before—that first time—you said you were expecting me. Why?" As soon as I blurted the question, heat flushed my wet skin. *Stupid*. Such a mundane query, when I might learn some secret of the universe.

But she dipped her head in approval. "A wise choice, as it speaks to the center of our dealings. Hear this, my answer: The Law of the Everlasting tells that all kinds reproduce themselves. Thus it was certain that one would be born to humankind with the gifts needed—blood that could perceive the beacon and follow the path it prescribes, and the proper talents to vanquish the boundaries between human realms and this fragment of the true and living world. To certain of my kind—those of us whose gards shine with starlight—and certain of thine own kind, thy gifts might be the answer to a long waiting. Or not. As my kin surely told thee, such strength, wielded in ignorance, brings dangers of its own, no matter thy intent. I cannot let thee cross until thy quality is proved."

"Cross what? What beacon? Take what path? An answer to what waiting? Please, I don't understand."

She hopped down from the niche, the silken draperies damp and clinging. My body could not but notice. Yet it was not lust but awe that drew my eyes along her long limbs and elegant curves and the fine markings—the very expression of living art. I longed to sketch her. Yet how dared I imagine my fingers could bring line and shape to such exquisite life?

Her lips quirked and the green eyes sparked brighter than the lightning that dazzled the horizon. "Come, *two* questions have I granted thee and not one hast thou answered in return. Here, an easy saying: What is thy name and parentage?"

It seemed right to bow. "Lucian, my lady, eldest son of Artur de Remeni and Elaine de Masson."

Impossible to raise my head as she stepped close, enveloping me in her scent of rain-washed springtime. "Good names all. Pleasant on the ear."

Her pleasure warmed me, filled me with such aching desire as I'd felt only once before in my life. Her finger on my chin set my knees quivering, and she lifted my jaw until my eyes met hers—a sea of emerald, spruce, and springtime that threatened to drown me.

"But a word on manners, Remeni-son. When we meet again, address me as *Sentinel. Lady* has no meaning here. Such naming would offend those of my kind unfamiliar with human ways. And the proper greeting is *envisia seru.* It says, 'The sight of thee delights my eye.'" A touch brushed my groin. "It seems quite clear you would admit this as a true saying. That pleases me. Thus I will grant thee a third answer: the Path of the White Hand. We shall welcome thee at its ending."

Throaty laughter rippled from her breast, and a warm breath shuttered my eyes. . . .

I blinked. My left hand lay on a dead man's brow and my right held a pen, new dipped and quivering with pent magic. No doubts plagued me this time. Before I could lay down my first line, my forearm had to swipe raindrops from my hair lest they dampen the page and smear the ink. And my traitorous body yet displayed its lustful weakness.

It would have been easy to stop and contemplate all that had passed, but the maimed soldier was patiently awaiting his due. For the next hour my magic was his.

"A full hundred count!" Bastien charged into the studio before I had wiped my pens. "Vanished entire! Not a soul breathed in this chamber!"

Pens into the case. Rag spread to dry. Ink cup covered. I could scarce spare thought to shape words. Half my spirit had fled to that place of rock and sea. "Seemed ten times that. Perhaps that's why it's named the Everlasting."

Bastien's mouth dropped open so wide and his wiry brows flew up so high, one might think the Dané woman had appeared naked in front of him.

Weary laughter burst from my soul, settling me deeper into the chilly studio. The real world.

The coroner tossed the portrait of the soldier onto the drying plank and hefted himself onto the bier at the dead man's feet. "You're not saying it was—?"

"My very question. But it was neither the Halls of Idrium nor the Karish Heaven. Rather it was but a"—what had she called it?—"*a fragment of the true and living world.*"

"She was there again. The Danae woman?"

I closed my eyes, desperate to recapture the shape of her, exquisite, elegant, yet . . . real. Alive. No goddess or mythic vapor, but a woman. Teasing. Warm. Inviting. "Aye. She said I was too ignorant, too dangerous, to stay wherever she was . . . then she sent me back."

A tap on the door brought Garen, Pleury, and Constance. The two young men stopped in their tracks and gaped. Constance rolled her eyes and twitched a hand at the dead man. "Well, be on it, then, dunderwits. Coroner's here, so's you're not gonna be struck pithless for lookin' at the blood's nekkid face."

Once the runners hauled away the dead man, Constance propped her hands on her scrawny hips and shifted her eye from Bastien, perched on the foot of the bier and quivering like a pup at a butcher's stall, to me on my stool, hands full of implements I could not think what to do with.

"Here it is naught but a spit till dark. And only now 'ave I got the while to say I've collected the garments you wanted. Seems like I was told to have 'em at dawn this morn or I'd be swimming in a dead-pit!"

"Garments?" Had I not been watching, I'd have missed the half an instant Bastien was as confused as one of the runners. But his wit quickly came thundering back. "Confound you, woman. I've been waiting all day. Thought I'd have to pull out needle and spool myself. Told you I'd be at the spyhole, didn't I, or are you gone deaf as well as thick?"

Constance pursed her thin mouth. "We both know what was told me and what wasn't, as well as who's thick and who's not. And no doubt the pureblood's magic can tell 'im who speaks true—and who don't."

From a bag dangling at her waist, she pulled a wrinkled apple.

Sweeping across the room as if wearing a queen's ermine instead of muddy canvas trousers and a kersey tunic splattered with dead spew, she removed the ink horn from my hand and installed the apple in its place. Then she glided from the room, smoothly laying the horn on the shelf and a glance of perfectly aristocratic disdain on the coroner.

When the door slammed shut, Bastien cast me a somber glance, and then we both erupted into raucous laughter. My ribs threatened to crack. A lifetime, it seemed, since such a torrent of good humor had made my sides ache so. When it was spent, naught remained of my enchanted visit to the Everlasting but a new mystery, my cold, soggy garments, and a ravenous belly.

I devoured the apple in three bites, as I told Bastien the tale of the Dané, every word as it was etched on my memory.

"So those you met in Palinur and this one are kin, but different. Squabbles between them, maybe."

I'd not thought of it that way. "She said their view of the world differed from her own. They both spoke of my need to learn, and how my strength, my magic"—delving, the blue-marked Danae had called it—"twisted the world and dissolved these *boundaries*. Both said my ignorance could be dangerous, even if I didn't intend ill."

"But this one didn't threaten your wits if you made a mistake."

"No, I think she was more pleased. If I proved my *quality*—whatever that entails—she and others would welcome me, while those in Palinur spoke of *trespass* and forging a weapon to use against me."

Though the female with the blue patterned fingers had known my name. "I couldn't choose one as friend, one as enemy. The female in Palinur expressed a belief that I could learn what was needed to keep out of trouble, while this one seemed . . . skeptical, perhaps. Cynical."

"And offered no guidance."

I shook my head. "It seems as if I ought to know what she's talking about. The Path of the White Hand, for example. I've never heard the expression. Yet something's nagging at me—Maybe the place itself. The land spreads into the sea like fingers, the rocks like bones. But I climbed one or two of them already in these visions, and I believe it's not so simple as that. The woman said I had *blood that could perceive the beacon and follow the path it prescribes*. But she never deigned to say what the beacon *was*."

"Doesn't matter." Bastien's elbows rested on his knees, fingers propping his chin. "She said your *blood* perceives the beacon—your blood that holds your magic. It's brought you to the same place each time. And your talents—the two together, used freely, just as you described to me—have certainly done the vanquishing."

"Truly, yes. But does following this path, whatever it is, mean I'm trespassing? How the devil am I to know?"

Bastien scratched his chin thoughtfully. "I'm thinking those that trounced you in the alley want to keep you out of wherever the magic can take you, and that's where the blue and the silver have differing opinions."

"So, by doing what she says—following this path to its mysterious destination and doing whatever in the name of all gods she thinks I can do there—I'm doing the exact thing the others said would make my wits forfeit. Gods!"

"Most of that, yes. But I think"—he wagged a thick finger—"she already named your destination. Listen to the words again."

I retreated inward, recalling each word, so precisely spoken. I had to prove my *quality* before she could let me *cross* and remain there, in this place that could be Magrog's realm, for all I know. She, the silver Sentinel, would either lead me astray or . . . "Sanctuary."

"It's such a particular word," said Bastien. "Not something to fear, I'd think. But of what sort? Is it only for purebloods or all them the Harrowers want to murder? For those of us the gods have decided to starve and freeze? Just for their kind, whatever they are, or just for you?"

The tangle of threats and enticement made me want to pound my head on the wall.

"I'll confess it," I said. "For a man who's spent his entire life getting educated, I must be the world's most ignorant soul. I don't even know what I have to learn. And if it is my dual bents that allow me to do these things, I have to ask: Did my grandsire know? Is this what my grandsire feared so deeply that he put my family in the way of the fire? But *why*? There must be a reason that every tale that lauds the beauteous Danae as the guardians of the earth also deems them treacherous."

Bastien grunted. "Had an uncle who swore by the Danae. Left out nivat bread every feast day. Spent many a night in the meadows, watching them dance, so he said, and spied on them at the seasons' turn when they came out of their lairs for the Great Dance. Swore he'd seen a pair of them mating in his field, and, sure to boots, he grew the best wheat in Morian."

I glanced up, eager. "Could we speak to him?"

"Nah. Sliced his thigh with knife one winter solstice and hit the great bleeder. Turned out he was using the nivat for more than feast bread."

"A twistmind." The word quenched my excitement. I'd seen them in alleys and ditches, those who wounded themselves while eating enchanted nivat paste to spike pleasure from pain. As years passed, they needed more pain and more nivat to make it work—slowly killing themselves as their craving drove them mad. I'd been taught that twistminds and Cicerons were the dregs of the cities. Though Demetreo the Ciceron headman had been more complicated than I'd imagined. . . .

Something nagged at me. I wandered over to the table and looked at the last portrait I'd done. Only magic could have assured me that the brawny, laughing soldier matched the half man on the bier. The hollow dullness in my belly suggested he had starved. Famine times made hard choices. Had he done it willing or had someone else decided he was not worth the feeding? Something in the body's disposition must have made Bastien suspicious.

How strange that drawing this sad fellow could transport me to another place and tantalize me with this Path of the White Hand. Bastien was sure to find someone that knew him, at least. His livery bore the blazon of the Guard Royale.

A *blazon* . . . Somewhere I'd seen or drawn a blazon incorporating a white hand. Indeed, *Cicerons* in my visions of the history of the Registry Tower had worn black tabards marked with the white hand . . . and somewhere else. . . .

"I did a portrait of an old Ciceron since I've been back. Do you still have it?"

"Aye. I've kept—"

A thump at the door announced Constance, or rather a pile of tatty velvet, stained linen, and torn brocade that comprised the promised clothes. So many things I needed and wanted to know, but the mysteries of the Danae and magic beyond comprehending would have to wait. Tonight belonged to Fleure and simple justice. I was off to Arrosa's Temple to steal the name of the lily child's murderer.

CHAPTER 22

"Word triggers are naught but whispers in the ear," I said. "Simple. It's one of the first magics a pureblood child learns, because it's easy and so very excellent for tormenting parents and tutors."

"I'm not 'feared." A bold statement considering how Garen's face was pale as the temple's marble steps across the courtyard. His quivering rattled the dead lilac limbs that sheltered us.

Garen the runner, the rangy young man of one-and-twenty, had been as cocky as always when we left Caton. He passed off burgling a temple as *scarce a bother* for one who had grown up in the rough streets of Wroling, and the enchantments I planned to work as *naught so very strange*. He had shepherded me briskly through the hirudo, telling Demetreo's sentries that his companion hunched in the ragged cloak and hood was one of Bastien's witnesses. We didn't want hirudo spies reporting me out and about. Indeed, it wasn't the burgling that frightened him. It was the magic. My first spell was for him.

"What's the word that will tell you it's time to move?" I said, hoping repetition would settle him. "And tell me what you'll do when you hear it in your head."

"Word's *snatchit*. And I go straight to the priestess's chamber and search out the scroll in the fifth slot to the right on the bottom row of her scroll case."

"Exactly so." Assuming she'd left the page I'd signed where I'd seen her stow it. "And what will warn of danger coming your way?"

"*Bolt*. Then I'm to take the scroll straight out through the entry gate without waiting for you."

"And what will *you* speak when you've got the scroll?"

"*G-grabbed*. Then I hide and wait for you to come do the magic."

"Good. But no stammering. The words must be exact. Speak it clearly—even in a whisper—and I'll hear, no matter where I am or what I'm doing. Is there a better word we should use?"

He shook his head vehemently. "I'll do it right. Swear I will. *Grabbed*."

I'd seen it before. Stiff as a flogging post, he was going to faint if I didn't distract him.

"I know you will. Now—did I hear someone out there?"

He peered out of the lilac thicket into the fog of incense smoke and moonflower-scented steam hanging in the temple's side garden. When he pulled back and shook his head, I shrugged and tapped both his ears as if to position him, and then dropped my hands to my side.

Chin held high and quaking damped, he eyed my idle fingers. "So, go on with the damnable magic. I'm ready."

Grinning, I wriggled my fingers that yet tingled with enchantment. "Already done." And then I covered my mouth and whispered, *"Snatchit!"*

He clapped his hand to his ears. A slow grin erased his awe. "Heard you clear as morning bells!"

I had been skeptical when Bastien insisted Garen partner with me. "He's been about the world more than you think," the coroner had said, with a firm grip on the young man's shoulder. "He's quick—feet and head both—and well-spoken when need be. Besides, who else would you have? Pleury would faint dead away when left on his own to do the snatch. And for certain none's going to swallow me nor Garibald nor Constance as a pureblood's servant. And it's not as if you'll leave him in any real danger. Not with your magic to see him safe, *right*?"

His ferocity had surprised me. Garen was a man grown.

I motioned Garen to straighten his collar, while I adjusted my vile doublet of puce and pea-green brocade, hoping to prevent Constance's row of pins from continuing to puncture my spine.

"You'll have to undress me at the baths. And carefully, too. Can't have an attendant noticing these damnable pins or the bloody knife hole in this shirt. I'll insist on privacy, but it's best to believe someone will be watching us."

"Not a worry," he said, Bastien's tough, confident assistant once again. "I've been in service."

"All right, then. Demonstrate absolute confidence at all times. Your master is one of the gods' chosen and no one can interfere with him—or you."

None but other purebloods. But I couldn't worry about that.

"And no matter whether it's a lamp boy or a temple priestess asking, you're not allowed to speak of me, even to reveal so much as my name. None who knows the law will think it strange. If they don't know it, they'd best learn."

How stupidly arrogant this sounded. Garen had seen me in chains and leather mask; he had seen me kneel to Bastien. But it wouldn't do at all for a pureblood and his companion to be discovered violating a temple's privacy. Arrest, disgrace, exposure . . . the Tower cellar for me, a quick hanging likely for Garen and Bastien. No end of consequences.

Nodding sharply, Garen tied his thick hair with a black ribbon, made sure his short cloak hid the old bloodstains on his own tunic, and held the lantern high. A comely fellow, no question.

I smoothed my new mask, a horizontal half as some families used. The mask surrounded both eyes, while leaving mouth and chin—and my month's growth of beard and mustache—uncovered. Bek, the barber-surgeon who explored dead bodies, had trimmed my hair and beard, and Constance the dead-handler had cut the mask from a not-yet-buried knight's silk grave winding. My lovely, refined, delicate mother . . . gods' save me, she would have collapsed in horror to hear it.

I swallowed a grieving laugh. "Lead me in, Garen. We'll make this work."

We headed across the garden and the courtyard, toward the faded grandeur of Arrosa's Temple. The sky had cleared, the moon was full, and one might imagine this a night from a happier spring. For the first time in almost three months, I walked free.

All the way from Caton, demon gatzé had whispered in my soul. *Walk away. Find Juli. Make a life somewhere far distant. Let these ordinaries solve their own nasty mysteries.*

Yet I was not yet ready to live as an ordinary—to betray the gods and their gift in my blood. Without magic I'd never be able to discover the truth of the altered portraits and whether they explained my family's murder. Without magic I'd never understand the mystery of my bent or the Danae or the mysterious place the visions transported me. I didn't even know whom to ask. Maybe old mad Cartamandua, the cartographer said to have walked out of this world into the realm of angels. Or maybe I was simply mad like he was. Else why did I persist in the impossible imagining that it was Morgan's voice that had spoken my name by way of a creature whose skin glowed with blue fire?

But there was a more profound impetus to be here. Bastien had saved my reason. I owed him.

Flames leaped from the great earthen bowl, setting the giant bronze figure of Arrosa gleaming. A raven-haired young woman in rose-hued silk stood beside the goddess's image. With perfect propriety, she waited, eyes lowered, for me to initiate our conversation.

"I've traveled a great distance to fulfill a vow," I said. "I seek cleansing and all comfort the goddess provides."

"Certainly, *domé*, Seeker of the Goddess's Favor," she said. "It is my privilege to conduct you to the Pools of the Gods' Chosen. Your servant may remain in the waiting chamber."

Eight or ten servants, a few in livery, a few plainly garbed, occupied benches about the walls of a poorly lit nook under the grand stair. Evidently temple stewards believed servants needed no lamp. Good. Perhaps none would note the shabby state of Garen's finery or get an exact idea what he looked like.

"My servant will tend my garments at the baths and then return here to wait."

Garen shuttered our lantern and hung it on the hooks beside the waiting chamber. As we followed the young woman into the steamy labyrinth, he positioned himself ahead of me, as I'd schooled him. I hoped his attention was fixed on the turnings and not the initiate's shapely curves.

Evidently so. His hand flicked toward the sloping side passage that led up to High Priestess Irinyi's chambers, telling me he recognized it from my description.

At the end of the passage, the initiate wished the Lady Arrosa's blessing on my devotions and motioned us through the short passage into the men's changing room.

A young man in a white loincloth, arms crossed and eyes lowered, awaited us in the small chamber with the latticework wall. He was not Leo. Relieved, I discarded the convoluted explanation I had prepared.

"Attendant," I said.

"Welcome, *Domé* Seeker. I am Herai, who will attend—"

"Await me at the tepidarium, attendant, with sacred wine and oil of ephrain in its purest form. I prefer my own servant to care for my garments."

"As you command, *domé*." He withdrew without lifting his eyes.

No common stealth burglary was going to work in a temple open to worshippers all night. Priestesses offered prayers at all hours, and we'd had no time to learn exact schedules and locations. So I would create a distraction elaborate enough and serious enough to draw the high priestess and everyone else who might notice us far from the wall of scrolls in Irinyi's chambers. And it had to keep everyone away long enough for Garen to snatch the scroll with my signature on it, and for me to rejoin him and use it to trigger my bent. With that scroll, magic, and a bit of luck, I would be able to locate the other scroll—the one with murderer's damning signature.

As soon as the attendant had gone, I removed my mask. Garen looped it over his belt and without a murmur began attending to buttons and laces. Indeed he was smooth in his service, deftly whipping off the insect-raddled purple cloak, unpinning the overlarge doublet, and removing the bloodstained shirt. My poor lost valet, Giaco, could not have done it better. Boots and hose quickly followed the neatly folded outer garments into the clothes chest. So expert and servile were Garen's postures, I began to wonder if he had once served in this temple.

When I nodded that he should remove my wretched underdrawers—also a gift from a Caton corpse—I lowered my gaze enough to glimpse the young man's face. His composure was perfect, save for a hard set to his lips and an angry twitch in his jaw muscle. Perhaps he had served somewhere even less savory than a corrupted temple.

He bowed and I dismissed him. As he exited the doorway, I cupped hands over my mouth as if to offer a divine invocation and whispered, "Well done," feeding a bit of magic into the words.

Garen's head jerked ever so slightly as the word trigger sounded in his ears, but he did not look back or do anything else to break role. A small test, passed well. Gods grant it was the only surprise awaiting us.

A moment to fix the structure of time and events firmly in my head and I strode out of the changing room to the mist-hung tepidarium.

Herai stood ready with a wine cup. I downed a mouthful, passed back the cup, and reclined on the bench beside the pool. As a harper plucked a lazy melody in some distant hall, the youth began to wash my shoulders and arms. Neither enjoyment nor cleanliness was my object, of course. We needed time. Garen had to get back to the waiting room and be noticed among the servants, and I had to prepare my spellwork. This was going to use every paltry spell I knew, and though each part was simple enough, I had never attempted any working so complex.

"How many worshippers avail themselves of Arrosa's gifts on such an evening?" I said.

The capable hands moved down my back. "Fewer of late than in the past, so I understand, *domé*. Ten or twelve in the public pools tonight, a nobleman and his two sons in the Pools of the Illustrious. It is a rare privilege to have anyone visit the Pools of the Gods' Chosen."

So fifteen or so Seekers. Young Pleury had spent the morning retrieving the information that Arrosa's Temple housed three priestesses and twelve initiates, all of whom were women, five male acolytes, twenty bath attendants, and fifteen or twenty servants. I had some seventy people in the temple to distract.

Herai moved around to the front of me, unstoppered a crystal flask, and passed it under my nose. Ephrain. Inhaling the pungent oil tuned the senses like strings on a lute until they worked together in harmony, waiting for the right hand to play them.

"Does the scent please you, *domé*?"

"Yes, but use only a little for now. More when I come out of the pool."

He spilled a few drops of ephrain onto his palms. I caught his wrist as his strong, attentive hands moved from chest to groin.

"Back, legs, and feet first," I said. "I've traveled a long distance and have no wish to hurry my devotions. In my own land, this day marks one year exactly since my dedication to Arrosa Triumphant. A prophet in the land of Cymra on the western sea told me that this temple, of all of her great houses, is alive with the goddess. And he says my pureblood gifts stem directly from my divine lady's hand. How can this not be a night of nights?"

I offered a silent apology to the lady goddess, reminding her that I hoped to cleanse her house of a great wrong.

"As you desire, *domé*. I am honored to aid in your celebration." He knelt and went about his work, while I readied my spellwork.

By the time Herai returned to my nether regions, most of an hour had passed. Garen would have had time to be seen, but not studied too hard. The initiates in the atrium would have greeted other Seekers or gone back to their gossip or devotions, or whatever they did between arrivals. It was time for magic.

I grabbed Herai's chin, rough but not cruel. "You make it difficult to control my urgencies, ordinary. But I am vowed to complete my year of celibacy entirely cleansed"—were relations between men *un*celibate?—"and my priestess in Cymra warned me that breaking my vow would offend the goddess. Bathing first."

"Certainly, *domé*."

The deliciously warm water of the tepidarium should have been soothing, but what pleasure could be had in the pool where the murderer had blacked Fleure's hair, choking the child to silence her sobs? I hoped to serve up a good fright to pay a small part of the debt the temple owed her.

Floating idly on the water, I propelled myself about the pool's periphery, occasionally ducking my head under as if trying to examine the chipped mosaic that lined its walls. Never did my right hand leave the wall, however, and I linked spellwork to the boundary I traced.

When the circuit was complete, I lunged onto the verge. Water cascaded onto the floor as Herai brought lengths of linen to dry me. Bidding him wait, I circled the chamber, making reverence before each of the four ugly statues that occupied the corners, as if I knew what nymph or godlet each one represented. At one of the female sculptures, my pious touch lasted a bit longer, and I infused the thing with another spell.

Beside another statue, in the very place where Gab, the sweeping girl, had spied on my ablutions, I touched my head to the floor as if to offer prayers. I swept up a pile of stone dust and infused it with the aerogen web I had created in the Tower cellar.

When all was ready, I leapt to my feet.

"Sweet youth, truly our goddess moves in me!" Breathing rapidly, I returned to Herai, while triggering a simple spell called an excitement, another favorite among pureblood children. Orange sparks should be visible in my eyes, my cheeks should display a heated flush, and my hair should be writhing in wet curls. "I must to the caldarium . . . now!"

Though his eyes grew huge as blue plates, Herai kept wit enough to escort me down the steps to the hot pool. "What should I—?"

I plunged into the scalding water, diving deep to its center. A touch linked my grandest spell to this pool—an illusion more complicated than the knife-and-pen illusion in the hirudo, but no more difficult.

Now to set things in motion. Noise, illusions, some smoke, and a void hole would have to do. I had to save true power for my bent.

My body pulsed with red and purple light as I rose screaming from the water. "She comes! Tell them all! The goddess comes in triumph and wrath!"

As I staggered forward, Herai retreated up the steps toward the tepidarium. "*Domé*, what's happening to you?"

Sparks flew from my spread arms. Growls and rumbles beneath my bare feet sounded as if the foundation of the temple crumbled. "Hurry! Gather her worshippers! The lady comes to greet us, to warn us, to punish."

I shrieked and spasmed as the steam swirled into cyclones and the screen of illusion took hold around me. My body would appear to swell. Blood would drip from my swollen flesh as purple fire appeared in the splitting seams of my skin. Bastien had said it was quite disturbing.

"Bring them all!" I cried. "She wants her children here—priestess and sweeping girl, Seeker and servant, initiate, attendant, cook—every soul who bides here this hour, else she will open the earth and swallow this house!"

Move, fool of a boy!

"Hurry! She has sanctified me to be her passage, the coals of her fire. Bring them. She must not . . . must not come to an empty—"

A scream I considered nicely bloodcurdling at last dislodged Herai from his paralysis.

The instant he vanished into the passage, I sped to the changing room, grabbed my undertunic from the clothes chest, and threw it over my nakedness. I had only moments. Still emitting bleats and shrieks, I rummaged deeper and found the tight bundle Garen had smuggled in under his own cloak. A small sack, a coarse shirt, and black hose. *Good lad—every bit what Bastien said of you.* Alas, the boots that were better than my own had to stay with the other things, to bear witness to my miraculous vanishing. Should anyone come investigating, naught must connect either the clothes or the ephemeral magic to Lucian de Remeni, closely confined in Necropolis Caton.

Back to the baths under cover of cloud cyclones and lightning. A touch triggered the voiding spell I'd laid on the tepidarium pool. Water and mosaic floor vanished, leaving an empty dirt hole. A touch of the floor here and there left jagged cracks.

To the caldarium and set an illusion of the hot pool bubbling. Unfortunately I didn't know how to heat the water to boil of itself.

To the corner statue and trigger the inflation spell to gradual increase and install the small illusion of Arrosa's silver crescent moon above the statue's ugly head.

Voices and footsteps echoed from the main passage and the upward stair from the caldarium.

"Corruption! Sin!" Punctuating my bellowing with an agonized cry, I dumped Garen's little sack of ashes on the top step and set a small whirlwind of true flame atop it. Then I snatched up a towel and ducked behind the statue nearest the changing room, waiting, hidden, as Arrosa's devotees flocked into the tepidarium.

Gasps and murmurs swelled into a terrified babble. Cries to kneel, to stay back. A rising chant to the glories of the goddess, sweet voices in unison. Good. Priestesses had arrived.

I twisted my fist. The blinding sunburst from the face of the illusory goddess lit the chamber as if the sun had exploded.

Frenzied babble burst out afresh. In the dazzle, none should notice my inflated statue's faded paint . . . or me, as I slipped from my hiding place, the length of linen wrapped about my head and shoulders, as if I'd just come from one of the common baths. The enchanted stone dust was tucked safely in my hand.

Seventy or more. Priestesses, silk-gowned initiates, half-dressed bathers, gawping sweeping girls, and sweating cooks. Gab's little face lit in wonder at the display; I believed she would welcome what I was going to show. I shaded my eyes and craned my neck to see, as if the spectacle was not already engraved on my mind. One person was yet missing.

"Quiet, my children. Let me pass."

The mellow voice halted the chanting. The wails were muffled. High Priestess Irinyi's cloud of wheat-colored hair was just visible across the sea of heads. Bodies pressed me back toward the wall as the crowd parted to let her through.

Flush with satisfaction, I whispered, *"Snatchit,"* feeding the word with magic. Goddess grant that Garen was listening . . . and careful.

Irinyi faced the spelled statue, now grown near ceiling height, across the voided pool. Her slender arms rose in supplication. "Divine Arrosa, speak your will! We are your handmaidens, your worshippers, your servants. Tell us the meaning of this apparition."

The crowd shifted uneasily. Unfortunately, a simple inflation as I had put on the statue allowed for no animation. I didn't know how to make the illusory goddess speak or smile or frown. The lightning and swirling clouds would have to disguise the rigid expression. I poked a little more magic into the thunder spell, as well, and flashed colored beams from the statue's empty eyes.

Irinyi spilled out prayers. When no answer came, she spun to face the crowd. Even from across the chamber, her painted eyes glared sharp.

"What's happened here?" The high priestess did not sound afraid, nor was she even so reverent as one might think before such a manifestation. Worrisome. But I needed to get on with things.

As the crowd shouted, *"The goddess . . . Pool vanished . . . Earthshaking . . . Fire. Terrible screams. Lightning and blood . . ."* I slipped backward and sidewise toward the lattice wall. Soon no one stood behind me.

"Hush, all of you!" Irinyi's command could have shattered crystal. "Did anyone witness its beginning? The *goddess* does not visit empty chambers."

"I, Sinduria." The pale-haired Herai stepped forward, his voice trembling. "It was the pureblood from Cymra at his devotions. His flesh swelled and split . . . his body burned from the inside . . . just there." He pointed to the pile of smoldering ash. "He spoke of prophecy, mistress. Of Arrosa Triumphant. He said the goddess was coming to punish corruption in her house."

Every eye was on Irinyi and the hovering apparition behind her—not on me. So I flung the dust high and infused the aerogen enchantment with magic.

Gasps filled the air as the dust formed into rings, sparking in the torchlight like black diamonds. Then I released the last illusion I'd hidden in the hot pool, the livid clouds that showed a child bent over the tepidarium pool, a cloaked figure blacking her hair.

Screams and pointing spun Irinyi about, where she could see the illusion as well. Another burst of light from the hovering goddess, and black dust began to shower down onto the crowd. Every person in the chamber stood transfixed, the high priestess at the front of them. The vile Motre Varouna, priestess and procuress, slumped to her knees just in front of me. I hoped the sight burnt holes in her eyes.

"Grabbed!" Garen's voice, straight into my ear.

No time for relief. My every scrap of wit was engaged with the magic. Laying a hand on a post supporting the latticework, I diverted all my power into a last enchantment.

A howling whirlwind snuffed every torch, candle, and lamp. Lightning and colored beams winked out. The private bath chambers of the purebloods were as dark as Caton's tombs.

The mob surged with the force of a sea tide. Wails and screams tangled with grunts and moans. Groping through the doorway at my back, I shoved the painted clothes chest to block any escape through the changing room, then fled blind into the steamy passages.

CHAPTER 23

Flame bowls and lamps yet blazed in the temple proper. The halls and stairs appeared deserted, as we'd planned. How long would it take for others to find their way out through the main passage or the caldarium stair? The cracks in the floor, one pool a gaping void and the other seemingly aboil, the noise and panic and the ever-present fear of encountering the angry goddess should grant me half an hour at the least. Lacking magic to feed them, the spells I'd used would slowly fade: the illusions and inflation going first, the void hole last. The dark would be gone as soon as someone had the wit to relight the lamps.

Half-dizzy with apprehension and heady magic, I raced up the stair and into the priestesses' household. Garen waited in the antechamber where I had first met the high priestess. The painted panel that led into Irinyi's private rooms stood open, her wall-sized scroll case in clear view.

Garen's glance darted from the outer door to the inner. "Sorry if I took too—"

"You did well," I said, snatching the scroll from his hand and spreading it on the floor. My false signature glared at me from the bottom of it. "Close the panel all but a crack and keep eyes and ears sharp. Lay a hand on my shoulder if you hear anyone coming."

Kneeling beside the spread parchment, I swept aside the scraps of common spellwork that lingered in my head like bones on a platter. My back prickled as if a spear were aimed at it; discipline banished that, too. With a quiet invocation, my fiery bent flooded through vein and sinew.

This artifact of vellum and ink, intent and contract—the false pledge I had signed to give a phantom child into corruption—was a gateway to the murderer's identity. Gab's Bear Lord with Shiny Boots had signed a document just like it when he left Fleure in Irinyi's grasp. I trusted this page to trigger my bent, allowing me to follow the threads of history to the scroll with the murderer's name and seal. Once we had that, we could run.

As the power in my hands built, I raised images of Irinyi's painted eyes, of a girl child with fair hair and rosy skin, of golden curls hacked off and left on the floor, of polished black boots and wide hands throttling a slender neck.

I set urgency aside, and only when my hands quivered with magic did I touch the scroll and let it flow. . . .

Flashes of candlelight . . . Smooth pale vellum . . . the seal of the temple. A walk down the steamy passages behind the mincing steps of Motre Varouna . . . divine terror, laced with the dizzying sweetness of moonflowers. The baths . . . busy with men . . . with women . . . oiling coarse skin . . .

No, I wasn't interested in the baths, certainly not the common baths. Fleure would have been kept back for the Pools of the Illustrious or, gods forbid, purebloods. I wanted to see the children, the contracts, the words. High Priestess Irinyi, who negotiated those most special contracts, wore amethyst rings. I searched for hands writing. . . .

Hard, thin hands; soft, plump hands; scarred hands; men's, women's, one and then another . . . vanishing as quickly as they manifested. But one ivory hand appeared repeatedly, adorned with rings of pearl and amethyst. I grasped that image and hunted the blooming child of Fleure's first portrait.

Images grown from my bent cascaded through my inner sight: *Sadness and terror, a blur of faces flushed with holy fervor, stained with tears. A small voice wailed, "Don't leave me!"*

Not that one. Fleure would not have cried out after the man she feared.

Another child, another. There! *Eyes as bleak as winter sky. Older than her tender years. She knew what was coming. Royal children learned early how things were done.*

"Voices in the passage, *domé*." A hissing Garen heralded the real world.

But I clung to the magic. Weave the other threads: *the parchment, the amethyst rings. A man's thick hand, black hair on its back, scribbled on a vellum sheet. . . .*

Garen gripped my shoulder.

"A moment," I whispered, and squeezed my own eyes tight so as not to lose the fading image. We were so close.

The handwriting blurred. *A gigantic, dark-furred beast—a monstrous bear bellowing rage rose on its hind legs. A gold collar circled its huge, stretched neck, and its great teeth were lancets and steel axe heads. . . .*

No, no, a big, hairy man had killed her, not an actual bear! I ripped the bestial image aside. If I could see the devil's name, we'd not need to locate the scroll.

The hairy hand had vanished, as the fingers ringed in amethysts rolled the page, tied it with a ribbon, and stuffed it into the scroll case.

That would have to do. "Fifth row from the bottom of the case," I whispered, counting, "ten, eleven, *twelve* slots from the right. Get it!"

But as I shook off the vision, the earth jerked and wobbled. My head flopped forward and my legs slid across the stone.

"Shhh!" Garen shoved me into the space between the end of the banquette and the wall, kicked my feet close, and pressed my head to my knees. The document and its ribbon tie landed on top of me, followed by a heavy blanket of musty wool—or Garen's cloak? Another soft *plop* on top could only be a cushion from the banquette.

"Who are you? What business have you in the high priestess's quarters?" The man's rumbling challenge pounded the air.

I dared not breathe.

"I am the servant of *Domé* Etan de Serrano-Pristé of Cymra." Garen's muffled voice sounded respectful but not servile. Urgent but not panicked. "A youth rousted me and others in the servants' waiting room, saying we were commanded by the goddess to go down to the baths. I could not, as my master had instructed me to await him in the servants' room. But when I heard the terrible screaming from below, I feared some disaster. And where should I inquire about one of the gods' chosen, save the most noble quarters in the temple? Please to tell me, sir, where I may rejoin my master."

"The Cymran pureblood! What was his purpose here?" *Damnation!* Irinyi was here already, voice brimming with suspicion. Had my enchantments been so transparently false?

"Surely all who come to this holy place are pursuing devotions to the goddess, my lady. . . ."

No, no, Garen. Do not tease her. You are not Bastien.

"But of course, I cannot discuss my master's business."

"I am a Sinduria of the Elder Gods," snapped Irinyi. "Your master has blasphemed! A Registry spy, isn't he? I was warned about him. What does he think to learn here?"

Warned? Who believed the *Registry* had any interest here?

"The law forbids— Ungh!" A grunt punctuated Garen's answer. *Gods!*

"Show some respect, belly crawler."

"Answer the high priestess," growled a second man.

If these were the thick-shouldered, well-armed bodyguards I'd noted on my first visit, even Garen and I together would never take them, not without magic. I crushed the stolen document and stuffed it under the lacings of my hose, then scrabbled through ideas—illusions, diversions, anything useful. I needed to be fast but not stupid.

"My apologies to the most excellent Sinduria, but I am not permitted—" Garen's unrepentant declaration dissolved into a choking gargle.

My own throat knotted. *Think, Lucian!*

"Sarat!" The high priestess's fury crackled. "Fetch the duc! Tell him we're holding one of our violators. Fal, remove this insolent vermin to the inner chamber and teach him reverence."

From the furious grunts, hammering feet, and sharp blows, Garen did not go easily. The panel to the inner chamber snicked shut. I had to get him out of there. Where was the priestess?

A muffled yell filtered through the layers of wall and cloak. A heavy thud shuddered the painted panels behind me. Unintelligible words rumbled. Another yell. And then another, louder, filled with pain.

I dragged my hands out from under my chest, ready to plow a fist into the wall if I could devise no better. The scuff of a slipper paralyzed me. Irinyi was still here.

Garen screamed in agony. I dared not wait.

The outer door was directly across the chamber from the banquette. I constructed an imaginary path from the exquisitely detailed stone frieze above the door to the cushioned bench, and then along the bench to my hand that rested on its painted surface. That line could serve as a conduit allowing me to feed a simple enchantment into the depiction of Arrosa's gardens. Thank all gods the room was small; such extensions drain a sorcerer's power like children devour sweets. A simple noise would be the least taxing.

As Garen's awful cry died away, I forced myself still. Silk brushed the floor, taking up a quiet ebb and flow. The priestess was pacing. Agitated.

When she was some halfway through her circular path, I released magic.

As the thunder of gushing water spilled from the direction of the door, I threw off my coverlet, lurched forward, and grabbed the distracted priestess from the back, covering her mouth and wrapping her arms beneath my own. She was tall for a woman and fierce, but thin and older and surely unaccustomed to an angry attacker. In moments I had her subdued. My bare foot kicked open the painted panel.

Garen lay face down on the floor beside the scroll case. The sight of his back, flesh striped with gore, did naught to make me gentle.

"Throw down the cane or I break this creature's neck." I growled and jerked tighter. As I linked a light spell to Irinyi's bead collar, my grasping fingers detected an unmistakable shape at her waist. The goddess of love's high priestess carried a dagger sheathed inside her gown.

Irinyi bucked and sank her teeth in my arm. As if on signal, the snarling thug brandished the bloody cane and lunged.

White-hot fire scored my cheek. I triggered the enchantment, and scarlet light beams blazed into the man's eyes.

"Up, friend, or die!" I yelled, shoving the priestess into her bellowing guard. Her blade remained in my hand. As priestess and guard stumbled backward, I swept a circle with my foot, crouched beside it, and laid my hand on the boundary. But before I could seal a void ring between us and our attackers, my magic sputtered and failed.

The roaring guard shoved Irinyi aside and rushed me again. I lumbered to my feet. Bereft of power, I swept Irinyi's knife across his path and struck flesh. Blood spurted across my arm as he dropped to his knees, his bellow reduced to gurgling dismay. The knife hilt slipped from my hand.

The guard toppled, blood gushing from a yawning wound in his neck.

"Murderer!" screamed Irinyi from somewhere beyond the fading scarlet glare.

Garen, head drooping, had made it to hands and knees. I heaved him up and dragged him through the panel door. Propping him against the wall, I shoved the heavy banquette across the broken panel to block the way. Irinyi screeched like a trapped wildcat.

"Hold on." I grabbed the wool cloak and threw it around Garen, and we staggered into the passage. Irinyi's screaming would draw a swarm of soldiers and servants up the atrium stair. I'd no choice but to retreat deeper into the household.

Doorways gaped on either side of the passage, some lit, most dark, all deserted. I picked a dark room at random. Spilled light from the passage revealed a barren little cell, a washing bowl and pallet with a thin pillow and a crumpled blanket its only furnishing.

We huddled in a corner hidden from any random glance through the doorway. Surely no one would imagine thieves hiding so close. Surely.

Footsteps raced down the passage, past the doorway, back again. Garen shook, his breathing erratic and tight between his teeth. The heavy cloak of scratchy wool must be torment on his lacerated back. Still we waited.

Shouts echoed, then faded into the quiet.

"Stay," I whispered, and crept across the room to fetch the blanket. But first . . . my bloody hand trembled as I scrubbed at it with the bedsheet. My jaw clamped hard, muzzling my rising gorge. I had never struck a wounding blow, never torn living human flesh. These hands were made to channel the gods' magic, not pain and ending.

The passage fell quiet. That wouldn't last forever, not when they hunted a murderer. Certainly not long enough for me to reclaim power for substantial magic. My spirit felt as empty as a dry waterskin.

Blanket in hand, I slipped back to Garen, catching him as he crumpled. "We're going to walk out of here now," I said. "Bold as brass down the stair and out the front gate, just as we planned."

Draped in blanket and cloak, we stumbled down the deserted passage to the top of the great stair. My intent to pass us off as two Seekers caught in the chaos of the baths was quickly proved idiocy. The atrium teemed with shouting, bedraggled people, surrounded by armed temple guards and other, more dangerous-looking warriors in black leathers—all with drawn swords. By my estimate every one of the seventy-odd occupants and visitors at the temple had been herded into the circle of soldiers.

A blood-drenched Irinyi watched over the chaos from halfway down the stair. A slender, bearded nobleman wearing a tabard of purple and gold—Ardran court colors—and a pectoral chain heavy with sapphires, stood at her side. Irinyi's duc, no doubt. He wasn't the murderer; Gab had described a big, hairy man. But the presence of a duc boded ill if we were caught. In the absence of an anointed king, a duc could interpret the Writ of Balance. He could condemn Garen and his pureblood master of violating the barriers between Registry and Temple—a crime much worse than simple burglary.

"They're questioning everyone," Garen wheezed. No one, whether initiate, Seeker, or servant, was leaving the atrium without challenge.

"Aye. And that fellow holding my boots knows my face. . . ."

A few steps below the priestess the bath attendant, Herai, clutched a wad of puce and pea-green brocade and my borrowed boots. We dared not go down. But not ten steps behind us gaped the archway leading to the sloping passage to the baths.

"But all's well. I know another way out."

The Pools of the Gods' Chosen were deserted. Half the torches were relit, and the tepidarium pool was no longer a void. One of the statues had toppled and lay in three pieces. Only a few cracks remained in the floor, but the tiles were littered with broken glass and puddled water, mud, and oil. The scent of ephrain near choked me. Garen leaned heavy on my arm.

"Just a little way and we'll be out," I said, guiding him past a godling's staring head.

" 'M all right," he mumbled through swollen lips. The poor man's face was rapidly taking on all the hues of the rainbow. "Not a milksop."

"Certainly not," I said. "Keep moving."

My dread of the journey to come was quickly distracted by a longing for boots. Negotiating patches of oil and broken glass with my bare feet took much too long. We had made it past the now placidly steaming caldarium pool and had started down the mold-slick steps into the drainage channel when voices rose behind us.

"We oughtn't come down here, Rafe." A young man's voice quavered. "None's allowed."

"I tell you I spied two fellows atop the stair. Sarat was so sure they'd head for the front gates, he never searched the women's cells. Man's got bricks in his skull. The pureblood was down here at the bath, so I'm guessing he'll come back to get out. Maybe we'll earn the livery if we find Fal's murderer."

Murderer . . . Please, gods, no.

"Oughtn't be here, Rafe. Goddess looked straight into my soul. What if she comes again?"

"She won't. Sinduria said 'twas all fakery."

I ignored the hisses of pain that squeezed through Garen's teeth and urged him faster through the hot passage and down into the cold dark.

The arguing voices dwindled. The rats clicked and scuttered over my bare feet.

Rafe's timid partner must have won the dispute, as none followed us through the sludge and the swarming vermin to the desolate spot where Fleure had died. And as far as I could tell none saw me kick out the grate or watched us creep through the drain hole and start down the muddy, ice-slicked ramparts below the Elder Wall.

The night wind whined and whipped across the exposed slope. My bare feet were quickly numb; my hands cut and frozen. A heart-pounding slide ripped cloak and blanket from our fingers, and the bluster sucked them into the night, threatening to wrench us from the slope as well. I kept Garen above me as we crept downward, pressing him to the rock lest he plummet all the way to Magrog's hell.

Garen mumbled repeatedly, "Please to hold on, *domé*." Before we'd descended halfway, he slumped into deadweight.

An eternity, that descent, but eventually, blessedly, my feet reached easier ground. I hefted Garen across my shoulders and stumbled and slid down the muddy slope of the lower ramparts, through the willow brake where Fleure's body had been found, and into the lane beside the hirudo piggery.

Shoulders on fire, I halted to shift the weight. The tortuous path to the necropolis plateau loomed above us in the dark. The ascent looked as welcome as the road to divine Idrium—and just as unreachable.

"Well, well, well, what have we here?"

Light flared from an unshuttered lantern. A blur of dark shapes sharpened and clarified into five Cicerons. So many knives and swords bristled in the lamplight, I might have been a rabbit in a thornbush.

"Sounded like a pack of dogs in the mud, *sengé*," said a gravelly voice. "Looks more like bumbling thieves . . ."

"Or perhaps someone thinks to dispose of another corpse amongst us." Smooth. Unruffled. Half-mocking. I knew this man's voice.

Hands shoved me to my knees in the icy muck. Others dragged Garen from my shoulders. Had they strangled me, I couldn't have lifted a hand to stop them. All I could feel was relief that I didn't have to move anymore.

"He's Coroner Bastien's runner," I croaked, my head drooping. "Bleeding badly. Would appreciate a message being sent."

A woman snorted. "Coroner's *runner*, he says. It's *Garen*."

"Fetch the coroner, Jadia. A small appreciation from his newfound riches would suit us well. Kalme, Ferde, take the coroner's man to the commons house. Hercule, wake the barber to tend him. I'll bring this one along."

The four hurried off, with scarce a footfall between them. The one giving orders remained. The *sengé*—the headman. Demetreo's smooth authority was unmistakable.

A callused hand lifted my drooping chin and his dark eyes memorized my face. "Not often does Serena Fortuna allow a Ciceron to see a pureblood unmasked. You appear quite human. Neither monstrous deformity nor divine beauty hiding in half the face."

The hand let go and my chin sagged again. The wet crawled up my thin hose and the hem of my tunic. The crumpled page bearing my signature had vanished from my waist. A small loss. But my failure was far worse than that.

The scroll case that contained the name and signature of the child murderer had lain a handsbreadth from Garen, and I'd not thought to grab the thing as we fled. And in accomplishing this nothing, I had gotten Garen beaten to raw meat. To top it all, I had taken life, sullying my family's name beyond repair.

All I could manage was a shivering bark of a laugh. "Indeed. A b-bumbler, as your man said. Most . . . ordinary."

I felt naked without a mask. Inside, too. The cold settled deeper.

"Come along." Demetreo hauled me up as if I were Fleure's size. "Wouldn't want the coroner to think I'd misplaced his prize. Though tonight . . . mmm . . . you may discover your true place in his regard." The thought seemed to amuse him.

Mercifully, the Ciceron babbled no more nonsense as he escorted me through his ramshackle domain. Perhaps he recognized that my spirit was leaden with failure and my sight smeared with blood. "Are you injured, too?" The top of Demetreo's plaited hair might come only to the height of my ear, but the arm, snaked under my shoulder and around my back, could have wrestled the bear in my vision.

"Just deple—" *Idiot, mind your tongue! Remember who you are.* "Just cold. Tired. Wet." I shrugged off his arm. "Don't touch me."

Given a bit of time, a bit of warmth, a drink, I could summon magic again.

He didn't protest—or laugh—but backed away, spreading his arms wide. His mockery stung. He directed me into a narrow alley.

"So, it wasn't just a common witness yon Garen escorted down our lane earlier this night," he said, as we trudged between huts cobbled from wood, leather scraps, mud, and straw. "I was right to discipline my watch for neglecting to identify the trespasser."

"We were on coroner's business. Pureblood business."

"Tell me, chosen of the gods, does the law forbid me to hinder a pureblood without his mask in the same fashion as one full-dressed? For I am determined to press you for more information. I must know whether to prepare for unpleasant intrusions from those who live so high above my little domain."

His question pricked like a lance tip. The temple servant Rafe might easily report the two he'd seen atop the stair, and if Irinyi's guards discovered the kicked-out grate, the priestess and her duc would know exactly where Garen and the pureblood murderer had ended up.

Honesty could complicate matters. But then again, I walked unharmed as yet.

"Be prepared, yes," I said. "Arrosa's Temple could very well send someone to inquire about a pureblood and his wounded servant tumbling into your lap in the deeps of the night. We were trying to identify the girl child's murderer, but it all went wrong."

How had Irinyi recognized my enchantments as fakery so quickly? They were good. I had tested them inside the prometheum. Perhaps it had been stupid to reveal what I knew about Fleure. Please gods the wind had snatched away the document with my writing on it. If I'd dropped it inside the temple, Irinyi could take the Registry a story about a pureblood who had conceived a child, betrayed his promise to give her to the goddess, and come back to use magic in a crime—stealing the evidence of his guilt and killing her servant. If someone was able to connect me with the page, they'd have a real murder to lay at my feet.

My head felt hopelessly muddled. "Does Bastien get his hands on me again, I'm thinking he'll lock me up for a year," I said. Or the coroner would be dead and I would be buried alive in the Tower cellar.

"I doubt that. You'll be in his good grace, if a fiendish bulldog can be said to have graces."

Now it was my turn to snort in disbelief. Bastien, the *fiendish bulldog*—exactly so. But good grace?

The outer wall—Caedmon's Wall—loomed huge over the muddy

lanes. Firelight here and there illuminated a warren of huts and shacks built up so tightly to the wall, a defender would have to barge through some family's hovel to find the steps up to the wall walk.

The hovels that clustered against the Elder Wall were, if anything, meaner. We ducked under a sodden length of ragged cloth hung on a stretched rope. Beyond a curtain of rain, a squat stone building roofed with black slate protruded from the Elder Wall's rocky underpinning like a wart on a toad. As we crossed a lake of muck to reach it, the building's red-painted door swung open as of its own will.

"Our commons house," said Demetreo. He vanished inside. My skin prickled. Was he so sure I would follow?

Soaked and shivering, ankle-deep in freezing muck on a starless, moonless midnight, I stopped to consider that. If the headman believed Bastien had riches to share, then clobbering me on the head as I walked in and making a bid for ransom was not out of the question. Who knew whether Demetreo's people had actually brought Garen here or had any real intent to help him? No one in his right mind would trust a Ciceron.

Yet truly, I'd left my right mind behind long ago. Demetreo's behavior had some purpose beyond simple ransom. And if I could regain a bit of power for magic, I could find Garen. I certainly wasn't going to leave him bleeding in this cesspool.

Filled with foreboding, I commanded my numb feet to carry me onward, through the red door into the den of thieves.

CHAPTER 24

If ever a man's expectations were confounded, so were mine when I stumbled into the hirudo commons house. Expecting grimy dimness, I found plastered walls and a dozen lamps beaming through panes of emerald, scarlet, and diamond clarity. Demetreo's pickthieves must have stolen a vat of oil to keep them lit.

Expecting dank and cold, I found a bonfire blazing in a circular stone pit. My frozen face stung with the glorious heat.

Expecting hostile, silent men twirling knives, I found a gallery of homely activity. Two ragged fellows diced in the corner, serious as if the rise and set of the sun depended on their continued play. A younger man, wearing hooped earrings and ribbon-laced braids, plucked the strings of a small harp. A swarthy giant chopped turnips as if the dusty roots were his enemies' heads.

Garen lay prone on a pile of cushions near the fire, surrounded by old women. One toothless crone held a tin basin, while her twin clucked and blotted his bruised face with a scrap of linen. Another elder wearing a necklace of bones murmured soft encouragement as she peeled the shreds of his shirt from his bloody back. Garen's mumbled protests had reached a reassuring vigor.

Trying to maintain a modicum of self-possession, I clamped suddenly trembling hands under my arms and looked away, only to find a cross-eyed girl boldly examining me sodden head to mud-splattered legs.

Grinning, she dropped a fistful of herbs into a pot steaming on the hob. My already heated cheeks blazed hotter than her fire.

Demetreo drank from a tin cup that sent out pleasant fumes of clove and lemon. A giggling girl child in a skirt woven of rags offered me one as well. "My granny's cider. 'Twill warm your bones and vitals and make your eyes keen."

I accepted the cup, inhaling the fragrant steam with gratitude. Lingering wariness prevented my tasting it right away, for, indeed, two hostile, silent men with blades had attached themselves to my flanks.

A lift of Demetreo's chin dismissed the two to the shadowed corners whence they'd come. "What happened to Bastien's man?" he said, pointing his cup at the prostrate Garen.

"A brute tried to beat secrets out of him," I said just loud enough that Garen might hear, "but he yielded nothing."

A rain-soaked breeze from the open door announced a newcomer.

"What's so urgent to fetch a man from his finest dream in a twelvemonth?" A great yawn punctuated this drowsy question.

Slight, rumpled, his greasy hair a wet tangle, Bek the barber-surgeon fixed his charcoal gaze on Garen and the flock of women. "I trust you've sent for Bastien. And where's our coroner's luck charm?" He twisted around. "Ah."

Waggling his eyebrows at me, the surgeon tossed his dripping cloak to the cider girl and stepped briskly to Garen's side. "What in all hells happened to you, fool?"

"Din' talk. No milksop."

Garen's slurred defense twisted Bek's hard mouth into a cadaverous grin. "I'd never think it. Here, let me do that. . . ."

He took one of the twin crones' rags, sniffed at it, and dipped a finger into the basin.

"Magrog's balls, woman! Get me fresh water and make it hot. I've told you; hot water will *not* boil a man's liver. I swear it on the *sengé*'s blessed grandmam."

I drained my cup of cider. Demetreo might hope for ransom, but he'd never have summoned Bek if he had murder in mind.

From his case Bek yanked out a steel pincer a little longer than my finger and proceeded to pick at Garen's back with it.

The younger man near rose off his pillows. "Ow! Stop that!"

"Be still," snapped Bek. "Do you know the Hansker cut their skin and stuff soot in their wounds apurpose to scar themselves? They believe it makes them look fearsome to their enemies. But I'm thinking you'd rather not wear such decoration if we can avoid it, so we needs must get all this mud and gravel out before you start to heal. Might have to stitch up a couple of these. Oldmeg, if you would . . ."

He motioned to the woman in the bone necklace to hold Garen's arm out of the way and blot the free-flowing blood just above the youth's left hip.

I winced in sympathy.

"No cutting on me, Bek." Garen, full awake now, came near twisting his head off trying to see what the surgeon was up to. "No pricking nor sewing, neither. Maybe you just ought to let the women do— Ow! Butcher!"

"Our family healer would recommend exactly the same," I offered. To my mind the surgeon was proceeding with admirable skill. "She always cleans wounds, sometimes even enlarges them a little. . . ."

But then, a pureblood healer could lay spells to discourage sepsis and charm the skin to prevent scarring. It was the magic in her fingers twined with the magic in her subject that made such healing possible—and thus *im*possible for ordinaries. My face heated. How boorish to compare my experiences with theirs.

Garen craned his head as if he'd just realized I was there. *"Domé,"* he whispered urgently. He yanked his arm from the crone and tried to reach his waist. "I've a pocket in my belt— Ow!"

"Be still!" The surgeon shoved Garen's arm back into Oldmeg's custody.

"Do as he commands," I said. Crouching beside the surgeon, I lifted a bloody remnant of Garen's tunic and found the canvas pocket tied to his belt. "Is this what you want?"

"Inside," he said softly, even as he flinched at Bek's next probe.

I pulled the bag open and poked my fingers inside, feeling a faint buzz of enchantment. Ah, gods . . . my mask.

"Good." What else could be said? The whisper of regret shadowing my spirit was nonsense.

I slipped on the mask made of a dead man's wrapping. Its enchantments snugged it around my eyes, ears, and the bony arch of my long pureblood nose until it felt like a second skin.

Garen dropped his eyes. And when I rose the lute fell silent, the chopping knife halted, and every eye in the room save Demetreo's hardened and looked away. Very proper. As if I had vanished.

Beneath his black mustache, the headman's lips twisted in amusement; then his expressive chin set the activities of the house moving again. But the talk was quiet and sparse, the chopping less exuberant, and even Garen's protests buried in the dirty cushion. When I held out my cup to the cider girl for more, her hands shook as she poured.

Fixing my attention on the flames, I turned my back to the others and moved closer to the hearth. Eventually life would move on more easily behind me—a technique hard learned in Montesard.

Why had Demetreo brought me here? He was no benevolent overlord, accustomed to harboring wounded burglars or humbled sorcerers. From our first encounter, his every move had been calculated. He had barred my passage through the hirudo that first night, asking for a glimpse of Idrium's glory, as if he'd never witnessed true magic.

On that same night my light spell attached to the iron grave marker had failed abruptly when I encountered Demetreo, yet once I'd escaped his snag, it had blazed anew down in the hirudo. That made no sense at all unless . . . Had another pureblood been here that night, working magic for Cicerons?

Curious, I spread my fingers wide before my breast, stretching my trained senses into the unexpectedly warm chamber. Magic! Faint, fragile, it riffled the hair on my arms, teased at my tongue like pepper, whispered in my ears like the drifting disturbance of a dead leaf come loose from a vine. Small enchantments wreathed the fire pit, just enough to slow the consuming of the wood, perhaps, or to send the smoke of damp fuel inerrantly through the dark vent hole overhead.

Reaching deeper, I discovered enchantments on every side of me, each slightly different in the subtle ways that testified to different sorcerers. More than one had been here. Strange . . .

I spun slowly in place as if I might see spells hanging here and there like cobwebs. Was it the lamps? What about the red door that seemed to open of itself?

My gaze roved the dusty dimness above the lamplight. When it reached the wall opposite the outer door, that which abutted the Elder Wall, astonishment swept aside my idle questioning. In the shadows beneath the timber rafters was a small fresco, its paint infused into the wall when the plaster was soft and raw. The image depicted a black lozenge bearing a white hand, thumb and fingers slightly spread.

I whirled to confront Demetreo, but the headman was no longer present. The others' quiet activities and banter ebbed and flowed around me as if I were but another hearthstone.

Were Cicerons somehow related to the Danae mystery? It seemed so unlikely. Yet I had sketched a blazon of the white hand on a dead Ciceron's portrait. And in the Tower cellar, when I had hunted dark-haired, long-nosed Aurellian warriors in the threads of history, I'd encountered Cicerons wearing black tabards marked with a white hand.

Ignorant folk had ever claimed Cicerons could work true magic. Only the children of pureblood parents carried the power for magic—that was a law of the universe as fundamental as the sun's rising. Certainly what magic I sensed here was weak and crude, nothing at all like the bent, yet it was far more than trickery. And though a talent for simple spellcasting was a rare possibility in first-generation halfblood children—those like Eodward's bastard youngest son, Prince Osriel, whose mother was pureblood—it would be wholly absent in any descendant. Proven time and again through generations: Interbreeding with ordinaries destroyed the gods' gift. Which meant purebloods or halfbloods had worked these spells. Did Cicerons make a habit of sheltering renegade sorcerers?

I turned back to the fire. Every pureblood was under obligation to report instances of true magic where it had no cause to be. If Demetreo had sheltered a *recondeur*, every life in the hirudo was forfeit. I didn't want to know.

My cowardice did not escape me. Had my questions arisen before donning the mask, before all these people knew what I was, I might have mustered the words to inquire what some of them knew of the history of this place or their lamps or the red door. I might have asked if anyone had heard the term *Path of the White Hand*. But the mask returned me to my proper place, and it was not in me to break the barriers it created.

The red door opened yet again to the pounding rain. Two newcomers ducked through the doorway, a lean, hard-faced woman in leather jaque and breeches, wringing water from her wet hair, and Bastien.

The coroner hurried across the chamber, sparing no glance for anyone but Bek and his patient. "Tell me."

"He'll be dancing your bidding in a day or three," said the surgeon without looking up, sounding wholly unsurprised to find Bastien at his side. "Give me half an hour to stitch up this hole in his side, and you can haul him off to the domain of the dead. To work, naturally . . . or whatever else might take his mind off his wounds. Carefully, I would suggest."

The hard-faced woman rolled her eyes, snatched a tin cup from a shelf, and joined the cider girl, who was refilling her pot from a barrel. The lute player, who had been studiously polishing his instrument, met the glance of the turnip chopper. They lifted their eyebrows in a unity of amusement.

The source of their jollity escaped me, right along with patience. I was happy to hear Garen would be well. And Bastien's concern for Garen spoke well of a man I was just beginning to know. But he would understand the significance of the white hand and would be better at the inquiries than I. "Coroner Bastien—"

"Errrggh!" Garen's pain leaked around a stick they'd placed in his mouth.

Bek's steady hands poked a needle into the tender flesh between the runner's hip and waist. He drew and knotted the stitch . . . without spells to ease it. And again . . .

My arms clenched my middle.

"Easy, bonecracker!" Bastien knelt beside the makeshift couch. From his expression, one might think the surgeon was stitching the coroner's own flesh.

All were silent, respecting the wounded man's pain.

"Done," said the surgeon at last, sitting up and twisting a cramp out of his shoulders. "Does the estimable Constance have an onion or three tucked away, do you think, Coroner? I'll vow she knows how to make an onion poultice, woman of many talents as she is. That would do as well as anything I've got to stave off sepsis. So near the gut isn't a place you want rot to set in."

"I can get onions."

"Won't smell nice, though, will he?" Bek grinned, nudging the coroner with his elbow. Bastien looked as if he might strike him.

Which flummoxed me.

Bek cleaned his tools, while Oldmeg blotted away blood and tied a strip of linen over the angry wound. The activities of the room resumed. Bastien noticed none of it. The coroner laid his wide hand on the runner's battered cheek and whispered something I couldn't hear. Garen gave a hoarse croak that might have been a laugh and fumbled about until his slender hand lay atop Bastien's. Then he opened his dark eyes and locked the coroner with a smoky gaze as could speak a vault full of secrets.

I caught my breath, understanding naming me a flat and utter fool. Even my sheltered experience of the wide world testified that theirs were neither the touch nor look of mere friends or even blood-kin.

My education in Montesard had encompassed many things. In one of my tutorial groups a quiet, well-favored young man was ever in close company with another man, their touch and conversation distinctly intimate. I had heard rumor of such relations, but never witnessed it. The university abruptly dismissed the two young men for indecent behavior, so it seemed the ordinary world disapproved. My parents had never mentioned such things, which implied the same.

I'd never quite decided what I thought. Though the exact mechanics remained a mystery and speculation left me queasy, I had wondered if such practices might provide a humane solution for older, unmarried pureblood men, who must live forever subject to the Registry's strict breeding laws. Clearly no children could result. But this . . .

Bek rose, swiped his brow with his sleeve, and yawned. "Anyone else need a swab or a stitch?"

No one responded, save the cider girl, who brought the surgeon a cup that he emptied in one long swallow.

"Time I got back to my bed, then. Coroner, see he doesn't rip out those stitches until I say. You can pay my landlord my fee; less chance of it going astray in these days of decadence. And I'd appreciate all of you refraining from bloody adventures in the middle of the night. *Sengé* . . ."

Throwing on his cloak and hefting his case, the surgeon inclined his back to Demetreo, who had appeared again, lounging against the outside wall. The red door opened by no apparent means, and the surgeon trudged into the night.

"Your care of my servants leaves me in your debt, *Sengé* Demetreo." Smoldering anger had enveloped all Bastien's sentiment. "But I would know how you come to have them in your custody—in such a state. We had an agreement."

The headman's chin jerked again. The turnips went into the simmering pot, the lyre into its skin case. The dicing men quenched the lamps. In moments only we three were left in the house, along with Oldmeg of the bone necklace, who was yet sponging blood from a sleeping Garen.

"*Custody* is hardly the case, Coroner," said Demetreo, emptying the cider pitcher into a cup and passing it to Bastien. "More like they imposed their inconvenient selves on my hospitality, and be sure 'twas in worse condition than you find them. Your pureblood will confirm this."

The headman perched on the rim of the fire pit. Bastien took one of the stools abandoned by the dice players and with a sharp gesture directed me to the other. A formal parley, then. Protocol forbade me from sitting as an equal with two ordinaries, but that wasn't why I remained standing. My curiosity was like to outstrip my patience for this dance between them.

"My apologies, then," said Bastien, unapologetically. "I shall, of course, offer a proper gratuity."

"We have reaped no ill from the dead child found here in the heart of winter. For that alone, I would offer you this consideration." Demetreo gestured toward Garen. "But if this night's work comes down hard on us, as your pureblood warns, our tally will be unbalanced yet again."

Bastien whirled on me. "You babbled our business to a Ciceron? Gossip outweighs gold in his trafficking!"

Demetreo seemed unmoved by Bastien's insult, but then, no masked pureblood kept his thoughts closer than did the headman.

"We'd no escape from the temple save the drainage channel," I said, "and Garen needed more help than I could give. When Demetreo and his people found us and demanded the reason for our trespass, I explained that we'd sought evidence of the girl child's murderer. The temple sits above the place where she was found. He is not stupid."

Demetreo dipped his head in mocking acknowledgment. The veins in Bastien's forehead pulsed. Perhaps I'd stated my case more forcefully than necessary, for my rendering wasn't yet complete.

"Though we got away, the danger is real. I lost the scroll with my handwriting—perhaps on the steps, perhaps in the temple—"

"And to remedy your bungling, you've put us in the debt of Cicerons." My master the bulldog, yes. "Are you determined to get us all dead?"

Patience held by a thread. "I'll tell you the particulars later. Removing ourselves and allowing *Sengé* Demetreo to see to his defenses should suffice for their safety, especially as his people seem to have resources I'd have sworn were impossible."

Demetreo's amusement stilled. Bastien noticed, his wiry brows rising. Curious.

I pressed on. "But before we leave or natter on about my incompetence, I must know about the hand."

The inscrutable Demetreo blinked. "The hand?"

Bastien echoed the headman's confusion.

I pointed to the fresco, almost invisible so high above the shuttered lamps.

"A white hand," whispered Bastien. "The same as in—" He caught himself.

"What do you wish to know?" Demetreo had shuttered his face again.

"What does it mean? Is it the emblem of your clan? A warding symbol?" The questions rolled out of me.

"What would you pay to know of it?"

One might assume Demetreo bargained his own knowledge. But Oldmeg had lifted her head as I questioned. The slightest jut of Demetreo's most commanding chin had set her back to her work. He knew something. Perhaps she knew more. But speculation profited me nothing when he held her reins, as Bastien held mine, when it came to that. Though the headman had directed his inquiry to me, I forced myself to defer.

"Master?"

"Such a trivial request to ease my servant's curiosity," said Bastien. He maintained the marketplace posture of a man who could walk away from trivial matters, though we all three knew full well that he and I had already betrayed the importance of my question. "I owe you Bek's fee to apply to his rent. Perhaps a small increase . . . say, double?"

Good. He did not scrimp.

Demetreo held up his hand as if to slow whatever river of coppers Bastien might produce. "Perhaps something less expensive." A cat's purr could be no more satisfied. "Keep the surgeon's fee and the generous excess. Instead we ask that you avert your eyes for one hour. A simple bargain."

"Avert my eyes from what? A murder? Thieving?"

"It is a matter of our safety and no violation of the law. You have my word—which has proved itself worthy of late, yes? Just leave the hirudo, taking your eyes from us for an hour. My men will carry Garen to your house—or wherever you want him. You can see to his recovery."

Bastien fingered his purse. "And in exchange, Bek's tally is forgiven for the month, and we learn what the pureblood would know."

"Exactly that," said Demetreo, rising, sober and sinuous as a snake.

"Done." The glint in the coroner's eye and the twitch of his profligate mustache as he pounced proclaimed him pleased. He didn't recognize Demetreo's trap, and I wasn't about to warn him. Not if the bargain would illuminate the white hand.

"Come along, pureblood. We've work . . ."

"Ah no," said Demetreo, apologetic as he sprung his trap. "I said nothing about releasing your pureblood just yet. We wish to consult with him on these private matters. Never fear, we'll send him back with his question answered and our debts squared, none the worse for our exchange."

"Private—!" One might have thought a rock blocked Bastien's throat. But shock quickly yielded to annoyance—whether more with me or the headman the only question. He had been fairly outmaneuvered and knew it. Had he been willing to risk Registry outrage by hiring out an hour of my service to other unscrupulous Navrons, he could likely have charged five hundred times Bek's rent for a year. I was well content. An hour was nothing.

Grumbling, Bastien shifted his scowl from me to Demetreo to Garen, who lay shivering despite the fire and blankets. He hated leaving, but, of all people, he knew how quickly evidence could vanish. By morning, the Ciceron could change his mind. Or the Registry could snatch me away. Or any one of us could be dead; Oldmeg looked as if she had cheated the Ferryman for decades. Bastien wanted to know about the white hand, too.

"My servant must be at the necropolis gate before the second-hour bells ring." He eyed my feet. "And if you've a rag to wrap his expensive pureblood toes before you send him up, I'll ignore the next dead Ciceron backslider shows up with his tongue stapled."

"Truly, Coroner Bastien, you ought to dress your servants for the weather." Demetreo's restraint in the glow of his triumph was admirable. His mouth twitched and his dark brows lifted, all false innocence.

Before Bastien could snap a retort, the red door swung open, producing a gust of winter and a Ciceron newcomer large enough to dwarf the coroner and Demetreo put together. Half the man's teeth were missing and his hair was parted into myriad braids threaded with gleaming wire. At Demetreo's direction he lifted Garen as if the young man were a sleeping pup.

Bastien threw his own cloak over Garen and motioned the giant out the door. After a last warning glare at me, he followed, spluttering in discontent.

As the old woman bundled bloody towels and rags from the piled cushions, Demetreo leaned his back on the red door. "What spurs this interest in the mark of the hand, pureblood?"

"My grandsire was a great influence on my youth," I said, picking carefully through the truth. "He used his magic to study ancient times, to understand our world by learning of our ancestors, their cities, and their wars. This white hand against a field of black appeared in a magical vision, worn by some who looked like Ciceron warriors, but he never learned what it meant. Seeing it here intrigues me."

The pulsing red-gold of the dying fire gave life to Demetreo's aspect. "Insufficient," he said after a few moments' contemplation. "What urgency is connected to a dead man's studies, especially for a knife-wit city coroner and a bloody, frozen sorcerer?"

"My reasons do not figure in this bargain," I said. "I've seen the mark before and wish to know more of it. Sooner, rather than later, if I'm to provide some service for you in this hour."

"Very well. Here is a bit of history," he said, his gaze like black needles. "Purebloods have an especial spite for Cicerons. Registry investigators pursue reports of our petty crimes through town and village. Registry witnesses testify in proceedings far beyond the concerns of their contracts. We but cross a sorcerer's path and we're accused of insolence or violation. Your curators would as soon sweep us from the lands of Navronne with jitter dogs and offal. Or, better, hang us all. Do you deny it?"

"Why would I? Respectable ordinaries would profess no different sentiment." No need to list the multitudinous reasons. "The only mystery is why you've not been chased out of Palinur long since." Indeed I'd never heard of Cicerons forming such permanent settlements as this one, even to having sentries and a commons house like a normal village.

"And yet unlike those *respectable ordinaries*, those chosen of the gods have little to fear from light fingers or vengeful knives," said the headman, digging. "Sorcerers who refuse to play our games of chance cannot suffer from our . . . skill . . . at winning them. What have we done to earn such spite?"

"If you wish to address matters of crime and justice, better you should consult Coroner Bastien," I said. "I've little experience to offer."

"Yet in no lawbreaking amongst ordinaries do purebloods take such an interest as in ours. Did you *never* wonder about it?"

"No." It was true that purebloods testified inordinately often against Cicerons; my uncle Patrus had been contracted to a merchants' fair and spent more than half his time witnessing to Ciceron thuggery, calling down raids on their caravans, expelling them. . . .

"Do you yet believe the god has provided us this sorcerer, *Naema*?" said Demetreo, shifting his attention behind me. "A stubborn prevaricator exiled by his own, one who gets his master's lover bloodied and cannot see beyond the prattle of fools?"

"How can you doubt, boy, when the sorcerer speaks to your questions before you ask them? Bring him." A woman's powerful voice came from the back of the house.

Naema! I whipped my head around. Oldmeg sat in a tall-backed wooden chair. A thick mantle woven of every color of nature overlaid her ruffled black skirt and bloodstained tunic.

I was no linguist, but all knew the title *Naema*—"grandmother" in the oldest language of Ardra and Morian, long before those became provinces of Navronne. It was a name associated with the Goddess Mother, Samele, or human women who wore her mantle, those who saw things others could not, those who read the signs of earth and air, those who spoke of past and future with wisdom beyond human knowing. No clan or family dared bestow it lightly. Even purebloods heeded those who wore it.

I bowed to her in deepest respect.

"What am I to make of you, sorcerer?" she said. "You ignore your kind's particular antipathy for Cicerons even as you read the tale of the reasons here in this holy place."

Was it only the dying fire sent a shiver up my back? The Registry was ferocious about those who made false claims to power for magic, naming them charlatans, deceivers, pretenders to the gods' gifts. And the terms of the Writ of Balance meant that neither Crown nor Temple could interfere with the Registry's retribution. And what did she mean, *this holy place*?

"'Tis only to set terms for our consultation that we speak of your kind's especial loathing," she went on. "Mayhap then you'll understand how much our need outstrips our shyness. In the usual course, we invite no dealings with Registry folk."

"I am hardly a Registry man anymore," I said. "But then"—Oldmeg had leaned forward on the arms of her chair, her whole body listening, observing me, her posture telling its own tales—"you know that." They had watched me since the beginning.

Oldmeg's head bobbed slightly in the way of the very old. "Indeed, your separation from your kind emboldens us," she said. "And my grandson deems you trustworthy." The old woman's faded lips squeezed away the beginnings of a smile. "But we cannot allow you to speak of what you see or hear in this chamber, whether to your own kind or any other; thus, we require your blood-bound oath of silence."

She produced a small dagger with a twisted hilt, and with a motion so expert as to be near invisible, nicked her paper-skinned palm. She extended the dagger hilt and her bleeding hand in my direction.

My stomach lurched with the remembrance of knife striking rubbery flesh and warm blood drenching my hand. The temple guardsman's blood had soaked my shirt. I stank of it.

"We do not draw our own blood," I said, staring at the scarlet beads welling from her palm. "It is touched by the gods, carries their magic."

Demetreo blocked the red door, his body a nocked arrow ready to fly. To refuse this oath would likely loose that arrow, for a word to the Registry about traces of magic in a Ciceron lair—even Lucian de Remeni's word—would be enough to bring down a bloodbath.

Yet to keep silent—to pledge my honor to it—would violate the discipline that was the foundation of my people's compact with the gods. I had devoted my life to Registry discipline. I had sacrificed my sister and my freedom to it. Yet my suspicions of those who proclaimed that discipline now festered like plague sores. What if our centuries of trust had been misplaced?

Oldmeg's hands remained steady. "Swear, or our bargain is voided and you learn nothing."

The white hand loomed behind her, a mystery bordering on the divine. Layer upon layer of spellwork teased at my senses. I could not leave here without knowing.

I snatched the dagger and pricked my palm, and then pressed the stinging wound to hers. Her hand was dry and cold, save for the blood.

"The secrets you tell this night shall remain with me," I said. "On my family name and blood, on our holy gifts, on the lines of magic unbroken. Witness my oath, great Deunor, Lord of Fire and Magic. Witness my truth, mighty Erdru, Lord of Vines."

I heaved a great breath. "Now, *Naema, sengé*, tell me all."

CHAPTER 25

Before I could blot my bleeding palm, Oldmeg was on her feet and Demetreo had dragged her chair aside.

"Here is our question and your answer all at one," said the woman, gesturing to the wall of smoke-stained plaster. "A marvel lies hid beneath the mark of the white hand. As my mothers before me, I've spent my days wandering the world in search of it, and once we found it, trying to unmask it."

Awe and reverence engulfed her small body as she gazed on the fresco, causing the hairs on my arms to rise. But when she reverted her gaze to me, it was only a wry, sad humor sparked her smile. "But my feet grow cold and my bones weary, and with these times—good Eodward's death, a new king of less scruple, no matter which brother takes the throne, famine, riot, winter, and everyone seeking to blame those who are ever scapegoats—we've no more days to spare. So tell us what a man with stronger blood than mine finds here."

Demetreo folded his arms across his breast. Oldmeg bowed her head and spread her arms. Waiting for magic.

Warmth and drink had restored me somewhat. Yet it was the need to *know* that drove me past depletion to dredge up every scrap and seed of power in me. Whatever mystery entangled my gift, a creature straight out of myth had told me that some *meaning* lay down a path marked with a white hand. I would have stolen power from the gods themselves to find meaning in the events of these past months.

Closing my eyes, I stretched my spread fingers toward the wall. Eerie enchantment flowed from the stained wall, an illusion that swirled around me like veils of silk, soft, smooth, flimsy, but not at all crude. The plaster wasn't real.

With a twitch of my finger, I expelled a single sharp burst of magic.

"Magrog's balls!" It felt as if the entirety of my blood had been sucked out through my eyes, drained by the unraveling veil.

Perhaps a third of the plaster had vanished, exposing a stony bulwark—not the even courses of pale blocks found in Caedmon's Wall, but age-blackened, undressed stones, laid and mortared as they were dug from the ground.

Centered on this crude expanse was a low, round arch, worked of bronze and decorated with vines, flowers, leaves, and beasts of all kinds. Exquisite work. Yet my eyes did not dawdle, for within the arch writhed sheets and strings of light, deep purples and blues and colors beyond those my paint pots could mime. They shaped and reshaped themselves into patterns of line and color—scenes of meadows and mountains and seasons, as well as purest abstractions—a living tapestry woven of magic as deep and rich and fresh as the grasses of Ardran meadows in springtimes that came no more to Navronne. Enchantment so complex, so far beyond what I knew, it made my chest ache with yearning.

"Ah," said Oldmeg, breathing a long sigh.

"What is it?" I whispered, unable to peel my eyes from the wall.

"Our elder stories tell of hidden doors across Navronne," said Demetreo with ill-contained eagerness. "We have ever been told that the sign of the white hand marks each of these doorways. We hope you can show us where this one leads."

Magical doors. A path marked. That connection made sense—astonishing, but reasonable. But surely they knew more. "The hand marks more than doorways, yes?"

"Naught else that we know," said Demetreo. "We hold the mark secret. Sacred. Some wear it inside their clothes, believing it will bring strength in time of need."

"But Cicerons once wore it openly, like a blazon. Why you? Who told you of hidden doorways? Who worked the magic?"

Demetreo's earrings glinted in the enchanted light and his dark eyes glittered. "Some tales say the doors were created by *your* ancestors in days when we were friends. Some say they were created by the god Valo himself—he you name Deunor, Lord of Magic—as a heritage for his lost children. There are a thousand stories. But in all the years of our wandering, this is the only one we've found."

"Deunor's lost *children*?" Unsure whether to laugh or yell or run, I threw my hands up. "You say these rogue magics are *yours*? This wonder, *yours*? You claim yourselves *pureblood*?" How could one express the death-inviting madness of it? "That is sheerest lunacy. Our bloodlines are recorded back to the earliest Aurellian invaders."

"Certainly not pureblood." Demetreo shrugged, unimpressed by my outrage. "We've no magic to match yours and would never be so foolish to claim so. Who knows where stories come from? At every fire, we sing and spin tales of those who wear the white hand—hero tales, magic tales. Oldmeg studies the stories; I do not. But if you can teach us more of this one, and it saves us from the next scouring"—Demetreo shrugged, his gaze never leaving the old woman—"perhaps I'll pay closer mind to them."

Oldmeg had approached the bronze arch close enough that the light of its shifting scenes bathed her face. Abruptly, she pressed her bony fingers to the magical artwork that for the moment appeared as concentric rings of sunlight. The tapestry of light dipped inward, but her touch did not penetrate. She withdrew and the pattern continued its shifting from a vista of rippling grass to a well of night, sprinkled with stars. At each change, she tried again.

I held my breath, half expecting, half hoping, entirely terrified that she would succeed. If a Ciceron elder could master such magic, then nothing in the world was as I believed.

After yet another failure, the old woman heaved a great sigh. "No further revelation comes to me."

She glanced up and read my question: What was she expecting? "Alas, naught in our lore tells us how to *use* the door. We've always believed we would know in our hour of need. And that hour is so near we can smell it."

And here, so near I could taste it, was the answer I craved—the key to mysteries that had grown to encompass matters far beyond my own life. "Use it for what?"

Neither of them answered. Yet as my question faded into their silence, logic and practice drew links among Oldmeg's words—concerns of war and winter and famine, reminders of powerful families who damned Cicerons for every wickedness—and Demetreo's desire to protect his people from the next murderous rampage that would drive them from their shacks and alleys. Rumors, sickness, plagues . . . all were laid at their doorstep. I had laid such slanders myself and believed them. They wanted to survive what was coming.

One could not have a much better back door from the hirudo than the narrow gate that led to the necropolis. But these two weren't just thinking of crossing Caedmon's Wall.

"You think to use this portal for escape." A Dané had spoken the word that brought the Ciceron's mystery and mine to a meeting point, as if some mystical circle was now complete. "You seek *sanctuary*."

"If the gods could grant us a boon, that would be its name," said Demetreo. "That name is whispered in our tales. We cannot abandon this place unless this door gives us the means to find something better, something safer. We need to know."

Why the Cicerons? How were they connected to the Dané and her cryptic references to a place of safety? Surely the clues to these larger questions lay in the magic. Craving understanding, I pressed my own fingers to a writhing nest of spiderwebs . . .

. . . and in the same instant yanked them back, clenching them to my breast until the burning agony went away, checking by the moment to make sure acid had not eaten away my livelihood.

"You didn't feel—?"

The two Cicerons watched me, brows creased. Oldmeg's bony fingers were folded at her breast, apparently unharmed.

Steeling myself, I tried again, pressing the shifting surface that felt like tight-stretched canvas woven with honed blades. With the last shreds of my magic, I tried to penetrate the barrier.

Again, nothing.

"I don't think I can tell you what you want," I said, when my jaw was no longer clenched against a groan. "The enchantment is seamless, impermeable. And I sense no hook or release point. Perhaps some other sorcerer could do better." Though how I, deemed a murdering madman, could persuade a pureblood to aid a Ciceron was beyond imagining.

Demetreo's foot beat an impatient cadence. "We've no time for bargaining, *Naema*. We should tell him."

With a small gesture Oldmeg agreed.

"We don't believe any other sorcerer would do," said Demetreo. "When we heard the coroner had got himself a pureblood, we rejoiced. Never before had a true sorcerer come so near the hirudo, much less walked amongst us alone. We schemed to capture and force you, but then you showed us your magic—"

"—and later you saw me in chains. And tonight I walked straight into your lair and gave you what you wanted with no trouble at all. Is your triumph sweet?"

Childish. Weak. I pressed the heel of my hand to my brow. The hour was so late and depletion had my bones rattling. I longed for a real bed. For clean sheets. For good wine. For Maia's roast venison. For warmth and peace and a family to surround and shield me from this cursed world.

"Your presence here is not by chance, not dependent on a failed errand to Arrosa's Temple or your damnation by your own kind," said Oldmeg, unfazed by my petulance. "Once we *saw*, we were prepared to ask you for your help. Can you not recognize your own gift? This door magic is unlike any other pureblood magic used in Navronne. Nigh on a hundredyear have I breathed the air of this world and read the lines of enchantments strewn about by Registry sorcerers. None is like to this, save only yours."

"The same as *this*?" I snorted. "That's ridiculous. I've never been here before tonight. My hand burns like acid when I touch it."

"Not that you yourself cast these spells, no. But I recognize the likeness in that way a master weaver can look at the wool, the stitch, the artistry, the rough or delicate hand and say for certain where a fine tapestry was woven—in the port of Morian or a particular warlord's fastness in Evanore, in the western cliff cities or in that Karish monastery down to Elanus."

"That makes no sense. I wish— Great gods, if my gifts could create something like this, I would be one of the Registry curators already. How could you possibly know anything of my work?"

The old woman smiled in sympathy. "Did you not demonstrate your magic for us one morning as you walked to Caton? And on that same evening, you knelt in the mud behind the willows and invoked a kind of power I had never witnessed, save in what lies behind this wall. Whoever created this portal could be your twin, Lucian de Remeni. If any sorcerer can explain its mystery, it is you."

She had been there. I recalled her now wearing her bone necklace, petting a dog, carrying a torch, watching as I made a grand show from a knife and a pen, and again when I explored Fleure's death place. I wanted to press, to ask how she learned to analyze spellwork and why she believed my simple enchantments mimed something so marvelous as this in front of us. Yet, in truth, my mind could shape no sensible argument.

"I can do no more for you tonight. Our hour's bargain is surely done and my master expects me. If you're so familiar with true magic, then you know a sorcerer's expenditures must be replenished. I can't explain what you perceive, *Naema*. Perhaps with some thought, once I'm refreshed, I might, and if so and Bastien allows, I'll send word. I need to go."

Yet even as I sagged against the wall, knees like porridge and the rest of me shaking so violently that my ability to reach Caton was in serious doubt, the words of the silver-marked Dané resounded in my memory, rebuking me for turning away from the white hand—and from where it had led me. *To certain of my kind and certain of thine own kind, thy gifts might be the answer to a long waiting.*

Thine own kind—humans, perhaps, not purebloods. And what humans had waited longer than a tribe of outcasts who'd spent centuries searching for their god's grace?

So follow the path, Lucian. Prove your quality. But how? The Dané said my gifts could vanquish boundaries—indeed, I'd done exactly that with each of my bents, and with the mystery of their entwined power that seemed to make each more than it was alone. If this daunting magic was one of those boundaries . . .

And in that moment, I knew what might tell us more. But no matter how I wished, I had no capacity for magic just then.

"Elsewise I'll have to have food," I said, "and a blanket, cloak, or rag of some kind to get me warm. Even two hours' sleep would restore me enough to try one more thing. But of course, I'd need a message carried to Bastien and someone to persuade him to send down my writing case and parchment and permission to use them."

The words were scarce out of my mouth before Oldmeg had my belly stuffed with sour ale and leek stew, and my quaking limbs bundled in a ragged rug beside the still-warm hearthstones of the commons house. At some point Demetreo vanished through the red door, while Oldmeg settled in her chair and began to hum. A most pleasurable sound, as my chattering teeth kept time.

"Tell me one thing," I said as drowsiness slurred my speech. "Why do Cicerons staple dead men's tongues?"

" 'Tis only for those who babble our secrets," she said. "You'd never do that."

The floor was hard. The hearthstones cooled. The rug itched me—fleas, my groggy instincts warned. And the subtle menace in Oldmeg's answer reminded me that she was no gentle, dithering gammy, but the Goddess Mother's heart in a clan of murdering thieves.

But it was the magic kept me drifting in the twilight verge instead of sleep. The scraps of enchantment hanging about the room—Ciceron magic? Oldmeg had so much as told me outright. And though my eyes were closed, the portal enchantment hung before me in all its marvelous complexity—lighting the darkness inside—a complete, harmonious image as if I had studied it my entire life. As if it were my own.

Oldmeg's humming eased my snarled thinking. Still, I knew that whenever she stopped, the questions these things raised would drive me into territory unimaginably dangerous.

Who and what were the Cicerons? My vision in the Tower said they had once been warriors, wearing their shield openly. More important, I had found them while seeking Aurellians, the ancestors of all pureblood families. Were we kin? And did the Registry know they could work true magic or did they only suspect? If purebloods were not the sole receptacles of the gods' gift of magic, then what were we?

And how was it possible that my magic and this extraordinary artifact were so like? Only the dual bent set me apart from other purebloods. Had others in the past risked madness to retain and wield two bents? My grandsire, the historian, claimed not—my grandsire, who had dared thwart Registry restrictions on my behalf, until he turned on me. . . .

Pale sunlight invaded the Ciceron commons house. The humming had yielded to soft murmurs. A sharp laugh pierced the frigid air . . . and the answer struck me like a spear in the gut.

Xancheira! I sat bolt upright. Threw the itchy rug askew. My bleary eyes were not yet focused, save on the unlikely, astonishing link. Xancheira, my grandfather's last historical investigation. Xancheira, the lost city of elegance, grace, and good governance, whose emblem had been a white tree with exactly five branches . . . something like a white hand with five fingers. Was it madness to think the two emblems were related? Surely it was lunacy to believe that my grandsire's investigation of an ancient massacre and a city that had been wiped from the earth was tangled with Ciceron magic and Registry restrictions and enchanted portals and Danae and cellar prisons.

And yet my life—my whole world—had changed in Montesard, but not when I had lain with Morgan. My small sin had not caused it. While I dallied in the university cloisters, Capatronn had pursued the mystery of Xancheira. And when he rejoined me in Montesard he'd told me *nothing.*

If Bastien was right, he had reported my dalliance himself. He had not only stuck me with a contract where curators could observe me, but he had resigned his post and never pursued an investigation again. Because he was afraid. For me. For himself. For our family. My vision of Tower history had shown me the fear on him as he tried to rip the magic out of me.

I'd thought Pluvius's visit to the Tower cellar a dream, a sign of madness, but what if it wasn't? What had he said to me? *You took something . . . his greatest discovery . . . something of extraordinary significance, something most secret and most dangerous because it propounded a great and terrible historical lie.*

Xancheira. What had Capatronn discovered?

"Are you revived?" Demetreo's braids and dark mustache obscured his expression as he stood over me. Naught could obscure the anxiety in his voice.

"Yes," I said, my emotions surely a match for his. Discovery was so near, my spirit rumbled like approaching thunder. If I could unlock this portal's secrets, the storm might break.

The headman and I were alone in the commons house. The hearth was cold, but the lamps sparkled. The magical portal remained unmasked, its weaving a riot of purples and blues.

"Best be on with the work, then. The coroner will be most annoyed if we keep you much longer. Scouts say Prince Perryn's only a few quellae from Palinur. Betimes, we'll see chaos in the streets and the deadcarts will roll."

And chaos would fall worst on the wretched corners of the city like this.

"Did Bastien send what I asked?"

The headman's expressive chin directed me to the dice players' table. My writing case, an ink horn and cup, and a single sheet of parchment sat waiting.

"And the permission?"

"Given."

"Then I need Oldmeg back here," I said, climbing to my feet. "I want to do her portrait."

"You *what*?" As a sword drawn from its sheath was the headman's true nature laid bare. Sharp-edged and dangerous. "Do you think to take her likeness round the city and see what witnesses make of her? I've heard what you and Bastien do, and you *will not*—"

"The portrait will go nowhere," I said. "It's but a way to access my most powerful magic."

Oldmeg's people believed the mantle of the Goddess Mother enfolded her. And the old woman had spent her life hunting for this place; she believed the portal was her magic to use. I believed that, too; *her* fingers did not burn when she touched it. She would be welcome, as I was not. Not until I proved my worth.

A first principle of historical study: *Impassioned belief* shakes kingdoms. And *belief* was the foundation of a sorcerer's power.

"Let her decide," I said. "If she says no, I'll go and our bargain is finished. Bastien would be pleased."

Demetreo slammed the door as he left the house, but in only a few moments, he returned with Oldmeg. She carried a bowl containing another portion of her tasteless soup. She looked more like Maia, our family cook who had died in the fire, than a temple priestess or a sorceress like my mother.

"Eat before magic working," she said, crinkling her eyes as she appraised my bedraggled turnout. "We'd not wish you to collapse again."

"Maybe after," I said, pushing the bowl aside and pouring ink into my cup. "We've people waiting on us. Sit in your chair." The tall-backed chair would be the symbol of her place in the clan. The bone necklace was likely the same, as was the woven robe she donned as she took her seat. I had placed the chair close to the portal.

"Naema," I said, bowing. "May I touch your hand? It serves—"

"I understand how it serves you." She held out her hand—coarse, dry, chilled, but steady, and when I squeezed it slightly, she squeezed back with an extraordinary grip and a twinkling eye.

With a fervent invocation, I began to sketch the seams and crags that defined the landscape of her face. The curve of her hollow cheek. The checkered brow. The sun creases at the corners of her eyes. The sagging lids above and the smudges of worry and short nights beneath. The heavy braids entirely gray.

A few strokes added the knife that had pricked her hand and mine. She was Ciceron as well as *Naema*.

The fire built inside me.

Even with her seated, I sensed movement in her posture. Alert, not at rest, not in that chair. Age had neither shortened her long legs nor curved her back, nor had time withered her will.

My own will summoned the pent flame in my breast, but before releasing it, I touched the center between my eyes and reinforced the web that linked my two bents. Nothing must be left to chance this hour. My own body as well as hers told me time was short.

For a moment my left hand moved from Oldmeg to the cool bronze arch and the scalding field of light. A radiant enchantment flowed through my arm and joined seamlessly with my bent.

Now! As liquid enchantment surged through my fingers, ready to transfer the true image to the mundane page, I shoved aside concerns of life and breath, mystery and spirit, and when I had reduced all the pieces I had assembled to their most elemental forms—dust and light and magic—I released the raging glory of my art.

"Well, what is it, pureblood? Failed, did you? I never believed this was going to tell us anything."

I passed Demetreo the portrait. He wasn't going to like it. The woman sitting in the chair would know it was true, though. As I did. *Naema*. She had been wrapped in magic and wonder since she was a girl.

The *sengé*'s dusky skin grew as dark as old blood. "A Registry man after all," he snarled. "Only one thing on your mind."

"Show her," I said, louder, where the woman could hear. "Ask her."

"I'll not!"

"You will." No fear or anxiety sullied Oldmeg's command. Perhaps she had felt the truth as I worked. She who had recognized how my magic and that of the portal fit together long before I did. Did anyone in the world comprehend the boundaries of her insight and her skills? If the time was as short as she believed—and the stench of war now assaulted my nostrils, too—then I would have no time to learn. One regret among many.

"You were right about the portal magic, *Naema*," I said, inclining my head to her.

She acknowledged in kind, eyes bright and pleased. For that moment we shared the exquisite sweetness of mystery and magic fulfilled.

Demetreo fought the truth, even as he dropped to his knees beside her chair and passed her the portrait. "He is pureblood, *Naema*. He is *Registry*. He's tricked us and thinks to steal our strength."

But the headman's insistence held no conviction, because he saw her face as I did. Her smile lit the room beyond the magic of the lamps.

One steady hand held the portrait and the other stroked Demetreo's gray-streaked hair. "Will you not stand in the vanguard to save us, boy? Of course you will. Why would you deprive me of the same joy? And, truly, it is not today."

It would be soon, though. There was no discrepancy of age between the woman and her portrait.

Demetreo kept trying to deny the tale of the portrait, even as his expression crumpled into sheerest grief. Oldmeg's joy made sense to me. She had searched for her path for a century.

The woman in the portrait sat straight and unbowed, as regal as any queen on her throne, as assured as the Goddess Mother herself. The knife had not remained sheathed at her waist, but lay in her lap, stained dark with the blood leaking from her wrists and heart—the same that smeared three precise places on the bronze arch. With the light in her eyes almost faded, a throng of people wearing dangling earrings of false gold and ribbons braided in their hair passed through the arch to a landscape we could not see. Beyond the commons house, the hirudo was ablaze. And apart from it all, a man in a half mask and a ragged pureblood cloak sat head on his knees and very much alone.

CHAPTER 26

The gray morning was well advanced by the time I climbed out of the hirudo. Thanks to Oldmeg, strips of dirty linen wrapped my hands, legs, and feet, and the flea-bitten rug was pinned about my shoulders. Thanks to Garen, my mask was in place. Thus protected against cold, threatening rain, and wandering pureblood investigators, I could prepare what to say to Bastien.

He wasn't going to like hearing that I couldn't tell him what I'd done for the Cicerons. Even less that I would be of no use to him this day. Two hours' sleep was not enough after my misadventure in the temple, much less to sustain me past the magic in the hirudo commons house. No enchantment of my working had required so much of me, summoned from so deep. Complex, intricate magic. Wondrous magic. A harmony I'd not felt for a long time, as Oldmeg's joy at the result balanced my own at the doing.

But as I threaded the muddy trenches between nameless graves, long-denied anger swelled in me. What *historical lie* could have driven my grandsire to destroy such a gift? If Capatronn had but trusted me, he might yet be living, for his attempt to excise my second bent had failed, and, as sure as my name, some unexpected detail in a curator's portrait had condemned my family to the fire and me to the dark.

Which ones of the six? Pons was so easy to blame. But Gramphier and Pluvius had witnessed the mutilation of my bent. And Pluvius had dogged me about the Xancheira artifacts, implying he had to destroy them to protect me. On the day I asked Gilles about the "flickering," my town house had burned. Whom had he told? His severe, traditional uncle Albin—or perhaps Damon, who valued loyalty from those beneath him, or Scrutari, who was ever coveting political advantage?

I had to question Pluvius. I had to see those portraits.

"Come back, have you? We were beginning to think you'd turned tail and hared back to your own kind." Garibald waited at the necropolis gates, long arms crossed over his gaunt frame. "Done damage enough, don't you imagine? Sent our runner back here ruint? And consorting with pickthieves and hoors—didn't think the likes of you would stoop even lower than dead-handlers."

Garibald had never been easy around me, but he'd never insulted me to my face. Perhaps the rags I wore made it easy. Perhaps it was the chains awaiting me in the prometheum. My hands clenched, aching to cast some astonishing enchantment to silence him. But discipline was not just for easy times. The sexton was Bastien's man and Garen's friend.

"Garen was brave beyond measure," I said stiffly, as if I wore brocade and fox fur instead of blood and threadbare linen. "His wounding grieves me. I was responsible and I failed him. As for the Cicerons, they saved us both. But then again, their business is none of yours." No stapled tongue in my plans.

Summoning what I could of dignity while wrapped in a rug, I hurried past Garibald through the gate tunnel. Bastien was waiting just inside, a steaming pot about to blow off its lid.

"Please tell me the runner is healing well, Coroner." Might as well get this contentious accounting over with. "Give me a moment to fetch water from the font, and I'll put my feet in your shackles willing and answer all the questions I'm permitted. Just don't ask me to do magic today."

"Insufferable, arrogant dunderwit, marching in as if you own us all."

Teeth clenched over his growl, Bastien grabbed my arm and dragged me around behind the merchant stalls, through a side door, and into Bek's windowless surgery. Only then did he speak again. "I'm sorry to tell you, O high and mighty lordship, that we've a small problem you must deal with right away, lest *I* get hauled off to your Tower and installed in your cellar dungeon or thrown off the top or whatever they do to people like me who *misplace* people like you. Now rid yourself of the rags and wash. You might dip your fingers in that ink horn as well, as I've put him off two hours claiming you're in the midst of sketching corpses out at the Hallow Ground. Summat's told him about my spyhole, so I couldn't claim you were in your regular place. Gods save me, I detest purebloods!"

Purebloods! And I just come from working enchantments for Cicerons after murdering a temple guard while using magic to attempt a burglary. Mighty gods!

A washing bowl and a mostly clean towel waited on Bek's bloodstained surgery table. Blood pounding, I stripped off the rags and the filthy remnants of my temple clothes and scrubbed at face and hands. Shirt and chausses had been left beside the washing things. They were dry, at the least, if not particularly clean or well fitting.

"It's not a group of them, is it?" I said as I fumbled with loops and laces. "Armed servitors in livery?"

"Stop dawdling or I'll drag you in there naked. It's only one and his servant, but I thought he was going to cut off my balls when I dared tell him for the fourth time that he had to wait longer."

Only one and a servant. Not so terrifying. But who? And why?

I pulled on the cheap cloth slippers, then thought better of it and settled for swabbing most of the dirt from my feet. If I'd been in the Hallow Ground, my shoes would be wet and muddy. No time to make these look right. As Bastien locked on my shackles, I ran conveniently ink-stained fingers through my matted hair.

"Enough," said Bastien, shoving me toward the door.

I slipped on my mask and clutched my pen case tightly enough none could notice my hands trembling. Bastien led me through the rotunda and around the right-hand passage. Only one visitor. I'd give three ribs for it to be Pluvius.

But the man in the pureblood cloak who gazed out Bastien's window was shorter than the Master of the Registry Archives, leaner, tidier, and his well-trimmed hair was solidly black. He pivoted sharply as we entered. His ivory silk half mask set off deep olive skin, a long Aurellian nose, and ungraceful ears slightly too big for his head.

"Why in holy Deunor's light does it take two hours for you to sketch a dead *ordinary*?" First Registrar Damon, the second-most-powerful man in the Registry—or third if Gilles's uncle Albin had anything to say about it. An extremely impatient curator. The one I knew least.

Touching fingertips to forehead, I bowed deeply, using the time to swallow my surprise, consider my response, and note the bulky bodyguard beside the door. Perhaps I should bend a knee. But Damon prized personal discipline, so I'd always heard, and discipline included pride and exact protocols as well as proper submission.

Thus I stood up straight and opened one hand to Bastien as if to receive a grant, hoping he would understand.

"You may speak," he said. Not for the first time, I felt thankful that Bastien and not dullwit Garibald had pursued my contract.

"I've had to adjust my technique in working with dead subjects, *domé*. As ever in matters of my contract, I do not withhold or offer less than my best. Though it takes more time than he expected, Coroner Bastien is patient. He, of course, must speak to his—"

"I am not come to this place to investigate contractual matters." The curator tightened his lips and waved a hand to dismiss the subject. I'd have wagered his annoyance was with his own display of annoyance.

Both Bastien and I held our tongues as the curator's silent gaze traveled my length, from my unbound hair to my shackled ankles. He squinted like a man who had spent too much of his life reading in weak light, and his eyes narrowed even tighter when he reached my bare feet.

"Do you allow him no boots, Coroner? You said he was working outdoors. Surely no such deprivation was specified in his restrictions."

"Boots were muddy." Bastien's complexion was far cooler than Damon's. "Bare feet seemed more respectful to your presence than graveyard filth or further delay. I understand he was kept naked in the Tower."

Damon's flush deepened to a new intensity.

Careful, careful! I could not but applaud Bastien's cut, especially as it struck a tender mark. But the line between plain speech and insolence shifted when addressing a curator of the Pureblood Registry, and Damon would not have considered it necessary to inform a mere ordinary of either his name or his rank.

"I would advise a study of respect, Coroner." Damon's clipped tone was cooler than his cheeks. "I will speak to both of you and then to Remeni alone."

Bastien bowed agreement without a hint of apology.

"Perryn of Ardra, the presumptive heir to the throne of Navronne, is but a few days from taking up residence in Palinur. He intends to solidify his support from the Pureblood Registry, the temples, and the Karish hierarchs by participating in various celebrations of Caedmon's Writ of Balance. One of these celebrations will bring the prince to the Registry Tower to offer his condolences on the death of King Eodward's late Royal Archivist, Remeni's grandsire—a historic link between Registry and Crown."

Though my heart's tempo increased, I kept my gaze politely lowered and nodded slightly. Perhaps Pons had failed to mention she had already informed Bastien of the prince's visit to the Tower. Why was a *curator* come to tell me this? That my grandsire had been a favorite of King Eodward would certainly not move the Registry to take sides in the ordinaries' war.

"What concern is that of mine?" said Bastien. "The dead take no holidays for such frivolities."

"Indeed." Damon's nostrils flared. "The prince has requested the curators to deliver a message to Lucian de Remeni-Masson. He is summoned to attend the prince in the Royal Antiquities Repository at fourth hour of the afternoon on the day of the ceremony. The prince wishes to review the historical collection with young Remeni, reminisce about his own youthful encounters with the grandfather, and then travel together to the Registry Tower for the official ceremony."

"No. The contract states—"

"This meeting will *not* happen." Damon cut off Bastien's indignation with the decisive efficiency of a headsman's broadsword. "Remeni is specifically and absolutely forbidden to attend it. The curators would not expose our prospective king to aberrant behavior or distress him with stories of murder or madness within a family he respects so highly. We have informed Prince Perryn that the grandson Remeni has been sent away to recover from a fever."

Cowards! Did they think I would so violate custom by airing their ignominious behavior before Perryn? Even if I'd reason to think the prince would care about my difficulties, I had not forgotten myself so much as that. Whatever was wrong at the Registry was not the king's to put right.

"Do both of you understand and agree?"

"Suits me well," said Bastien. "And my pureblood has no say, so what does it matter if he agrees?"

"*Honor* matters," said Damon, cold now, as if lecturing an idiot child. "Even with madmen. If Remeni says he understands and agrees, I will believe him."

My breath slowed. *Honor? Belief* in what I said? A desire to hear *me* speak? Did he mean it? It seemed so unlikely, yet might explain why he delivered the prohibition in person.

"Well, tell him your thoughts, Servant Remeni," said Bastien, flailing his arms as if to say purebloods were impossible idiots. "I've five more corpses out there need drawing before you're finished for the day."

I looked straight into Damon's eyes, a flagrant breach of protocol, but of all times, this communication must be clear. "Honor and truth matter a great deal to me, *domé*. I understand your message, and in faithful submission to the curators' command, I agree that I will not attend this royal meeting you speak of. My contracted master is my witness in this matter. As is the shade of my late grandsire."

Fitting that Capatronn should be witness to a swearing that was true but not entirely the truth.

Damon did not avert his gaze. Nor did his expression register disapproval—or anything at all—when I refused to drop my own. "I would speak with Remeni privately now, Coroner. The conversation will not concern you, thus I prefer we remove to his studio. I understand it was not entirely secure when my colleagues inspected it, and would ensure it has been improved."

"As you like. We've buttoned up your madman quite fine and keep the shackles on for extra. Show him the way, Remeni. I've work to do here."

I bowed Damon out of the cluttered chamber. The bodyguard remained with Bastien as I led the curator around the passage and up the stair to my little domain. As ever, the hobbles made my progress slow and awkward.

It would have been easy to let expectations rise at a chance to speak with a curator who seemed open to listening, but Bastien said the visitor *knew* of his spyhole. So did Constance and Garibald, Garen, Pleury, and gods knew who else. Whatever we said would be no more private than what was spoken in Bastien's chamber.

Once we were alone, I removed my mask. Damon did not. Clearly, manners were not on his mind. He swept briskly about my little chamber, taking in the shutters, locks, and furnishings.

"Need for the bier is obvious, but what purpose does this other table serve?" he said. "Loose planks and bricks in the chamber of a sorcerer under restriction are not usual. And these materials on the shelf . . ."

"I must lay out my drawings to dry," I said, "and to remain dry until the coroner collects them. The shutters leak, you see, and puddle the floor. The materials on the shelf are cleared away at the end of the day's work, lest I be tempted to corrupt them with wicked enchantment."

His attention reverted sharply to my face. "And are you tempted?"

"To afflict or harm or frighten the people here? Never. To escape this restriction—the shackles, the silkbinding, and the leather mask, which is Magrog's own invention—and the consequences that could result in the end of two most honored bloodlines? Every moment of every day tempts me. But will I ever succumb to that temptation? No. I have sworn on my beloved dead to do what is required of me until I can convince the Registry of my honor, sanity, and innocence. I did not commit the crimes of which I am accused. I am not mad."

More bitterness had spilled out than I intended. He would likely disapprove. But to speak my truth at last to a *pureblood* was irresistible. I certainly would not weep or grovel, not to one of those who had put me here. Perhaps only two or three of the curators had conspired in my downfall, but I trusted none of them.

Damon made no answer in either words or expression. Instead he took down the leather mask, attempting to flex it—an impossibility. He riffled the stack of parchment and unstoppered the ink horn and sniffed at it. Again, no comment. Then he rejoined me in the center of the chamber, standing uncomfortably close—close enough I could smell wine and garlic on his breath and the perfume covering his body's odors.

Perhaps he hoped to intimidate me. Perhaps it was merely to allow a weak-sighted man to gauge the nuances of my expression. I did not retreat.

"My colleagues are divided on many matters, including your future. Several believe you more trouble than your life is worth. At least one of our six, maybe more, believes you would make a fine pet in a very dark cage."

The phrases were tossed out like scraps, without feeling. Foolish that they could churn my bowels and chill my skin so; he spoke naught beyond what my night terrors conjured.

"One of us is convinced that your back will be a stepping-stone to a position of authority—the preeminent position of authority among our kind."

Would that be Albin, aiming to replace Damon as Gramphier's successor? Why would my life or death aid such an ambition?

Damon continued. "Several would prefer that you walk free and justified, yet are willing to see you dead for their own causes. All see you as dangerous; two believe you are the most fearsome danger to our way of life that has ever existed."

My asking would certainly not affect his choice to tell me which curator believed what. Yet his pokes struck steel inside me. How dare he dismiss my life, my bloodlines, or my young sister, whose fate none of my Registry visitors had deigned to mention, in so flippant a manner?

"Explain this to me, *domé*," I said. "Tell me why I am a danger to anyone or of any use in a cage. Tell me why I deserve death."

Not for murdering a pureblood. If my sister had done as I commanded her, then Damon surely knew that charge was false. Yet to admit that *I* knew Juli lived was to imply collusion, putting her and Bastien at risk. I bit my tongue before I could lose control of it and waited for an answer.

Not a blink or a word acknowledged my outburst. "Your life hangs by a thread, *plebeiu*. Each day a thinner thread. Even in this chamber."

He twirled a finger and lowered his voice, but not so low a spy would fail to hear every word. "I am included among these partisans I've outlined, certainly."

An exquisite enchantment settled over and around me like tendrils of steam from Arrosa's baths. As mists and fogs distort sight, so did these fogs distort my hearing, so that I could scarce distinguish which words my ears heard and which were laid upon me so delicately that they must be absorbed through my skin.

"But I have not declared my opinions to the others. I know you only by hearsay, thus decided to come see for myself."

A cold dismissal, but at the very same time I heard him say, *"But some among my colleagues have dispatched me with a proposal that might preserve both your life and bloodlines. You would be required to leave Palinur for at least a year to reside in a house of healing and reflection. It is a strict house, known but to a few. You would voluntarily submit to the rules and practices of the masters there, as you do for this ordinary."*

No matter this strange dual message, no matter my resolution, I could not stay silent. "Coroner Bastien has enforced his agreement with exactitude, and I have obeyed every restriction the curators imposed. Save for particular instances of my master's business, I exist entirely in this room, shackled. I have written no letters, begged no relief, served this humiliating contract in every nuance, and worked no magic without my master's permission. What further submission could you possibly require? Must I walk into my own cage?"

My speech took on a different quality, as if it, too, occurred on some other plane of hearing, some phrases audible to anyone, some floating in the air where only Damon could grasp them.

My spirit heard him continue. *"It is not the Tower cellar we offer. It is not a cage. For your safety, none but those who send you will know where you are. The Registry will name you* recondeur, *but because of the nature of your submission, your good name and family honor will be restored on your return."*

Run away and reap no consequence? What fool would believe that?

"Your behavior will determine which faction earns my support," he said . . . or so my ears heard. "It has been decided that you must willingly forgo all use of your bent."

"*Forgo?* Stop? Break my vows . . . my contract? Never to use—?"

Shock and disbelief left me stuttering. To be forbidden magic as a punishment was terrible enough, but to stop of my own will?

A savage fury rose from my belly and infused my veins and sinews, setting my hands trembling, threatening to shatter every remnant of self-control. Perhaps that's what he wanted: an excuse to haul me away. I could not give him the pleasure, so I did not call him the spawn of Magrog or a rock-headed fool; I did not even yell, but snapped my words quietly like dry sticks. "You would have me dead by my own hand, *domé*. I will *not* do that. My gift is from the hand of the gods. I cannot—will not—abandon it."

A flick of Damon's hand, heavy with gold and gemstones, dismissed my outrage. "This necropolis is not secure enough to contain a sorcerer of aberrant mind—one capable of kin murder. Your choices are severely limited. If Coroner Bastien's contract is revoked, your future will certainly be meted out on much crueler terms."

And in that other place, he added, *"Consider the opportunity. When the time is right—and only at that time—two men will present the stipulations of the house of healing and ask if you will accept and abide by them. Refuse and you give up the chance for all time."*

Without ceremony or additional word, he departed, leaving me speechless with fury and frustration. If he wished me dead, then how better to entice me into incaution than suggesting conspiracies at every hand? If he were the one who wished me in a cage, he had served up the very plan to accomplish it. He must think me an idiot even to propose such a scheme. Yet his warning was chillingly real. If one of the most powerful men in the Registry reported that Bastien's restrictions were inadequate, the contract would be voided and I would be returned to the cellar. Why would he bother to give me a choice if the end was the same? And if not the same, as he claimed, then what in Deunor's mighty name was it?

Great gods, if I only knew more about the man, about the Registry's secrets and lies, and about what, in the name of all gods, this *proposal* meant and who it was had proposed it. Was giving up my bent a condition of this house of healing, too, or just the goad to make me choose it? Did Pons know? Did Gramphier, a man of passions that only my grandsire had seen? Or did blathering, ineffectual Pluvius?

Heavy footsteps raced up the stair, warning of a more immediate problem. I chose to make my stand beside the window, unlatching the shutters and pulling them open. I could always jump out head first if need be.

CHAPTER 27

The coroner's rant began before he was fully in the room. "An invitation to stand in a room with Prince Perryn himself and you *swore* not to go? You vowed it on your family, you damnable cretin, and I know what that means. I should have expected it after last night's farce. Solving the lily child's murder is *my* part of our bargain, so who cares if you fumble away a chance to make right your blundering?" His meaty finger shook, accusing. "You've a glib tongue on you when you want. You could have found a way. But perhaps you've decided to throw in your lot with Demetreo and his band of murdering knife throwers now you're so friendly."

"Are we alone?" I couldn't have him gabbling about our agreement with the Cicerons in front of a spy.

But he paced in tight circles, ignoring me entire. "Did Demetreo provide you a fresh corpse, so you could draw his picture with my ink and dance off with the Danae, leaving the rest of us to bleed for you like Garen did? Was that what the white hand was all about? Or were all your tales meant to confuse an ordinary too stupid to understand magical marvels?"

"We shouldn't—I can't talk about—"

He threw his hands up. "Well, of course, you can't talk about what you did for them, nor what secrets you learned, because all I'm here for is to pay for you to do favors for damnable Cicerons!"

"Bastien, listen to—"

"I should chase down that Registry prick and tell him to take you. Let them bury you alive or chop off your hands or whatever they want."

"By the name of every god in this universe, Bastien, will you just shut off this self-pitying nonsense and *listen*?"

My bull's bellowing stopped him in mid rant.

"First and most important, can we speak *freely*?" I swirled my eyes around the room.

A brief puzzled squint and understanding dissolved his angry frown. Then he bolted from the chamber as if I'd stabbed him in the backside with one of my pens.

The hard slam of a door and the rattling of keys jostled the ink horn standing in its holder on the shelf. An examination of the ugly and ornate brackets that held the shelf would surely reveal the elusive spyhole.

Bastien returned, the patches of skin revealed by his bristling facial hair only a modest crimson. "Don't think you've—"

"Clearly you didn't listen to me in front of our visitor." I spoke quietly, but with all the forceful clarity I knew how. "You taught me well to think around a problem and be careful with my words. If you had *listened*, you would have heard me foreswear only one particular meeting. We will accept Prince Perryn's kind invitation, just not at the time of his choosing. I've not a notion in the world why Perryn would want to meet with me, unless he thinks a Remeni would be a prestigious escort to the Tower ceremony. We mustn't let him find out that it's not true anymore, so we'll have to be careful on our approach . . ."

Bastien opened his mouth, but I didn't let him start, hoping to get through everything I had to tell him before his tongue blistered me again.

". . . and we will only venture the visit when we know the right questions to ask. I'm so very sorry Garen was hurt so badly. I pray he'll be well and wish with everything in me that I knew some magic to ease him. But, Bastien, our venture was not so much a failure as I first thought. Though I can't speak of last night"—I held up a hand to keep him silent—"Just listen! What I did for Demetreo—a portrait, yes, and for now I'm sworn on my honor and the prospect of a stapled tongue to keep it secret—made me believe in what I do with my dual bent. More deeply, more certainly than before. I think the curators are afraid of me."

It sounded prideful, but I didn't feel so. Damon's outlandish proposal had confirmed my suspicion: My bent was what bothered them.

"You don't know—"

"Please *listen* to me." Now I'd cracked this skin of detachment that I'd grown over six-and-twenty years, I could not seal it up again. "I've pronounced the words my whole life: Magic is a gift of the gods or nature or whatever greater power can bestow or withhold such benefices in a man's blood. I have accepted that with my entire being, shaped my life around it. If my parents or some aunt or uncle had argued convincingly that my magic was not divine, but merely elicited impressions from my own senses, I would have believed that, too, and still considered it a gift worth the discipline demanded to use it well.

"But now this gift has transported me to a place I've never been. Has made me feel sensations that belong to other bodies. Has shown me truths I could not possibly know. And, yes, I learned something new from Demetreo that I cannot reveal without betraying my oath to him."

I had recorded an event that had not yet occurred and believed in my every bone and sinew that it would come to pass.

"The responsibility of this power fills me with such awe I can scarce breathe, and such dread I don't know where to turn. They're going to kill me, Bastien. Or they're going to lock me in a cage. Or they're going to force me to run. That's what our pureblood visitor came to tell me."

"So you're actually going to speak about this prickly fellow came today and his square-headed henchman who sat on me like Magrog's own fiend?" Though not yet ready to relinquish his fury, Bastien could produce little more than a harrumph and a sour breath. "He was no simple messenger boy."

"No. No messenger boy," I said. "Our discipline forbids me speak of him or our conversation."

Stupid even to consider such rules when I had been skirting the law with Bastien since my release—speaking to him of curators' portraits and family matters, urging Juli to a great lie. But transgression did not unravel the value or meaning of law. Registry discipline had been a foundation of my family, prescribing how we honored and worked with each other, as much a part of me as how I ate, how I walked, the very languages I spoke. I believed Bastien and I had been born to different purposes in this life and that my place required certain things of me, no matter that they felt awkward or difficult or unkind. Yet, my master . . . my partner . . . needed to know what danger he faced.

"But I'll speak of them anyway."

Damon was different from the others. For good or ill, he had listened to me; Bastien had likely noticed that, too. And he had done his strange magic to communicate out of public hearing, which confirmed that the dissent among the curators made him wary. I just didn't know whether that made matters better or worse for us.

"His name is Damon. He is a curator. I don't know him well, but he is immensely powerful and we disregard him at our peril. I think he prefers the running to the axe or the cage. But I can't run. I won't. Juli remains in their hands, and she would suffer for my rebellion. And if the slightest whiff of collaboration clings to you, then you and Constance, Garibald, Garen—all of you here—will die, no matter what the outcome for me. It's not right that it should be so, but it is."

He could not be more astonished at my words than I was.

"You have to be wary, Bastien. To prepare."

Bastien had settled on my stool. "Go on," he said quietly. "None can hear us."

Shaking off anger and horror, I bent my mind to the present and matters I could control. To learn who my enemies were I needed Bastien, and I already owed him my help.

"I've got to find out what's going on before one faction or the other wins out," I said. "But we have a problem here at Caton. My ruse at the temple didn't work as well as we planned because Irinyi was *expecting* something to happen last night. She said she had been warned about a Registry spy. She had a duc from the Ardran court there with a cadre of at least twenty armed men. They were not there to bathe. Someone has been carrying tales."

"A spy here?" he murmured. Voice and body spoke denial.

But my spirit was sorely frayed and I couldn't allow it. "Think! The curators told me that someone reported the hour I left the necropolis on the night my house burned. That departure time became evidence to condemn me. At first I assumed some Ciceron had sold them the information, but how would the true villain know I wouldn't interrupt his setting the fire? What if the spy told someone that I would be on an errand from you once I left here? It gave the murderer ample opportunity to make it seem as if I had come home and set the fire myself."

"It must be someone else." A weaker protest. "Only a few knew what you were about."

"I told you about the shadows and dreams I had in the cellar, how they were always trying to get me to draw. What if those were no dreams? What if someone from here had reported that my presence flickered when

I worked, that you felt it necessary to move me inside the prometheum to avoid alarming your patrons? And then I stupidly mentioned the very same thing to Gilles. Would they have believed such a thing possible if I'd only posed the question, or was it the two events together that convinced them? Because the night after I so stupidly asked the question, someone made me responsible for a crime so terrible that I could never again walk free."

Someone who wanted me in a cage, perhaps, or someone who considered me *the most fearsome danger to our way of life that had ever existed.* Or someone who wanted me to run away to . . . what? A madhouse?

Bastien's hand plowed the forest of hair and beard slowly. "Five years at the least I've known most of them—the runners, the scrubwomen, the diggers," he said, softly, "and Garibald and Constance for more than a dozen. I'd trust my life to any one of them." He glanced up to the shelf and its suspicious brackets. "But you've made a case worthy of my inquest chamber."

I did not tell him about Constance's gossip with Demetreo in exchange for *necessaries* in my first days here. She had freely admitted her offense and promised to keep my business private. Even then, I had believed her. Knowing her better, knowing how she valued her position and flourished in it, I was even more convinced. I had sworn silence on the matter, and until I had more evidence against her I'd keep my word. Bastien would look at his people fairly.

"Damon himself warned me that someone might be listening."

"I've locked the closet where I sit to watch you. Not even Constance has a key to it. I'll get back the key to this chamber, too. Constance and Garibald keep it, but they pass it around when there's need. I'll find the spy."

"Then I'll leave the matter to you," I said, relieved that he believed me. "Because I've got to tell you about the temple. . . ."

Bastien was up and pacing by the end of the tale. I could almost feel the heat of his racing mind. "A *duc* from the Ardran court, ready to pounce. He was wearing Ardran colors, then—those of Perryn's household, not his own?"

"Yes, but he's not our murderer."

"Why not? Bayard or Osriel might suborn just such a man. How many lords come running at a temple priestess's beck? Perhaps one who frequented that temple. One who owed her favors. So who was he?"

"Never heard a name," I said, trying to recall everything about the man I'd seen with Irinyi. "Never saw his boots. But the nobleman with the priestess was no bigger than me. Yes, he was hairy—black-haired with a beard. But I can't see even a child calling him big."

"You're sure she said he was big?"

I closed my eyes for a moment, recalling the interview in the tepidarium with the forlorn little sweeping girl. "She said, 'He were dark and hairy, as Fleure always told me . . . and his boots were shined like a black mirror glass. I called him—' " My palm slapped my aching forehead. "Aagh, that must be where the image of the bear came from. Gab named the murderer the Bear Lord with Shiny Boots. I assumed that meant frightening and hairy and . . . big. The knife teeth could signify he murdered her."

"So, we've a starting place. A duc of the Ardran household. There's only five. Noplessi is old as the sea and bent like a spoon; he's been there since before Eodward. The others—Marcout, Tremayne, Vuscherin, and Comlier—I know the names but not the men. But he'd be dark, hairy, bearish. . . . Maybe *big.* Maybe not so much. If you're going to be a witness, you must be precise. But we can find him. My runners know how to talk to servants, tinkers, grooms—them that will know."

"One of your runners *did* talk to servants. Is he—?" Bone-deep weariness shoved aside every other thought save the consequences of the night's failure. "Great gods, Bastien, why did you send someone so important to you on a temple burglary with an inept sorcerer?"

He folded his arms and propped himself on the bier. " 'Tis not my way to tell Garen what he can and cannot do. I'm neither his da nor his wife nor his jailer. You needed someone. I chose our best for the job and asked if he was willing. He wanted to go. As for what you did . . . he told me. How you got him out through the drain tunnel, down that damnable wall. How you killed a man to save him. 'Twas your first, wasn't it? And I'd guess it's hit you wicked hard."

Too tired to shut out the memory of rubbery flesh and spilling blood any longer, I couldn't stop my hands from knotting or my thumbs from trying to wipe them clean. Bile stung my throat, and I had to swallow multiple times before I could speak without disgracing myself further. When I had more time to dwell on it, *wicked hard* might be too mild a description. "More than I expected."

"Good. It shouldn't be easy." He paused, continuing only when I'd gulped in enough air to suppress the urge to spew. "But mostly we don't have time to go through all the rights and wrongs of a deed. We have to trust our nature. If our nature makes us lash out too easy, we have to tame it. But if our nature prevents us saving a good man's life, then we'd best examine what we believe. I doubt you have a murderer's nature, Servant Remeni."

"Never thought I did." But then I'd never thought lies could be such a part of me, either . . . or madness or such deep-rooted panic at losing everything of importance to me.

"Once I spent my spleen, I would have told you how it was with Garen and me. Some don't hold with our way, but it's our business, not theirs. Figured you, of all men, would understand that. But I lost one like him years ago, and seeing this'n bloodied threw me off the cliff a bit."

"I swore I'd bring him back unharmed. I tried, but—"

"And so you did." From behind his sand-colored thatch beamed a smirk. "I've a stone cot a quellé or so out the back gates. Near had to lock the young fool in this morning to make him stay abed, but his worst injury is that an *older fellow* like you, brought up soft, had to carry him out. Mayhap I'll go ask if he ferreted out anything about the temple's noble visitor."

Relief shone a bit of sunlight on the day. "Good . . . most excellent."

"So, what do we do about all this?"

"Keeping me locked away will be good. Make sure all who work here know you do it. Watch your own back and keep a clear head."

Stillness fell over him. Shame and guilt and no small amount of anger that a decent man and his friends sat in such danger at the hands of purebloods kept my eyes averted. My bones felt like lead; my spirit hollow. The straw mattress lay in the corner like the gods' own sanctuary.

Drawn as if by enchantment, I hobbled toward the pallet, chains rattling on the stone. "With your permission, Master Bastien, I'm going to sleep for a while. If you wake me while there's still light, I could likely do a drawing or two. But instead, I might suggest we concentrate on our plan to catch Fleure's murderer. I would very much like to accomplish that before doom falls."

I felt his eyes on my back. "Aye. A good notion."

The stool scraped on the stone, and his footsteps crossed the room, pausing when he reached the door. "You'd best watch your insolent tongue, Servant Remeni, bossing me around and all," he said. "What did you mean, *self-pitying babble*?"

A gust of wind rattled the shutters, as if all the pent anger in the chamber wriggled its way out. I curled up on the straw mat and pulled the thin blanket to my chin, an unlikely grin teasing at my lips. "As you noted early on, I've become quite familiar with self-pity," I said between yawns. "I can recognize it in all its forms. You have perfected one particular variety—the *this idiot was brought up rich and coddled and gifted with magic, while I had to scrabble and work and skirt the law for everything I've got, and where's the justice in that, so I'm just going to yell at him and make sure he is shamed by his pomposity and show him that he's not the only one in this world with a mind* variety. You've made the point very clear. Thus you can just stop pummeling me with it. Elsewise I might devise an enchantment that will give you boils, so young Garen will never look at you in that unseemly fashion ever again."

I believe he laughed. And locked me up securely on his way out. But in truth, I knew nothing more for a very long time.

"Tremayne. Laurent de Buld, Duc de Tremayne."

I tried to parse the odd words that yanked me out of a sound sleep, riffling through every Navron and Aurellian dialect my tutors had ground into me. When none fit, I rolled over to bury the problem in my pillows and got distracted. No pillows. A thin, scratchy, pricking thing lay under me instead of herb-sweetened linen and a great bolt of feathers. And the room was horribly damp and chill. "Giaco! What are you—?"

"Attend, pureblood! The lily-child's murderer, we've learnt his name. Laurent de Buld, Duc de Tremayne and *consiliar prime* of the Prince of Ardra's household. He's the man who wipes Prince Perryn's ass." Bastien stood over me like the messenger of doom.

The lily child . . . a would-be king's murdered bastard. And Giaco was not waiting to bring me a tisane or to bathe and dress me, but had burnt to death in his bed.

I sat up and rubbed my head vigorously, shoving the scattered fragments of dream, memory, and grief into their proper places. "The bear . . . you found him?"

"Garen told me a noble's body servant was pawing at one of the temple girls who was in and out of the waiting room with messages. Garen stepped out to speak a word with her, saying she should report the man's ill behavior. She told him who was the fellow's master and how he came round now and again, being great friends with the high priestess, so's the girl didn't dare complain. The Duc de Tremayne, he was."

I pulled the blanket around my shoulders. The tail of it was sodden.

The deluge drumming on the shutters had puddled half the floor. How long had I slept?

"Seems flimsy," I said. "Like I told you, the noble with Irinyi on the stair was no *bear* of a man."

"While you lolled here most of the day, I sent runners to ask around the market and the districts where ducs are known. Reports say Tremayne is smallish and tight-bodied, but hairy as a black goat and fanatical about his boot polish. Were it only that I'd still have doubts, but the image struck me as more than a child's impression of a man. So I sent Pleury looking for something else. Our clever lad twinked this from a goldsmith in the Council District. Seems the fellow crafted a new ring for the Duc de Tremayne not a tenmonth ago. . . ."

From his jaque Bastien whipped out a small sketch of a nobleman's blazon—the heart of the family's arms. The device was a rampant bear, a bouquet of bristling knives in its mouth.

I sat up straight, all torpor banished. "Deunor's fire! We've got him!"

"No. We don't." Bastien's biting denial quenched my flaring excitement like a pail of slush. "Tremayne's as rich as a pureblood, with a young wife kin to half the nobles in Ardra and two formidable sons by his first wife. Between the duc, the two sons, and the wife's kin, they've enough men-at-arms that Perryn can never, ever in the world give up the bloody villain to hang for murder."

Bastien's foot shoved the studio door shut with such a bone-shaking thud the iron slab almost passed through its frame to fall out the other side.

"But we've witnesses now," I said to his broad back. "Gab. The servant Garen spoke to. Others in the temple could witness to Tremayne's presence on the night of the murder."

"And what weight would such testimony hold against a drowning prince's lifeline, when that prince sees his brother's legions bearing down on his royal city? None. Not even when that prince is Eodward's noblest son."

That we could know who committed such a crime and have no way to see justice done was outrageous. There had to be a way.

"What of the child's mother? Do we know who she might be? We don't even know Fleure's real name." Irinyi would know, but a priestess could not be forced to testify without incontrovertible proof of her own crime.

"We've one possible lead, again from Pleury. He was talking with a scullion from the palace whose mam was wet nurse for Prince Perryn's own children. When Pleury asked her if her mam suckled other nobles' babes, the girl said she did, and mentioned that the woman had even been called in by Prince Perryn's mistresses a time or two, as her milk set so well with his blood. Pleury's thinking to talk to the wet nurse herself tonight when she goes home. I'm leery of it, though. It's a risk to prance around the noble districts, talking of a prince's mistresses and a dead bastard. Purebloods, if they gave a pig's snout about a dead ordinary, might live through such a folly, but not the rest of us with heads less protected."

A certain desperation possessed me, inspired by the doom-saying Cicerons and Curator Damon's threat. The time to accomplish anything of worth was so short. "What of the other dead children? I could copy their portraits and brush out the royal lilies. If we could learn their names . . . find witnesses to their deaths . . ."

But Bastien denied me even as I babbled. "Don't you see?" he said, when my arguments ran dry. "Were the shades of all five dead bastards pointing their bony fingers at Tremayne 'twouldn't make no difference to the outcome. No matter his own character, Perryn needs his every ally. I was hoping we'd come on a weaker man, one out of favor or—I don't know. It was ever a fool's hope. If only you were— Pssh!"

Words could not encompass his frustration. Nor mine. In any other circumstance Bastien could hold his inquest on the steps of the palace, because the testimony of my bent would be unassailable. But not if my own kind proclaimed me mad.

Rain dribbled around the shutters and spattered on the floor, the quiet sounds not peaceful but infuriating as they emphasized our dearth of ideas. Bastien strode round the chamber, his jaw like rock.

"Perryn must be told his own servant is a murderer," I said at last. "Tremayne is surely a spy—Prince Bayard's or the Harrower priestess's—which means Perryn's *legitimate* heirs could be next in line for poison or strangling or trampling. How could an honorable prince, Eodward's noblest son, ignore the death cries of his own blood? With your persuasion and my magic, we can convince him to give up Tremayne. If he's not honorable . . . well, then we'll know."

"And we'll be dead as well." Bastien kept walking. A determined hammering on the door halted him midstride.

"Coroner, come out!" It was Constance banging and rattling the latch.

Bastien rolled his eyes and yanked the door open. "How thick-headed are you, draggletail? I told you never to interrupt me here."

Constance, hair lank and garments dripping, did not flinch. She was quivering with excitement, the smoking torch in her hand not half so fiery as the spark in her colorless eyes. "Get to the wall and lay your eyeballs on what's come. Him as is in there with you might ought to see, as well."

Without a question Bastien unlocked my shackles and jerked his head to the door. I grabbed my mask and my already damp blanket and followed them down the stairs, through the deserted prometheum, and across the lane to the eastern wall.

The necropolis walls weren't thick enough for a wall walk. Who would need to guard a city of the dead? But every few hundred quercae of the wall's length, a stone stair led up to a height where one could reach one of the stone cauldrons mounted atop the wall.

I doubted Garibald's linkboys ever had occasion to light the cauldrons; the quantity of oil needed for such grandeur would far outreach any but a king's funeral fees. But as the gray afternoon lapsed into rainy night, surely everyone who worked in the necropolis crowded the stairs or perched on the wall, looking out. Eerily quiet. Even the rain seemed to tiptoe across the dirt lane and the courtyards.

"Move aside!" Bastien's command split the air like a lightning flash.

Linkboys and washing girls scrambled away or jumped from the sides of the steps to make way.

Clutching the damp wool about my shoulders, I hurried behind him up the nearest stair. The view beyond the wall took my breath.

The land fell away quickly from the plateau where the necropolis stood. Below us the rolling hills of Ardra lay as soft and smooth as women's breasts. Rivers of torchlight flowed through the pooled night between the hills, a gathering flood as they neared the eastern gates off to our right beyond the tarry canyon of the hirudo. I had never seen so many torches. Thousands.

As we gaped, a deep and throaty roar rolled through that throng and a fanfare of trumpets blared welcome and warnings to every creature with ears to hear them. Perryn of Ardra had come home, dragging with him his battle-weary legions and his war.

Part IV
Harsh Magic

CHAPTER 28

If the rest of the morning's plan was going to proceed as badly as its beginning, Bastien and I might as well skip our meeting with Prince Perryn and offer ourselves straight up to the local hangman.

"Look out!" In a single deft move, Bastien dodged a rattling dung cart, shouldered me out of its way, and sent it careening down the steep lane. The erstwhile driver of the cart grappled in the mud with the fool who had tried to steal the stinking rattletrap.

I hoped both thief and drover drowned in the cold muck. I hoped the cart flattened a few of the drunken louts whose pawing, vomiting riot had caused us to lose two hours on our way to the palace and my meeting with Perryn of Ardra. We were almost out of time.

Five days since Perryn had marched into Palinur, and he had yet to impose any sort of order. He could not have picked a worse month to make a stand in his royal city, when the long winter had depleted meager stores and famine dug its claws into every citizen's belly. My own gut ground its sides together, raw from naught but a lump of pignut bread.

And to shut thousands of soldiers behind city walls after months in the field was madness. Amid the cartloads of pikemen dead from battle wounds and the increasing numbers of the diseased and starvelings were hundreds dead from riots and no few from licentious usage.

Matters would certainly be worse if the Prince's thuggish elder brother took the city or, gods save us all, if Sila Diaglou and her Harrowers grew bolder than they were already. Garen and Pleury reported the Harrowers wore their orange scarves openly, demanding sacrifice, destruction, and burning to appease their angry Gehoum. Rumor had both brother prince and priestess racing toward Palinur like wolves toward a wounded buck.

Most citizens of Palinur blamed Perryn's generals, his soldiers, or his Guard Royale for their terror, thereby fueling the constant brawls between townsmen and soldiers; others blamed the Elder Gods, the Karish god Iero, twistminds, or witches. None blamed Perryn. Good Eodward's fair-haired middle son held all their hopes. And ours.

We squeezed past the thief's dull-eyed brood. Bastien's powerful elbow battered a reeling thug into the wall, clearing us a path through the narrow alley. His sword had been in and out of its sheath so often, I expected to see the leather charred.

"Damn and blast, Lucian, can't you do something?"

"No." I kicked a clawing hand from my ankle and yanked my rucksack from a hard-eyed woman's grasp. "I can't. Not unless we're desperate."

Over and over I'd reminded Bastien: *no magic.* If we were to expose a murderer this day and live to see him hang, then I needed to hoard every scrap of my power. Nor did I dare call attention to us. In blatant violation of law and custom, I wore no mask and no cloak of a pureblood's claret hue, but a hooded cape of dingy brown. In part, this was to deceive our necropolis spy; we had sneaked out of the necropolis gates in a flood of mourners. But my disguise was also meant to save us trouble weightier than an unruly mob. Until order was restored in the lower city, I could not count on fear- or drink-maddened fools to let a lone pureblood pass without challenge. To stop and teach idiots the law would cause more delay we could not afford and grab Registry attention.

We'd thought we had more time. But early that morning, Bastien's runners had brought in two critical tidbits of gossip. First, despite the continued unrest, the Prince of Ardra's conciliatory venture to the Registry Tower—and thus my long-awaited opportunity to see the curators' portraits—was set for the morrow. Second, Perryn was feasting with his household knights at midday. Such a meal could extend long into the night. If Fleure and her half siblings were to have justice, it had to be now.

Both purebloods and ordinaries would call us lunatics to pursue a resolution so small amid the agonies of a kingdom. Yet the cause of a few dead children had become the cause of Navronne and the cause of a good man.

The noble line of Caedmon and Eodward was at risk, and Bastien believed the case would tell the tale of his worth.

The Registry would say I had no business risking my safety for either cause. And yet my venture into the Registry Tower on the morrow was where the truer danger lay. I hoped the curators' portraits would tell me who had murdered my family and why, but my chances of evading capture were wickedly small. If my fate was imprisonment, whether in the Tower cellar or Damon's mysterious house of reflection, even one small success in the cause of right might make the future bearable. Besides, a Remeni always fulfilled his contracts.

And so with brazen foolery we'd set out for Perryn's palace, not knowing if we could so much as get past his gates. Faith in Bastien's sword, my magic, and good Eodward's blood that flowed in Perryn's veins had brought us this far. We were determined the riot would not turn us back.

"Not that way!" I grabbed Bastien's arm as he turned into a refuse-choked lane that led toward the *pocardon*. "We save half the distance if we cross the Council District instead of the market, and you'll not have to fight our way through. Believe me, no one will bother us today."

Skeptical, Bastien snorted. But he followed me up a long stair toward the city's fairest heights.

The chaos of the streets fell away with every worn step. By the time we reached the top of the stair, one would think we'd traveled to a fortunate land that had never heard of war or beggary. A tree-shrouded lane followed the winding course of an ancient wall. Behind the wall, sheltered by trees and spacious gardens, great houses sprawled so that every chamber could catch the fairest breezes of Ardran summers. Purebloods, high-ranking clerics, and members of the royal household occupied these grand estates, built by our Aurellian ancestors two centuries past.

"Oughtn't be up here," said Bastien, shifting his shoulders uneasily.

"Everyone who lives here will either have left the city already or be holed up behind magical wards or private armies. And we *must* make ourselves presentable. There's a perfect place along our way." As he was just now, guards would sooner throw Bastien into a pigsty than admit him into the house of Navronne's kings.

The hoary wall was far older than the houses. A few hundred paces from the head of the stair, it was interrupted by a knob of native rock. Water bubbled from a moss-lined notch in the rock into a pool the size of a wide-brimmed hat. Palinur lore said that the pool, called the Aingerou's Font, never dried up and never froze, and that every spring a different variety of flower grew out of the cracks in the rock. Perhaps so; perhaps not. No enchantments lurked there. Nonetheless, it was a pleasant place, an islet of peace in the noisy city. Before the weather had taken its wretched turn, I'd often sat and sketched the views or the passersby or the font itself—something other than pureblood faces.

Glancing nervously from side to side, Bastien scrubbed at his hands, face, and hair, then dabbed at his leather jaque, but only succeeded in grinding the filth into it. With a grumbled curse, he pulled it off.

"Best wear it," I said, pointing to the left side of his ancient green velvet tunic. The seam must have given way in his wrestling match.

Meanwhile, I switched the ugly cape for a mask and the fine wool grave wrapping Constance had spent five days cleaning, dying, and stitching into the semblance of a pureblood cloak. It had been too late to keep my Tower visit secret, though Bastien swore fifty times that he himself could sooner be our spy than Constance. He refused to believe any of Caton's people could betray him. But he'd also made sure no one knew of *this* day's venture.

"Let's get out of here," said Bastien, his gaze flicking from shrubbery to either direction of the deserted lane. "This place gives me the willies."

"I'll be quick." I dipped my own hands in the clear water, astonishingly unsullied by Bastien's mud.

"Aagh! Magrog's fiends!" I clamped my hands under my arms. Hard.

"What's wrong?"

"Don't know," I said. "Water felt like acid."

I stared at the little font. I'd drunk that water fifty times. Splashed my face on a long-ago day when the sun burned hot. Why would it affect me in exactly the same manner as the White Hand portal in the hirudo? As if I were forbidden to use it anymore.

The tower bells rang the half hour. Bastien shouldered the rucksack and nudged my arm. "We've got to go. Once Perryn sits down with his knights, we'll never get a hearing."

Indeed. I dipped a corner of my cloak in the font and used it to dab at my hands. No sting. And then I slipped my father's ruby ring onto my finger. What pureblood would appear at court without a single jewel?

To my sorrow the light of my father's enchantments that had once instilled a richness to the ruby's blood-red heart had faded. Though only to be expected, it struck me hard. As we hurried toward the palace, I could not shake off a sense of profound estrangement, as if the world I knew had taken some path without me. As if I had somehow become disconnected from my own self. What had Pons told me? *You are a deviant soul, Lucian de Remeni-Masson. . . . You have no place in this world.*

"The prince expressed a particular wish to meet with me in the Antiquities Repository *before* his visit to the Registry Tower," I said to Hugh de Orrin, the court functionary summoned to the palace gate. "Inform His Grace that the gods have healed all trace of my illness. As the divinities so clearly favor the Prince of Ardra in this sorry conflict, I took that as a sign that I should heed his invitation immediately on my return to Palinur. *And*"—the properly deferential young man had bowed and half turned away—"my man must be brought immediately into the bailey and offered suitable refreshment. Fail in this and I shall take it as a personal insult as well as interference in my business."

"Of course, *Domé* Remeni. As you say." Orrin failed to mask his disapproval. "Yet I must repeat that even for one of the gods' chosen from such a noble house as your own, an unscheduled audience is extremely unlikely. I'm sure His Grace will arrange to meet with you another time at a place of his choosing."

The gate guards had escorted me to a waiting room inside the palace's west gate and comfortably out of the damp wind. But they had looked askance at my dead men's finery and Bastien's rough turnout and insisted my servant remain outside the walls. I didn't like it. No riots had erupted so near the palace, but the approaches teemed with nervous men-at-arms, gossips, and brazen thieves. Any one of them could be a spy. We couldn't afford for Bastien to be caught up in a fight.

My fingers tingled with magic as I readied a simple illusion of fog and fearsome noises. Magic might keep us safe, but only if we were together.

Anxiety would not let me sit on the padded bench, but I commanded my feet not to pace and my hands to stay relaxed at my back. The bells would ring midday any moment. If Perryn was prompt to his feasting, we could be cooling our heels all afternoon. Time for the necropolis spy to figure out that Bastien and I were not closeted in my studio with a difficult corpse. Time for news of Lucian de Remeni's disobedience to reach the

Registry and news of Lucian de Remeni's madness to reach Perryn. We had chosen not to apply for this meeting, but rather just to present ourselves at the gate to avoid those very eventualities.

The bells rang midday. Then a quarter past. Had Bastien been brought inside the walls? The gratings in the waiting room wall gave me no good vantage on the outer bailey. Two guards were posted at the open doorway, and no pureblood would ever peer through the grate to judge if his orders had been carried out. I had to wait. Whether for admittance, arrest, or a Registry guard with shackles and silkbindings, I wasn't going to know in time to do much about it.

As the first hour past midday rang, hurrying footsteps crunched on the gravel outside the waiting room. Orrin, flushed and breathless, bowed much deeper and more sincerely than earlier. "My apologies for the delay, *domé*. Prince Perryn will be *most* pleased to give audience to Lucian de Remeni-Masson in the Royal Antiquities Repository."

I gave the young man a cold nod. That I did not sag into a puddle of relief was a monumental accomplishment.

Orrin extended his hand to the arch. "If you will follow me, *domé* . . ."

"My man accompanies me."

"As you wish, *domé*."

Sure enough, as we left the waiting room and circled around through a wicket gate and into the inner bailey, Orrin's wave brought a grim Bastien into our party. Another strand of anxiety released.

Veterans were gathered around fires of the inner bailey, some with families alongside. As we traversed courtyards, arcades, and dormant gardens, servants and courtiers clotted every doorway and corner, gabbling excitedly. Rumor infested both city and palace.

We hurried past a bakehouse, yet smelling of the morning's bread, a scent surely more sacred to any god than incense. But it was when we came to the armory—an endless fascination when I was a boy—that my pulse began to thrum, for just beyond a hedge garden stood a long, low building of limestone blocks. Carved into the pediment atop its columned portico were glyphs of ten ancient languages that named it a house of clarity, philosophy, wisdom, and destiny—the Royal Antiquities Repository, the king of Navronne's own archives, where my grandsire had held sway for seven-and-twenty years.

My gut clenched as we approached the portico. No liveried Guard

Royale, but ten battle-dressed lancers flanked the bronze doors, presenting arms as if I were a foreign potentate—or a rogue sorcerer to be arrested?

Simple justice. Navronne's safety. Bastien. The reminders helped.

Orrin paid the lancers no mind. Opening one of the bronze doors, he motioned Bastien ahead, properly allowing my servant to assume the risk of first entry. The somber coroner marched through, his hand near but not touching his sword hilt. We both knew this venture was chancy.

"I'll leave you here, *domé*," said Orrin, bowing. "His Grace will join you soon."

"Your guidance has been useful, Hugh de Orrin. One more matter . . ." I pulled three rolled messages from my waist pocket. "Give these to the porter at the west gate to be delivered within the hour. These additional members of my party will arrive this afternoon in answer to a Crown summons. They should be brought here immediately. You can be sure the prince will wish to see them." Unless he'd had us executed by then.

Orrin accepted the ribbon-tied rolls. "As you command, *Domé* Remeni. I shall return and stand doorward for your guests as soon as I've discharged this mission. The grace of the gods be with you on this day." He hurried off, leaving the heavy door to swing shut behind us on its own.

Clerestory windows cast a soft light on the cavernous space. Bastien, hands on hips, frowned. "What the devil kind of place is this?"

I could not help but grin. No one ever expected what they found beyond the grandiose entry.

"A treasury of igniters for a pureblood historian's magic," I murmured as I came up beside him.

The Repository appeared to be more of a castle undercroft than a temple of learning. There were no chambers or passages, but only ranks of columns to hold up the roof. Every quat of the stone floor was crammed with stacked crates and leather trunks, scroll cases, canvas bags, and barrels packed with straw. Shelves were scattered with caskets and tins, rusted tools, and dusty vials filled with everything from buttons to coins to dried beetle husks. It was a panoply of miscellany, a chaos of Navronne's refuse.

While the Registry Archives held documents, portraits, and magical artifacts from pureblood history, the Royal Repository housed every kind of relic both from Navronne's history and from times before the kingdom's founding. My grandsire had brought me here often as a child, allowing me to explore his treasury of pots and scraps. He had taught me how to interpret their making and glean what they could teach us. Only in Eodward's reign, he'd told me, had Navronne gained the luxury of studying our own history that we might understand what our past could teach about present and future.

I'd cared naught for such abstractions early on, only for the curiosities and the individual puzzles. But as my bent developed, and I was able to discern connections between battles and bowstrings, castles and trade routes and oranges, I became enraptured with the grand portrait of our kingdom and its people that these bits and pieces could sketch. Only then did I begin to appreciate Eodward's great-great-grandsire Caedmon and his monumental work of uniting three disparate peoples: the fierce warlords of mountainous Evanore with their mighty fortresses and rugged caves in the south; the wily traders, merchants, and shipbuilders of the river country, Morian of the north; and those who tended the sweet, fertile hills of golden Ardra, the farmers, artists, students, and philosophers nurtured by the land's beauty. Caedmon had made them one kingdom, far stronger than the sum of their individual might.

It gave me heart to believe Prince Perryn valued what my grandsire had tried to teach him. Enough, at least, that he had tamed Orrin's suspicions and disregarded my inconvenient timing. And he had agreed to my suggestion that we meet in the same venue as his original invitation. All could change easily, of course. If he arrived with his wife and a crowd of court ladies, he likely wouldn't thank us for bringing up such delicate matters as his bastards, debauched children, and his murderous duc. And then, of course, if we presented our case and Perryn refused to believe . . . That trouble made all others seem small.

"Wait here," I said to Bastien. "I'm off to hunt my grandsire's missing secrets." I'd told him of Capatronn's last investigation and my surmise that the white tree of Xancheira might be related to the Path of the White Hand. He was not stupid. He had recognized right away that my secret dealings with Demetreo and the Cicerons had spurred such an insight.

Pluvius believed I had taken something from the Registry Archives, something important and dangerous, having to do with Capatronn's Xancheiran investigation. I hadn't. But my vision in the Tower cellar had shown my grandsire kneeling before a small painted wooden chest, examining artifacts marked with Xancheira's tree. If my grandsire had wanted to hide something from the Registry, he might well have taken it home to

Pontia, in which case it had burned with everything else. But he might very well have moved it here, protected by preservation spells. No pureblood had the authority to search these premises. I had to look.

There was an order of sorts to the chaos. Not markers or labels; my grandsire had disdained those as ephemeral—misplaced or out of date as soon as they were installed. Instead he had grouped things by logical association. Moriangi artifacts here, Ardran ones there, relics of Caedmon's era distinct from those of the years since Eodward's coming. Maps, charts, and notes were not stored in one place but left with objects from the sites they described.

Unfortunately, Xancheira fit nowhere. We had no solid artifacts . . . or so I'd thought. Fortunately my grandsire *had* set aside a corner for unsortable oddments. Blood heating with excitement, I headed for the northeast corner of the building, scrambling between stacks of Moriangi shields and a dusty worktable piled with bows and arrows. I bypassed the larger trunks and casks. No time to search them. Capatronn's favorite place to store mysteries was a knee-high crate with a lid of woven branches—itself a curiosity he'd found before I was born.

No sooner had I spied the crate under a dented breastplate than a sharp hiss from Bastien shifted the dusty air. I couldn't stop, though. I unhitched the worn leather loop that held the crate closed.

The bronze doors boomed and torchlight flared from the entry as I set the breastplate aside and raised the square of woven leather and sticks. And there it was. Amid some rusted knives and swords, a bronze cauldron, and a rolled tapestry sat the small rectangular chest, straight out of my vision. Patches of red and yellow paint still shone bright on the dry wood.

The chest reeked of enchantment, which encouraged my belief in its importance. I snapped the first layer—my grandsire's private locking charm—with a familiar twist of magic. But inside the lid lurked a blanket of deterrent spells that churned my gut and blurred my vision. I'd no time to devise a counter; thus I fumbled blindly through the contents: small boxes, a leather pouch, some shards of stone, a rusted dagger. What I wanted was one of the small stitched journals where he described his findings and their provenance, his theories and conclusions. I searched for enchantments rather than shape, for his journal would bear the thickest layer of protection, especially if he were hiding secrets. Something not at all journal-shaped kept stinging my fingers.

"His Grace Perryn, Duc of Ardra, Prince of Navronne!" A herald's cry. I had to go.

Still no journal. I needed something to take with me. I might never get back here. Again I encountered the enchantment that pierced my hand and eyes like shards of heated glass. The protected object felt like a small roll of canvas or linen wound on a wood spindle. It must have *some* importance. I stuffed it inside my doublet and replaced the woven branch lid.

Bastien had ducked behind a man-high barrel of oil lamps. I hurried past, then paused to calm my breathing when I reached the last row of columns before the entry.

Three men and a woman stood with their backs to the gray daylight streaming through the double doors as footmen set torches in nearby brackets. Though I had not seen Perryn since we were boys, I could have picked him out of a much larger party. It was not his grand apparel—the deep, rich blues of satin and brocade, the trailing sleeves of intricate lace, the thick ermine ruff, or the diamond pectoral glittering in the torchlight. His companions wore equally elaborate garb. Rather it was the golden hair so like spun silk, the milk-fair complexion that spoke of pure Ardran lineage, and the long, lithe body that would be graceful whether dancing, riding, climbing trees, or fighting barbarians. Not so muscular in chest or shoulder as his father, and less ruddy in the cheek, despite months on campaign. But with such a noble presence, clear eye, and fair, open visage, he was most definitely Eodward's son. My hopes soared.

"My lord prince," I said. "You are most gracious to receive me with so little notice. Your summons was relayed to me only recently, and I've rushed here straight from the road, lest I miss this opportunity."

"Remeni . . . Lucian!" He abandoned his party and hurried forward, his hand extended in welcome. "Indeed, it is our pleasure! What a fortuitous day! I was most distraught when I heard you were out of the city . . . ill, I was told. But you're better now?" He was near bouncing in his jeweled slippers.

"Very much better, Your Grace. It was but a mild upset."

I would not kiss his ring. Instead I touched my fingertips to forehead and inclined my back just enough to acknowledge his rank, while leaving no impression of subservience.

He gave no appearance of pique, but cupped his extended hand and clapped it to his breast in exuberant drama. "Good! Good! The message from the curators made your illness sound quite dire. For a month or more I'd been determined to meet you here, but gave up all hope."

This was all so strange, as if we were longtime friends instead of two men who had crossed paths two or three times in our very different childhoods.

"I could not gather a great party to come." He leaned close, as if to whisper a great secret, but did not modulate his voice in the least. Perhaps his high spirits had to do with spirits—he reeked of wine. "When I told them I was meeting the grandson of my father's pureblood historian in a dusty warehouse, almost every member of my household found some more urgent task to be about. So these are now my most stalwart friends." He beckoned them over. "Hierarch Eligius of the Karish cathedral . . ."

I squinted into the light. The broader of the two men, gowned in red silk, would be the Hierarch of Ardra—the highest-ranking Karish clergyman in Navronne. The red cap atop his frizzled brown hair and his gold pendant shaped like a sunburst confirmed it. His presence was surprising; I'd no idea the prince dabbled in the new religion.

Eligius and I exchanged nods of respect.

". . . and one of my most intrepid field commanders, Fallon de Tremayne . . ."

Tremayne! But *Fallon*, not Laurent. Young, beardless, and slight of stature, his hair dark but trimmed close to his skull, he was not the man I'd seen on the temple stair. He'd be one of the Duc de Tremayne's formidable sons, I guessed, for despite his youth and slender build, the planes of his face were chiseled granite and his well-fitted black satin bespoke steel sinews. When he rose from a crisp bow, his gray gaze met mine straight on. Very bold indeed. A scarce-healed slash on his face spoke of recent tenure on the battlefields.

The formidable son intrigued me. Bastien had issued the murderous duc a summons to ensure his presence. But the son might be useful as well. Only two days since Bastien's runner, Pleury, had spoken to the palace wet nurse who told tales of the Duc de Tremayne's second wife. It happened that the young wife had borne the much older duc a girl child some nine years since. Nine years. Perhaps Fleure was his daughter's friend.

". . . and the Ducessa de Spano, the merriest lady in any court."

The woman was slight and fair, a perfection of form and face, exquisitely gowned in white satin and dripping with rubies. Though her years could not yet have numbered twenty, her sapphire gaze was locked on Perryn like that of a lynx on a roe deer.

"I've learnt to trust your entertainments, lord prince." Her silk mantle floated behind her as she twined ivory arms about his waist. "None can match your jongleurs and masques. I've not danced so much in a year as these few days since your return. How could I stay behind and miss such glorious amusement as a treasure hunt?"

CHAPTER 29

A treasure hunt? An entertainment for his mistress? Had no one told Perryn that his starving city was in chaos and his enemies on his doorstep?

"Fickle woman, now you've spoilt the surprise!" The prince drew his finger across the ducessa's parted lips in a most intimate manner. Then he nibbled at her ear, stopping only when she giggled and pushed his hand away.

"Dearest Your Grace," she said, squeezing closer, "we must be about our fun with the pureblood before my lord husband and your other knights grow restive in your hall."

"My lord, it is ever my pleasure to fulfill your wishes," I said, uneasy, "but Palinur's streets are not safe today." I wasn't even sure what kind of treasures they'd wish to hunt.

Perryn's hand waved to encompass the repository. "Well, of course, it is the treasures of Navronne we seek, else why would I summon Vincente's favored grandson?"

Keeping confusion beneath my mask, I fumbled onward.

"I understood you wished to reminisce about my grandsire, lord prince." Gods, I sounded insufferably priggish. "Of course, one could say his life was something of a treasure hunt."

"Exactly so!" said the prince, dragging his attentions away from the woman. "That's what spurred me to fetch you here. I was always jealous of you, you know. When we were boys."

"Jealous? A son of history's noblest king?" I almost laughed aloud at such a ridiculous assertion. But a certain bite in Perryn's speech registered danger quick enough to turn my course. "Indeed, lord, I doubt a pureblood youth forever bound to his rules, studies, and contracts could hold any advantage over a young Prince of Navronne. Both were chosen by the gods for their roles in life."

"Yes, yes, 'tis only in one matter." He sniggered and waved a limp hand, dismissing my serious reply with a ripple of lace. "But it's time to set it right. My father forced me to spend interminable hours in this dreary house of dust and rust with Vincente, who preached at me endlessly of battles and lawgiving and naked savages who lived in Navronne before the gods were born. I felt quite abused, because he said that when *you* came here, he set you to seek Navronne's most valuable treasures buried amidst all this rubbish. 'None can find them so well as my clever Lucian,' he told me. Indeed that must be true, as my own pureblood and I came here not a year ago and found little beyond a few emerald chips and some bent medals. So I decided that *you* must show me where these treasures might be."

He spread his arms wide as if to embrace the entire Repository.

"You seek valuables . . . like gems or gold?" My faith in Eodward's blood dissipated like frost in sunlight.

"Maintaining a kingdom is very expensive," he said, sniffing the ducessa's hair and fingering the rubies dangling round her neck. "And this damnable war empties my coffers as quickly as this lady here empties my bowls of oranges."

"Lord prince, I regret to tell you—"

"Do *not* say this is holy pureblood business or that somehow the valuables in this repository belong to you or the Registry!"

As Perryn's tone sharpened, young Tremayne stepped forward, alert.

"Certainly not, lord," I said. "Everything here belongs to Navronne's righteous king. It's only . . ."

If I told him the truth—that when my grandsire spoke of treasures, he meant these very rusty bits Perryn so disdained—besotted pique could ruin any chance of justice for the dead children. I had to twist the truth into Perryn's expectations.

"My grandsire was a most excellent student of history, lord, but no judge of worldly value. I recognized that only as I grew older and realized what men with experience of the world consider precious. The 'treasures' he sent me to find were a jade game piece or an ancient wax tablet—things no practical man would value. I'm thinking your own noble father recognized this. He incorporated any cache of gold or excellent gems into the Royal *Treasury* in the same hour my grandsire revealed them. But if it pleases you, we could seek out the best of what is left—surely a few pieces."

Though his exuberance was damped, the prince agreed. "Use your best skills. Convince me not to have all this burnt."

Bastien had said he would step out to begin the inquest when the time seemed right. So why didn't he? What reason to wait?

I knew why, of course. Because our three witnesses would not arrive for an hour yet. We had allowed time in our plan to accommodate Perryn's wishes.

"Certainly, lord prince."

I buried my disappointment, and for most of an hour sought out what salable objects I could recall. Many were missing. Perryn's pureblood must have found the ten jeweled daggers of a Moriangi prince, and the goldwork jewelry, goddess figures, cups, and fibulae from gold-rich Evanore. I hoped something would please him before our witnesses arrived.

Hierarch Eligius, his puffy face sagging like overwarm cheese, trailed after us, sniffing frequently—whether at the dust or the poor display, I didn't know. Young Tremayne didn't seem at all interested. He wandered off on his own, shuffling items on shelves, poking idly into boxes and peering into crates and barrels. The ducessa, however, twittered like a canary, especially when I found a silver comb set with pearls, and a necklace of rare moonstones from the western shores.

The lady's delight should have cheered Perryn a little, expressed with such bold intimacies as it was. But he grumbled at the paltry haul and dispatched the ducessa to have wine brought in. It was curious he'd brought no servants.

Fortunately, the Repository was quite as I remembered it. No Royal Historian had been appointed after my grandsire left the post. The rise of the Harrowers and the worsening weather in the last years of his reign had likely distracted Eodward from naming a replacement.

From a buried leather trunk filled with King Eodward's documents, I pulled a Cartamandua map of Navronne's western coast. Besides its superb illumination, which made it a work of art in itself, the spells worked into a Cartamandua map could keep a traveler's road inerrant. Some said such maps could take its user to places no common traveler could find—holy places, places of legend. As my finger traced its inked borders, exquisite magic teased my senses. I hated giving it over.

"What's that?" Perryn peered over my shoulder.

"Your father commissioned this in the first decade of his reign," I said, pointing to the date and the words *Eodward Regne* scribed in the map's cartouche.

Perryn beckoned young Tremayne—Fallon—who wore a leather satchel hung over his shoulder. "See what Lucian's found in this collection of my father's things. Cartamandua maps fetch a fine price. Keep this with my lady's baubles."

The taciturn Fallon stuffed the map into his bag and wandered off again. How wasteful to have a seasoned veteran in his prime serving as a footman.

We moved on from Eodward's era to Caedmon's.

From a crate of tins and boxes, I drew a handful of gold coins struck with a man's noble likeness. My grandsire had believed the face Caedmon's own—probably the only likeness of him in existence—which made the coins far more valuable than the weight of gold in them.

Delighted to see gold of any amount, Perryn again summoned Fallon and his sack.

My fingers slipped two coins back into the crate as I handed them over. I could not allow such a treasure to vanish entire.

"Have we searched enough, my stalwart?" said Perryn, once all was stowed away.

Fallon met the Prince's gaze and nodded. "I serve your pleasure, Your Grace."

"And your opinion, Excellency Eligius?"

"As long as we are finished here by the holy hour of Vespers, I am content, lord." The hierarch's words burbled up from the depth of his wide body.

"Well, perhaps a little more hunting, then, Lucian." Perryn's spirits had shot upward again. "We cannot let the Lady de Spano return to find us flown. The wine she brings shall fortify us!"

Perryn was not at all interested in the sonnivar, the booming signal horn from Evanore's mountains, its length twice the height of a man. "Barbarians' trash," he called it, though the intricate silver inlay had been worked over generations of craftsmen. "If those decorations were gold I'd have them melted out of it."

"Lord!" Fallon's bellow whipped us around. His wanderings had taken him back to the trunk where we'd found the Cartamandua map. "See what lies here."

Perryn hurried over, the hierarch and I on his heels. Scrolls, bound pages, and loose sheets of parchment were scattered outside the leather trunk. Atop the remaining contents was a scroll the length of a man's forearm. The vellum was the finest that could be had in Navronne. Three leather straps bound it shut, each fixed with a heavy seal.

"What do you make of it, Lucian?" Perryn's voice throbbed with excitement.

Kneeling beside the case, I examined the wax impressions. "This one is your father's own seal, lord prince. This the seal of Kemen's Temple. And the third you will recognize, Excellency Eligius." The seal of the Hierarch of Ardra. Which meant . . .

Eodward had made three copies of his will. One was to be hidden in some place of safety where it would be revealed at his death. The other two he had entrusted to the two clergymen who had borne witness to his lineage before he took the throne—the High Priest of Kemen Sky Lord, and Eligius's predecessor as the Hierarch of Ardra. But the two holy men had preceded Eodward in death and no one could find any copies of the will. The lack of a writ naming one of Eodward's sons as his successor was an ongoing mystery—and a tragedy. It was the cause of the war. Lord of Light, this document could end it.

And yet . . .

How could I have missed a document with unbroken seals as I searched for the Cartamandua map? And my grandsire had never mentioned the will.

My fingers lingered on the scroll. If I invoked my bent while touching it, what might I learn?

I was wholly aware of Fallon standing behind me, the leather satchel over his shoulder, and his lord, one of the partisans in this conflict, kneeling beside me. If they were determined to press a falsehood, my protest would not alter it, and the shades of four children stood at my shoulders, begging for justice. If I discounted them when we had some slim chance of a hearing, what right had I to demand justice for the unnamed thousands? Perryn might yet be the kingdom's best hope.

"Break the seals, Your Grace," said Fallon. "You've witnesses enough. If this is what it appears . . ."

"I recommend you proceed carefully, lord," I said. "The chancellor of the realm must be the one to break the seals before witnesses of his own choosing. He can call any of us to testify to its discovery."

"Wise, Lucian. Very wise." Perryn's voice quivered. "Excellency, could I prevail upon you to carry this to Chancellor Ruthais? Tell him the circumstances of its finding and the names of these witnesses. Assure him that I will most certainly not interfere with his duties in the matter. Have four of my lancers escort you. See to that for him, Fallon."

The hierarch bowed deeply. "With all humility I accept this charge, Your Grace. By holy Iero's mercy, may it prove the hope of us all."

"Lucian . . ." Perryn motioned me to take the scroll and give it to Eligius.

Clever of the prince not to touch it. If the chancellor called in a pureblood to examine the thing, that one would certainly look for evidence of Perryn's hand on it. I could have offered to mark the scroll with an indelible imprint to validate that it was the one pulled from the trunk, but observing Perryn this last hour . . . these odd circumstances . . . his pent eagerness . . . I chose not to be an active collaborator.

Eligius marched out as if he bore the crown jewels themselves, as I supposed he did. Fallon accompanied him as far as the entry and gave orders to the guard commander.

"I had hoped our meeting might lead to a few treasures," said Perryn, hands clasped to his breast, watching through the open doors as the hierarch's scarlet pelisse vanished into the fog-draped hedge garden. "Never did I imagine this possibility. Truly the gods are with you, Lucian."

"May the result be the salvation of Navronne," I said, meaning it in ways he would likely not approve. Surely somewhere there must live some true inheritor of Caedmon and Eodward's legacy. Not Bayard—the Smith, they called him, for his hammer hand, capable in battle but lacking education, generosity, moderation, or mercy. Not Osriel, the crippled bastard who lurked in Evanore, the secretive halfblood rumored to steal the souls of the dead. But not this prancing caricature of greatness, either.

As I lamented the desperate courage and bright light I'd seen in Fleure and the horse boy, Fallon pulled the bronze door shut. "Are we finished here, Your Grace?"

Perryn surveyed the cluttered room. "What treasure could we find to match hope?"

I glanced toward the barrel of lamps. Bastien had already read the signs.

"If I may, Your Grace . . ." The coroner stepped from his hiding place and dropped to one knee before the prince, his fist on his breast, conveniently covering his coroner's pendant.

"Who is this?" demanded Perryn. Fallon darted to the prince's side, sword drawn, before Bastien's words had faded. "How did you get in here?"

"I brought him," I said. "Your Grace and my lord Tremayne, may I introduce Bastien de Caton, a loyal and faithful city official of Palinur? As a measure of his exceptional honor and distinguished stature, the Registry has deemed him worthy to hold a pureblood contract that links him to the noblest bloodlines of our kind. He is, as it happens, my own contracted master."

"You hid him here . . . why? So he could listen in?" Perryn's frown deepened.

"Certainly no spy, lord prince. Master Bastien and I have ventured your patience on the chance to present a matter of justice before a prince of the realm. As a holder of the gods' magic, as well as the grandson of your royal father's loyal servant, I request you give my master fair hearing, for the matter in question is one that touches on your royal person. Has he your consent to do so?"

"Surely there are better times and venues for matters of justice?" snapped Fallon.

"My lord?" My gaze remained focused on the prince. We had rehearsed this introduction for hours, devising the precise words so that any assent on Perryn's part would, by crown law, allow Bastien to convene a formal inquest.

"Your grandsire was contracted to a king. How is it possible you are contracted to this Bastien?" said Fallon. "Is the Registry now giving away its sorcerers to peasants and tradesmen?"

"The Registry only recently extended my contract an additional three years," I said. My tongue did not even sting.

"A matter of justice that touches my royal person?" Perryn's gloved finger massaged his lower lip. I could imagine him riffling through his secrets and indiscretions.

The ducessa flew through the doors with a salver laden with flagon, pitcher, cups, and a bowl, handling the burden as deftly as a serving girl.

Perryn brightened and waved her to hurry. "Come, come, dear lady, bring the wine. We've a new diversion. And, Fallon, find us stools that we may sit and hear out Remeni's bound master. I'll wager he tells us that justice demands Lucian paint my likeness when I become king. Proceed, noble Bastien de Caton."

Only one who knew how to read expressions behind a mask could have noticed the predatory gleam behind Bastien's wiry red-brown thatch. Perryn's mocking consent would but hone Bastien's waiting knife.

Bastien rose from his genuflection and waited politely until the young noble had brought three stools and wiped the dust from the seats. Fallon did not take the third stool, but remained standing beside his lord. Protocol forbade me sit, but I would not have done so anyway. Better I stay to one side, halfway between Bastien and the others, ready to defend my master if need be.

Once the prince and the lady were settled with wine cups and entwined arms, Bastien uncovered his pendant. The bronze hammer of his office shone in the torchlight.

"Your Grace Perryn, Duc of Ardra, Prince of Navronne, by your consent, witnessed by these men present, and with the power granted me by the Crown of Navronne, do I, Bastien de Caton, Coroner of the Twelve Districts of Palinur, here convene an inquest into the untimely death of a girl child known as Fleure, found strangled in the vicinity of the hirudo Palinur and Necropolis Caton."

He turned to me. "With the lawful capacity of my office—and forgoing any control or duress implied by my contract for your service—I do summon thee, Lucian de Remeni-Masson, to give witness in this matter, thy truth verified by the grace of the gods' favor born in thy blood."

I nodded.

Then he turned to the young noble. "With the lawful capacity of my office I do summon thee, Fallon de Tremayne, to give truthful witness in this matter, any perjury to be punished with all force of law."

Yes, Fallon could tell us of his stepmother's daughter, who had been suckled by the same wet nurse as Perryn's own children. Perhaps not Fleure's friend at all. Was it possible a prince would cuckold his *consiliar prime*? This one surely might.

And then back to Perryn. "Out of respect for your interests in this matter, Your Grace, I have not summoned every possible witness to this inquest. We can do so afterward, if you please. But a few additional witnesses will be arriving shortly, summoned upon the chance of this hearing."

Perryn looked puzzled; Fallon, disbelieving. The ducessa, however, bloomed with a slightly bloodthirsty excitement that disgusted me. "A strangled girl? How intriguing! Tell us more."

Bastien needed no encouragement to proceed apace. He must get his case flowing before Perryn realized what was happening.

"Step forward, Fallon de Tremayne. I wish you to identify the subject of this portrait."

"My lord prince?" Fallon, increasingly wary, looked to Perryn.

"As he bids." Perryn, brow creased, eyes narrow with uncertainty, waved him forward.

Fallon took the rolled parchment from Bastien and spread it open. "Why do you have a portrait of Ysabel? And this—?" His head jerked up, steel-hard eyes riveted on Perryn. Then they shifted to Bastien. "Where did this come from?"

It seemed as if the world gave a great sigh. The lily child had a name.

"Ysabel," said Bastien, with polite interest. "And who might she be? Recall that the law obliges you to answer to the best of your knowledge."

"She is born of my father's wife." Each word was broken ice.

Like a beggar's pustule, my hatred for both the Duc de Tremayne and this prince swelled and burst all in that moment. I had not wanted to believe the connection. *Naive and stupid, Lucian. Was Pontia not enough to teach of the world's savagery? Was the second fire here in Palinur not enough? Were the lessons of Necropolis Caton not enough?*

No wonder the elder Tremayne wanted to tear out Fleure's pale, shining hair, so like that of the master who cuckolded him. No wonder the child feared the devil lord so. Whether or not she knew of her mother's fault, she would recognize her erstwhile father's spite. Had he violated Ysabel in his own house before abandoning her to debauchery?

"You speak of his current wife, Annitra de Rosine, who is not your own mother?" said Bastien. His self-discipline was worthy of a pureblood. I wanted to spit fire.

"The whore, yes. But the child is innocent . . . and *safely* housed, cared for—"

"That will be all, lord."

Bastien took the portrait from Fallon's hands and showed it to the prince. All color faded from Perryn's cheeks save the flush of wine. He chewed a fingernail like a nursery child and looked away.

As for Fallon, his narrowed eyes peered at Bastien and me as if we were messengers from the netherworld. I'd swear he had not suspected his liege of fathering Ysabel. Nor had he the least clue that the child was dead or how. And he cared.

"*Domé* Remeni, step forward." Bastien passed me the portrait. "The Writ of Balance requires you to validate your blood heritage, if you please."

I crouched down and drew a circle in the dust on the floor. Bastien had wanted to see the prince's reaction if a void spell emptied a hole in front of him. But Perryn had lived near pureblood magics all his life and would not be so impressed as Bastien. On a whim, I invoked my aerogen spell, scooping the dust from my circle and tossing it into the air. The torchlight colored the enchanted particles with every hue of flame as they showered us like a rain of stars.

The ducessa's face lit with delight. Fallon blinked, which I considered a success. Perhaps it did not instill Perryn with awe, as Bastien wished, but Ysabel would have liked it.

Bastien released a great breath. "Sufficient. Now, *domé*, tell us of this artwork."

And so I began my tale. "Some half year since, on the first day of my contract with the Coroner of the Twelve Districts, the body of a child was brought to the necropolis. A beggar child, by the look of her, she had been found in a ditch below the inner ramparts of Palinur. . . ."

Imitating Bastien, I sped onward, giving no opportunity for interruption. ". . . and I released the power of my blood and began to draw her. As Prince Perryn himself has spoken today, my grandsire believed that I inherited not only the gift of true portraiture from my Masson lineage, but his own bloodline magic of envisioning the connections of history. Within me these two bents have merged, and so the work of my hand and my visionary investigations can produce truth that is beyond the evidence of my eye alone. By the gift of the gods that resides in me, I swear that this portrait is the result solely of my magic. . . ."

I had just shown them the second portrait depicting Fleure—Ysabel—with dark hair and a blood-stained shift, when the grand doors opened.

Our guide and doorward, Hugh de Orrin, announced the arrival of a new guest.

Like a whirlwind of silk draperies, High Priestess Irinyi swept into the Repository, a rolled page clutched in one hand. She lifted the veil covering hair and face, and her painted eyes took in our unusual surroundings before settling on Prince Perryn.

I stepped backward, hoping that between the wavering shadow, my new growth of beard, and the different mask, my identity would remain concealed for the moment.

"Your Grace," she said, bending slightly in deference as she would to none but a king—or a prospective one. "What a pleasure to meet you at last. Your summons was at one so gracious and so mysterious, I hardly knew what to think."

Her gaze swept across the rest of us. I merited no attention. Nor did Bastien. More surprising, Fallon's face elicited no recognition, either. The ducessa, however, received a scornful twist of the priestess's thin lips.

"Why have you brought me here, Your Grace? I was given to believe that certain other members of your household would join us in a *private* meeting."

Perryn waved her off with a mirthless laugh. "I'm as mystified as you, priestess. Strange magics. Portraits of dead girls. Witnesses popping in and out. You'll not imagine who is this roguish fellow!"

Bastien bent in a modest acknowledgment of her rank, but did not lower his eyes. "Sinduria! Greetings of your divine mistress."

Her nostrils flared in distaste. "Who are you to address a high priestess of Arrosa?"

Bastien touched his pendant. "I am the Coroner of the Twelve Districts of Palinur, conducting an inquest sanctioned by the Prince of Navronne. It is my lawful summons has brought you here to lay before your prince and these varied witnesses the parchment you carry. . . ." He repeated his warning against perjury and held out his hand for the document—the one I had tried and failed to steal, the one Garen had bled for.

Eyes narrowed to slits, Irinyi stepped backward, clutching the scroll to her breast. "You've no right to temple privacies."

"Lord prince, perhaps you could remind her?" said Bastien.

Perryn wagged a finger for Bastien to do the explaining. The finger flew back to his teeth. He would have no fingernails left by the end of this.

Bastien continued. "My authority is direct from Caedmon's Writ, Sinduria. Matters of murder transcend petty privacies, whether those of a temple or the royal household."

"Murder?" Was a trace of fear mingled with her shock?

"Aye. Murder. Even purebloods must open their secrets to a murder inquiry that falls within my jurisdiction. Surrender the document, Sinduria, else I shall step out and ask one of our prince's lancers to bring fetters suitable for a noble lady."

Her glare flayed Bastien and Perryn equally as she flung the scroll at Bastien and turned to go.

"Alas, priestess," said Bastien. "You are not dismissed." We could not have her running tales to the Duc de Tremayne.

"Surely the accursed Writ does not permit this cur to dictate my comings and goings." Irinyi spun in place, her hand flying to her waist.

"'Ware, Coroner," I snapped. "Dagger!"

Irinyi's hand jerked away from the hidden sheath, and the blaze of her fury focused on me. "Who is this pureb—?"

As if Magrog's own dagger had pierced her soul, she froze. "You," she whispered. "Sneaking, lying, weaseling . . . murderer."

"Your testimony is not yet complete, Sinduria." Bastien's insistence could not quite drown her accusation, certainly not its bitter echoes in my own soul. "Tell us of this document."

"I'll tell you nothing."

Bastien remained cool. "Then perhaps another witness can explain what this page will tell us. *Domé*, would you continue your tale?"

"My master may, of course, command me to undertake any task he sees necessary to forward his business," I said. "I began by locating the place the child's corpus was found at the base of the eastern rampart of the Elder Wall. Magic revealed the girl child did not die there. . . ."

With Bastien's help, I had carefully rehearsed my tale of unraveling Fleure's murder, eliminating all mention of the Cicerons who found her. Nor did I announce my conviction that the high priestess was complicit in debauching children. Though my suspicions of Irinyi had long become certainties, I had no proof. Bastien insisted that it was better to bring a solid case against one, and then see how the pieces fell together. It was a rule difficult to swallow.

"I agreed to sign a document to relinquish all connection with this false child, to forgo contact, interest, comfort, discipline, education, leaving all parental duties to the temple. The high priestess has brought a document like to the one she had me sign. But this particular document will be the one used to consign Ysabel de Tremayne, known as Fleure, to the Temple of Arrosa. Of course the signature itself cannot reveal the murderer, unless the one who delivered the child and the one who slew her are the same. I needed to investigate how children were used in the temple. And so I spoke with the high priestess of my particular circumstances, and she offered me the solace of the goddess's devotions. . . ."

I spoke in a measured pace, making sure I did not take the listeners too far into the Pools of the Gods' Chosen until Orrin announced our next expected arrival.

"Varouna!" Irinyi's wrath came near shoving the soft young woman in pink ruffles back out the door she'd just entered. "You will not—"

"Silence, priestess," said Perryn, straightening on his stool. "Let this shocking testimony continue."

Bastien's gaze met mine and unspoken words flew between us. Perryn had at last decided his roles in this scripting. *Noble adjudicator. Horrified prince.* Would *indignant father* follow?

"Step forward, Mistress Varouna," said Bastien, and, as with the rest of us, he called her to witness under pain of the law. "You serve at the temple of divine Arrosa, do you not?"

"Yes." If it had been possible, the woman would have split her fearful gaze equally between Bastien, the prince, and Irinyi, who'd taken possession of the empty stool.

"What services do you perform there?"

"I . . . I care for the temple's younger charges . . . initiates . . . bath girls . . . serving girls, sweepers. I see to their prayers and that they eat properly and wash themselves. I teach them manners."

Even as she spewed these commonalities, I wanted to scream at the vile woman. *Do you black their hair? Do you remove their undergarments when you bring them to tend naked men?*

"Of course," said Bastien, with the sinuous glide of an adder, "it makes sense that young children living in such a holy place would need someone devoted to their tending. We wish to know if you recognize this child"—Bastien passed her the lily portrait—"or this one." He passed her the second portrait, Fleure in the bloodstained white shift.

"Mistress?" she said, pleading.

"Why look at me, Varouna?" Spite tainted Irinyi's offering. "Arrosa's child servants are entirely your responsibility. You're the only one who even knows them all." Irinyi, too, had chosen who would take the blame.

"Yes, I know them . . . her. It is only one. Her name was . . . is . . . Fleure. A hateful child." She nodded to herself. "She thinks because she's highborn that she's better than the others, entitled to privileges. Yet all our aspirants, initiates, and serving girls are equal in the sight of the goddess. One day when Fleure was cruel to a sweeper, I punished her. I cut the hair she was so proud of. Put blacking on it to quench her pride. Dressed her like them." She indicated the second portrait. "This one's wrong. Sweepers don't wear pretty shifts. Never . . . and why would there be blood?"

"You put her in gray tunic and leggings," I said, unable to keep silent longer. "Coarse cloth."

"Yes, gray. All our sweeping girls wear gray. And simple fabric for dirty servants." Only then did Varouna look up to see who had spoken. When she recognized me, all color left her cheeks. She knew I had seen what she did. She had offered me a half-naked child in a fine embroidered shift to do with as I pleased in the name of her divine mistress.

Bastien took back the reins. "Mistress Varouna, can you tell us when you last saw Fleure?"

Again the pleading gaze at the hard-faced Irinyi, at the Prince of Navronne. And again the cold indifference. She'd begun to shake.

But when no one offered any relief, she stiffened. "Fleure hated the punishment and somehow sneaked out a message to her family. To a brother, I think. He came and fetched her away, and I didn't tell the high priestess, as I thought she might punish me for losing one of the goddess's pledge children. That's it, her brother fetched her and I've not seen her since."

"He did not." Deadly quiet, Fallon denounced her lie. "No brother fetched her from the temple. I know this girl's brothers and both have been in the fields of Ardra and Morian, fighting for their prince for more than half a year. She was a spritely child. Be sure of it—either brother would have slain the one who treated her meanly."

Varouna's mouth opened, but no words came out. How grievous that Ysabel had such a champion only in death.

Bastien seized the moment. "Would you change anything of your testimony, mistress? Perhaps you now recall the name of the one who came and *fetched* the girl called Fleure."

Speechless, she shook her head. The pink ruffles quivered like aspen leaves.

"Then I think it is time we heard what happened that night the girl disappeared, for the gods have opened the past to the magic of our witness. *Domé?*"

I told them how I had felt the hand of the goddess in the tepidarium pool and she had sent me the image of a man holding Ysabel over the water and blacking what was left of her hair, as most of her pale locks were left in her bedchamber. I did not mention that this image was not sent through magic, but through the eyes of a grief-stricken sweeping girl. Who is to say how the gods do their work?

And then I told them about the drainage channel. "I invoked my magic again. In my visions the gods . . . the earth . . . divine magic . . . showed me that this dark place was indeed the place where Ysabel died. Below the hellish heat of the hypocaust, down in the dark and the slime and the cold, with the only music the cry of rats, she battled a nobleman with thick, dark hair and well-shined boots. A man she looked on with eyes the color of a winter sky and called the devil lord. Because she knew him. Because she knew that if he came for her, it would mark her end. She fought him with the stalwart courage of her incomparable lineage. But she died there. And the devil lord unlocked the drainage grate and tossed her out into the winter night."

As I told the story, Fallon de Tremayne's anger had grown so large that it felt like night and storm had taken up residence in the Repository, no matter what the day or season beyond the doors. Only at the end, when I spoke of thick dark hair and well-shined boots did he stagger backward as if someone had kicked him in the gut.

Bastien noticed, too. He handed Irinyi's scroll to the prince. "The high priestess can tell you the name on this scroll. But it is my thought that you must read it for yourself. You should recognize the hand. You may be able to fit details into this terrible story that we've not had time to review. Reasons, for example. We can surmise, but you, lord, know the man as we do not."

Then the Coroner of the Twelve Districts stepped back—well out of reach—and waited.

Perryn ripped open the scroll, glanced at it, and then dropped it to the floor. "By Kemen Sky Lord's holy balls . . ."

The ducessa clucked in disappointment when she was unable to read the name over his shoulder. But Fallon de Tremayne dared pick up the discarded evidence and read it for himself.

The document flew again, and the young man walked away, his hands clasped atop his head and his elbows squeezed tight as if crushing his skull was the only way to erase what he had just seen. Moments later, from the depths of the Repository, came a bellow speaking grief and disappointment and helpless rage. I recognized them.

Fallon's cry had not yet faded when the bronze doors swung open yet again, and Hugh de Orrin announced, "His Grace, the Duc de Tremayne."

CHAPTER 30

Tremayne strode through the door, a striking, dark-haired, thick-bearded man. His tabard was the purple and gold of the Ardran household, his mantle lined with fox fur, his position immediately affirmed by the onrushing power of his presence. His calf-high boots gleamed.

"My good lord"—he swept a bow—"your knights are near devouring the tables in your great hall. I've done my best to stave off their hunger with your ale, but truly we ought to get back before that pays us ill—or drains every one of your casks. Fortunate that I knew where you might be at this hour, though I wasn't at all sure this came from you."

He twirled the summons that Bastien and I had labored over. We'd tried to make it just intriguing enough to draw him, just official enough to make him chary about not coming, just conspiratorial enough to ensure he wouldn't mention it to anyone beforetime, even Perryn.

"What an odd venue for an illustrious gathering. Greetings, Sinduria, Ducessa, mistress—"

Perryn leapt to his feet, hands raised in a flourish of jewels and lace. "By the gods, Laurent, what have you done?"

Tremayne's glance glided over me to settle on Bastien, who bided his time, his hands at rest behind his back.

"Nothing but serve you, I hope, my lord. May I ask what transpires here? Your summons speaks of secrets unveiled. It said you had a question that only I could answer."

"*I* have the question, Father." No pureblood sculptor could have chiseled a more perfect image of a god's fury than what Bastien had wrought in Fallon de Tremayne. If Kemen Sky Lord felt such wrath at human failings, then ravaging winter, plague, and war were only the beginning of our punishment. "Where is Ysabel?"

Tremayne's curiosity vanished. Arrogance remained, however, and contempt.

His glance whipped around the circle of light defined by the diminishing torch flames. To the ducessa gaping alternately at the damning document and his own face. To Irinyi launching daggers from her eyes. To quivering Varouna, back to the wall, creeping quat by quat toward the bronze doors. To an inexpressive pureblood, who wished he dared create a void hole as deep as his loathing under Tremayne's feet. To Bastien, calmly waiting, and his prince, not so calm. Tremayne judged his audience and chose his defense.

"She is dead, my lord prince, as was necessary. As are five others whose lives should never have been. I will not apologize for it. This is wartime. Deaths are necessary for the future of Navronne. You and I preach it every day on every battlefield. Do we preach a lie?"

"You *admit* it," said Fallon. "You *strangled* a child who brought nothing but love and brilliance to a house bereft of both. You thought your young strumpet would fill the emptiness left by my mother's death. And so she did, not with her own vicious vulgarity, but with her child. And you took that brilliance and snuffed it out in a *sewer*? How can you live with such sin?"

"Duty sustains me through every battle," said the duc, unapologetic, "whether with Bayard the Smith and his hired mercenaries, or Sila Diaglou and her lunatics, or corrupt nobles who would use bastard children to tear Eodward's kingdom apart. Who would you have sit Eodward's throne? Did you think the brat might carry *you* there?"

Fallon crossed the gap between them and touched a knife point to his father's neck before any one of us could react. "How *dare* you profane her—and slander me for defending her?"

Tremayne displayed no fear. But he, as all of us, held quite still. Had one of Perryn's lancers glimpsed the unsheathed weapon, Fallon would already be skewered.

It was Bastien who stepped up and with a dagger pulled from his boot lifted the son's steadfast blade. "Let us hear our prince's judgment, young lord. We are not here to witness a new crime, but to uphold the Crown's law—the Crown you have shed blood to defend."

Did I wish Fallon to plunge the dagger through its mark or withdraw? Surely, it would take all his strength to step back. But so he did. And then pivoted smartly to face Perryn, sheathed his dagger, and dropped to one knee.

"Forgive me, Your Grace," he said, bowing his head. "To hear that one's honored parent has slaughtered one's young sister sets mind and heart at odds. His slur upon my honor must await another occasion's resolution. I serve you only, as you well know. But laying my service, past and future, at your feet, I beg your justice for this child, an innocent who did not deserve such an end."

Tremayne blew a note of indulgent scorn. "In the hour our prince is proclaimed, you'll see the wisdom of my course. Until then, mewl about bastards as you will."

Perryn had sagged onto his stool. His mistress had crept to his side, rubbing herself on his arm like a cat seeking warmth and attention. But he wrapped his arms about himself, not her. "Of all the wretched, nasty messes. What am I to do with you all?"

Pitiful. Not even Tremayne's admission of his victims' identities seemed to strike Perryn ill. Was he too much the fool to understand the crimes committed in his name or was he complicit and too much the coward to admit it? Did any of those who yearned for a resumption of Eodward's kingly path, who fought for Perryn and died with savage, mutilating wounds, have a notion what rubbish hid beneath Perryn's comely figure?

Bastien, knife returned to his boot, stepped forward. Never would I doubt *his* courage. "May I speak, Your Grace?"

"Have you not spoken enough, you and Remeni here?"

Curb your tongue, prince! To hear my name spoken in front of Tremayne and Irinyi chilled my marrow. I imagined minds reaching for half-remembered rumor regarding that name. My testimony, exposing the inner workings of my gift, had been all I could contribute to this trial. We needed to finish it before Registry lies made that testimony worthless.

"I would go, lord," said the priestess. "I have answered what was asked of me, and it is time for prayers. The goddess beckons." Varouna seemed already to have vanished during the father-and-son confrontation.

"Yes, yes, be gone from here. No accusation has been made against you. A good thing I've not been asked to challenge the Elder Gods!"

I'd never seen a woman move so fast as Irinyi. We needed a quick resolution. She had Temple guards with swords and knives at her disposal, and the fury in her departing glance at Bastien and me vowed her intent to use them. She knew our names.

"There are yet formalities to observe, lord," said Bastien, a similar urgency tugging at his calm.

"Speak, then, before I order every one of you hanged. This grim tale is not at all what I wished to be hearing on this day of all days."

On this day . . . He referred to the scroll, I supposed. He believed he would be king by the morrow. Perhaps he would, gods save us all.

A sneering Tremayne jerked his head at Bastien. "Who is this windbag who presumes to lecture the Prince of Navronne on formalities while stinking of a midden?"

"He is Palinur's coroner," said Perryn, "and evidently more reputable than he looks or smells. The Registry thinks highly of him. And he's presented a formidable case against you and certain of your acquaintances." He glared at the bronze doors closing behind Irinyi. "All of it is vouched for by pureblood testimony and now your own confession!"

Perryn was far too easy with Tremayne, talking as if judgment was a matter of discussion. That did nothing for my rising anxieties.

"I am bound by Crown law to render judgment in cases of suspicious death, my lord duc," said Bastien. "If I judge a death murder and am satisfied that I know who has done it, the verdict is published to the citizenry of Palinur. The appropriate magistrate must then assess punishment. In all cases, the final arbiter is the Duc of Ardra—our own Prince Perryn."

"Appoint a new coroner, lord," snapped Tremayne. "No commoner should get the idea he can interpret the law or insert himself into the Prince of Navronne's plans. He wrests his livelihood from corpses, for the gods' sake. No doubt he'll soon come begging for his fee—likely a prodigious fee when he aims his righteousness at Ardra's *consiliar prime*."

"This is no minor indiscretion blown to scandal," said Fallon, pacing in a tight circle like a chained bear. "Those of us in this chamber have heard the entire sordid tale. The prince. Myself. The Ducessa de Spano." She looked most alarmed at the mention. "That high priestess was responsible for Ysabel, and that unnatural woman debauched her. Witnesses can be found to the other deaths, I have no doubt. The gods themselves have taken pity on Ysabel and sent the pureblood these visions. What retribution might they demand do we bury the truth?"

Perryn shuddered. "Speak as you will, Coroner. Just be done quickly."

Bastien bowed yet again—this time to Fallon as well as the coward prince. He gripped his pendant and I imagined the bang of his gavel, giving weight to his saying.

"It is my judgment that the child known as Fleure is proved to be Ysabel de Tremayne, daughter of Annitra de Rosine and an unnamed partner of the blood royal. It is my judgment that Laurent de Buld, Duc de Tremayne, is responsible for a crime that every god in every heaven deplores—the willful murder of an innocent. So say I, Coroner of the Twelve Districts of Palinur."

Bastien released the symbol of office, returning his hands to his back and his voice to a more natural timbre. "I have fulfilled my duty by the Crown, by the people of this city, and by the dead. The crime is verified. The guilty party is established. The preliminary report of this case has already been turned over to the chief magistrate of Palinur for recording and displayed this hour in every district square. And now, my lord prince, punishment—justice—rests in your hands."

If a man ever looked less willing to take on such a responsibility, I could not imagine it. Perryn looked like a limp stocking tucked in upon itself. He disgusted me.

"This is lunacy!" Tremayne threw his hands up and turned his back. "I took on the hard work of power. Will you not do the same, lord? Will you throw away your triumph? For if you think you can prevail without me—"

"Silence! All of you!" The prince jumped up from his stool and wandered over to the tables and stacks. "What have I done to get so foully entangled with priestesses, children, and over-diligent servants, some of them sporting priggish purebloods? It's as if you all conspire against me!" He shoved a pile of helmets to the floor.

As the helms clattered and bounced, the pouting ducessa refilled her wine cup. She drained it and launched the delicate vessel into the scattered armor. Then, as if her pique was satisfied, she joined Perryn and led him away from the mess.

"Sweet lord, it grieves me to see your generous heart so torn." She drew his arm to her breast. "That poor child. Your loyal ally. That must be why the gods favor you above all men, both upholding you and testing you, so that those of us privileged to stand in your shining circle might be uplifted as well. How perfectly right that it is in your power both to *do* and to *undo*."

She brought his hand to her lips for a soft kiss. Relinquishing his arm, she returned to her seat and folded her hands modestly in her lap.

Perryn, his back to all, wandered a little farther. Stopped. After a moment he spun sharply and returned to the wavering circle of light transformed. Standing straight and fair and sober, the light gleaming in his pale hair, he was the perfect model of noble justice. *Great Kemen, Lord of Sky and Patron of Kings, let him not be just a model, but an extension of your hand. . . .*

"Such a terrible crime as the murder of innocents must reap punishment."

"My lord—!"

"Silence!" Perryn's roar aborted Tremayne's protest. "You need not remind me of your loyalty, Laurent, or your might, or our long history of great deeds and shared pleasures."

Fallon held still, his steel gaze fixed on the man he served, his pain raw as any battle wound. He could not win this day, no matter how Perryn's judgment fell.

"Coroner Bastien, we thank you for bringing this crime to our attention. Your knowledge of Navronne's law and your firm adherence to it in face of this most difficult situation is wholly admirable, and we hereby confirm you in this post for as long as Ardra remains in our care. In the writ of confirmation, I shall stipulate severe penalties for *anyone*—peasant, pureblood, or noble, even my own friends—who dares threaten or enact retribution upon you for bringing a case to the fore, no matter what the magistrate's ultimate verdict. Bear witness to this, all of you."

Good. Unexpected. Tremayne's jaw was near cracking with rage. Perhaps I had rushed to judgment of this prince. . . .

"As for this judgment. We are engaged in war. As Lord Tremayne has reminded us, death is ever present and sacrifice necessary. But deliberate murder of innocents is cowardly and casts an ill odor on our cause. Therefore I deem that the proper punishment for this crime is the punishment for cowardice. Laurent, Duc de Tremayne, you are hereby sentenced to be stripped and displayed in the public market alongside a description of your crime, and you shall receive fifty lashes at the hand of the captain of the Guard Royale—"

"Fifty lashes! For *cowardice*?" Tremayne's rage shook the foundation of the Repository. "How can you imagine I will tolerate this? My men and I have bled for you, lord. I have killed for you." He held his fists in front of him, ready to crush the first person who tried to drag him to a flogging post.

Fallon dropped to one knee and bowed his head, his expression unreadable. His father's shame would cling to him until the end of days.

Bastien's lips were pressed hard together. It was not the judgment he hoped for. Tremayne would likely not die. But the humiliation, the judgment of cowardice, and the crippling punishment would ruin such a powerful man. A victory, even if tempered.

Satisfaction filled my own spirit. Questions answered. A resolution. Rightness. If only somehow we could persuade Perryn to judge Irinyi and Motre Varouna . . .

"However"—Perryn's abrupt continuation brought every head up—"Palinur is under siege, or soon will be. In the hour before I came here, I received word that my traitorous brother and his legions will be camped at Palinur's gates within days. Every hand, every sword, and every cadre will be needed in service to Ardra and Navronne. Therefore all civil judgments are suspended indefinitely, this to be proclaimed throughout Palinur by dawn tomorrow. So say I, Perryn, Duc of Ardra, Prince of Navronne."

As if in a flash of magefire, hope was transformed to ash. Rightness to jarring corruption. Appalling, despicable . . .

Both Tremayne and his kneeling son gawped at the prince, who preened at his cleverness.

Fallon moved first and dropped his gaze, arms crossed on his breast, fists clenched, as if to collect and contain the fragments of his beliefs.

The duc's stormy countenance began to glow. Perryn would be king, perhaps this very night. No one who stood with him would suffer the inconvenience of a murder judgment. Tremayne dropped to his knees and bent his back. "I am, as ever, your devoted ally."

Perryn wagged a finger, his mistress already distracting him. And so when Tremayne rose again, the duc's gimlet gaze and twisted smile was all for Bastien and me. *Kings* could pardon capital crimes. *Kings* could even forgive acts of vengeance against upstart coroners or arrogant purebloods. Perryn's promise to protect Bastien held no more worth than the Registry's vow to heal my "madness."

The power to do and to undo. A knowing smile teased the ducessa's generous lips, as she drew the prince close. He plunged his fingers into her red-gold hair and stroked her jaw and neck with his thumbs. Not gently, but she didn't seem to mind. She held his wine to his lips.

What a fool! Perryn believed he ruled her . . . all of us. He believed himself handsome and clever. He believed his parentage made him kingly. But even an inexperienced pureblood could see the truth. He had deceived everyone in Palinur, himself not least.

Tremayne laid a heavy hand on his kneeling son's shoulder. Forgiveness, reconciliation . . . or another warning? Were I Fallon de Tremayne, I would make sure to keep out of range of my father's archers, lest one of them mistake me for the enemy.

"No, no, no . . ." The snarling denial resonated in my soul, but it was given voice in a whisper behind me . . . and then beside . . . as Bastien moved forward. "You lily-livered wastrel. You sniveling, mindless, murdering moron. You poisonous excrement of greater men. You—"

Before anyone could hear, I wrapped my arms around the coroner from behind and dragged him deep into the shadows. Clamping a hand over his mouth, I hissed into his ear, "Your life is worthy. Your death will not bring back the dead. Or justice."

He growled and wrestled inside his skin, but not with me; he could have burst my hold with one harsh thrust. He wanted to. Gods' grace, how he wanted to.

"Listen to me," I said. "We must get out before Tremayne turns on us. Before Hugh de Orrin or Varouna runs to the Registry with reports of a mad pureblood, or Irinyi sends her temple guards to put knives in our backs. We have a bargain. I've a mystery to solve tomorrow, and I need your help. Now bow and thank him, or I'll conjure your prick into a dog's tail."

Though breathing as hard as if we'd battled, his muscles stilled and I let go.

"*You* speak," he said, through gritted teeth. "I dare not."

And so we approached the would-be king, and when he could unlatch his attention from his fawning mistress and his wine, I offered a modest deference. Bastien dropped to one knee, eyes down.

"Our duty is done, lord prince," I said in my chilliest hauteur. "The law is satisfied. Final justice shall await the day of Navronne's safety, for which we all petition our gods. Accept our gratitude for your forbearance. My master is yet speechless at your generous appointment and will strive to be worthy of it as he seeks justice for the dead."

"A toast to the balance of justice and those who serve it." Perryn raised his cup, tottering a bit. How many had he downed? "We visit the Registry tomorrow, Remeni. I'll sing your praises to the curators."

My throat clotted. "Unnecessary, my good lord. Tomorrow is the day to honor my grandsire. I'd not distract attention from his memory."

"Perhaps I'll tell old Gramphier I want you. I'd wager I could wrest your contract from this worthy coroner. Then I'd install you here to dispose of this flotsam and send you off to find me barbarian treasures."

Perryn did not wait for my appalled response. He and his ducessa were already tittering at some private jest as they strolled toward the bronze doors where a smug Tremayne awaited them.

Fallon had sat back on his heels, hands resting on his thighs, a sculpture of cold steel, not warm bronze. As Bastien fetched our rucksack, I approached the young lord, halting at a respectful distance, feeling the necessity to speak though I'd no idea what to say.

"Did she suffer overmuch?" he said, before I could begin.

"It happened very quickly from his arrival to her death. But she was her grandsire's worthy descendant. She fought bravely and with all her strength. Yet she was dead before he threw her down the rampart. I hope that is some comfort."

"None." He did not look up. "She was a merry sprite. I knew early on she wasn't Father's. But I never suspected . . . I should have seen it. I could have shielded her."

"Would you like to have her portrait? I could copy it for you, as true as the first. I could make it small, easy to carry."

He glanced up, his eyes lance points. "Not the first. I will ever recall her well enough as I knew her. But I'd like a copy of the other one, the one with the bloody shift. For now, I've no choice but to forget everything you've said of this matter. But when the time is right, I'll pull out that drawing and release what I must bury tonight. If the gods have not wrought justice by that day, I will."

"Good enough," I said. "After tomorrow, find Constance at Necropolis

Caton. She'll have the portrait for you, and she can show you where the child is laid."

He nodded and looked away. "Beware. My father, as you've seen, bows to neither sentiment nor the law."

I left Fallon to bury his sister and his hatred. So unlikely an encounter. I'd not forget him.

Bastien fidgeted beside the door, his sword already in hand. "There's arguing just outside. Hope you've magics to scare off some angry partisans."

The Xancheiran spindle remained tucked inside my doublet. I would have to leave the painted chest and the rest of its secrets here for the time. One more regret among many.

"Better we use the back door."

CHAPTER 31

Bastien and I crept from the rear of the Antiquities Repository and scuttered through the hedge garden like startled hinds, keeping as far as we could from Perryn's lancers . . . and the four men in black and white arguing with them. Black and white, the Duc de Tremayne's personal colors. A chill, foggy night, and I was already sweating.

Once away from the Repository, we slowed to a steady—unremarkable—pace. People stepped aside to let me pass. Bastien kept a few paces back so none would guess we were together.

There were far too many people and too much torchlight for the quiet departure we'd planned. Eights and tens of servants and courtiers choked every nook and colonnade. The excitement was yet spoken in whispers. *I've heard . . . It's said . . . Rumor is . . . Closeted in the chancellor's chambers . . . The Ardran son always favored . . . The Smith's bound to give up the claim . . . No more war . . . The gods will be appeased.*

They were wrong. Even if my suspicions about the newfound will proved incorrect, villeins would still face fields of frozen mud at sowing time and plagues at hearth and sheepfold. The decline of the world had begun before Eodward's death.

A blast of damp wind swirled the smoke of torches and roasting meat. I shivered.

A skeletal young man, leaning heavily on a stick instead of a right leg, stood gossiping with two grizzled veterans at the apex of an arched bridge. If the conflict ended, at least the bloodshed and maiming might stop.

Just past the bridge and a columned arch, a steep stair led down to the inner bailey. I stepped into a niche between the arch and a wall to wait for Bastien. We had a new problem.

"Holy gods, do you smell that smoke? I'm going to drown in my own slobber," he said, slipping in beside me. "I didn't think there was meat to be had in the city."

He abruptly shoved me deeper into the niche. A quartet of men in temple livery hurried past in the direction of the Repository. My own stomach ground with nausea more than hunger.

"You need to get out of that cloak and mask," said Bastien. "Tremayne's livery is everywhere, and now the priestess's, too."

"Not just them, I'm afraid," I said. "Look down at the wicket gate. The Registry's here as well."

Our position offered a good view of the brightly lit courtyard below. Vielles and hurdy-gurdies sawed raucous tunes for a dancing, eating, laughing mob. Two pureblood servitors flanked the narrow gate we had to traverse from the inner to the outer bailey. They were deathly sober.

"We could make our way round to the postern. Might be fewer people between."

"Masked, disguised, naked, west gate, postern—it doesn't matter," I said. "If they've come for me, they'll recognize me—and you—and they'll be watching every gate."

"So we need a distraction. As you didn't blast the royal snake and his murdering friend into Magrog's hells, you've magic to use, right?"

"The problem is what to do with it." I didn't like what I was thinking. "I suppose I could lead them off while you get through. I could circle around, get back, release my fog enchantment, and run through the wicket before they catch me up."

His skeptical grimace reflected my own opinion. "Constance could come up with a better plan! You'd never get back in time. And what if there are more of them waiting in the outer bailey? I think one of those void holes would do us better." Bastien had yearned to see a void hole since I'd told him of my grand enchantment in the temple.

"No. Firstly, I'd have to lay it down right under their noses. And secondly, if it's too big or too deep, it's going to kill someone when the ground caves. Thirdly, if it's close enough to snag the guards, we'd not be able to get past it to get out the gate, while smaller and farther away is useless, as they'll never leave their post just to gawk, unless . . ."

I *truly* didn't like what I was thinking. Timing would be everything.

"Back by the parapet was a young man with a walking stick," I said abruptly. "Buy it from him before he gets away. Just do it. And leave me the rucksack."

He grumbled but didn't question, which marked a level of trust I hoped would prove out.

While he bulled his way back the way we'd come, I squeezed deeper into the dark space between column and wall. From the rucksack I dragged the ugly brown cape. From under my doublet I pulled out the small canvas-wound spindle I'd snatched from the Xancheiran chest. No time to unlock its stinging enchantments just now. The spindle went into the bottom of the sack. The brown cape I draped over the wine-hued wool I wore, tucking the pureblood cloak out of sight. Then I yanked off my mask.

The common penalty for being caught *out of dress* in the presence of ordinaries was a caning before representatives of ten pureblood families. I'd heard the punishment was sufficiently painful to ensure no repetition of the offense, and certainly did not wish to test what the *uncommon* version of it might be. But that was my least worry just now.

I needed something that would not only hold a linked spell, like the iron grave marker or my silver bracelets had done, but a great deal of pure magic. The number of objects that could do that was small—gemstones, pearls, the black glassy stone found near volcanoes, and such rarities. Fortunately my father's ruby would serve, though to taint his ring with violence scarred my conscience. Patronn had been such a gentle man, his talent fine but narrow compared to my grandsire's—or mine. Generous, too. I'd never considered how much. Not once had he chided me for spending my youth so eagerly with his own father instead of him.

Believing he would appreciate his ring's saving my neck, I shaped a voiding spell and linked it to the gold ring. Then, eyes closed, I laid three fingers on the ruby itself and let my magic flow. The fire in my blood erased the chill and damp. *Such sweet fire . . .*

"Got it. You owe me— What the devil are you doing?"

"Wait . . ."

I couldn't stop, not until I'd stored enough power to ensure the enchantment worked. There'd be no recourse if we failed. Keeping only a little in reserve, I lifted my fingers. "Done."

"Didn't think you dared undress yourself." His eyes were on the ruby ring that gleamed with an unnatural fire. "A ruby and a cripple's stick and an unmasked pureblood. I hope this plan isn't crazier than the last."

"I take the stick; you take the ring. It won't burn you or anything . . . unless you were to run off with it."

My attempt at humor didn't help. He glanced from the ring to my face three times before touching it.

When it didn't explode or scorch him, his shoulders relaxed. Slightly. "You and your steel spine," he mumbled. "Make a man do things he knows he oughtn't, just to keep up."

He was wrong about the steel. My spine felt like soggy bread. "Whatever you do, keep this safe as well," I said, opening the rucksack and showing him the spindle tucked inside. "I've no idea what it is, but if anything happens to me, bury it in your graveyard and never speak of it. Doesn't matter how important it might be or how useless; it's naught but trouble should any ordinary be caught with it."

He opened his mouth, but no words came out.

"Now I'm going to walk a very particular loop down in the bailey. Watch me and mark the placement and dimensions exactly. If you're off a finger's breadth, this isn't going to work." Actually, there would be a slight overspill on either side of the line, but he had to get it right. "Be ready by the time I get back to the place I started, and when the Registry men cross the boundary nearest them—you can judge the timing—touch the ruby to any spot on my path. *Exactly* on the path. Farther from where I'm standing would likely be better, but be sure." I tugged the brown hood lower and the flapping, stinking wool about my chin. "Keep trying until it works, and, whatever you do, stay on the *outside* of the loop."

Bastien's grin blossomed hugely. "So I get to see one, eh?"

"If I do it right. Elsewise I'll see you in Idrium."

"Won't come to that," he said, quickly sobered. "I've got my sword. Besides, you're mine for most of four years to come, bought and paid for. We may have sucked a dry tit today, but I'll be damned if I let you loose till I know what's in those accursed portraits and what's this Path of the White Hand and if that was truly a Dané that talked to you about it. Would hate to think you're a loony after all."

"I must be," I said, lifting my eyebrows at him for a change. "I'm thinking . . . we partner well."

A knight caught in battle unarmored must feel this way, I thought, as I limped down the stair and across the yard without pureblood cloak and mask. I couldn't shake the sense the two Registry men could see straight through the wretched brown cape.

Begin at a spot straight out from the wicket gate no more than thirty paces. I didn't want to leave us too far to run. *Five paces straight toward the man sawing on the vielle . . .*

I limped as fast as I dared through the crowded bailey, bobbing my head to the music while dragging the stick to create the enclosing loop. Inside my head, I held the spell of the ring, weaving its edges to the line I walked. Not the easiest way to work a void, but it should do.

Left at the hurdy-gurdy man; now past the knot of singers toward the soldier turning the spit . . . I made the perimeter as nearly rectangular as I could estimate. Easier for me to get it right. Easier, I hoped, for Bastien to find a place to trigger the spell. My stick left a line in the dirt as well as the thread of enchantment, but jigging dancers, messengers, mule carts, and dogs quickly erased most of the visible boundary.

More rumors pattered on my back like rain. Maybe Perryn started the rumors even before meeting me at the Repository, when he first realized I'd come to provide him an unimpeachable witness to the finding of his father's will.

Concentrate, fool. Six . . . seven . . . weave boundary and spell . . . eight, turn . . . Ten steps this direction to keep the proportion . . . I walked the gate side of the small rectangle, the Registry servitors so close I could smell what they had eaten last. Their faces were alert, scanning the shifting crowd.

I ducked my head. Mumbled. Dragged the stick. Wove the spell. *A slow collapse. Just deep enough it would take time to climb out.* I waved my hand at those standing in my path and muttered, "Get out the way. This be a cursed spot. I can smell it."

Back at the beginning, midway along the boundary farthest from the gate, I closed the loop with a dollop of magic.

One of the purebloods jerked his head in my direction.

Heart dancing its own jig, I ducked my head and shuffled a few paces backward—enough I wouldn't get caught in the void and tumble into the hole. *Be quick, Bastien.*

The pureblood on the left edged forward a little. Called softly to the other. Waved a finger in a loop. As long as he didn't figure out what spell I'd laid . . .

Come on, Bastien, come on! The fleeting notion that the coroner had taken the ring and escaped on his own shamed me. But truly it seemed a month already.

Bastien strolled into view. He bought a pocket loaf from a bread seller, and stopped beside the boundary to munch on it, nodding his head in time with a rattling tabor.

Taking that as my signal, I ducked my head, slipped on my mask, and offered a heartfelt invocation. I crouched down, grabbed a handful of dirt, and in one grand gesture, lunged upward, threw off the brown cloak, and enchanted the flying cloud of filth and dust into a whirlwind of colored light.

Horrified dancers scrambled away, shoving, pushing, yelling in panic. But cries turned quickly to laughing wonder as the drifting sparks tickled and did not burn. None stepped closer, though. I stood alone and exposed in the center of the bailey. Unfortunately, the purebloods, too, hung back, peering into the mottled light behind me . . . beckoning urgently.

I spun around. Two men in masks and wine-hued cloaks shoved through the crowd on the stair. *No, no!* I needed the gate watchers inside the void perimeter.

"Fire!" Bastien's shout whipped my head around. He was pointing at me. "That madman's firing the palace!"

Taking his cue, I grabbed more dirt and sent up another burst of sparks, along with gouts of flame and a roar. Then I backed away a few more steps as if poised to retreat.

That was enough. The two at the gate bolted toward me. And Bastien touched the ground and the earth collapsed inward, almost floating, carrying the two purebloods and perhaps three others along with it. The bailey erupted in panic.

I released the spell of fog and noises into the melee, then sped around the small pit toward the wicket gate, happy I'd imprinted its position so firmly in my head. I kept my head down, tried not to get tangled with panicked ordinaries. . . .

A missile slammed into my back, jolting me forward. My limbs seized, heated enchantment spreading through spine and sinew like cracks in shattered ice. Strength fled. No one around me seemed to notice.

Stay on your feet, fool. I was so close. The dancing gleam on my right would be the soldier's roasting fire.

Invisible lightning crackled through the fog on my left and thudded into my side. The impact staggered me. Threads of spellfire ripped through lungs and heart. One hand touched earth, as I stumbled forward, my feet like clubs. Pain threatened to shatter my bones.

The wall loomed through the wisps of enchanted fog, a handsbreadth from my nose. Bastien, sword drawn, manned the wicket gate, encouraging people to pass through in an orderly fashion. When he glimpsed me, he stopped the flow, holding the frenzied crowd back with his blade. "Let him pass! Registry business. Godspeed, chosen!"

I lurched toward the gate.

Another crackling from behind me and the wicket gate exploded, battering all with shards of wood and iron and billowing black smoke. My right temple burned. My eyelids sagged.

Panicked screams shrilled from every side. I needed to move, but my body just hurt. . . .

Someone nearly wrenched my arm from its socket.

"Don't touch me." But I'd no strength to draw my arm away. "The law . . ."

"I *am* the law. Remember?" Bastien's growl in my ear would have made me smile, had my knees not taken that moment to collapse and my stomach to empty itself of pignut bread and bile.

The world spun and jostled and settled upside down with a boulder in my belly. My lacerated face bounced on leather that stank of horse muck.

"Over here!" Bastien's bellow rumbled in my ribs. Yet I seemed to be *here* already, wrapped around his broad shoulders.

Jostling. The clash of steel very close . . . how was that possible? Bastien's arms—both of them—pinned me tight. Had he grown extra?

"Stand down, all of you!" A new voice, scarce distinguishable from the steel. "Stand down and move aside, by order of Prince Perryn's *consiliar prime*!"

Registry servitors? Tremayne the devil?

I yelled at Bastien to drop me and run, but it came out a muddled mumble. He only yanked my arm and leg tighter over his shoulders and around his chest until I thought my side must rip.

"One of the gods' chosen has fallen in service to his prince," spat the steely commander. "Get him to his people. A madman's on the loose inside the walls. Bar the gates behind us."

Deeper darkness. More jostling. Hands grappling and then a dreadful sensation of slipping . . . falling. My limbs refused to answer my commands. Magic sputtered through my fingers and fell dead. My tongue produced gibberish.

"Silence, conjurer." A snappish whisper. Strong arms held me up from each side as if my rescuer had split into two. "Get him over behind the stables, and, for gods' sake, hide that cloak and mask."

A hand ripped off my mask. A whipping of cloth, and a mantle fell over me. My feet whisked and bumped on the ground. Two men, then. One on each side, breathing hard. One of them smelled like fresh corpses. I knew him. I wanted to ask who the other was, but my tongue was a dead fish. The night grew darker, interminably.

"His head's bleeding, lord. We ought to take a look."

"Time enough for that. I've a horse kept here for dispatch riding. Have her back here by dawn."

"Done."

They propped me up against a splintery wall. I promptly crumpled. On the way downward, my throbbing side struck something very hard. Pain obliterated thought and sense entire.

Water splattered and dribbled over my back. Hot water. Blessedly hot. My head—or the pounding granite knob that had replaced it—rested on two bony lumps. Knees. My own, I guessed, though the knees themselves gave no evidence of it. I couldn't feel anything that far away. Ridges of metal dug unpleasantly into my upper arms—my naked arms—propping me up, but everything beyond my elbows was dead, too.

"This'n? Are ye sure? Seems cruel with slush floatin' in it?" The woman's voice bounced about the bottom of a well, and I was—

A frigid downpour atop my head robbed me of thought, though it confirmed I was, indeed, naked as a babe. "M-m-m-erciful Mother!"

"Ah-hah! You see, it worked." The man bellowed from a barrel. "Just as the young lord told me. Do it again. From the front this time."

Wait! A scalding flood on my legs and feet that—gods in all heavens—splashed over my groin. And before I could beg mercy, another dousing straight from Magrog's icy heart stole every whisper of breath and shriveled every quat of my flesh.

"Again!" said the cruel man, laughing as a flashing pitcher emptied its hellish liquid on my head.

And with the slurry of snow and water that quickly followed arrived the snap of a fire, the smells of ale and wet wood and greasy smoke, the sounds of muffled laughter, the stomp of boots in rhythm with a trilling pipe, and a murderous ache in my side. Water slopped just behind me—pitchers being filled.

"Wait! Stop!" I yelled. "No more!" I would have leapt up and proved my state, but the female tittering all around kept me crouched in— My half-frozen, half-scalded forearm blotted my bleary eyes. I crouched in a bathing tub scarce bigger than Maia's largest cookpot.

Shrinking into a defensive knot, I glared at Bastien, who stood at the foot of the tub, grinning through his thicket of beard. Though chips of stone and wood were yet stuck in his tangled hair, he appeared to have suffered no injury from the exploding gate.

"Welcome back, *servant*. And say thank you to the gentle ladies of the Bucket Knot, the finest sop-house in Palinur, for rousing you from your *drunken stupor*."

Two stringy-haired girls in wet aprons held dripping pitchers at the ready, while a third poked at a blazing fire. A tall girl with red cheeks and red-gold curls stood by with a length of not-so-clean linen, inspecting me with an experienced eye and a friendly grin. "Seem he has 'is wits back, Coroner. Do you s'pose 'e rathers the towel or should we get 'im up dancing to get him dry? Your runners always like the dancing and drinking well enough, though they never seem to fancy us girls!"

A sop-house. Baths, beer, and bawds. A haven for thieves and twistminds and other low sorts, so I'd been warned. But the girls looked cheerful, the hearth fire merry, and the low-ceilinged room, lit with the smoky yellow glow of rushlights clipped in brackets around the walls, felt safe and friendly. Inexplicably so, when all the forces of Magrog's hell were after us.

"Mayhap we'll have a dance later, sweet Tansy," said Bastien. "For the present, give us the towel. And draw us a mug of whatever's decent, now the fool's breathing. We'll come out to fetch it and celebrate the *news*." He waggled his eyebrows as he did whenever he wished me to take especial note of his words. He thought I oughtn't mention that it was magical thunderbolts from the Registry had paralyzed me. As for *news*, I wasn't sure.

The giggling girls bustled out, leaving only the ruddy-cheeked Tansy. She tossed the wadded linen to Bastien and winked at me before strolling out. "I'll be waiting!" she called over her shoulder. "Dorrie's a merry piper."

A man with more wits and fewer enemies than I would surely find her airs most inviting.

"So, you've bones again, eh?" said Bastien, dangling the towel over my head.

"B-brutal," I croaked through chattering teeth. "That was brutal." Thoroughly chilled, I sat in a finger's depth of cold water. Every shiver wrenched the pain in my side.

He dropped the towel over my head. "But you can move now . . . control your limbs, you see. Such paralyzing magics are oft thrown in battle, and his family's pureblood told him hot and cold dousing was the only way to shake them off in a timely fashion. We owe him in a number of ways."

I climbed out and blotted myself, happy to note my garments draped over a wooden rack next the fire and that my forehead was the only part of me seeping blood. "*He* . . . the swordsman with the horse? The one who got us out."

Bastien leaned close and dropped his voice. "Fallon de Tremayne. When his father's men barged into the Repository in search of us, he sent them off one way and followed us out the other. Said he wasn't going to let his da get away with another murder tonight."

"Gods, he could hang for thwarting the Registry's hunt. And his father's wrath could be worse." Such courage was humbling. He didn't owe me anything.

"Aye. I've already sent his horse back to the stable. It's trusty folk here at the Knot." Good cheer fallen away, he passed me the warmed clothes. "More so than my own people, I suppose."

I'd no answer for Bastien's angry hurt. I laced the baggy chausses around my waist and pulled on the stained shirt. There was no sign of my purple cloak or mask or the threadbare brocade doublet I'd worn to the palace. "I take it that *this* servant is to remain half-naked."

"Aye. I told them you gave your outer garments to a starving lady, as you had no food to offer. The girls think you're one of these Karish saints. Tansy will cobble up something for you before we go; she's near as good as Constance at providing what's needed."

"We need to go now. Your people at Caton are in terrible danger."

"I sent Garibald a warning soon's we got here—two, three hours ago. We've no chance to get there ourselves just now. The celebrations have clogged the streets worse than the famine riots."

"Celebrations?"

"The criers are out. Despite the *mad Harrower who used stolen magics in an attempt to fire the palace this evening*, the chancellor of Navronne has announced the discovery of King Eodward's will. Seems it names Perryn, Duc of Ardra, as his heir."

Expecting Perryn's victory didn't make it more palatable. But the other part . . . "They named me a *Harrower* using *stolen magics*?"

"Several onlookers reported the dastard wore an orange scarf, though others swore he was a dragon, breathing fire. Certainly it couldn't have been a true sorcerer, as the Registry is entirely loyal to our new king." Bastien wagged his head wearily. "For our safety, Servant *Filon*, I believe we should remain in this merry company and drink to King Perryn—at least until the rest of Palinur falls down drunk and allows us safe passage to our beds."

"Which are likely not safe, either." Nor would they ever be, my gut told me.

"Likely not. But the sexton will see our people safe. And, I've a notion where we might take refuge and assess the outfall from our day's work . . . our cursed, lunatic, *useless* work."

Face twisting into righteous rage, he lifted the copper tub and threw it into the wall. The dregs of my dousing extinguished half the rushlights and dripped in ashy rivulets to the floor.

CHAPTER 32

It was in the sop-house called the Bucket Knot on the night after the inquest into Ysabel de Tremayne's murder that the Pretender to Eodward's throne was born. This fourth royal son was strong, intelligent, courageous, and nurtured far from Navronne, destined to be the hope of all who learned the truth of Perryn the Weasel, Bayard the Smith, and Magrog's rival, Osriel the Bastard. Of course, this virtuous youth was not birthed of a human mother and good King Eodward, but of a disgruntled coroner and a drunken pureblood.

I'd been starving and tight wound as a crossbow, knowing half the city was after us with murder on their minds. In a few short hours I was to sneak into the Tower, and examine the curators' portraits to learn who wanted me dead. Meanwhile, I had to sit, unmasked, amid a taproom full of ordinaries, expected to talk and jest as they did. And though my side seemed only bruised, it hurt fiercely, worse even than my head. Concentrating on the cups of stout ale rosy-cheeked Tansy kept setting in front of me eased all these discomforts. I'd never imbibed so much with a gut so empty. An hour in and I was giggling like the sop-house girls.

Bastien whispered that he'd best get drunk like me or he'd be hauled out for the happy mob to dismember. He was furious with himself for expecting better of the loathsome Perryn.

When Tansy's mistress arrived to complain that we had dented the Bucket Knot's prized copper tub, Bastien waved toward me, mumbling that his servant had some delicious gossip to repay the debt, and somehow in my onrushing inebriation, I came up with the rumor of Eodward's fourth son. Bastien pounced, imbuing our creation with the necessary virtues. As the night wore on and everyone in the common room grew louder and unlikely to remember their own names, much less ours, we'd thought it a great joke to whisper of it with each of the sop-house girls, swearing each to forget where they'd heard it. Soon everyone in the house was talking of the Pretender.

Yet in the pitchy hour before moonset, as the two of us stumbled down the hill toward the hirudo, I could not imagine why the prank had seemed so amusing. The moon's dull light stabbed my eyes like a poignard. My mouth tasted like a stable floor. We had to stop every few steps to gather our wits, get a better grip on each other, or puke. I repeatedly asked Bastien where we might sleep that we wouldn't be slaughtered in our beds. He kept answering, "Head homeward."

That *homeward* should lead me toward a city of the dead seemed a kind of blasphemy.

"Halt!" Three Cicerons stepped out of the brush at the base of the slope. Lantern light revealed bloody knives and clothes, and a smoking rubble where two huts had once stood. Reason rushed back.

"Fetch Demetreo," I said, swallowing bile and hauling Bastien's heavy body upward yet again. "Tell him it's the coroner and his servant. We need a safe place to sleep."

Bastien's snores could have waked the entire population of his necropolis. The dawn that reddened the sky had not yet reached the hirudo when I wandered outside the flimsy lean-to in search of quiet. I found a piece of broken wall to sit on and pulled my grandsire's canvas-wrapped spindle from under my baggy shirt. Bastien had kept hold of the rucksack through magic and melee, dousing and drunkenness. He felt no sensation from touching the spindle, which was astounding. Even yet, its enchantment had me wanting to claw the skin from my bare hand.

The whole was no longer than a woman's hand, wrist to fingertip, the cross-section no thicker than my thumb. Only the outer wrapping was sturdy canvas, the material my grandsire used to protect fragile documents when he had no supple leather to hand. Examining the end of the tight little roll revealed a more fragile fabric underneath the protective sheath.

The frayed edge and mottled color spoke of age. Carved into each end of the wood spindle was a five-branched tree. Xancheira.

I exhaled a pent breath and began to work on the layered protections. First my grandfather's knot spell that locked the ribbon tie, easily countered. The canvas sheath bore a protection against fire, but naught else. I removed it, exposing a roll of fragile linen.

But then matters became most discouraging. The harsher enchantments that pierced and itched my hand were bound to a locking spell so complex I wasn't sure I even knew how it worked, much less how to undo it. Cursing, I set to work . . .

. . . and at the first touch of my magic, both spells vanished. A delicate flap of linen fell loose, inviting me to look. Such an odd combination of spells—the fire that pained only me, a lock that kept no one out, unless . . .

Without magic, I touched the linen wound on the spindle. Pain coursed through the sinews of my arm. The hem of the fabric began to smolder. But with the slightest infusion of my power, both pain and thready smoke vanished. Magic was as distinct as an artist's brushstrokes, thus it did not seem farfetched to conclude that my grandsire wanted me, and no one else, to notice the spindle.

Excitement sharpened my attention. *O Serena Fortuna, let this not be some ancient house dam's inventory!*

I unrolled the fragile linen, spreading and folding it over my knees, ensuring its trailing ends didn't fall into the muck. Bordered in intricate spirals of gold thread, it was longer than my estimate. Surely it was a *stola*, an Aurellian ceremonial scarf made to hang from one's neck and invoke blessings or interventions from the gods. Fine stitches of colored silk formed fans of words and symbols along its length, arranged from the center so that both halves of the array would appear right side up when the garment was worn.

Hope of enlightenment faded as my eyes devoured its length. The inscriptions were no household inventory, but almost as mundane. At the tail of each half was a single name—one side *Domenica*, one side *Eruin*. Stitched above each was a genealogy, each fan marking a generation of parents and children. This was certainly a wedding *stola*, worn by a Xancheiran woman of Aurellian heritage—a pureblood woman—as she assumed the responsibility of carrying on her new husband's bloodline as well as her own. It was a beautifully crafted record of a sacred heritage, for each name was accompanied by the symbol of a pureblood bent, just as Registry documents would display my own lineage. Here was an eye for a diviner, there a loom for a weaver, crossed chisels for a sculptor, and—

I shifted around so that the rising sun would strike the fabric more directly. Some symbols were missing. Not worn or rotted away, for the threads where the symbol should be lay flat and smooth beside the names. Henik, the great-great-grandsire of the bride, had no designation. Either the sewing woman had been careless—difficult to believe with such exquisite and significant work—or the *stola* had been wrought before the Registry formalized the breeding laws, for indeed Henik was a Moriangi name, not Aurellian. He was an ordinary.

Henik's wife, Neria, was a pureblood sculptress. And the same symbol appeared beside the name of their daughter, Regan. Their *halfblood* daughter, if I was reading this correctly.

My skin prickled. In the next fan down the *stola*, Regan's name was linked to one Philo. The mark of the sculptor's bent was repeated beside Regan's name. And beside the name of her husband, two marks had been stitched—the pincers of a goldsmith and the quill of a scribe. Two marks—a dual bent.

My gaze snapped down to the names of Regan and Philo's children. And there, the tiny stitches of this ancient garment proclaimed the impossible. Marcus, a scribe. Philomena, a sculptress. And Jullian, no mark. Two grandchildren of a pureblood and an ordinary were marked as bearing pureblood bents. Impossible.

My gaze darted to another name that lacked a mark. The bridegroom Eruin's grandmother, an ordinary named Cymra, had wed a pureblood, Leonid, who bore the dual bents of a linguist and a singer. Each of their five children had been gifted, and so, too, their grandchildren, including Eruin himself, a singer—one whose songs could make his listeners see visions.

The Registry declared our blood sacred, because no descendant of a halfblood could carry the bent. Never could purebloods and ordinaries interbreed without committing the blasphemy of destroying the gods' gift of magic. To protect that gift, we had devised the disciplines that kept our kind separate, that forbade us simple friendships and the choice of what life to pursue or what person to love, that allowed the Registry to punish any of us who strayed from our rules and destroy any ordinary who dared interfere in our ways or claimed to work magic. This simple fact of nature had created a way of life that kept our gifts precious . . . and rare . . . and our family treasuries full, and the Registry powerful enough to rival and balance Crown and Temple. Only that *simple fact* was a lie.

"Great gods, sorcerer, you look as if you've seen the end of the world."

I glanced up, vision blurred and mind slowed to a crawl as two centuries of history and lies and vanished cities and massacred populations clogged my thinking. But as surely as the indistinct features resolved into Bastien's grimy curiosity, so did the fullness of our danger strike me harder than any magical thunderbolt ever could. The end of the world indeed. *Holy Mother! Lord of Light!*

No wonder Capatronn had stopped speaking to me. No wonder he had tried to excise my second bent—the very talent that might reveal the truth he'd learned—in front of the First Curator of the Registry. No wonder he had buried me in the Registry portrait studio, where all could see how ignorant I was. He had been terrified the Registry would find out what he knew and assume he had told me.

This flimsy bit of cloth explained the Registry suppression of a second bent. For if those with two bents could reinvigorate a broken bloodline, we could make the impossible possible. The gift of sorcery could spread outside pureblood families. Loyalties and disciplines would be upended. The Registry would lose its stranglehold on magic.

"This is—"

No. Bastien could not know. He could not even suspect. If he and his friends were to survive, he had to be able to swear without hesitation that he had no idea what I might have discovered about my grandsire's investigation. They would question him under enchantments of confusion; they would probe his mind and memory. The least glimmer of this truth, and he and anyone he might have told would die . . . as my family had died.

"A sample of Xancheiran needlework," I said, rolling the fabric on the wooden spindle and relocking its protective spellwork.

"So I'm naught but a rock-headed ordinary again. Good for swordwork and rescuing, but not to be trusted with pureblood business."

"I trust you beyond anyone in this world. With my life. With my sister's life." If I so much as hinted that the scroll was dangerous, a Registry investigator would ferret it out . . . and assume I'd told him more.

Closing my eyes, I pressed the spindle into his hand. "Bury this with the lily child to remind us of our failures. My grandsire thought me useless and ignorant, and so I am. If Tremayne or the Registry doesn't clap me in a dungeon, you should see to it yourself."

"You're a wretched liar, and I'm not stupid!"

"No, you're not. That's why I will *not* speak of this again." *Think, Bastien. Use your logic, and draw your own conclusions. Then you can say* truthfully *that I told you nothing.*

I set out through the hirudo's narrow lanes, leaving Bastien to follow. I regretted his bitterness, but I couldn't apologize and I couldn't retreat. The knowledge I bore could change Navronne . . . the world . . . forever, and once changed, there would be no going back. The word *pureblood* would have no meaning.

Who at the Registry knew the truth? Gramphier, most likely. And Pluvius. Albin? Pons? What if my portraits of the curators had not exposed *personal* faults at all, but rather which of them knew the truth, and thus bore the stain of my family's slaughter?

"It's even more important I see the portraits tonight," I said. "If the curators tell Perryn I've gone crazy, Tremayne will never wear a noose." Nor would my dead ever have justice. As for the lie . . . and changing the world . . . I'd have to consider what to do about that.

The hirudo was awake and wary. Every shadow held an armed man. There were no dice players. No children. No laughter. No syrinx. Even through my own fear and tumult, the air felt taut. When would they go? Would Perryn's ascension and the promise of peace keep them here a while longer? To pass through an enchanted doorway and into an unknown realm was no easy choice, no matter legend or promise or a mad sorcerer's assurance.

We'd just reached the piggery when Demetreo took shape from the crowded trees.

"We thank you for the hospitality," I said. "Our eyes are open and minds unclouded this morning."

Perhaps the Cicerons *were* Deunor's lost children. Had their own ancestors worked the true magic in their commons house?

Demetreo's dark eyes darted from me to Bastien. "Just thought you should know, Coroner, your messenger passed through safely yesternight. But not long after, we turned away some dangerous men. Some insisted on passage . . . to their sorrow. Others retreated. But of course, we could not prevent those from taking other paths to the dead city."

Not even casual admission of killing could astonish me anymore. Nothing could.

"Wasn't born an idiot," grumbled Bastien. "We'll not go prancing through the front gate."

"No insult meant. Only concerned for those who've done amicable business with us. Being of sneaking, suspicious minds as we are, Cicerons pay attention where others might not. The world grows more dangerous by the hour. We hear Prince Bayard doubts the newfound writ and will fight on."

"We appreciate the warning," I said, before Bastien could interrupt. "How fares your granny, headman?"

"She holds," he said, "but not for long. She sorely mislikes the state of the world and fears the coming dawn beyond any change she's known. If need be, she will act."

I nodded and tugged at Bastien's arm. "We'll be off, then. May Kemen Sky Lord and the Goddess Mother defend your path, *sengé*."

"And yours, pureblood. And yours, worthy coroner."

Demetreo vanished into the undergrowth, even as I quickened my own steps up the hill. If Oldmeg feared the dawn so much that she would initiate the destiny shown in her portrait, our time was short to get things done.

When the slot gate and the dawn-kissed graveyard beyond came in sight, I halted.

"Show me your hidden way, partner mine," I said, hoping to lighten Bastien's rightful anger.

"Happy to be of use, *domé*." He spat the honorific.

I could not apologize. They would test him.

He led me through a ditch at the base of the outer wall that none but an eagle could see, circling halfway around the necropolis and through a pureblood graveyard to enter the prometheum from the rear. The necropolis was eerily quiet. Carts stood unloaded. Hawkers and merchants huddled in their stalls.

"What the devil?" Bastien's steps accelerated, until we saw the silent crowd of runners and washwomen jamming the stair to my studio.

"Out of my way," snapped Bastien as he plowed through. I stayed right on his heels, dread darkening the sunlight.

. . .

"He'd chose to patrol the deadhouse," said Constance, voice cracked with grieving. "I put him on it, saying I'd a worry for the oils and the lock-chest if crazies got inside. But I never estimated no hurt to 'im, as they'd have to get past Da and the gates first, and then the merchants' men."

She stroked Pleury's blood-matted hair. The soft-bodied youth, who had so carefully arranged the corpses he brought me to draw as if their pose mattered, sprawled on the floor of my studio, his head caved in by one of my shackles. Blood and hair coated the iron band.

"How the devil did they get inside?" roared Bastien. "I sent warning!"

"They must've come over the walls, as Da kept the gates barred all the day."

Bastien badgered Constance for answers, but I could do more. Speechless with outrage and dread certainty, I touched the bloody metal and called up the magic that burned between my eyes, right in front of every person who could crowd into that fouled chamber.

My shackles. My ankles. The proximity to my own experience narrowed my search quickly. The shackles spurred visions of Tower storerooms and my own prison cell. I knew it from the stink, from the dark, from the dust and desolation, and from my smirking jailers, Nelek and Virit. They dragged me shuffling through the Tower into the Curators' Chamber and into cells I didn't recognize. They had locked my chains to chairs, to walls, to hasps set in stone in rooms where undead men lay on biers, and unseen hands shoved pens and ink, brush and paint, into my hands. . . .

I could not linger in those mysteries. A youth lay dead, and I needed to know who had wielded my chains as a weapon.

Digging deeper, I drew in threads, searching for Pleury, who always had a laugh at ready, who had puffed his chest and vowed to beat Garen in a wrestling match before he turned twenty, who liked to tie a bit of thread about a dead infant's finger so the Ferryman would know that this one was too young to answer his three questions.

"A wasted night. Where is he, vermin?" Cold fury wielded enchantment that pierced the mind like heated nails, that bound the gut with invisible blades, ever tightening, cutting. "The old man says he always sleeps here."

"Don't know . . . don't know . . . don't know. You was told right . . . always

sleeps here. Don't hurt me, lord . . . domé *. . . I don't know . . ." Words and sense dissolved in screams.*

"Finish the useless wretch before he wakes the dead. And erase this mess."

A flash of copper and a flash of enchantment, like an explosion viewed in a mirror glass, blanked out the vision. I had to drop the bloody shackle before all my senses were ripped out, too.

". . . the merchants left men behind to guard the stalls, and I made assurance that we had some posted everywhere." Constance's litany of sorrow continued. "But a broken head like mine only *thinks* she's got things right, don't she? There's no help for stupid. And now our cleverest boy—"

"It's not your fault," I said, trying not to choke on anger. "It was purebloods. Sorcerers. *My* people killed him. They were after me."

The *stola* explained why. Some simply wanted to hide the secret that could bring down the Registry, changing the balance of power in Navronne forever. Some likely wanted to find out if my grandsire had uncovered solid evidence of it or how dual bents worked—perhaps so they could destroy a bent more reliably or use my particular combination to gain advantage in the coming realignment of the world.

But this wasn't solely a pureblood matter and was certainly not just about me. These villains had profaned the gods' magic, using it to induce agony for their questioning. Cynical in their evil, they had finished Pleury with the chains so as to blame the death on ordinaries, and then they'd hidden their true identities with enchantment. And a spy had let them in. The spy. *The old man.* Garibald.

Pleury had no family that anyone knew. No one wailed or fainted at his loss. Death was too familiar at Caton. Yet all of us at the necropolis mourned. After we laid the boy in the Hallow Ground, and the carters and washwomen and hawkers' folk had gone back to work, I promised Pleury's closest friends—Bastien, Constance, Garen and the other runners—to bring down the purebloods who had murdered their friend and expose the ordinaries who aided them. I fixed my gaze on Garibald as I swore on my family's blood and honor. Though the sexton jutted his chin and ground his teeth, his ruddy skin took on the hue of the dead. Bastien saw it.

The work of the necropolis creaked forward again. I copied Fleure's portrait for Fallon de Tremayne, as I'd promised, and left it with Constance.

When I tried to take Bastien aside to speak of the traitor, Bastien shook me off. "I know what needs doing. When the time is right, he'll tell me what he knows or he'll be dead. He won't know their names, will he—the purebloods who did it—the ones he spied for?"

"No. They would have made sure he could not identify them."

"I'll get you to the Tower. I want you to find out who did it."

"On my family's name, I will."

The iron-visaged coroner dispatched his determined runners, even bruised and battered Garen, to glean every scrap of information about Prince Perryn's movements, the Tower festivities, and any estimates of Prince Bayard's arrival. He told them that we were worried about the riots starting up again.

Garibald spent the afternoon hauling in two trees to make new barricades for his gates. The veins in his brow nigh on bursting, he hacked off the weakling limbs as if each were a pureblood's neck. It was me he wanted dead or gone, not Pleury. He had ever warned Bastien of the trouble I'd bring. And so I had.

When a young baron was left by his grieving mother for Garibald's evening burning, I stole the silk pall from his coffin. I needed a new and different mask. My mother would have mourned her eldest son at hearing this; the Lucian she knew could never have been so base as to steal from the dead. But indeed that Lucian was as dead as the young baron. As dead as Pleury. *That* Lucian's life had been based on truth and honor and centuries of discipline grown from a divine trust. And all of it had been a lie.

Nose red, eyes dripping, Constance fitted me, yet again, with dead men's finery, and sewed the mask, readying it for my enchantments. "You could open a market stall for pureblood masks," I said, when she brought me the slip of blue silk. "Your stitches are as fine as any tailor's, and the shaping's better every time."

Wordless, she kept her eyes to the stone floor. Did she know of Garibald's perfidy as yet?

I touched her chin and raised it, hating what I had to say. "No one can know of these preparations, Constance, nor anything of my comings and goings. Especially not your father."

"Sworn—on Pleury's soul, it's sworn." Thin lips pressed together hard, she hurried away.

No matter what happened on the night's venture, I would fulfill my own vow, even if I had to come back from the dead or rise from a living tomb to do so. The portraits were all. Something in them would tell me who had murdered my pureblood family, who had murdered this youth of my new family, who wished me dead, and who wished me in a cage, forever in the dark.

CHAPTER 33

"*Aperite, porte mordé!*" Open, door of death.

The iron door in the Tower foundation swung open, waiting for me to step into the cellar where I'd spent five months buried.

So many years I'd known the meaning of the opening incantation. I'd always thought it a macabre reference to the Tower's troubled past. But history is a tapestry where every thread is connected to every other. The ancient kings of Ardra and Navronne had dragged their secret prisoners to the Tower cellars. And so, too, had these vainglorious villains of our own time who thought to rival kings, who had built centuries of wealth and hoarded power on a lie.

Outrage at murder and corruption had brought me this far, but not even that made it easy to cross the threshold.

Bastien had seen my fear. Likely my trembling hands told him, or perhaps the fact that I couldn't swallow so much as a walnut all afternoon. But he hadn't tried to talk me out of it.

"They're already after you," he'd said, as we threaded the alleyways of the Council District in early evening. "Even if none sees you tonight, they know where to find you. But I've friends in Cymra who take in strays. They'd keep you till your people tire of looking."

"I can't run," I said. "They won't tire. Not ever. Only one *recondeur* has ever eluded them more than a few months. I have to see who I'm up against and find Juli. Then I'll decide what to do."

"But you'll have a care. No use to any if they take you."

"No one knows about this back way in. And I'll be fast. An hour at most. All I have to do is touch six paintings. But of course, if I'm not back here by tenth hour . . ."

"Yes, yes," he growled, "I'll bury the worthless needlework that illumines nothing, as you ask. But I'll not run away, either. If I've got to haul the First Curator himself in front of Perryn the Weasel to get justice for Pleury, I'll do it."

Empty words. He knew it. I knew it. But what else did one say at such a time?

"I still owe you most of four years' service," I offered, "pitiful as the stipend was."

He shrugged and spat. "Maybe I can get the Registry to return my money for defective goods."

"Maybe." I grabbed his hand. "But if not, this will make up for it."

When he opened his fist to find my father's ruby ring, his jaw dropped in most delightful astonishment. I wished I could linger and tease him about it, as I had with my brothers in that life that was gone. But we'd come to the last turning before the Tower, and I had yet to pass on Demetreo's warning.

"There's good reason to run, Bastien. This war's not over, no matter what Perryn or the chancellor or drunkards say. Demetreo says Bayard won't accept the will as valid. And his granny, who is the wisest of wise women, sees a doom of mortal danger befalling her people—and likely the rest of us as well—at dawn tomorrow. I swear on my family's name that if I'm alive, I'll be with you to help, whatever the dawn brings. Then you can give this back to me. If not . . ."

"Your sister should have it."

"It's for you to use it as you need. If Juli walks out of this door today or arrives at Caton on another day, tell her I said to serve you better than I did. I hope Demetreo's granny is wrong about the dawn. I hope I'm wrong about everything."

"This is maudlin shite," he grumbled. "In and out. Be quick. And come back with something you can tell me."

I had left him at the turning of the alley. He'd wait there to help with my escape.

Now the cellar yawned in front of me, and the door swung closed behind.

No one pounced. My heart did not stop. I did not start gibbering, though the darkness and the smell of dust and iron gnawed on my soul like rats.

Don't think. Just move. With as little ripple in the web of the world as I could make, I cast a pale light and slipped through the corridors. Juli was not there. No cell was occupied. With that weight lifted, my feet did not dawdle. The need to know drove me onward to my grandsire's hidden entry and up the servants' stair.

The portrait gallery occupied the second level. If Garen's information was correct, Perryn would arrive within the hour. The curators would receive the king-to-be in the atrium, exchanging gifts and compliments before a short ceremony to honor my grandsire's life. I should have most of an hour to see what I needed to see. In and out. Easy.

I peeked through the arch into the gallery and mumbled a curse. A Registry servitor was posted not two steps in front of me. And I'd no time to go anywhere but forward.

A pureblood, properly disciplined, should not startle easily. "Servitor. If you please . . ."

The youth swung around. More curious than alarmed, he could be no more than fourteen.

"I require assistance. I've just arrived in Palinur and wish to familiarize myself with the curators before I am introduced. I understand their portraits are quite fine. But of course, I've no idea which is which. You must walk with me and tell me the names. What are you called?"

"Rigaro, *domé*." The boy trailed after me. "Naturally, whatever you need, though I must attend another guest when he arrives—an ordinary. I'm charged to carry his messages."

"The Prince of Navronne, you mean."

"Nay, a district constable."

Unease hollowed my gut. A *constable*, the man who fetched thieves to the pillory, was scarce more respectable than a dead-hauler. "Such a low ordinary wandering the private reaches of the Tower? Surely our restrictions have not changed so much."

To my relief, the boy kept his voice low. "He's to watch for assassins and other nefarious persons, *domé*."

"Nefarious persons in the Registry Tower?" I said with a disbelieving air, trying to mask my rising alarm. "Who would come up with such idiot notions?"

The boy glanced over his shoulder. "I was told that Constable Skefil is a low sort who knows these types of criminal and is to make sure none slip inside with the prince's party. My captain says it's a curator brought him."

"I see." But which curator? And did this constable await a mad portrait artist? The boy likely wouldn't know either answer, and I could not afford to seem interested. The portraits waited within arm's reach.

"You will, of course, remain available when he arrives, but I've no time to delay. I'm expected below." My heart surely thumped like a tabor as the youth and I approached the wall of portraits.

The gallery stretched around the entire circumference of the tower and was fronted by a waist-high rail. The grand stair opened onto the gallery level. At the far end of the arc wall where the six man-high portraits hung, a narrower stair climbed to the higher levels of the Tower.

An easel stood in the middle of the space, black ribbons draped over the small work it held—the outdated portrait of my grandsire I had hoped to replace. The curators must be planning to bring the prince up here for their condolence formalities. I'd best be quick.

"This is First Registrar Lares-Damon—*Domé*, what are you doing?"

"My eyesight is quite poor," I said, squinting as I lifted my three fingers from the canvas. "I've spellwork that allows me to see such works clearly if I do but touch them. My own Master of Archives has assured me that a light touch will not damage the surface." Lies flowed easily nowadays.

In truth, there was no need to compare Damon's portrait to the true image hidden inside me. That first touch told all. No alteration had been made to the painting from the day I completed it. Which was not to say there was nothing untoward about the depiction. Valuable moments passed until I figured out what bothered me.

I had placed the diminutive Damon in the courtyard of the Hundred Heroes, the statues that ringed the palace precincts, thinking it an interesting setting for one so unheroic in physical appearance. His face and posture were delineated by pride and discipline; his arm was extended, and his palm open in largesse. But almost undetectable among the mottled patterns of the paving stones beneath his feet my gift had hidden tormented faces . . . a young woman . . . a child . . . a king . . . and countless others. In my own artistic pride, certain that the pleasing depiction shaped truth, I had not even noticed.

Fancy suggested they were those Damon had trampled in his rise to a curator's seat. Whoever they were, he'd not bothered to have them removed. Perhaps he thought the image gave him authority. I'd no recollection of putting them there, but the painted image was identical to that which lived in me. Truth. Nothing in the portrait hinted that he had ordered my family's murder.

Pons next. My eagerness to expose her secrets should have shamed me. But of course, it didn't. Stolid as ever, her gaze cold, she sat in her curator's chair inside a walled garden, facing a closed gate. Outside the gate a rope swing hung from a walnut branch, the swing tossed and twisted by the wind.

My first glance told me a hand other than mine had altered the painting. The vines on the wall, the tree branches, the long grass . . . none were at all moved by the wind that affected the swing. I'd not made such an error since I was fourteen. The color and texture of the ropes were off here and there, as well, and the closed gate lacked the assurance my hand would have brought to it.

When I touched the canvas, my head near split in two. My bodily eyes recorded one version of the portrait, while my mind insisted that the inner version was the only reality. And the truth . . .

"Lord of Light!" How had I missed the significance of the country scene?

Rigaro glanced up.

"Move on," I said. The gallery remained empty. No sign of the constable.

One of my uncles had ever insisted that to identify the person who had committed an offense, you had only to look at those who pursued offenders most vigorously. Pons's true image, created by my bent, shimmered behind my eyes. Pons herself was unchanged, but the true image showed the gate in the wall open, a boy child in the swing, and a fair young man giving the laughing child a push. The young man was clearly an ordinary. My art had portrayed the truth of the scene, but hate had blinded me to its significance. As Pons gazed on man and boy, her eyes were not cold, but empty and sad.

Pons had proclaimed to the Registry that I should be whipped and disgraced for lying with an ordinary, and then commanded her own offense be obliterated. But would she murder to hide her crime? I didn't believe so. The painting spoke clearly of her own punishment.

"And who is this masterly gentleman?" I said, setting anger aside for later.

I needed no answer. Pluvius stood before the grillwork doors to the Registry Archives, clutching a scroll labeled as the Writ of Balance. It was quite an ordinary pose, properly denoting his historian's bent, but a good likeness. Every stroke was recognizably my own work, yet something teased at me. I touched the canvas and summoned the true image.

A startling difference! The painted pattern of the grillwork doors was an abstraction of knots and curves and swirls—as were the actual Archive doors. But in the true image—the image magic had created and transferred onto the page last summer—the iron strips had been wrought into the shape of a tree with five branches. Xancheira.

That Pluvius was somehow associated with the Xancheira mystery was not the surprise. He had pressed me for information about my grandsire's last investigation. At the least, he suspected what the *stola* had revealed.

But there was another difference. Pluvius's right hand held the scroll. His left was scarce visible in the convoluted folds of his full sleeve. The glaring dissonance of the enchantment drew me to his left. The true image showed the hand hidden in the sleeve grotesquely withered. That I would repair such an error was reasonable, but it was inconceivable that I—drawing on the power of my magic—could have made it in the first place.

The image inside me was truth. I felt it. I believed it. And I had altered it. Why, in the name of all holies, could I not remember doing so? Unless . . . those times in the cellar . . . the dream shadows forcing me to draw and paint . . .

My mind revolted. This had surely been changed by someone else. I reached for magic.

Stunned, I watched a corner of Pluvius's robe darken at my touch. No alien hand had broken my connection to the portrait. Should I choose, I could revert it to the truth.

"The next, *domé*?"

"Yes, yes, move on."

Three more portraits. It was all I could do to control my shaking. Which was more terrifying? That someone could force a sorcerer to work magic without his consent—contravening a precept as old as Aurellian bloodlines? Or, assuming I had consented, that someone could so effectively obscure my memory of doing so? What else could I not remember from those days in the cellar?

"Boy! Are you my messeng—?"

A bony, gangle-limbed man, standing in the stair arch, bit off his question at the sight of me. His worn cape of unadorned black wool scarce reached his knees. It was not the cloak of a pureblood and was certainly not the cloak of anyone who should be staring boldly at two purebloods in the heart of the Registry. Yet I'd seen the same man here before, in the Curators' Chamber on the day I was judged to be of aberrant mind. Just as I'd seen him when his long pale hands, ringed in plain copper bands, had dragged me from the fire that burned my house and killed my servants.

"Drop your eyes, ordinary!" I snapped, as I commanded my feet not to run and rage not to burst through my flesh. Copper rings . . . I'd seen flashes of copper in Pleury's death vision. And this man had worn Harrower orange on the night of the fire. "Tell me your business here or I'll have the guards gift you a flogging you'll never forget."

He bowed, eyes dropped and arms spread wide. " 'Tis only your own masters' business I tend, *domé*," he said in a nasal tone that slid past the ear like oil and honey. "I be Skefil, Constable of the Council District, at the service of the lordly Registry. This lad's charged to guide me, I ween."

"Ah, the assassin watcher!" I said. "My superiors in Morian will be amused that Ardran purebloods must call in *ordinaries* to protect themselves. I've use for the boy. I'll loan him if you note a nefarious person sneaking up on us."

I motioned Rigaro to the next portrait. "Which curator is this?"

Skefil's eyes were hot on my masked cheek. But as the boy and I strolled along the portrait wall, he turned away and leaned over the gallery rail. Beaded sweat dribbled down my back.

Ascetic, cold-eyed Gramphier loomed tall above us, portrayed half in shadow. The First Curator of secrets and mysteries. Again, no evidence of a second artist's work. Yet again, the painting failed to match the true image I carried. I had removed a shadow from the First Curator's hand, a shadow the ominous hue of blood. From the murky floor behind his feet, I had removed all trace of a dagger scribed with the white tree of Xancheira. The true image testified to a man willing to murder to protect the Registry from Xancheira's secret.

Drums and trumpets sounded in the distance. The crash of doors and a burst of sunlight from the atrium announced the arrival of the royal guest. Rigaro glanced over his shoulder at Skefil, whose attention focused entirely on the scene below.

"Only two more," I said, tight as a drum skin. "He'll call if he needs you."

The boy ducked his head and led me on. "This is Curator Albin."

Wide brow, olive skin, raven hair. The man likeliest to succeed Gramphier, if rumor was true. The changes between original and the portrait on the wall were immensely subtle. I had portrayed Guilian de Albin standing on a hilltop, overlooking the harvest in his expansive vineyards. I remembered choosing it as his defining environment. On the distant horizon a fiery sunset blazed behind a dark line—the silhouettes of carts laden with grapes.

Again, my own hand had altered the portrait, but where? The true image seemed very like. Forcing anxiety aside, I studied the painting carefully and then closed my eyes to examine the true image alone.

The horizon . . . The jagged silhouette backed by garish orange was not heaped carts framed by brilliant sunset, but broken structures, charred roofs and towers against a sky darkened with ash and glowing with rampaging flame. And among the vineyard laborers, half hidden behind a mound of autumn flowers—flowers of Harrower orange—was such a perfect likeness of the man pacing the gallery behind me, I might have thought I'd transported him from life to art right then. A torch blazed in the painted Skefil's hand. It's five white-hot flames mocked Xancheira's tree.

Albin. Skefil. Harrowers. Fire and ruin. Truth.

Blood-hot rage, murderous rage, boiled in my belly. The dagger sheathed in my boot sang its readiness. Constable Skefil leaned over the gallery rail, picking his teeth with a wooden toothpick. So casual, as if he belonged here.

I clenched my hands behind my back to force them still.

"This time has been well spent, Servitor Rigaro," I said, my jaw rigid. "I feel as if I know these people now."

Albin—the most traditional of purebloods. What arrogance, what cruel and vicious apostasy to attack his enemies with the most despicable of all weapons. Harrowers denied the gods, denied magic, and scorned our responsibility to use our talents for the world's good.

If Gramphier, the powerful protector of Registry secrets, and Albin, the powerful defender of Registry tradition, suspected what my grandfather had learned, they would have feared him above all men. They would have wished him dead alongside anyone he might have told. But they would never have dared kill without confirmation of their fears. And with that understanding came devastating truth.

Last summer, ignorant and blind, reveling in pride at my advancement, I had given them the assurance they needed. All the curators knew of my second bent, supposedly excised. And I had proved its danger—seemingly flaunting the evidence that I could reveal the corrupt secrets they most wished to hide. Not ten days after I'd finished these portraits, my family had been burnt alive. Save for Pluvius and his extra work assignment, Juli and I would have died with them.

Holy Deunor, I should burn *this* place down or create a void hole beneath it so deep that all within were plunged unto Magrog's hells. And then plunge after it myself. *I* had done it. My arrogance and ambition had killed them all.

A noise escaped me—a groan, a curse, a sob, or all three at once.

"There's one more portrait, *domé*—Curator Scrutari-Consil." Rigaro glanced up, puzzled. "Do you not wish to know him?"

Rigaro's innocent stare reminded me of poor, dead Pleury. I wanted to scream at him: *Run away, boy. Get out of here that their infamy of blood and murder will not taint you. Nor will my own.* But paralyzed with guilt and anger, I let discipline provide answer. "Yes, quickly. I'd not wish to slight him."

The devil Skefil did not turn as we moved to the next portrait.

The snappish little curator with the twisted spine glared out of his frame like a demon gatzé. He sat at a writing desk, pen in hand, the document in front of him the finest vellum. A window behind him framed the palace of Navronne's king and the unfinished tower of the Karish cathedral. No Registry Tower was included, as might be expected, yet the scene was entirely appropriate to his office as Hierarch Eligius's contracted pureblood.

I had altered Scrutari's portrait, too. And only because of our venture on the previous day did I recognize the significance of the changes. On the writing desk lay three leather straps as were used to bind and seal a scroll. And dangling from them lay three unbroken wax seals, one bearing the blazon of Eodward, King of Navronne, one the seal of the Hierarch of Ardra, one the seal of Kemen's Temple. A puzzle waiting to be assembled. Innocent, one could say, but for the very fact that someone had seen fit to hide them. No contract permitted forgery of a royal will.

My plan had to change. The web of lies and murder detailed in this gallery were going to be the end of me one way or the other. I would take at least four curators with me.

I darted to the gallery rail, keeping well away from Skefil.

"My lord prince, welcome!" I cried, raising my open palms in the gesture forgoing magic.

The glittering assembly of purebloods and courtiers fell silent. Two hundred faces, male and female, masked and bare, fair and deep-hued, gaped up at me. Skefil withdrew from the rail quickly, keeping out of sight. But he, too, stared. He would not stay back long.

"I've come here to meet you as we agreed, Your Grace. You and your *consiliar prime* must come up here to view what I spoke of yesterday." The Duc de Tremayne stood on Perryn's right.

Nonsense all, but it would give them pause. Outright assault before so large a company would require too many explanations, so I hoped. If I could live past these first moments . . .

"Curators of the Pureblood Registry and all who've come to celebrate my grandsire's unique service to Registry and Crown, I beg your indulgence. I've come here to surrender, to confess infamy before you all, to submit myself to my righteous masters and beg forgiveness of noble Eodward's heir, of my grandsire's respected colleagues, and of every pureblood who holds the gods' gift of sorcery precious and inviolable."

When no thunderbolt slammed into me, I bowed, touched fingertips to brow—and smiled. By the hand of holy Deunor, I was going to expose them all.

CHAPTER 34

Young Rigaro stood paralyzed, his jaw sagged at such audacity as shouting at princes and curators from the gallery.

"You ought to leave now, boy," I said, nudging his shoulder. "Matters could go ill." Very ill. Tales said purebloods had once been able to call down whirlwinds. It must have felt quite like this—exhilarating, though carrying a very slim chance of survival.

The curators charged up the stair. Prince Perryn, not to be ignored, marched behind them as if they were beaters scaring up game. The Duc de Tremayne remained behind, pointing at me as he consulted with Fortieri, the commander of the Tower Guard. An inducement to speed and forcefulness in my arguments.

Skefil had taken the opportunity to creep up from my left, one long pale hand outstretched. His copper rings glinted so brilliantly in the lamplight, I guessed they carried spells. Surrounded by enchantment, I couldn't tell. His other hand held a very long dagger.

My attention halted him a dozen steps away. My palm was no longer innocently open, but rather shooting small, hungry flames in his direction.

"I'd come no closer." I hoped he recognized my will to murder. "Our masters are on the stair. And my flames can melt those rings right through your fingers. You've no idea of my power." Having three younger brothers had taught me how to state the most ludicrous claims in tones solemn enough to evoke belief.

Unfortunately, a nasty smirk gashed his long, bony face. "You'd no skills to douse my pretty fire that night your sister burnt." His voice mimed a snake slithering through long grass. "And I watched you grovel naked in the dark. You couldn't raise a hand to them snivelly guards."

He took another step. And another.

"If you deem my behavior in the cellar a sign of weakness, then you know *nothing* of pureblood discipline." Had he, an ordinary, been one of the shadows?

"Lucian!" Pluvius topped the stair first and hurried to my side.

Skefil halted a few steps away. "Best keep away from 'im, Curator. Mad sorcerers must be put down like dogs with the hopping fever. I've skills can do such." He wriggled his empty hand, making the copper bands on his fingers spark in the light. Spider feet pricked my skin.

"Both of you, stay away," I said, retreating toward the portrait wall. I'd allow no one to touch me.

Pluvius ignored the ordinary. "What are you doing, lad?" Soft and intense. "Let me help you— Ah, hand of Magrog!"

The prince arrived at the top of the stair, curators on either side of him, forcing a babbling crowd of courtiers and Registry folk to stack up on the broad steps behind.

Pluvius's nostrils flared in annoyance. "Young Remeni's been ill, Your Grace, suffering delusions. I'll take him away."

"But he was quite lucid yesterday." A flush of anxiety colored Perryn's milky complexion. "Prudish like his grandsire, but clear-headed. Must we talk again of crimes and infamy, Remeni? Is that rough official around here somewhere?" He peered behind me, as if Bastien might pop out of a painting.

"Muzzle the lunatic!" Gramphier's order would have been more alarming had any Registry servitor been able to press through the clot of curious dignitaries on the stair. Nor did Skefil move to enforce his command. The constable had thrust his dagger behind him and retreated. But dutiful young Rigaro had returned to his post, conveniently blocking Skefil's access to the back stair.

My hope lay in keeping the two parties—Registry and Crown—in a standoff, each unwilling to expose their sins before the other. To maintain their grand posturing before the world, they each needed the other's support.

Perryn was key. I kept my eye on him, even as I addressed Gramphier.

"Alas, First Curator, I cannot be bundled off before confessing my crimes to His Grace, crimes that imperil our righteous king at the very beginning of his rule. Only yesterday he expressed his wish to see me here—did you not, my lord? Just after I witnessed the god's hand at work in Navronne's interest."

"I suppose I did." Perryn's flush deepened. He could not afford to disavow his unimpeachable witness. "What crimes do you speak of? And what do you mean, my rule in peril? Perhaps we should speak alone." His glance shifted uneasily from me to Gramphier, who seethed at his side. The Duc de Tremayne was nowhere in sight.

"Treason must be proclaimed before witnesses, Your Grace. Some here will call me mad, but rather I was entangled in tradition and faulty discipline. Through your generous reception yesterday—and your considered judgments—I have recovered enough to see the right. And when I found this evidence of treason . . . well, I could not stand by and see such injury done you—your noble father's favored son."

"*Pureblood* treason?" The prince grew ashen. Even a lackwit could see that such a rupture in the fabric of Navronne could prompt a conflict that would make Prince Bayard and Sila Diaglou's Harrowers seem no more than mosquitoes.

I dared not let my focus leave Perryn, but Pons and Damon shifted sidewise away from the others, as if to circle behind me. Old Pluvius shuffled across the gallery toward Skefil and the boy. Albin, like a squat toad on Perryn's left, clenched a fist. Before long I'd be surrounded.

So I raised a warning hand, first at Albin and then sweeping from one side to the other so as to include all of them. "Stand down, masters, if you've naught to hide. Once I've had my say, you may do as you will with me, for indeed I must have been aberrant to participate in this scheme."

Perryn shook his head. "If this is but an argument between you and the Registry—"

"Nay, lord. The scheme I speak of involves some few of these curators. They have aided in such deception as to undermine your peaceful ascension. They induced me to conspire with them to hide their treason. In honor of my grandsire, your noble father's trusted ally, I must reveal—"

"You will be *silent*, Remeni," snarled Gramphier, "or you will wear a steel mask and tongue binding for the rest of your days. Your spew of lies is unworthy, unholy, a grievous result of madness indulged."

Perryn's agitation increased. One of his attendants touched his satin sleeve, but the prince wrenched his arm away. "Leave off this jangling, all of you. I would hear what Remeni has to say. Treason is a Crown matter; the Writ is quite specific. Speak, Lucian, and be quick about it."

Touching fingertips to brow, I acknowledged his warning. "As was proved yesterday, the gods have deigned that my art reveals truth beyond my knowing. Summer last I was commissioned to paint portraits of these six who administer the Pureblood Registry—the very paintings you see before you. Proud and ignorant and blind, I brought my fullest power to the work, not realizing that my fingers spoke secrets—"

The crackle of lightning gave an instant's warning. I twisted around and ducked. The impact drove me to the floor, the bolt glancing off my shoulder, instead of full in the heart.

I rolled into a ball to make a smaller target. It was Albin's fist raised in my direction.

By the gods, Guilian, stop this disgraceful show. What are you thinking? Damon's command snapped, not in my normal hearing, but inside my ears. *Inviting low ordinaries to troop around as if they belong. Expressing your resentments before Eodward's idiot son and his associates, who have tongues, for the gods' sake! A man would think Remeni had murdered* your *sister instead of his own. Let the man prove his lunacy once and for all. He's the grandson of Vincente de Remeni, and before we decide what to do with the fool, we must put to rest this royal puffin's interest in him.*

"Get up, Remeni. Show the noble lord the state of your wits." Assuredly Damon's voice, too, only this time audible to all.

Damon's magic, the same duality of speech he had demonstrated at Caton, left me itching and queasy. Gods, what a talent! But when he extended a hand to pull me up, I yielded him a modicum of trust along with my hand. He had let me hear his admonition. My mother had once told me that a man honest in his faults tended to be more reliable than one who denied them.

"Domé." I inclined my back to Damon, cradling my left arm, lest it drop to the floor like a dead fish. "Observe, and judge my wits."

"Someone explain all this!" The crowd on the stair seemed the only thing preventing Perryn's abrupt departure. "How dare you throw wild magic about my person!"

I stepped forward. "In brief, Your Grace, by virtue of my magic these portraits exposed several disturbing stories, and I was ordered, as a loyal and disciplined pureblood, to alter them. I did so. I do not seek to absolve myself, for any pureblood artist could tell you that four of these six works have been touched by my hand alone. But that is a *fortunate* circumstance, for a pureblood artist can reshape the work his hands have created to more perfectly match the truth the god has granted him. Let me show you."

"Do not dare!" Gramphier and Albin spoke as one. Scrutari-Consil swayed against the banister as if he would faint.

"Note these regions here and here." I pointed at Gramphier's painted hand and at the bare paving where the bloody knife should lie. Then, before anyone could flatten me again, I summoned magic.

"Lord of Light and Magic, guide your gift. . . ." Forcing away fear and distraction, summoning strength and will to answer my call, I touched the dry surface and called up the *quadreo*, the spell of harmony and reversal.

In a torrent of heat and color and truth that near caved my chest, the world blurred and then reasserted itself. The bloody shadow stained the First Curator's hand and the dripping knife lay in the shadows.

"Open yourself to judge if the portrait is a true likeness," I said when I caught my breath, "and then note the pieces I was commanded to remove. Others might speak to what these artifacts signify. I cannot."

"Fakery . . . this has no meaning . . . lunacy . . . murderer . . ." Denials, outrage, accusations of fraud and perversion of magic rained like ash.

I moved quickly to Albin's portrait and drew their attention to the dark horizon against the sunset and the clumps of orange flowers. Again I invoked holy Deunor and bled his gift onto the canvas.

Prince and curators closed up behind me—Damon closest—as I pointed to the flowers of Harrower orange, to Skefil and his torch that had been so carefully removed, to the blaze that was not sunset but horror lighting the night sky. Indeed the charred towers and ruined houses might have been Pontia itself, the vineyards my family's own. Had my bent detected the plan fermenting in Albin's mind, or, gods forgive, had I given him the idea for it?

Only discipline could hold my voice firm. "When I painted Curator Albin's portrait, the concept of Registry involvement in Harrower attacks was as impossible to imagine as walking into dreams. To consort with Sila Diaglou's fanatics is to condone the slaughter of the gods' chosen, as well as ordinaries, both noble and mean. A Harrower massacre has near wiped out a pureblood family your noble father held in favor. Is that not treason?"

"Lies!" bellowed Albin the toad. "Who could believe—?"

"But the torch wielder himself is right here!" Pluvius's sharp accusation came from the direction of the stair. "You brought him here tonight, Guilian. And you brought him to testify at Remeni's judgment about the other fire, the one that killed his sister."

Astonishingly, the white-bearded Master of Archives had Skefil in a lock hold. The old man's arms—powerful arms—wrapped underneath Skefil's shoulders, and his hands gripped behind the Harrower's neck.

"Pull open his coat, boy. Sila Diaglou ever requires her minions to carry her telltale."

Skefil writhed and snarled as young Rigaro pulled an orange rag from the black coat.

"Harrowers!" Curator Scrutari, the forger, whirled on Albin and Gramphier, spitting like a cat. "Are you mad? We agreed—"

"The Registry consorts with *Harrowers*?" Perryn's protest sounded wheezy compared to Pluvius's booming outrage, but his horror rang huge—and genuine. "By Kemen Sky Lord's mighty hand, I'll have your heads!"

"This is but trickery, prince," said Gramphier, "and proves naught but this madman's disposition to evil works. We tried to protect you from his obscene ravings."

"Master of Archives," called Damon, as clear as the gods' trumpet through chaos. "Is Remeni's demonstration honest? Can he do this—revert changes to his works? Reveal truth?"

"Aye," said Pluvius. "Not every artist can wield the necessary spell, and certainly not so easily, but Lucian has always exhibited extraordinary talents." The old man grinned at me. "Show them the truth of my own portrait, lad."

Pluvius's support made me question my intent to expose him. But then again, he was no innocent. He had consented to my condemnation and confinement. He had known of what was done to me in the cellar—whatever magic had forced me to the work and stripped my memory of it. And he certainly knew something of the Xancheira secret.

"Lord of Light and Magic, guide my hand. . . ." I dived into the enchantment yet again.

"What crime does this one tell, Lucian?" Perryn's sharp query, spoken from just beside my shoulder, startled me as I raised my hand from the canvas.

I couldn't answer right away. After three quick invocations of the most difficult magic I knew, body and spirit felt riddled with bruises.

"Lies and secrets," said Pluvius, also at my side. "A lifetime of lies. Centuries of secrets. No treason, however. No murder. I doubt Lucian can explain."

Damon had taken Pluvius's place as Skefil's warden, but with much less strain. Cool as always, the diminutive curator stood beside a kneeling Skefil, twirling a sparking finger above the man's head. With every circuit, the Harrower snarled through clenched teeth. He tried to rise but could not.

"All right, Lucian," snapped Perryn, moving down the row of portraits. "You spoke of other crimes. . . ."

Pons stood silently behind Albin and Gramphier. Eyes of gray marble in a face of stone, she'd spoken not a word in all this endless hour. I could tell the world what had been removed from her portrait, but as my hand had not altered it, I could not revert it to the truth. What was I to think of her? We were enemies. She despised me. Yet her portrait hinted that she had judged herself with the same ruthless standard and punished herself as severely as she had wished to punish me. The root of our enmity was her excess of righteousness, and her crimes hypocrisy and ambition . . . not savage murder, nor stealing Eodward's throne.

I pointed to Scrutari's portrait. "This one, lord prince."

"Your Grace!" The bent-shouldered curator's panic was palpable. "Surely you've seen enough. Though I cannot imagine what personal foibles Remeni's magic might show, I am ever your loyal servant, as is His Excellency the Hierarch. Clearly there are serious matters for the Registry to address, but . . . sire . . ."

Perryn glanced from Scrutari to me, his blue eyes wide. Only now did he seem to realize the possible implications of my exercise. There were many kinds of treason. Forging royal wills would certainly count among them.

"Perhaps we do not need to waste our time with this one." The prince spread his hands, inviting, all smooth reason and accommodation. "It's clear that this Harrower disease has not spread to all six of your masters. Your revelations read true, and exposing such vipers must certainly see you vindicated amongst your kind. Indeed, you should have a hand in rebuilding the trust between Crown and the Registry. We shall certainly value your advice, now and later. So, tell us, Lucian, what do you advise in this case?"

To live with magic prepares one for the extraordinary, but the choice Perryn gave me could alter the course of a kingdom . . . tens of thousands of lives . . .

I didn't want that kind of power. Had I the least notion that Perryn's brothers were more intelligent, more large-minded, more suited to kingship, I would not have hesitated to expose Scrutari and the hierarch and with them Perryn's scheme. But to reveal their lie was to ensure the war continued—a burden of lives and fortunes too heavy for my shoulders. And if I let it go, I could perhaps right one great wrong. Surely the world would be the better for that.

Thus, I met the prince's gaze and tapped my fingers on the portrait. "Curator Scrutari well knows what this altered version hides. As I recall, the particular discrepancies have to do with a matter we discussed yesterday, of which there were only two, both of them quite personal to you, lord prince. One touched on a matter of present justice; one on an incident of history. In my mind, matters of justice trump every other consideration, even incidents of history. For *justice's* sake, I am willing to allow these private concerns to remain private. But that is *your* decision, lord."

I did not, even for a moment, remove my fingers from the portrait.

The prince's fair visage twisted into ugliness; his blue eyes grayed to iron. Never again would I imagine Perryn of Ardra a man of fickle attachments or passing enmity. So I might as well give him the rest of it. When I removed any way for him to weasel out of the bargain, he wasn't going to hate me any more than he did already. His kingdom or his duc; he had to give up one.

"And I must see firm evidence of that decision before we leave here, lest some misfortune happen to this painting. When I am assured that *justice* has triumphed—the appropriate sentence for such a crime carried out—I will ask one of my non-treasonous masters to affix a binding on Curator Scrutari's portrait that will prevent me ever unmasking its private revelations. Curator Pons-Laterus, whom, as anyone in the Registry can attest, loathes me, could do such a thing. She would surely be pleased to thwart any backsliding on my part."

"You can lock this portrait as he said?"

"If he allows me access to the true image he holds," she said, "I can."

That must be the reason they'd not sealed these changes when I was a prisoner. Even in my madness they had not subverted my will entire. A bit of encouragement going forward.

"And can you ensure he is unable to speak of the personal matters involved?"

"I can. A tongue block can be keyed to certain words or phrases."

Perryn's question did not surprise me. Nor did Pons's answer. Certainly she—likely all of them—had guessed some sin on Perryn's part was involved. But Perryn's concerns were thrones and wars and allies. The politics of ordinaries did not concern righteous purebloods like Pons.

Albin stood mesmerized for the moment—curious, questioning, complacent, his meaty arms crossed stubbornly over his chest. I hoped that would change very soon now. Surely Perryn could not ignore a pureblood Harrower, even if our own curators could.

"Noplessi!" Perryn whirled and beckoned a wiry, bent old man who wore the same royal household tabard as the Duc de Tremayne. Though older than Pluvius, I judged this man more dangerous, his wrinkled face reflecting no more human feeling than a storm wind. "Send up Vuscherin and Comlier. You yourself must deal with another matter."

Perryn murmured in the old man's ear. Whatever he said made the old man twitch, a reaction likely worthy of an earthquake in anyone else. Noplessi recovered quickly and bowed deeply. "As you command, Highness."

Even the jammed crowd seemed to recognize a force of nature and parted to let him through. Perryn shouted after, "Yourself to see to it, Noplessi, and return with proof."

Then he turned to the curators. "I came here tonight to join with the Pureblood Registry to ensure our mutual interests according to the Writ of Balance. Instead I've found a nest of traitors, arrogant ink dabblers, and quivering cowards. I could dissolve the Writ on the day I am acknowledged king of Navronne. Tell me why I should not. Who speaks for the Registry?"

A snarling Gramphier stepped forward. "It is my—"

"*I* do"—Damon crushed the First Curator's assertion as a smith's hammer flattens molten iron, and only then inclined his head respectfully to Gramphier—"until my fellow curators consider these revelations."

With a smooth touch of their palms, Pons assumed Damon's sparking control of Constable Skefil. The diminutive Damon folded his hands at his back and strolled into a position equidistant from the prince at the head of the stair; Pluvius and me beside Scrutari's portrait; and Scrutari, Gramphier, and Albin, who formed a bulwark of pureblood indignation halfway along the portrait wall.

"We are as disturbed as you by these strange matters, prince," said Damon. "You must excuse us for short while as we consider these portraits, Remeni's recent illness, and the demands of our position."

"Consider as you will," said Perryn, bristling. "But I want this business settled tonight, so I need never set foot in this blighted tomb again." He could not leave. To hold the throne, he needed the Registry neutral, at the least.

The curators drew into a circle, all save Pons, who kept Skefil immobile and his curses trapped inside his purpled skin. The discussion grew heated, all of them speaking at once, but was shielded by some enchantment that left the words unintelligible. From time to time, Pons nodded or shook her head. Perhaps Damon included her in the conclave with his extraordinary way of communicating without words. This time I was not privy to it.

What had Damon said to me at Caton? *One of us is convinced that your back will be a stepping-stone to a position of authority—the preeminent position of authority among our kind.* Perhaps Damon himself? That might not be the worst outcome.

Prince Perryn and I waited. Or, rather, I stood guard over the painting, while Perryn stood guard over me. The true image of the prince in that moment would surely show him watching me burn at the stake or laughing as I turned to stone while he held a quarry hammer at the ready. But my fingers rested on Scrutari's portrait—on Perryn's crown. He dared not touch me.

After a short while, Pluvius stepped away from the circle and dispatched Rigaro down the back stair. The boy returned in moments with several Registry servitors—big men who remained in the shadowed arch. My heart near seized when I glimpsed shackles and the spool of white silk cord.

Observing Albin did not reassure me. He seemed unperturbed, asserting himself as authoritatively as ever, chest thrust out, flinging dismissive gestures in my direction. The rise and fall of his scornful basso was unmistakable. Had I overplayed my hand?

Two court nobles bulled through the crowd on the stair and took a martial stance at Perryn's side.

As if that were a signal, Damon stepped forward. "We, the Curators of the Pureblood Registry, request parlay with the Prince of Navronne, according to the Writ of Balance. Our purpose is to offer judgment of the serious charges Lucian de Remeni-Masson has brought before us all."

"Get on with it, you blighted fossils!" Perryn's diplomacy had been seriously compromised.

I forced breath in and out of my constricted lungs. Six curators. Pluvius and Damon, perhaps, believing in me. Gramphier, Albin, and Scrutari my implacable foes. And Pons, where would she fall? How could right prevail?

"First Curator Gramphier is accused of no civil crime," said Damon, unperturbed. "For the present the Registry assumes all responsibility for him. If we determine that the unsettling artifacts of his portrait bear on a crime against the Crown, we shall inform you."

No surprise there, though I believed Gramphier complicit in all. Nothing happened in the Registry without his approval. But one side or the other had to buy his loyalty with a pardon. Damon's face revealed naught, either beneath or outside his mask.

"The Harrower ordinary is yours, of course, to do with as you will," Damon continued. "He has murdered purebloods, and the Writ mandates his death. As with all Harrowers, who defy gods and men with their savagery, we assume he will receive no mercy."

Again no surprise. Skefil, bound in Pons's ring of sparks, growled and wrestled his invisible bonds. The great veins in his purpled forehead bulged.

Damon cleared his throat. My heart stilled.

"Guilian de Albin has consorted with Harrowers and solicited murder of purebloods, treason to our kind as well as the Crown. The evidence against him is judged unimpeachable—revealed by the gods' design through the truth of Lucian de Remeni's magic."

"What?" Albin whirled about, not facing Perryn, nor even Damon. His bile was all for Gramphier. "You would yield to this royal *vermin* on a madman's word? Remeni will be our—"

Damon tweaked one finger and a sparkling rope arced toward Albin and circled his neck. The big man dropped to his knees, words transformed to unintelligible roars.

"Albin is ours to punish, prince," said Damon. "As of this moment, he is silenced. As of this hour, he is dead."

Damon raised his open hand, and three Registry servitors fell on the writhing Albin like dogs on a fallen hind. While one man held him down, a second forced his hands together, and the third bound them in silken cords. A full-faced mask lay beside them at the ready. Iron, not leather.

Justice.

I sagged against the wall, squeezing my eyes shut. Albin's feral bellowing and Gramphier's strident protests were drowned by the echoes of death screams and the choking scent of burning flesh. Discipline kept it all inside me. These soulless beasts would not see a Remeni weep, though I drowned in such a flood of pain and grief as must reive divine Idrium itself. . . .

"Lucian . . . Lucian, heed. Drink this before you collapse." Pluvius pushed a cup into my face.

The world recovered its shape. Marble floor underfoot. Mosaic ceiling above, shimmering with magic. A wall behind my aching shoulders—one still throbbing from Albin's thunderbolt, the other from the strain of keeping my fingers jammed against Scrutari's portrait.

Albin and Skefil were already gone, as were most of the crowd on the stairs. Perryn paced alone, shielded by five attendants. Scrutari twitched nervously halfway between Perryn and the other curators. Damon and Pons conferred with Gramphier, one and then another of them casting hooded glances at me—altogether too comfortable with each other. The danger was not passed. Did Damon or Pons know what the *stola* revealed? Did Pluvius?

"Take this, lad. Let me help you."

I shook my head. I would not drink in the Tower.

Pluvius leaned in close. "What bargain have you struck with this rogue prince, Lucian? Interfering in ordinary affairs taints all purebloods."

"Justice should not depend on bloodlines," I snapped. "And sometimes there are no clean bargains. I think you know that, master."

He either didn't understand or chose not to take offense. "You've put yourself in a terrible position."

"A terrible *position*? My family—two hundred and fifty-three souls, two hundred and fifty-three pairs of hands that graced this world with magic, the entirety of two bloodlines, save only me—died in agony. Fifty ordinaries who were part of our lives for generations died with them. All were innocent of any crime. I should not have had to endanger myself or anyone else to find justice for them. And if I can squeeze out a bit of righteous truth for a few ordinary children as well, I'll wager the gods will forgive my lapse in pureblood discipline."

"But I fear no one else will." He dropped his voice to a whisper. "I can help you get away."

Boots tramping up the marble stair silenced his offer. Two young members of the Guard Royale arrived first . . . and Noplessi just behind them. The old, bent noble bowed to the prince and showed what he carried. The prince motioned him to me.

The cold-eyed duc handed me a gold ring bearing the device of a bear with lancet teeth, a well-used dagger with the same device scribed in its plain hilt, and a purple and gold tabard. Even such witness was no good untested. I closed my eyes and dived once more into enchantment, hunting justice and death. . . .

"Are you pleased, pureblood?" Prince Perryn bit off each word. "You can go out and view his corpse if you wish. The crime of royal murder is blazoned on the gallows."

I tossed the evidence to the floor. "Satisfied, lord, not pleased. And I've no need to see his body to know you have fulfilled your part"—my bent had shown me a bound and kneeling Tremayne and this very dagger opening his throat—"even if he was given a *noble's* death before he was hanged."

Old Noplessi paled. I turned to the curators. "*Domá* Pons, if you would, please."

Pons, cool and efficient, laid one hand on my forehead and one hand on the painting. "Open the true image."

As soon as the image shimmered in the front of my mind, a cold hand enveloped it. The astringent burst that followed felt quite like a pureblood healer cleaning and sealing a wound. The hand withdrew. Naught seemed changed.

"A test only, lord," I said to Perryn, and laid a finger on my signature.

Not even that, the most personal detail on Scrutari's portrait, responded to my touch. Once the internal image faded, would I even be able to retrieve it?

"I'll create the tongue block if you wish, prince," said Pons, "but I'll not excise *paint*, *ink*, *portrait*, or any other common word or phrase that properly belongs in a pureblood artist's vocabulary. So you must give me a particular phrase—*Prince Perryn's brindle cow* or the like."

Perryn considered for a moment. How could he forbid a secret without admitting to it?

"I forgo the tongue block. I'll know if Remeni speaks of my privacies." The eyes of a basilisk could not be so murderous as those of our king-to-be.

Indeed, the sooner I removed myself from the festering resentments around me, the better. Four curators might have supported my actions in the face of public scrutiny, but I had forced their hand in the same way I had Perryn's, and their retribution was like to be far more serious. I believed Gramphier and Albin partners in conspiracy and murder.

"As you say, prince." I touched my forehead but did not bow. "Our business is done and we can take our leave. What greater honor could we have done my grandsire, who served Crown and Registry so faithfully, than to dispense justice in the murder of both purebloods and ordinaries?"

Perryn didn't seem to appreciate the balance. He shoved a young courtier aside so viciously, the young man crashed down three steps before grabbing the rail. As the prince and his retinue marched down the stair, the unfortunate baronet clutched his ribs and hobbled after them.

The curators summoned guards to clear the remaining gawkers from the stair and the atrium. Hoping to take advantage of their preoccupations, I sped across the gallery toward the back stair.

"Hold him, Pluvius." Gramphier was near spitting in his wrath.

"*Arriet*, Lucian!" A sharp, nasty enchantment nailed my feet to the floor. The shadowed arch to the stair taunted me, only an arm's length ahead.

"Do you imagine you can walk away from this disaster, *plebeiu*?" said the First Curator. "You've shamed the Registry before ordinaries, transgressed rules that that have maintained us for two centuries. You will answer for it."

No unlocking, unraveling, or freeing spell I knew budged my feet from the marble floor. So I spat over my shoulder. "When will you answer for your deeds, Gramphier? You have solicited murder and harbored its instrument, a man traitor to everything we revere. All to preserve—"

No, I could not list every grievance. To reveal what I knew of the Xancheiran secret could end my life right here.

"Do you forget, First Curator? As long as I breathe, I must serve my contract. My master has not given me permission to be gone all night."

"Oh no. Not this time. If he's allowed you to come here without silkbinding and chains, then he's violated your restrictions. Your contract is void."

"So am I to be murdered right here or shall I be buried in the cellar, where you can corrupt my magic yet again?" Rage, not fear, made my voice shake.

I had thought I would be satisfied once my family's murder was explained, the treachery exposed, and Tremayne punished for his crimes. I had believed I could accept whatever Serena Fortuna parceled out, whether death or imprisonment. But here at the brink of ending, I could not bear to leave it at this.

If it was divinities who sparked the magic in a person's veins, then who were we to constrain such a blessing, much less to punish that person . . . or kill him? If my family had been slaughtered to protect this secret, hundreds of others had suffered the same throughout two centuries. Others, like the Cicerons. Someone should hold us to account for that.

"You are far too much trouble to be allowed to live, Lucian." Gramphier's breath scorched my neck. "Insolent boy. You think you know so much. But your perverse magic cannot unmask a soul, not even those you know best."

"Gramphier, no!" yelled Pluvius.

I dropped to the floor, twisting and reaching behind to grab Gramphier's knees. But my arm flailed empty, as others converged and dragged him backward. At the same moment, my boots broke free of the floor.

I scrabbled forward and lunged to my feet.

"Wait, Lucian!" called Pluvius.

"Stop him!"

"Pons, alert the guards!"

Without a backward glance, I dashed around and through the archway and onto the back stair.

CHAPTER 35

Not three steps down the back stair and I knew the hidden door was out of reach. Leather creaked below me. Boots scuffed—ascending. Of course, the Registry commander would have men guarding every way out.

So I reversed direction and raced upward. But to where? One thing certain: The higher I went, the more surely I was trapped.

The fourth level was familiar ground. They'd certainly come looking for me in the Archives, but a drainpipe descended from the roof just beyond the window of my former studio into a long-neglected well yard. Gilles and I had forever joked about using it to escape Pluvius's inspections—a ludicrous thought for two privileged portrait artists, whose greatest adventures had consisted of hunting expeditions or hiking across country to a historic ruin. Yet if the pipe was solid . . . if I didn't think about it too much . . . if my bruised shoulder would hold up . . . No one would be guarding the well yard.

I crept quietly through the grillwork doors, then sped through the deserted labyrinth of nooks, shelves, and worktables, only to stop short and strangle a breath. Candlelight gleamed through the open door of the studio. Gilles sat at a worktable, his dark head bent over a page, pen in hand, though not moving. Gilles, whose uncle had just been hauled off to his death on my word.

I couldn't attack; Gilles was no Harrower. But the drainpipe was my only way out.

"Grace of the Mother, Gilles."

His head popped up, his expression blank, as if deep in thought or magic-working. "Lucian!"

The pen dropped to the floor as he leapt to his feet and examined me head to toe, smiling. "Grace of the Mother, indeed! You look a wreck. Does your master not feed you? And what in Magrog's realm are you wearing? Lest you've no looking glass, the bird's nest"—he wriggled his ink-stained fingers under his chin—"it just doesn't suit. I thought your family discipline was clean— Well, I suppose it doesn't matter. I'd no idea you'd be allowed to attend the celebration, else I'd have come down. But I'm so behind on all this." His shoulders lifted helplessly at the same jumble of portrait folios I'd seen here before the fire. Before the cellar.

On a normal day, I'd have swallowed his disconnected ramble. But the smile had not touched his dark eyes and his left hand twitched, picking at his doublet—a very fine velvet doublet—and his jewels and his lace, fitting garb for the scion of a great pureblood house meeting a new king, not a junior portraitist catching up on his work. His cloak and mask were tossed on my old stool, as if he'd just come in.

"He *is* guilty, Gilles, your uncle Albin. He corrupted his position, consorted with Harrowers, ordered them to slaughter my family. He brought a Harrower *here* tonight—brought a *murderer* to the Tower to do his bidding. But his taint won't reach you. You've done nothing wrong."

"Did you come here to tell me how fortunate I am?" Bitterness crackled like frost. "I was out there on the stair and heard it all. You've won the day, you and your perfect discipline and your superior talent."

"What did I win? Friends? Hardly. Safety? Do you know what the curators did just because they were *afraid* I might expose their corruption? Your uncle's Harrower burnt the house where my sister and my servants were sleeping. Six innocent people *died* that night. . . ."

I kept talking, hoping to find a friend beneath the deadness in his eyes. But I edged toward the window, as well. Purebloods weren't allowed friends.

". . . and your uncle and his constable made it look like I did it. They buried me in the dark for half a year, Gilles. They corrupted my magic, corrupted my memory. I was on the verge of madness. Tonight I need your help, because you are *not* a murderer, and if the curators take me, they're going to kill me this time—one way or another, fast or slow."

Shouts rang from the stairs, much too close.

"Please. You know me better than they do, as I know you." I waved at his cloak and mask only an arm's reach away atop the wooden stool. "If you lent me those, I could walk out of the Tower. You could say I threatened you. You're a good man."

He squeezed his eyes closed, pressed his lips together, and shook his head. "Tell me why, Lucian. You didn't explain why a sorcerer of my uncle's noble history would do those things. If my uncle is guilty, Gramphier and Scrutari and the others corrupt, and only you are honorable, then tell me what any of them thought to gain. Why would any pureblood want your bloodlines destroyed?"

The Archive gates clanked. There was no time to explain Xancheira, even if I dared.

"I will not answer that; I cannot. Help me now. Live to share your gift as the gods intend."

Face bleak, he heaved a great breath and pressed a clenched fist to his mouth.

I dared not trust him. Laying my hand on his cloak and mask, I drew up a bit of true fire and my well-used illusion.

"Run, Gilles!" I bound my puny fire spell on the clothes and the wooden stool, then raised a curtain of false flame and smoke behind it. Hidden by the illusory blaze, I twisted the latch and threw open the casement.

Wind whipped the little fire and set pages and portraits alight, whirling them through the smoke-filled chamber. Sleet pelted my face. The dented, rusty drainpipe, just within reach, disappeared into blackness a long way below.

Just as I slung my leg over the sill, enchantment lanced through my feeble barrier. The air exploded from my chest as if I'd slammed into a wall. Thought disintegrated. Chest burning . . . lungs starving for air. Sleet and night swirled around me, as vision darkened.

My hand fell away from the window frame. Fire on one side; the abyss on the other. *Will not burn . . . cannot burn . . .*

"Stop right there!" A crackle and a thud accompanied the woman's command.

The flames—both real and illusory—vanished. A huge whooping breath returned sense, relief, and puzzlement. Pons's thunderbolt hadn't struck me, but rather startled the breath back into me. Perhaps she hadn't as good aim as her colleagues. Pons. Gods of all idiots, save me. I clung to the casement, coughing, just happy I could breathe again.

"Bring your foot back inside, Lucian de Remeni," she said, "or my next exercise *will* topple you right out."

While I was deciding whether to jump and save my tormentor her trouble, the smoke cleared enough that I saw Gilles sprawled on the floor, dusted with ash and scorched pages. "Lord of Light, Pons, did you kill him?"

"He'll not die of the blow." She closed the door softly and pressed her back to it. "But I was not trying to pat him on the head and tell him he was a good boy. If you had developed any skill at observation, you might have noticed him preparing the *aeroviar* spell as he begged enlightenment. Had I not intervened, I estimate your lungs would be entirely ash by now, and your body the height of a griddle cake spread on the cobbles below that window. Now climb back in. Slowly and carefully. And do not imagine you can bewilder me in magical fog or drop me in a hole or terrify me with flames that couldn't fire a haystack."

Would she do as she said? Of course she would.

I climbed down, but risked her wrath by hurrying to Gilles. He was limp as a rag mop but warm and breathing. I'd no idea what an *aeroviar* was, although the Aurellian syllables meant *air* and *starvation*.

"Why should I believe you about Gilles?" I said. "Were you not the one who called me a deviant soul who has no place in this world? I've seen ample evidence of your own capacity for lies and hypocrisy."

"Do you feel better getting that little jab off your chest? Now perhaps you might take a moment to *listen to me*. We've very little time."

Her square-shouldered figure blocked the doorway. A wall of cocked crossbows would have been less daunting.

"Your *friend* here—who told his uncle the location of your town house, by the way, and assured him gleefully that your sister would burn in Skefil's fire, too, as she rarely went out—is going to wake up and imagine he and I are allies. And I have to know—"

"*Imagine* . . . *Gilles* assured . . . ?" She might have been speaking in a foreign tongue.

"I have to know how much you've learned. When I heard you were in the Antiquities Repository yesterday, I hoped you'd located Vincente's painted chest there, a place so obvious I never thought to look. But then I learned you met *Perryn* to assess blame in a murder of one dead ordinary child. Has any bloodline birthed such a sentimental idiot as you?"

"The Duc de Tremayne murdered at least six children and was—"

"He might be Magrog himself, for all I care. Lucian, you cannot leave the Tower without understanding what you are."

"Leave here?" One would think I had passed into another world as strange as the five-fingered land beyond my visions. But Pons's obdurate urgency rammed home the truth, leaving a great void where my every perception of the woman once festered. "You—the inquisitor of Montesard—you're going to let me go?"

"Despite what you *think* you know of me, I prefer you neither dead nor a mindless husk. I need you to comprehend the stakes in this struggle—the reasons why your enemies cannot, will not, *ever* leave off, whether you hide in Palinur or run. *If* you know what you are, and *if* you understand why your grandsire cut you off and installed you here in the Tower, and *if* you take the trouble to learn a bit of magic, you might survive. And that, my young fool, could change everything we know."

She could be probing my knowledge of the Xancheira mystery, deciding whether she preferred to kill me or cage me, but somehow . . . my bent had shown her in the Archives with my grandsire and his painted chest, speaking to him with the same urgency I saw here. Gods save me, I wanted to believe her. Of all things in this world, I needed an ally, no matter how unlikely. But one great obstacle remained.

"Tell me what's become of my sister." The other curators yet named Juli dead from the fire.

"Only three people in the world know that she lives, and now you do as well. She is as safe as anyone can be in this city. And she is a far better liar than you. When I finally got the truth from her—that you had sent her to me—I thought you must finally have grown beyond your childish grievances with me." Pons threw her head back with a caustic laugh. "She is quite comfortable. Her only sadness is for you and those you've lost. She will survive if you do."

I wanted so much to believe. "Where is she? I'll tell you nothing until I know."

"Juliana lives in the Temple of the Mother under the personal protection of the high priestess. Now can we—?"

"You put her in a *temple*!" Horror near sent me flying through the casement, be damned whatever Pons might throw at me.

"Think, fool! The Mother's temple is not Arrosa's. Yes, the old man told us about all that, too. Believe me, your sister is protected in *all* ways.

She does not share your gifts, but she shares your blood . . . and the hope that comes with it. Now tell—"

"The old man—the spy—Sexton Garibald."

"We've already established that *you* are a fool. But your coroner could use lessons in conspiracy as well. The sexton babbled your every move to Pluvius, who, naturally, being a lackwit on your own scale, shared them with everyone who might loan him a pinch of salt at table. Now tell me: Was it there in the Repository? The painted chest? Do you comprehend why you are anathema to the Registry? If I'm to help you, I must know."

Fear for Juli and relief at Pons's assurances warred in my soul. After so many years of enmity, how could I possibly trust her? Yet she had not used me in the cellar, and her portrait displayed her grief for an ordinary and a halfblood child. Perhaps her hopes were for the future of her own bloodline. And truly, if Pons wanted me dead or captive, I would be dead or captive.

"I've seen evidence that explains why a strong dual bent and any mention of Xancheira terrify the curators. Pureblood life—the Registry, the breeding laws, our wealth and power—is built on a lie."

"Good." The set of her sturdy shoulders softened slightly. "Vincente's harsh reaction to your childish misbehavior fit no pattern I understood. Early last year, I confronted him about it. To his dismay, I picked the hour he was attempting to sneak that chest out of the Registry Archives. He had to explain some things to me before I let him take it."

"Great gods, you *knew*? You could have—"

"I could *not* have prevented your family's murder. I was naive, too—a horrific blunder. But sacrificing myself on the altar of indignation would not have brought them back. To keep silent and retain my position protected you—as Vincente begged me to do that day we talked. Think. Your sister lives."

"*You* sent the warning message about the second fire."

"Yes. I thought I'd gotten you out of the Tower and into a situation where you couldn't make things worse."

Thus my unnegotiated contract.

"But then your offended pride brought you whining to Gilles de Albin, confirming Albin and Gramphier's worst fears. You *must* survive, Lucian. What you've learned is only a beginning, I think, for the story of Xancheira encompasses far more than bloodlines and magical inheritance.

Our ancestors did something dreadful at Xancheira, something that left a great wound in the fabric of the world. Vincente was unable to plumb the nature of that wound, but he believed you could. He saw you *vanish* once while working magic, and believed you truly went somewhere else. Is that so?"

A wound in the world . . . the Danae in Palinur had spoken of the world as broken. The silver one said my talents were ones they waited for. "Yes. But I don't know where. Did he?"

Pons blew a sharp exhale. "I don't think so. He just wanted to destroy the chest and forget what he'd found. He believed it would be your doom as well as his. As it proved. I persuaded him to hide the thing instead, even from me. But it is not righteous to ignore such a matter."

Gilles moaned, bringing Pons instantly to his side. Like a statue of ice, she stared down at him.

"Do it again, whatever you did to him," I whispered, my pent questions ready to explode. "What does this have to do with the Danae?"

"Danae?" Her puzzled look crushed my hope. "I've no idea what you're talking about."

"You *must* tell me. I've drawn a portrait that shows the future more clearly than a diviner's cards. I've existed in another place. A Danae woman has spoken to me of something I need to do, but in riddles impossible to unravel. I'll listen to you. I'll learn. But I have to know whom to trust and where to find answers. I am not mad, Pons. I swear it."

"Our time is done," she snapped. "My colleagues will be here in moments. Give me your hand." She extended hers. "*Now,* fool, or die here and end our hopes."

"Lord of Light, Pons, hopes of *what*?"

But she refused to speak. Her hand waited.

No matter how formidable her magic, we could not stand against four curators. Perhaps her skills could hide me. I extended my hand.

Pons grasped my wrist. Her hand was not cold as I had always imagined, but warm and womanly and unbelievably strong. She knelt beside Gilles and drew me down, too, but on opposite sides of him. She maintained her grip on my wrist across Gilles's body and she fixed her eyes on mine.

"Vincente de Remini was a coward, Lucian. Your family died for it, and we very nearly lost you, the first matured dual bent in more than half a century. I am going to lay the blame for all the ills of the Registry at Vincente's feet—and *your* feet—blackening your name beyond redemption. It was love for you that weakened Vincente's knees. Sentiment, a terrible lesson you must learn as I did. To make this right, you have to run."

Every bone in my body protested. I would not abandon my sister.

"I won't. I am not you."

"Exactly so." She averted her gaze, her mouth grim, her body rigid. "So you have to change."

She jammed my fingers into Gilles's chest. Explosive magic—brutal, ferocious, scouring turbulence—raced through my arm, through my fingers, drawn from my centers of power, as if a god's hand stripped out my entrails.

"Gods' bones," I gasped, "what are you doing?"

Gilles's fine doublet charred, orange embers flaring as it shriveled and revealed his shirt, already blackening, and then his chest, each wiry black hair flaring and curling. As the fire gouged into his thick, raw flesh, his eyes popped open and he screamed.

"Curse you! Stop this!" I tried to pull away, but she held on, her grip like a steel manacle bolted to stone.

Inside me and without, all was fire and screaming and raging power. I could not slow it. I could not stop it. Horror-struck, dizzy from the draining magic, I twisted and dragged at my hand until it seemed the bones must snap. She would not budge. So I lunged across Gilles and plowed into her. Crushing her with my entire weight, I wrenched my hand free and scrambled back to Gilles's side.

Too late. His back arched in a single great spasm of agony. Then he collapsed, a smoking, fist-sized hole where his heart should be.

"Ah, gods!" Shaking, disbelieving, I could not draw my eyes from my onetime friend. "What have you done, witch?"

"Only what is necessary." Pons knelt at my side.

As I closed Gilles's eyes, she grabbed my wrist again. Using both hands and inhuman strength, she pressed my fingers to her own body and dragged a second gout of magic from my soul. How was this possible?

"No!" I yanked my arm from her weakening grasp and leapt to my feet. She remained kneeling, back curled, head down, as flames of scarlet and vermillion devoured the pale flesh of her shoulder.

"We'll find you when the time is right," she said harshly. Her whole body spasmed. She clenched her teeth. "Now run and don't look back."

A wisp of a smile, and then she screamed as if her soul was ripped from her body and slumped to the cold stone. Insensible. Dead? Her shoulder smoked. The enchantment had eaten halfway through it.

"Elaia, where are you?" Closer. Running footsteps in the passage. Hammering fists. "Pons!"

I backed toward the window, aghast. Any pureblood who examined Gilles would determine that I had worked the enchantment that killed him. Magic turned to murder was the most heinous crime a pureblood could commit. They would execute me—slowly, painfully.

"Down here, Pluvius! This lock's been melted!" A blow left the door splintered at the hinges.

"Get out of my way!" Gramphier.

I scrambled out the window to a boot-wide ledge, closed the casement, and then stretched to reach the drainpipe. Clutching the rusted conduit with hands and knees, I levered myself downward, heedless of wind, sharp edges, the blackness below. My boots scrabbled for footholds in the stone face of the Tower. Bits of mortar crumbled out from under. I prayed for fog, for blizzard, for direction, for redemption. . . .

When the casement burst open two stories above me, I gripped the pipe with cold, bleeding hands, closed my eyes, and kept moving. Magelight flashed around outside my eyelids. But no crackling discharge slammed me to the earth so far below.

"Get Fortier down there to greet the murderer," yelled Gramphier. "And hurry, or the royal prick's men will take him first. He must be ours."

"I'll see to it myself. We'll have him." Damon.

The magelight faded, and I moved downward faster, terrified my screaming hands would not hold. I passed between two arrow slits and risked a pinprick beam of my own. Rain-slick cobbles gleamed far enough below to hollow my belly. And even so small a magic left the world swirling like soup in a kettle.

A dozen years it had been since my brothers had challenged me to such folly. I had always been overcareful, always well disciplined, so Germaine was forever goading me into competitions, sure that his focused determination must win. Emil had been wild in all ways, while clever Ari, the youngest, save Juli—

My hands slipped and tore again. My toes gouged holes in old mortar. I clutched the iron pipe with arms, elbows, knees, and will, until my heart slowed and I dared resume my downward creeping.

I had to find Juli. Assuming Pons survived her wound, how long would it be until the madwoman chose to sacrifice Juli for some noble purpose? My sister was not safe anywhere in Palinur.

Another quat and one foot slipped and dangled free. Rusty metal ripped my palms yet again. I gripped with knees and forearms, kept from falling by one precarious toehold. But my hands could not squeeze tight enough to support me while I found another foothold, so I took a breath, let go, and dropped.

The cobbles slammed into me sooner than expected, jarring one knee. But I stumbled to my feet and ran.

CHAPTER 36

My spine shivered with a foretaste of magic. Searchers ahead and behind.

Before the searing magelight could expose or blind me, I reversed my steps yet again and pelted into a slotlike alley I'd passed earlier for fear it was a dead end. Muck seeped into my boots; the air stank of decay and mold. I flattened my back to the wall and closed my eyes as white flares pierced the night.

The maze of narrow lanes surrounding the Registry Tower had become another trap. Every time I headed downhill toward the corner where I'd left Bastien, I'd run into Damon's search party and their cursed magelights. An eternity of dodging and hiding and I was thoroughly lost.

What was the hour? The city bells pealed from time to time, but I'd had no concentration to spare for counting. Now the eerie quiet taunted me. Surely it was near midnight. If he'd kept his promise, Bastien would be safely returned to Caton, though his safety was like to be as ephemeral as my own. *Magrog devour your bones, Pons!*

The brilliance beyond my eyelids faded, and I took off down the alley, stretching my arms forward. The slimed walls were scarce farther apart than my shoulders, and high enough to keep the alley dark as an oubliette. *Best not think of cellar prisons.*

Aagh! A solid lump tripped up my foot, threatening to buckle my twisted knee.

My hands flew outward to hold me upright. Gritty brick scraped another layer from the raw flesh of my palms, the pain entirely out of proportion to the injury. Pressing the heels of my cupped hands hard to my forehead, I let my sleeves absorb my ragged breaths.

"Help me. Sweet Magrog, help me." The slurred entreaty originated at my feet.

"Who's there?" I whispered. No light or voices behind me as yet, but the pounding chase rumbled deep in the earth. Or maybe just in my own chest.

The mumbling continued uninterrupted: "Help me . . . help. . . ."

I shrouded a risky wisp of magelight with my cloak and exposed a filthy man of indeterminate age, bleeding from deep gouges on his face. His bloody fingers trembled as he desperately sucked a black paste from a twist of cloth. A twistmind, then. Locked into cycles of self-injury, pain, and pleasure by the spell-wrought paste of nivat seed, he didn't even know I was there.

The familiar disgust did not manifest itself. I could not judge corruption. Pride, arrogance, willful ignorance, lust for vengeance . . . who could measure my own sins that had left my family, servants, and young Pleury dead, and Gilles with his heart burnt away?

But there was no help to give a twistmind. I snuffed the light and stepped over him.

Fingers of enchantment tickled my back. The faint snap of orders sped my steps.

Damon had offered me refuge in a house of reflection. Now he drove me like prey before the hunt. Pons had claimed interest in my survival, then proceeded to blacken my name beyond redemption. Had everyone gone mad? Had they killed Pleury, too, trying to force me to run?

Pons's lunacy answered one question. I could trust no pureblood.

A thin slot of flickering light ahead—torchlight? bonfires?—proved the alley no dead end, though the mold-slicked walls closed in so tight I had to squeeze through sidewise. No one of any bulk was going to be able to follow me through there, much less take me captive. As long as I could fit. As long as the flickering lights ahead weren't a second search party.

But it was a broad expanse of cobbles that awaited me, lit with torches and populated by the remnants of a dispersing crowd. Knots of men and women lingered in agitated conversation, while other groups hurried into the dozen streets that opened off the square.

Each of the twelve districts of Palinur centered on such an open yard where all the principal streets came together. The focus of each was the district well, fed by Aurellian pipes and conduits from the deep-buried springs. Here—the heart of the prosperous Council District—water sluiced over magnificent bronze representations of Kemen Sky Lord and his sister, the Goddess Mother Samele, surrounded by their three offspring: Deunor Lightbringer; Erdru, Lord of Vines; and the Goddess of Love, Arrosa.

But it wasn't the imposing bronzes that had drawn gawkers so late. District squares also housed a pillory and flogging post for meting out punishments for local miscreants, from thieves to scolds. And because the Council District housed the Registry Tower and Hall of Magistrates, its square also sported a gallows for timely executions.

Magical vision merged into the scene before me, as if I'd walked into a memory. A man dangled from the gallows, just as I'd witnessed hours earlier. Even at a distance I recognized the Duc de Tremayne.

Four of the Guard Royale stood watch, preventing thieves from stripping the corpse or mutilating it. And someone else stood close, surveying the thinning crowd. A broad man clad in leathers and sporting an unruly thicket of brown hair and beard. Bastien.

Blessed gods! A hard knot in my gut untied itself. I squeezed out of the alley and hurried around the dark peripheries of the square to join him. But as if my relief had conjured them, Damon and a dozen men in Registry livery hurried into the square.

I ducked into a shadowed colonnade. The search party passed right by Bastien, but then the damnable fool yelled and flailed his arms to catch their attention. In moments he was surrounded.

Mumbling curses, I scuttered through the shadows, aiming to get as close as possible before Damon's men noticed me. The Registry was not going to harm Bastien right in front of me. I dug deep for magic and readied my pitiful catalog of spells.

Pons was right about the inadequacy of my training. Working alongside my grandsire, reading a rare codex borrowed from the Karish monastery at Pontia, or walking out with my favorite drawing master on fine days to sketch the countryside had ever tempted me away from boring lessons in common spellwork. I'd never gotten past the childish amusements of void holes and fire, excitements, inflations, and sketchy illusion.

By the time I got close enough to Bastien to do any good, half of Damon's men were jogging toward the alley I'd just escaped. Bastien remained unbound and unwounded, ranting at Damon in undecipherable complaint. I imagined words about contract rights and his pureblood property.

Damon waved the rest of the Registry guards after the others, snapped a few words at Bastien, and then hurried after his men. As the coroner bowed to their backs, untouched and free, I could not hold back a grin. Some ordinaries carried their own magic.

Bastien strode toward the corner where the Riie Segundo branched off the square. I set out to intercept him. While I retrieved Juli, he could—

No. My steps slowed. Better if he got back to the necropolis and looked to its safety. And better if he had no idea where I was if or when the Registry came calling. But I would keep my vow to be with him at dawn. Whatever danger Oldmeg feared would drive the Cicerons to the sanctuary beyond the portal would surely endanger the necropolis as well. Then, if we survived it, Bastien, Juli, and I could map out a plan for the future. I felt safer, stronger with Bastien at my side, but just now the night was too dangerous. *I* was too dangerous.

Once he was out of sight, I sped down the Riie Domitian toward the Temple District.

A cadaverous young man and a woman heavy with child ascended the broad steps of Mother Samele's temple into its forest of painted columns. They were the first supplicants I'd seen in my hour's watching. I ran lightly up the steps and followed them, dodging from column to column to see where they would go, hoping to find the high priestess without anyone taking note of me.

The temple was replete with sights to awe and inspire. Great bronze cauldrons billowed fire. Statues of the goddess and her minions stood taller than three men. Stone altars, large and small, bore the stains of blood sacrifice, and baskets of charred bones sat beside glowing braziers, where supplicants burnt their offerings. And every lintel, every column sported its impish aingerou, waiting to carry the sweet odors of blood and smoke to the Mother.

I cursed as the pair knelt before a bronze of the seated goddess.

A careful circuit of the temple peripheries had convinced me that it was not being watched. But the labyrinthine temple was entirely open to the night air. Where were the priestesses?

Conflicting anxieties gnawed at me. Despite Pons's brutal madness, I believed she wanted me to live, just as she'd said. She had killed Gilles and maimed herself, at the least, to force me to run. She had pointedly not pressed me for what I'd done with the painted chest so she could not testify as to its whereabouts, but she *could* be made to tell where Juli was. And she had admitted that a fourth person besides her, me, and the high priestess knew my sister's hiding place. To fetch Juli would be to plunge her into my danger, pointing Registry and Albin arrows at her back as well as mine, but I dared not leave her here.

It seemed an interminable time before the bony husband helped his wife rise. Before they could begin some other devotion, I stepped out.

"Goodman," I said, "where would I find the Mother's gatekeeper?" Every temple of the Goddess Mother had at least a gatekeeper—a crone bound to answer a Seeker's questions.

The man's slack mouth gaped at my mask. The wife's dull eyes locked on my bloody hands, trembling with magical depletion.

I drew my hands into my cloak and bit back rudeness. "It is permitted to answer me. It is required."

The woman's stammering direction led me to an unpainted column deep in the temple. The massive column measured at least twenty quercae in diameter and was chiseled to mime a sheaf of wheat, the heads sprayed out across the ceiling. An ancient woman sat cross-legged at its base, nibbling a withered apple while the damp breeze fluttered tatters of gauze about her birdlike limbs. At her feet sat a basket holding a sparse collection of coins, twigs, bundles of herbs, and scraps of parchment. Behind her, an arch of midnight opened into the column. That's where I would find them.

"Naema," I said, crouching beside her. The title was perhaps overmuch, but the Mother's gatekeepers were certainly holy elders. The old woman might have been the high priestess herself at one time. "I bring the goddess a problem of mortal urgency. It is necessary that I speak with the Sinduria."

"Look round you, chosen of the gods. The wind blows from every quarter. The birds have abandoned the city. All matters of the Mother are of mortal urgency, are they not? Especially in an hour of portents. 'Tis an awful and perilous thing for any to interrupt the goddess's rites on such a night, most especially"—her bony finger tweaked my cloak aside, exposing my torn hands—"for a male creature with blood on his hands, not all of it his own."

Fear seeped from that deep-buried place inside where ancient stories shaped us. This had been the Goddess Mother's place for centuries before my ancestors had invaded Navronne. I tugged at my cloak, as if it could hide the blood taint from the goddess's eye.

Since leaving boyhood, I had passed off such old-woman pronouncements as artifice and clever guesses, contrived to frighten those of lesser mind. My spine had no longer prickled at my grandmother's tales, nor had my stomach hollowed at talk of omens. But all that had changed since my magic had taken me into visions . . . since Oldmeg and her portrait . . . since Necropolis Caton.

"Tell me more." The old woman's broken teeth tore off another bite of the leathery apple and chewed slowly.

"I cannot," I said. "My question is bound in . . . divine mystery . . . and vows of silence. I *will* go to the high priestess. I prefer to go with your blessing."

"The dark is fraught with pain. You bring it . . . and bear no small portion of it." She shrugged. "Yet the Sinduria is of your kind. That in itself gives you no privilege, but I ween she would wish to understand a wild-hearted, blood-marked sorcerer who brings her mortal urgencies on a dangerous midnight."

The high priestess was *pureblood*? It certainly made more sense that Pons would have hidden Juli with one of us—a woman powerful in her own right, as well as protected by her office—than with some ordinary. Purebloods who took on the mantle of clergy did not serve contracts, only their gods.

The old woman ate the last bit of her apple, seeds and all. She grinned and patted her scrawny middle. "Planting time is coming! Not long now. Enter as you dare."

Trying not to imagine an apple tree growing from her decaying belly, I bowed and walked round her to the door in the column.

The tight spiral of the downward stair was well lit, and the scenes of bountiful fields, lush forests, and healthy sheepfolds painted on the close walls were beautifully wrought, their brilliant colors only slightly dimmed by smoke stains. But I detested every step of that descent. The stair plunged deeper than Arrosa's baths. Deeper than the Tower cellars.

The lower temple that opened out from the bottom of the stair was almost the twin of that above, like a reflection in a calm lake, save that columns and altars and smoke-stained murals were right side up. The vastness smelled of earth and smoke and musty herbs, with a pungent trace of lavender that seemed somehow out of place.

No priestess or initiate, but a man in the Mother's green livery awaited me. Large ears protruded from his dark straight hair and green half mask. A pureblood, too.

He touched fingertips to forehead. "Greetings of the Mother, *eqastré.* I am Silos, attendant to Sinduria de Cartamandua-Celestine. What business brings you to the goddess and her priestess so late of an evening?"

He seemed a soft man, his voice pleasant and polite. But I felt as tight wound as a clockwork. I needed us to be out of this pit . . . out of the city.

"My name is for the Sinduria's ears alone, *Eqastré* Silos. Please inform her that I've come to retrieve a valuable that was left in trust with her a month ago. The circumstances of its leaving have changed."

Perfect composure graced the man's features. "I shall inform her."

"And time is of the essence."

"We live by the goddess's time here," he said.

The quiet reprimand did naught but grate. But indeed he returned in moments. "This way."

He led me between the columns—squat and thick. The farther we went, the more oppressive the place felt. Older. Heavier. Who could say what really went on down here? In ancient times, the goddess required a healthy young male die every spring to ensure an abundant harvest. Tales said the priestesses drove the unwary sacrifice to mating frenzy and then stabbed him, leaving him to bleed slowly into the earth. Deep in a cave. Naked, in the dark.

I pinned my gaze to the wide back in front of me. Silos must be a brave man to serve in the Mother's fortress. Or perhaps his Head of Family had simply committed him to a terrible contract.

"The Sinduria will join you as soon as she is able."

Silos motioned me through a doorway into a candlelit chamber. Water trickled into a laver set into one wall. A stone altar stood before a crumbling fresco on the end wall. Even half-peeled away, the images were recognizable—the story of Kemen and Samele, the twin brother and sister born of Light and Darkness.

"Sit, if you like. I'll bring wine."

"No wine, *eqastré,*" I said, wanting only to be gone with Juli at my side.

"But I would clean my hands before greeting the priestess." Pureblood healers forever warned of sepsis from dirty wounds. Without hands to release it, my magic was dead.

"Certainly. Be free of it." He gestured at the laver and took his leave.

Both palms were scraped and raw and threaded with cuts. The cold water stung as it washed away filth, grit, and blood—only the visible blood, of course. A deep and dirty laceration on my left palm continued to seep. I rinsed it until my skull threatened to crack and blotted it with my cloak. Then I sat beside a small stone writing table and waited. Pacing would have worked better to prevent me grinding my teeth to pulp, but I knew I was more tired than my anxieties would admit. The night was like to get no easier.

A person's worktable can reveal many things. The Sinduria's held pens, an ink cup, a box of sand, a stack of blank parchment, and implements to impose a temple seal, laid out in precise order. An iron clip and a box of cheap rushlights bespoke a mind for thrift unusual in a pureblood. And a cedarwood box held a stack of beautifully painted, well-used cards.

Sinduria de Cartamandua-Celestine, Silos had named the priestess. Cartamanduas were the family of cartographers, the mapmakers cursed with a drunkard son who had become a *recondeur* while still a boy. But the Celestines were diviners. The painted cards could be those of a pureblood soothsayer.

I wasn't sure I wanted to know more of the future. My own pen and ink had shown me sorrow enough.

As the hour crept onward, my thoughts raced in ever more chaotic circles. My fingers took up one of the pens and a little knife. I soon found myself sketching on a scrap of parchment from the stack, summoning memory and what magic remained in me. . . .

"Who are you who dares make free of my implements?"

The accusation, cold and low, lifted my head from the drawing. A youngish woman of robust figure stood not ten steps from me.

I leapt to my feet, my cheeks heating. What had possessed me?

Heavy black hair had been twisted and piled atop her head with jeweled combs. Even so she would scarce reach my chin. But the interlocking beads of lapis, malachite, and gold spread like a shield across her ample breast proclaimed her a Sinduria.

"I don't recall your leaving any valuables here in trust," she said before

I could answer. "Indeed I wonder what you must value, coming to the goddess with such unseemly dress and deportment."

Eyes were the mark of a pureblood diviner. The priestess's wide silver bracelets were graven with eyes, and instead of a mask, her own eyes were enlarged with thick outlines of kohl and swaths of blue paint. Once my gaze met hers, it was difficult to look away.

No reason to play games with a woman granted such a rare, difficult gift, and a character so formidable as to be named the Mother's high priestess while near my own age. She would never house a fugitive pureblood without knowing exactly what she was doing and for whom.

I inclined my back and touched my forehead. "Grace of the Mother, Sinduria. And I beg your pardon for the late hour and my unseemly dress. My name is Lucian de Remeni-Masson. I've come to fetch my sister, Juliana, given shelter here by your divine mistress's grace."

"The Goddess Mother frequently shelters supplicants. Some have names. Some give up their names in humility before her. If you are the person you say, you are condemned as a deviant and a murderer by our superiors. Why would I do aught but send for the Registry? And do not tell me *because I am your supplicant's family*, as family can be the most treacherous of all enemies."

Silos had materialized in the doorway behind her. I doubted insisting on privacy would alter that. Indeed, I seemed entirely bereft of argument, save perhaps . . .

I passed her the page in my hand. "I am the person I claim. If you would look at this, lady, you might recognize the one I seek. And by the gift the gods have granted me—and the one they've given you—perhaps you can see that I mean only her good."

The drawing depicted Juli on the night she'd told me about her friend Egan the linkboy and how she'd found us a place to live. I knew I had captured the truth of her—earnest, intelligent, flushed with righteous indignation, and afire with youthful passion and laughter as she had called me *the most priggish, solemn, dearest* ancieno *in this miserable world.*

The Sinduria examined the page, then tossed it onto the table.

"The Mother's grace must be profound in your family," she said coldly. "Your sister is quite safe. I understood you would leave her until those responsible for your family's murder and the slander on your person are rooted out. Although . . . I've no illusions that purebloods are free of sin,

Remeni, but for someone highly placed in the Registry Tower to be involved in such savagery is exceedingly difficult to accept."

Determined not to anger the woman, I worked to shape the right words. "The motives for our family's murder are not entirely clear. That my sister survived two deliberate fires was a matter of sheerest chance on one occasion and a timely warning on the other. But the gods themselves have revealed through pureblood magic that someone in the Tower was responsible. And due to certain events of the past few hours—which I'm sure you'll hear of on the morrow—our danger has become even more critical. In short, the secret of my sister's refuge is no longer secure, which means neither of you is safe if Juli remains here."

The priestess clasped her hands at her breast and, in thoughtful silence, strolled toward the frescoed wall. I hoped she didn't plan to pray. We needed to be gone.

She pivoted sharply. "The Mother's fortress has withstood blasphemers since the days of barbarian raiders. Where could you take the girl that would be safer than this?"

"That must remain my secret, lady. You understand the difficulty of Registry interrogations."

Her eyes grew even larger with dawning understanding. "Only a curator would dare interrogate a member of the Sinduri Council. You deem a *curator* involved in murder!"

Pons must have told the Sinduria next to nothing. The priestess was neither warm nor ingratiating, but she deserved to know her danger.

"The Registry will execute Guilian de Albin this night for consorting with Harrowers. Justly so, his guilt revealed by the gods' magic. At least two other curators are entangled in a web of lies, corruption, and murder that extends not only throughout the Registry, but taints the court of Ardra, the Karish hierarchy, and Arrosa's Temple. I've no freedom to judge individual guilt or innocence and no impartial wisdom to outweigh the horrors done to my family. I simply must get my sister away from Palinur until the problems at the Tower are resolved. You yourself, *doma*, must be wary."

And here I had to lie. The priestess could not be allowed to think of us as *recondeurs* before I had Juli. I didn't trust her that far.

"Curator Pons has made provision to shield the Remeni name from dishonor. Fortunately, my contract master has business interests in a western city where my family has powerful allies. There my sister and I shall persevere in our duty until we can return safely."

"Silos!" The Sinduria's sharp command displayed neither shock nor disbelief, only urgency. "You and I go to the Registry within the hour. Prepare. Our guest will leave by the Ox Gate. I'll have a message for my father and a letter for the abbot before we go."

The soft man bowed and vanished.

"Now you, Remeni, must explain your inference about Arrosa's Temple as I write. Yes, the whole thing."

I felt a bit silly recounting the story of Ysabel, Tremayne, and Perryn to the Sinduria's back as she wrote and sealed a number of letters. But she listened, peppering me with questions about Gab the sweeping girl, Motre Varouna's bath girls, and High Priestess Irinyi's exact words. By the time I spoke of the inquest, her writing was finished, and she listened with her entire attention. And when the tale was done, she laid down her pen with an excess of deliberation.

"The matter of divine Arrosa's Temple shall be dealt with," she said, cold fury locked in every syllable. "The Sinduri Council has heard this accusation before and failed to act; thus, these sins rest on our shoulders as well as Irinyi's."

She rose. "We're finished here. Silos"—I'd not seen her aide return to the doorway—"I'll be ready to depart for the Registry as soon as you've taken care of these."

She passed him the letters, gestured his attention to me, and swept from the room.

"But what of my sister?" I called after her.

"Luka!" A blur of green silk from the direction of the doorway resulted in an impact sounder than any magical thunderbolt, and I was lost in the joy and confusion of blessed reunion.

". . . Never thought to see you . . . that last time when you were so cruel . . . terrified . . . came to understand . . . so much time to think . . . drove me mad. Old Pew-Pons locked me in a tiny closet . . . sure I would die . . . but never harmed . . . Well, all right it was just a vile, bare, cramped room . . . Then brought me here . . . No one told me *anything ever* . . . only 'behave yourself' . . . or 'his life depends on you' . . . But I knew you'd come. Years . . . oh, Luka, I thought it would be years!"

Juli's flood of words had not ceased since she plowed into me like an attacking legion. It was just as well, for weariness and relief had robbed me of words. As we hurried after Silos through the underground, I whispered "Decorum, Juli" and "Later, *serena*" though the phrases were but placeholders for all the things I wanted to tell her.

She looked well, her dark braid glossy, her flushed cheeks smooth, her eyes sparking with excitement and pleasure that buoyed my spirit beyond measure.

We came to a . . . barn was the only thing to call it, though it was merely another vast extension of the underground temple. Mosaics depicting fire and bloody sacrifice adorned the squat columns; straw covered the stone floor. Wood slats divided pens holding a few goats, a dozen sheep, and a pair of rare white oxen. There was naught divine about the beasts; their stink overwhelmed the more ordinary perfumes of a temple. A wide ramp led upward to a great bronze door hammered with the image of the Mother's favored beast. The Ox Gate.

"You look so thin, *ancieno*! Are you hungry? These beasts are offerings to the goddess. Most of the meat goes to the poor, but we residents get to share a bit of it. We could ask the lady if we could take some. Silos would see to it. He's most helpful."

"We must go, *serena*. Silos, has she cloak and mask?"

"I have them here, *domé*. Her other things—"

"We'll send for them when we're settled." But I doubted that was to happen anytime soon.

Men in temple livery hoisted two great beams of oak. Magic snapped and hinges ground as the bronze door swung inward. Beyond the door the city bells pealed and clanged in relentless cacophony. Perhaps Perryn wanted everyone awake to celebrate his anointing.

Silos hurried Juli into a claret-hued pelisse, its fur lining thick and clean, and passed her a finely embroidered mask.

Against all protocol, Juli clasped Silos's big hands. "You've been so kind, Silos. I've been a terrible nuisance, forever pestering and pouting, but you've taught me much of patience and duty."

Though his half-naked face remained impassive, Silos smiled beneath his mask. He bowed to each of us. "It has been an honor, *Domé* Remeni, and very little trouble, *doma*. May the goddess protect you both through these perilous hours."

"What hour is it?" The clamor of the bells continued as if it were the first day of the new year. The world pressed on my spirit, a swelling clamor to match the bells, as if I had touched the earth and invoked my bent.

"We're at fourth hour of the morning watch, *domé*. For the last hour the bells have not struck the hour or the quarters." He dropped his voice, eyeing Juli, who had gone to pet a bleating lamb. "You must be on your way quickly. 'Tis the *alarm* they peal. The Sinduria has Seen Prince Bayard closing on the city."

The Sinduria—a pureblood diviner—and *Seen*, pronounced in that way that raised the hair on my neck.

Silos exhaled a long breath, clearly wrestling with himself about saying more. "The siege will be long and difficult. Months. Perhaps years. This war and this winter threaten to lead us into an age of darkness such as Navronne has never seen."

So it was a tightening noose I felt. Was this Oldmeg's seeing, too? "Come, *serena*, we must go. Express our deepest gratitude to the Sinduria, Silos."

Juli nattered on about putting fat on my bones as we hurried up the ramp and into a yard that smelled of beasts and ash. The bronze gate crashed shut behind us. Two ponderous thumps told me the defensive beams had been lowered.

Juli quieted and grasped my hand. The pale, unmasked half of her face was all I could see of her in the sudden dark. I longed to enfold her in my arms and promise that I could keep her safe. But I would not lie to her. The bleak truth had settled in my gut like lead.

More than anything I wished to return to the necropolis. I'd given Bastien my word, and I desperately needed his aid. He knew so much more of the ordinary world where we would need to live. And surely his incisive wit could help me discover the Path of the White Hand. But he would never abandon his dead-city, and I dared not enter Caton. The Registry would be waiting. One glimpse of me inside, and my people would kill them all. Juli and I were on our own.

"Stay close," I yelled in her ear. Now we were outside the thick walls of the temple, the jangling timbre of the bells made it near impossible to hear. "This way."

Before choosing our escape route, I needed to see if the attack had begun, if there were riots or fires.

The beast yard was but a part of the mundane workings that stretched behind the arc of temples facing the Temple District square. On an ordinary day, servants would be pounding laundry or tending the priests' horses. The bells must have chased them all away.

We hurried past deserted stables, kitchens, and washhouses, and cut through an abandoned aviary whose wire cages gaped empty. The cloying stink of rotted fruit welcomed us to an ancient orchard that should have been sweet with cherry blossoms. We halted only when I glimpsed the torches of Temple Square blazing through the last rows of trees.

I pulled Juli close. Her heart raced and she was breathing hard. "From the Elder Wall we can spot the best route to the city gates," I said. "I'd leave you hidden here, but—"

She shook her head vigorously and clung to my arm.

No pureblood search parties were in evidence, yet neither was the square deserted. Servants missing from their usual haunts mingled with priests, initiates, and guards to gossip, pack carts, or simply mill about the stair to the Elder Wall. Silos must have been wrong about the hour; a pale glow in the sky insisted dawn was near.

Juli and I passed through the babbling crowd like ghosts; temple servants and the Guard Royale were not ones to forget pureblood prerogatives. Unhindered, we climbed the stair to the walk atop the ancient wall. Six months previous, I had walked this very stretch of wall to spy out where Ysabel de Tremayne's body had rolled down into the hirudo. Below us, Demetreo's demesne filled the seam between inner and outer walls like a moat of tar.

"Oh, Luka, is this the world's end?"

It was not sunrise that lightened the sky. Dotted over the dark landscape to east and west, at least three villages burned—the dwellings of those who planted, tended, and harvested food for Palinur and much of central Ardra. Worse for us, ribbons of flame marked the merchant camps, the inns and stables and sop-houses that served the east and west gates. Outside the main gates, it was difficult to distinguish the fires of destruction from those of the enemy encampment that sprawled southward like a second city.

"Certainly not," I said.

She touched my arm, drawing my gaze, her face intent on reading what I was not saying. "We can't stay with your master . . . or Egan's mam, can we?"

"No. We have to leave the city before the siege takes hold," I said. But how?

The three principal gates were already blocked. The small postern sported no merchant stalls, for the rugged rocks and defiles that led northward were impassible for wagons or carts—and entirely choked with ice and mud in winter and spring. The only other gate I knew was the slot gate at the end of the hirudo. If we could slip through the slot gate without being seen, we could hug the wall and follow it northward to the far side of the necropolis plateau. Instead of entering the necropolis, as Bastien and I had done on the day we returned to find Pleury dead, Juli and I could circle around Caton to the cart road that would take us east, well away from the fires and growing siege lines. It seemed the only way. A good way, except that we would have to traverse the hirudo. Therein lay the greatest danger. . . .

Fire marked the protective ring of Caedmon's Wall, as well as the enemy's approach. Atop the great outer wall torches and cauldrons burst into flame, one and then another, like gems being added to a sparkling necklace. Only the span that bounded the hirudo remained entirely dark. Palinur had been immune from siege so long that the Cicerons' dank settlement had blocked the stairs that would take soldiers to the walk atop the outer wall.

The city's defenders would not allow it to remain dark. It was only Cicerons in the way. And Oldmeg had foreseen disaster falling on the hirudo at dawn. We had to hurry.

"Come," I said, urging Juli down the stair and across the square. "As soon as we're out of this crowd, we're going to run. Can you do it?"

"Faster than you if I hitch up my skirt."

Lamps flitted like fireflies in the dark side streets. People clustered in front of their houses, questioning their neighbors, exchanging news and rumor. I tugged Juli into a deep doorway. "Fix it," I said.

With a deft twist she gathered the muddy hem of her gown and left it a knot dangling loose at her knees. "Now."

We gripped hands and ran, our pureblood masks and colors forging a path through growing crowds. Some citizens were armed and ready to defend their homes. Some were armored and riding out to honor debts of fealty to their duc. The lower streets would be dangerous as panic grew, so I diverted us through the *pocardon*. The market would be less confining.

No one had time to delay us. Tradesmen were packing up their wares in hopes of salvaging something if worse came. Gangs of soldiers dragged men and boys from shops and stalls, pressing pikes or staves into their hands and marching them off to the walls. Bread women passed a loaf or a bun to each of the defenders, until their barrows were empty. Chaos was coming . . . an age of darkness, so the high priestess had Seen . . .

Juli and I slowed to a more dignified pace when a troop of men-at-arms quick-marched past us, heading down toward the main gates. We swept along in their wake, as if to add our magic to their defense, until I spied the familiar lane of deserted alehouses.

"This way." I dragged her into the dark lane redolent of yeast and mold. At the far end we'd find the broken arch that began the steep path down to the hirudo. Half an hour more and we should be at the slot gate and our path to freedom.

The high walls of the empty alehouses muted the clangor of the bells. Halfway down the lane, all but one of them fell silent. It tolled a double peal and paused. Over and over. Perhaps it was just the echo in my ears and not a bell at all.

"Stop . . . stop." Juli dragged on my hand, gulping air.

I stroked her hair and glanced at the sky, perceptibly paler behind the sheen of smoky orange. "We can't stop, *serena*," I said, tugging her forward. "Someone extraordinary warned me that this way will become impassable when dawn comes. Her name is Oldmeg, an intelligent, generous, ferocious, powerful woman—quite like you."

She glanced up and smiled, flushed and panting—a sight that would someday ravage the heart of a besotted man. "Wondered when you'd notice. Come on, then!"

Laughing, we jogged onward. I felt whole again, my family together, as was right.

Ten steps from the arch, two Registry servitors stepped from behind the broken bricks. I grabbed Juli and backed away. But an implement sharp enough to pierce my layered garments pricked my back, and two more servitors appeared on our flanks.

"Be very still, Lucian," came a voice from behind me. "We've no wish to harm you. And who is—? Lord of Light be thanked; the dead now walk!"

Master Pluvius.

CHAPTER 37

Pluvius pulled off his mask when he stepped out from behind me. Magelight gleamed bright on his white hair and beard, and his visage revealed naught but kindness and concern. A genial old man nearing the end of his days. But he had restrained the much younger Constable Skefil with physical strength as well as magic, and it was *his* magic that had locked my feet to the gallery floor at Gramphier's command. I had underestimated him. Everyone did.

As if privy to my thoughts, he chuckled and waved off his guards. "Lucian is not dangerous. Not in combat at the least, eh, boy? Though put a pen in your hand and matters are entirely different."

"Has everyone in the Registry gone mad, *ancieno*?" Juli did not temper her tone in the least. "Isn't this Curator Pluvius?"

"Sssh." I gathered her into my arms, her back to my chest, as Pluvius's men retired a short distance away. I remained wary. It had been no pen that pricked my spine.

My lack of mannerly greeting didn't seem to bother Pluvius. "*Doma* Juliana, it gladdens my heart to see you alive," he said, touching fingertips to forehead. " 'Tis a bit presumptuous, but I take your survival as the gods' affirmation of my attempts to preserve your family."

Juli's spine stiffened against my chest. "You must not be very skilled at preserving," she said. "I saw the ashes at Pontia. And those who died in our town house were my friends and good servants. I hear their cries in my dreams. And was it not the Registry curators who treated my brother so despicably?"

"Discipline, *serena*." I tightened my hold on her. "Master Pluvius kept me—and you—in the city on the day the Harrowers attacked Pontia. We do owe him our lives."

Pluvius drew his clasped hands to his heart. "Truly, *Doma* Juliana, I had no idea of the horror that was planned at Pontia. I heard whispers that Albin wanted your brother dead for some inexplicable reason, and that he bragged that such would be accomplished within two days. Lucian had told me that the two of you were traveling to Pontia for a sealing feast. To thwart Albin, all I had to do was to change that plan—so I imagined. As to the second fire, I had no idea of it. Old fool that I was, I feared the reports of Lucian's . . . derangement . . . must be true. Regrets accomplish nothing, *doma*; I understand that. But we must turn our minds to the future."

So smooth his explanations. He'd thought me deranged, yet had repeatedly offered me help.

"What possible future awaits me after this night, master?"

"What was difficult has become more so, it's true." He shifted into a conspiratorial quiet. "That detestable harridan! It violates every protocol to speak ill of my fellow curators, but I don't blame you in the least for avenging five years of her vitriol. When heads are clearer they'll see you had good reason to take her down. Even Damon rebuked his precious protégé over her spite."

"Pons is Damon's *protégé*?" I'd never heard that . . . never imagined . . .

"He mentored her, supported her elevation to curator. They are kin as surely as arrogance and ice in their veins can make them."

Pons and Damon. That could explain a great deal. Pons's acts could not have been better crafted to force me to run. Perhaps she intended for me to run straight to Damon's mysterious *house of healing*. Such murderous manipulation. Why not just capture me and throw me into the cage they wanted?

"As for Gilles, he was very much his uncle's tool. Though I'm sure we can clear your name of his demise, as well, it will take some care and some time. The Albins are very powerful and very angry. They won't understand how Guilian's crimes were uncovered, or why he would ever consort with Harrowers or conspire in your family's murder."

"Murder! And *Gilles* dead? Harrowers! What is he—?"

I squeezed Juli quiet again, lest Pluvius be diverted. He had locked onto my gaze.

"*No one* is going to reveal those reasons," he said. "Be sure of that. The Albin family will remain your enemies, and therefore your sister's enemies, until the day you're both dead. But if *Gramphier* could be made to understand that you are no threat to the Registry and those it represents—that you might even be a help to us—he will force the Albins into line. So we must convince him that *you* are ignorant of those reasons as well."

I choked a laugh. "Most unlikely. Gramphier saw the paintings—including the symbols of all he fears." My dual bents. Xancheira's tree. "He consented to Albin's crimes. And not four hours since, you—or someone—barely prevented his strangling me."

"Gramphier views you as an ignorant, impudent boy who plays with matters he does not understand," said Pluvius. "You were careful tonight. You mentioned nothing of the . . . um . . . far-reaching implications of your talent. Or of your *dual talents*, should I say?"

For five years I'd considered Pluvius a kind and doddering fool of weak talents, an opinion skewed by his self-deprecating manner and my own pride. I had thought him my grandsire's friend, my protector, and fond of me in his way. Yet he believed me deranged or vile enough to fire my own house? He believed I had wounded Pons and killed Gilles, yet blithely dismissed both crimes? His scruples were no better than Albin's. He didn't know me at all.

"What do you want of me, master?"

"Only to protect you. Your grandsire's painted chest holds everything he learned of Xancheira. You will never be safe while it exists. If you've looked inside it, then you know why. The time is not right for that kind of upheaval. And we must hurry. Damon could be here at anytime."

So Pluvius, Damon, and Pons were not working in concert. Pluvius, like my grandsire, wanted the evidence destroyed. *Cowards*. I'd never thought to ascribe that word to Vincente de Remeni. And yet if Serena Fortuna offered to let me change all that had happened . . . bury the evidence . . . return my family to life . . . start again . . . would I not?

A wave of homesick longing flooded through me in that moment, filling me with memory of laughter and music, good wine and summer, strong arms, running children, endless study and hard work—*good* work for both body and mind . . .

"Luka, stop. You're hurting me." Juli squirmed in my arms. "Let go!"

I eased the crush of my embrace yet kept her close.

Let go. Indeed I had to let go of such mad notions. There was no going back. Nothing would ever be the same. And even if every Elder God and Goddess stepped forth with the very offer I yearned for, I would not accept it. For the price would be this strange, rare magic grown up in me and every worthy deed that it had done and might ever do: justice for Perryn's murdered bastards, sanctuary for the Cicerons, exposure of Registry corruption . . . and whatever duty or destiny might lie beyond the Path of the White Hand.

Juli craned her neck to look up at me, her face pale in the night, her dark eyes throwing off sparks of curiosity. "Much as I would relish your explaining what all this is about—chests and *dual* talents, murder and paintings, Capatronn, and *Xancheira*, of all things, shouldn't we be leaving? I thought we were in a hurry."

"Yes . . ."

Another illumination. Pluvius had no intention of giving us a choice, any more than Pons or Damon did. He would never have let Juli hear about Xancheira or the chest or that there were *far-reaching implications* of a pureblood with two bents, if he intended to let her walk free.

"I cannot deny we are in need of help, master," I said, scrabbling for some idea of a plan. "I just didn't know where to go other than the necropolis. My duty . . ."

"Come, now, Lucian. None but you ever took that contract seriously. Certainly the worthy coroner cannot protect you. You'll be far safer in my house tonight—and then I'll get you out of the city. We should go now."

How were we to deny him? What power I had was depleted, and he evidenced more determination and more dangerous skills than I'd ever imagined.

If Oldmeg was right, dawn would bring disaster directly to the hirudo—an attack over the walls or within them. The confusion might give Juli and me cover to get away, if we could make the time work out. Dawn was perhaps half an hour away.

I squeezed Juli's hand. "Master, does Gramphier know the chest exists?"

"He suspects something of the sort."

"Why?"

Foot tapping against the cobbles, he bit the words hard. "Had your grandsire been contracted to anyone but the king of Navronne, Gramphier would have outright forbidden a new search for Xancheira. He claimed it a waste of magic. And when Vincente's reports from the north stopped coming, Gramphier threw fits. He questioned me, of course, because of the history connection, but I knew nothing at the time. Only when Vincente contracted you to the Archives did he confide in me about his findings and how he was determined to bury them in order to protect his family. Now we must—"

"If I were to agree to your plan, how could we possibly convince Gramphier that the evidence he fears doesn't exist or that I know nothing? A Registry inquisition will reveal all."

"If I were to take Gramphier the chest and claim Vincente gave it to me—which, in a way, he did—Gramphier could destroy it himself."

"And me along with it?"

"Certainly not!" The old man clucked and dithered, even as his sharp gaze raked the shadowed alley. "You will be safely tucked away at a fortified house near Casitille, a fine house left me by one of my own mentors. These men, loyal to my family, will get you and your sister to Casitille safely, and the two of you can make a new life far from the Registry's dominion—work, practice your magic, study, whatever you like. I promised your grandsire I would keep you safe. And so I will."

Not a strict house like Damon's refuge, then, requiring submission to some unknown masters. What I would not give for a spell to parse his thoughts! Truly I needed to learn more magic.

Pons had also claimed she promised Capatronn to keep me safe. But she wanted the chest to survive and me to run. No matter how mad her actions seemed, she had spoken of a wound in the fabric of the world, an eerie echo of the Danae's words. Pons had not lied about Juli, whom I had found unharmed exactly where she'd said. And Damon, who valued loyalty and had offered me a place to hide, who had supported me in the Tower gallery, and who had not caught me tonight in four hours chasing, was Pons's mentor. They had spoken of hopes and a future.

Pluvius didn't care what I knew. He'd not even asked whether I had examined the chest's contents.

"This is a great kindness, master, to risk yourself for us. But distance will not slow the Registry in this case. My art can reveal things people want to remain secret, and to hold back or destroy those nuances is to compromise the truth the gods build in me."

Holding so firmly to this belief was likely foolish, considering all I'd learned of the Registry and its corruption. But Juli, magic, and the discipline required to serve that gift were all that remained of my life . . . and I refused to turn my back on any of them.

Pluvius did not drop his gaze, but a shadow altered it, as if his steady magelight flickered.

"Only a small compromise," he said. "I had to compromise when they imprisoned you. Others wanted you dead and the paintings destroyed. I convinced them you could be more useful alive. Having you alter the paintings was wiser than destroying artworks everyone in the Tower knew of."

"Earning my thanks yet again, master."

I deliberately did not ask him how they had forced me to it. Let him think me a fool. But someone had destroyed my memory of those events, and all of them had let me believe I was going mad. *None* of the curators had freed me from the cellar. Only Bastien.

Pluvius chuckled. "I didn't think you would make a show of their unveiling so soon. I'd hoped I'd get a chance to warn you! But for now . . . if we're to get you two away safely, it must be tonight, before Bayard the Smith starves out the city or burns it. Where is the chest?"

Behind the orange smoke the sky was gray. I had to choose now—for Juli as well as for myself. I rested my forehead on her hair. She was quivering. Cold? Afraid? Angry? Or just bursting with curiosity? What had I done, dragging her into this madness? The most powerful sorcerers in the world believed I could destroy their way of life. Every pureblood in Navronne would soon be convinced I was a murderer. The largest, wealthiest pureblood family in Navronne bore a mortal grudge and would expend their every resource to hunt me down, and the would-be king of Navronne would cheer them on.

Pons was right. I had to run . . . fast and far, without experience, without worldly skills, and without the help of magic. How could I protect a young girl—I, who had survived this long only because of the kindness, sacrifice, or callous self-interest of others? My grandsire, Fallon de Tremayne, Demetreo, Bastien, Garen, Constance . . . and, yes, Pons and Pluvius . . . so many. Pons had kept Juli safe, but she could be preparing to sacrifice my sister for her ends, as she had sacrificed Gilles and herself.

Weariness weighed heavy as I glanced at the graying sky, on the brink of a terrible dawn . . .

. . . and there I found my answer. So obvious, and it must surely rip my heart asunder.

"I'll give you the chest, master," I said, "and then my sister and I would be grateful to accept your offer."

Pluvius spread his arms and beamed brighter than his magelight. "Holy Deunor be praised! We shall see the right of all this together and make a fine future. Where is the damnable chest?"

"I'll guide you."

I spun Juli around to face me. "Will you accept what I choose, *serena*? I've mucked up things terribly and the last thing I want is to take you into unknown dangers. But I'm not skilled enough to protect you, so your part will be very hard. Uncertain. More so than ever before. But you are strong and intelligent and you've proven yourself resourceful, everything good and worthy of our bloodlines."

With a grave curiosity, Juli touched the naked half of my face. "When you forced my oath before, I hated you. But you were exactly right. Our magic and our bloodlines must be preserved before all. Though clearly there are matters here I don't understand . . . *yet* . . . I trust you to keep doing that, *ancieno*. You are wiser than you know."

I crushed her to my breast, grateful for her trust, glad of her discretion, and fearing she might see too much if she looked at me too long.

"Leave your men here to wait for us, master," I said over my sister's head. "Those guarding the chest will not welcome any stranger, especially pureblood, on a morning like this. I can vouch for one—you—but they'll never accept so many."

"Where are we going?" said Pluvius, frowning.

"Down there." I pointed into the inky darkness beyond the arch.

"The *hirudo*?"

"Can you think of any safer place to hide secrets from the Registry?" I wrapped Juli's steady hand around my arm and led her through the broken arch.

CHAPTER 38

First light had not come to the hirudo as yet. Halfway down the path I asked Pluvius to mask his magelight, and I cast one of my own. Using my cloak, I exposed the light in the pattern Bastien and Garen had used to secure safe passage: three times quickly and then once more. Sky Lord grant the signal had not changed.

"You've become friendly with thieving vagabonds?" said Pluvius.

"My sojourn at the necropolis provided me a number of new experiences. Business with Cicerons is only one."

"Clever. Never in my wildest imaginings would I have guessed the chest was here."

At the bottom of the hill where the path turned into the hirudo, I halted and allowed the light to reveal my face.

Pluvius's fingers twitched. His foot tapped. "What are you waiting for?" he blurted. "We need to be on our way. Damon and his hounds are on your scent."

"Manners can ease life amongst ordinaries as well as purebloods," I said.

"Manners are wasted on brutes. You are pureblood. Exert your will."

Soft footsteps crunched on the path.

"Sengé." I touched my forehead as Demetreo stepped from the deeper shadows.

The headman's razor eyes could have sliced stone. "What brings the coroner's pureblood so early of a dangerous morn? And with strangers of your kind? More even than these two, I think."

"I request safe passage for three only. My sister and I are in sore need of *sanctuary.* This Registry curator has offered us a refuge in the long tradition of our kind, which you and I discussed not so long ago." I willed him to hear the words left unspoken. "Before I go with him, I must retrieve an item from beyond the piggery."

After a moment's study, Demetreo's gaze slid to the ground. "Go on."

"While I attend to the curator's needs, I wish my sister to visit your honored grandmother. Is the hour propitious?"

"Luka?" Juli's puzzled frown heated my cheek.

Demetreo bowed. "Your trust honors us, pureblood. The hour is yet propitious. Any later and my grandmother would be sleeping."

"Juliana, *serena,*" I said, holding her chin steady, "*Sengé* Demetreo has proved himself an honorable man and his followers likewise. While I attend to the curator, I wish you to go with Demetreo and offer our family's blessings to his grandmother. Heed his instructions exactly, lest you lose your way in the dark. I'll join you when my business is done, and with the help of our friends, we shall set about rebuilding our family name."

"But—"

I pressed a finger to her lips. Her dark eyes were troubled but not frightened. "Discipline, *serena pauli.* A terrible dawn is upon us. We must be gone from the city before the day storm breaks."

She dipped her head. "As you say, *ancieno.* I'll be waiting for you."

With the dignity of a woman twice her years, she opened her hand to the headman in invitation. Demetreo nodded and bade her follow him into the dark warren. He did not touch her.

For a moment I couldn't breathe. But I did not, would not, relent.

I believed that Juli would be able to find sanctuary with the Cicerons. The Danae had not charged her to wait and learn, as they had me. Whatever dangers she might encounter, were it to be death itself, I could not imagine them worse than those she would face at my side. The Cicerons were survivors, and Juli would see their worth quicker than I had. I had to trust Demetreo's honor to see to her safety, because unless something had changed with the portal, I'd not be able to follow her. Not yet.

I still had work to do. The Danae—both silver and blue—had warned that my magic twisted the fabric of the world. Perhaps proving my *quality* meant exploring the mechanisms of my power and how to control it, assuming I could hole up somewhere the Registry couldn't find me. But first I had to get free of Pluvius.

"What was all that?" snapped Pluvius under his breath, as we threaded the night-choked lanes of the hirudo. "You revealed my *rank* to a lord of thieves, an ordinary. You entrusted your sister to him. Are you wholly naive? We *must* see to your education."

"The headman saved my life once, just as you did, master. I can tell you of it as we travel. But first the troublesome chest, yes?" Pluvius's condescension struck sparks inside me. But I would not let him see.

An eerie quiet lay over the hirudo. No dice players. No racing urchins. No bony dogs. One man lounged beside a small fire, an unsheathed blade across his lap. A second sat on a stool, sharpening a knife as long as my forearm. The hard-faced woman, Jadia, twirled her sling. Were the rest of them gathered in the commons house, waiting, or had Oldmeg been sure enough to begin their journey and her own beforetime?

I didn't hurry as I led Pluvius toward the piggery, though my own nerves thrummed. A fight was my last resort. No matter our difference in age, I'd no confidence I could best him. I'd spent far too much of my life buried in books and ink. Whatever was coming down on this place would be my chance to run.

"Well, where is the chest?" he said, his own patience fraying.

"Beneath the ramparts of the Elder Wall. I buried it in a great hurry once I found it." I held back the wet willow branches, allowing him to go ahead.

Blaring trumpets from the far end of the hirudo jolted me alert. I scrambled up the slope to get a better view beyond the willows. "Master, come look!"

Fire cascaded down the path from the city to the accompaniment of shouts and steel and drumbeats, bringing the hirudo's doom with the rising light.

Pluvius joined me on the slope. "Hold, Lucian!" he said, reaching for my shoulder.

I backed away. "I've got to go!" I said. "Juli's back there."

"Arriet!"

My dash for the willows was halted abruptly, as if my feet were shackled to the earth.

"You *cannot* go back," he said. "What if Damon's with them? He'll protect your sister, but you he wants in silkbindings and a tongue block." His clenched palm relaxed.

I shuffled my feet, my own will ruling them again.

A woman's war cry shrilled in the distance. "Perhaps you could distract them long enough for me to get her. Please, master, she's not safe . . . soldiers . . . brutes . . ."

"Discipline forbids us interfere with the ordinaries' war," he snapped, all benevolence vanished. "Get the chest and lead us out of this rats' nest. I'll send my men to fetch the girl."

I had chosen rightly not to trust Juli's life to Pluvius.

"The path climbs up to Plateau Caton from the far side of the pigsty," I said, feigning acquiescence. "None would dare stop a Registry curator from entering the city through the east gates. But it will take an hour at the least, and we'll have to leave the chest. It's buried deep, and we'll be overrun before I can dig it out." My beam of magelight illumined the steep incline to the necropolis. Perhaps I could push him off the rocky steeps.

"Magrog's plagues on these wretches and their wars! Damon must not have that chest—or you. We have to get back to my men."

But the line of torches crept inexorably downward. Blue and yellow flame burst high above the fray—one of the huts. Another. And another, choking the ravine with smoke and thundering flame. The commons house was stone, its roof slate, its magics powerful enough to have kept it safe for centuries. Had I not been sure of that and Oldmeg's resolve, I'd have risked Pluvius's wrath and run back.

Footsteps, accompanied by muffled curses, pounded the path beyond the willows. I released the magelight and dragged Pluvius down behind the brake.

"Where'd the vermin go?" The frustrated whisper was not ten paces away. "More'n a hundred of them nest down here. And I saw lights."

"Maybe some's hiding in that pig wallow." A second man snorted in grotesque humor.

"The fight's done," snapped a third voice. "Gerro's troop will purge what's left. You two get up there where the path narrows and finish any strays. Once the Guard mage damps the fire and cools the steps, we've real work to do. The Smith and his Moriangi scum will *not* get over our stretch of the wall."

The determined guardsmen gave me an idea.

"Master," I whispered, as soon as the two had scrambled away, "if I go back and tell the soldiers I'm a Guard mage come to cool the wall stairs, I can fetch Juli. We'll meet you here, take down these two ordinaries, and be off."

Unwilling to lose the chance, I pushed harder. "Master, we are the last of our bloodlines. Without my sister safe, I cannot accept your kind offer. Surely you can see that." *Exert your will*, he'd said.

"Have you skills to cool stone?"

Pluvius's fury scalded the air around us, so his lack of argument astonished me. Why did he yield so easily? And yet all these months, it had been the same. He had repeatedly offered me help and waited for me to accept it. I had thought it a sign of indecision or weakness. Yet he could lock my feet to the ground if he chose. And Damon could throw ropes of lights and confine a man with circles of sparks, yet required I run to his refuge of my own will. . . .

Will was an essential component of every magical working, but usually it was the will of the practitioner, not the subject. But when Pons stole my magic to kill Gilles, it was only after offering me her hand and after I, like a naive child, had taken it without reservation. In prison it was only when I was near undone with madness and despair that I had smelled ink and paint on my hands. Had I consented to change the portraits, thinking it a lesser evil than my crazed fantasy of stealing souls, and thereby given them the very means to corrupt my memory of the event?

More than the dawn chill sent shudders up my spine. What use did these people have for me that required me to yield my consent?

"I've never actually managed spellwork so grand as to control heat and cold," I said, "but I'm sure I could bluff."

"Magrog save us! I'll have to go, then." He could no longer mask his anger. "My authority will quiet any question from the purebloods attached to the Guard. I can demand custody of your sister and send for my men. Meanwhile *you* find that damnable chest and wait here with it until we're back to fetch you."

"Bless you, master. I'll be forever grateful." And I would run as far away from him as fast as I could go. I would not yield.

Elated, I held the branches aside to let him through. . . .

Just as rope snagged my ankles and yanked them out from under me. I grabbed for the willows. Prickly branches tore at my hair and scraped my face.

A kick unlocked my knees, sending them hard to the ground. Iron fingers manacled my left hand, and a long arm wrapped around my neck. The bare flesh was twined with blue light that shimmered like strands of sapphires.

"Shhh," he hissed unnecessarily, as his tightening hold strangled all possibility of speech. Whispers drifted behind us, quieting as something heavy was dragged into the brush.

My feet dug into the rocks and mud, and my free hand clawed at his strangling arm.

He held firm. Planting a sharp knee in my back, he bent me backward like a bow, and with honeyed breath whispered in my ear, "Did we not warn thee of trespass? About the danger of delving so deep? This very dawning hath a boundary been violated and Aeginea opened to human feet. 'Tis thy doing. Where did they go?"

"Aagh—" My choking spurred him to relent slightly in his grip. "I didn't—I mean, the portal was already there. I just showed them how to pass through. They would have died in this fire—women, children, people desperate for your sanctuary."

"Sanctuary!" His grip slacked enough to speak the depth of his astonishment. "What dost thou know of sanctuary?"

"Why should I answer a brute?"

He twisted my left arm harder. "Thou'rt the violator. We warned thee."

I tried to will away the pain. "Warnings are useless without knowledge. You and your companion told me nothing but how ignorant I am. Though her manners were not so crude as yours, the sentinel who offered sanctuary told me the same." Yet perhaps I could use her tactic. "A bargain: Answer a question of mine and I'll answer yours."

"A *sentinel* offered . . . What sentinel?"

"She told me no other name. Her marks—gards, she called them—might have been drawn with starlight. An eagle—"

"Starlight? True silver, then, not pale, not tinged with blue?"

"Entirely silver. She called you her . . . uh . . . kin whose gards shine the color of day sky." Her *excitable* kin.

He dropped his lock hold on me as abruptly as he'd taken it. I scrambled out of his reach and planted my back against a leafless oak. I wanted answers, yet for a moment I could only stare and whisper the greeting the silver one had taught me: "*Envisia seru*, Dané." How could the wonder not move me? How could the sight *not* delight an artist's eye?

I had seen his like sculpted in marble and painted on urns and the walls of ruined temples, the finest work of the ancients. Nowhere had art come near the truth. He was tall and comely, his chestnut hair braided with vines. His flesh housed such taut muscle and sinew as I would draw in a portrait of Kemen Sky Lord or his sons. And scribed on every quat of his long limbs, torso, face, even his privy parts were drawings of light—birds, fish, plants, and creatures I had no names for. But the growing daylight revealed his lean face riven with shock.

I snapped a dead branch from the oak and felt slightly better armed. My throbbing neck and back could attest that his sinews were not just handsome, but extraordinarily strong. Pluvius was nowhere in sight.

The Dané drew his gaze from some far-off distance back to my face. "*Silver* gards . . . *entirely* silver? And it was night?"

"No mistaking." I reached for calm and determination. "Once in day, once at night, both times entirely silver. That was *your* answer. Now one for me. The old man—did you harm him?"

He waved off my concern, even as the creases in his brow deepened. "The long-lived do not wreak mindless hurts as humans do. The elder will wake elsewhere. Truly, his airs bespoke him no friend of thine."

"No. But neither are you that I can tell. I'd not have him dead." Though to have Pluvius *elsewhere* was the finest gift of fortune's goddess. "Now your turn for a question."

He shook his head as if to clear it. "Where did you meet her, this sentinel marked with silver?"

"On several occasions when I invoked my magic—that which you say twists the fabric of the world, which I swear I did not know and did not intend—I was transported to another place, one unfamiliar to me. A rocky hillside, green and barren with five—"

"Five promontories that protrude into the sea, each one ridged with white stone." I'd not thought his eyes could open wider.

"Yes. On two of those occasions, she was there. She called it the Everlasting and said she could either lead me astray or offer me sanctuary."

"Impossible." His whisper was for himself, not me. "*Sanctuary*. Found by a human."

So urgent, so passionate was his fervor, I voiced a question without considering the others clamoring inside me. "So this place she called the Everlasting is the sanctuary?"

"The Everlasting is not a place. The Everlasting is *all*—the human realms; Aeginea, which is the true land, and the great ordering that lies beyond the lands we walk. Sanctuary was—is—"

He glanced up, as if taking note of me for the first time. He hesitated, frowning. But any disciplined pureblood would recognize the sharp exhale and the moment's silent invocation when he chose to say more than he should.

"Sanctuary is a memory that encompasses naught but the name itself. There are a few others, places or names we believe of great importance, though we cannot say why or why we cannot remember more about them. Thou'rt certain she spoke that word and that it is where the humans went this dawning?"

He had moved beyond crude threats and bargaining. I answered in kind, telling him of the hidden door marked by a white hand and blocked with patterns of light, and of what the sentinel had told me. "And until then, she said I could not pass."

"Clearly the sentinel has closed her ways to thee, just as we have done, though I know naught of this path she requires. But how are her pathways not of Aeginea? I must speak with the Archon. We may have use for thee after all to smooth this confusion."

He turned his back, his gards shimmering, fading. . . .

"Wait! You can't go yet. You've no right to *make use* of me. Give me answers, tell me what you want of me, and then I'll choose to help or not. But I must know who is the woman with the silver marks—and who is she that companioned you in the city. You spoke before of dangers, but I thought— You're not going to harm the humans who crossed these boundaries?" Fear and anger and exhaustion had me shaking. "You damnable villain gatzé, you *must* tell me where they've gone."

He strode across the muddy rocks and ripped the oak limb out of my hands. "I need tell thee nothing, Remeni-son. Thou'rt ignorant and proud, like all humankind, breaking, meddling, and strutting as if all the Everlasting is thine to rule. Let me show thee a touch of the torment we have long crafted for the human who twists the boundaries. Perhaps it will humble thee to imagine its fullness until the end of your days."

I spun from his grasp and ran. But when my feet skidded out from under me on a mud-slick rock, he pounced and pinned me to the slab. Raising his head to stretch his throat, he sounded the screech of an eagle diving for prey.

For a moment I was paralyzed, sure my bones had shattered with the sound. When he rubbed his thumb on my lips, I could not stop him.

Nasty. Bitter. As I wiped my mouth and spat, small feet scrabbled on my legs. Chittering shrieks accompanied stinging nips at my ankles . . . through my hose. Rats! I kicked at them. Tried to scramble away. But I needed my hands to brush away feathery spiderwebs that blurred my vision, to swipe at the fleas, ants, and spiders under my clothes, crawling into ears and nose. Disgusted, horrified, I curled up in a ball, batting and flailing. Blood seeped through my clothes. Gods, it would bring more rats.

Real? Imagined? It made no difference. Mud and smoky sky swirled together until I could not tell up from down. I might have been plummeting *upward* or soaring into solid earth. Reason melted like lead left too close to a forge.

"Please." My muscles seized as I tried to keep from falling, while slapping at spiders and vermin. "Make it stop!"

The Dané stood above me, coolly watching me writhe and whimper. As howling madness swelled inside me, he crouched down. "These things only can I tell thee, Remeni-son." Surely it was kindness softened his speech. "We know nothing of this place you saw, save what comes from a wisp of song that speaks of a five-horned land and the sea. But that is a song of sanctuary, and *sanctuary* is a word we honor with the same regard as the Law of the Everlasting and the Dance that is our purpose and our glory."

A hint of better humor played over his sober mien, like darting sun glimmers in the wood. "My companion of our first meeting has vouched for thy ability to learn. I choose to believe her. But trespass again before we come for thee, and thou'lt have these vermin with thee always. Be sure we *shall* come."

He brushed his hand across my eyes. A blanket of peaceful dark enfolded me as his last words faded. "The matter of silver gards does not concern thee. Nor does the matter of my companion."

My eyes flicked open. I sat on damp ground, my back to a wide-boled tree. Yellow-brown smoke choked the windless daylight, and I could scarce see, much less breathe without coughing. Shouts, drumbeats, and trumpeting horns both near and far spoke of siege.

There was no sign of Pluvius. No sign of the Dané, either. With a frenzy of horror, I brushed at my face and neck and soiled clothes, though neither sense nor inspection revealed vermin, spiders, blood, or bite marks. Every muscle and joint ached.

Had it been an hour or a day or a year since encountering the Dané? It would take an hour of concentration to reconstruct our exchange. But I clung to his last mercy and scarce controlled a sob of gratitude. Sanctuary was holy to his kind. Those who had crossed this boundary . . . perhaps they would be all right.

I needed to run—fast and far. But I could not leave the hirudo without making sure Juli had crossed the portal. If ever the gods had mercy on fools and lunatics, perhaps on this morning I could follow her through it.

Keeping behind the line of willows, I scurried back toward the charred settlement. When the ramparts became too steep to traverse, I adjusted my mask, pretended my clothes were silk and brocade, and strode with proper hauteur onto the path.

Little was left of the Ciceron settlement. Here and there a cracked hearthstone protruded from charred rubble. Dying rills of flame hissed. Puddles from the night's rain had turned to tarry mud. Gouts of steam and the heavy stench of ash rose from my left, where the soldiers had fired every shack or shed that blocked the outer wall. They were here to defend Palinur. The Cicerons had just been in the way.

Armed men were everywhere. Shouted orders sent archers and newly armed pikemen swarming up the wall stairs.

"Who goes there?" The halberdier who barred the path with his pole looked younger than Juli and more nervous than I felt.

I flicked sparks from my fingers. "Avert your eyes, ordinary, and lower your weapon. Where is the mage who's come to quench the fire? I've messages from the Registry."

He dropped his gaze and pointed to the outer wall.

"Have any prisoners been taken?"

"None, lord . . . sir. We were told no prisoners."

Swallowing hard, I strode past and, as soon as I could be sure he was not looking, dodged into the strip of shacks and sheds that hugged the Elder Wall—the inner lane where the Ciceron commons house was tucked away. Wary pikemen were kicking down unburnt huts and flimsy shelters, hunting any remaining resistance. The only Cicerons I saw were dead.

Less than a dozen altogether, piled in a heap—Jadia, the dicers. As I peered out from behind a charred baking oven too hot to touch, soldiers threw another body atop the pile. It was Demetreo, one side of his head caved in.

Goddess Mother embrace them; Lord of Light honor their sacrifice. And please, please, please, let Juli be safely away.

A pikeman tore off the headman's earrings. When I stepped from my hiding place, he blanched and darted away. Would I knew how to heat the false gold and sear the skin from his fingers.

Search parties had passed the commons house three times and never given it a look. Only when I held it steadfast in mind did my attention stay fixed long enough to stretch out my hand.

The red door swung open. All was as I expected. No sign of fire or slaughter. Dice lay idle on the small table, and a scattering of dropped items littered the floor—an empty cup, a bent spoon, a bundle of rags. The hearth was cold, the lamps dark.

Oldmeg's chair remained where I had last seen it, and the *Naema* herself sat straight and unbowed, bloody knife in her lap, blood drying on her wrists and breast. The light had long left her eyes. Behind her, the white hand glared stark above the shifting colors of the portal. Enchantment shimmered inside me like moonlight on rippling water, taunting me with beauty and warmth and scenes I could not touch.

I tried, of course. Oldmeg's blood yet stained the carved markings on the arch. The first attempt was sufficient to remind me that the scrapes and cuts on my hand did not deserve the word *pain*. Yet pain alone would not deter me.

I pushed harder, trying to force the barrier with hand and then shoulder, burying my mouth in my sleeve as the enchantment threatened to dissolve my bones. I pushed until my teeth felt like molten lead and my skin like the cinders outside the commons house. The tapestry flexed inward slightly, but it would not yield. And I'd no magic to try more.

Pureblood searchers would be hard on my heels, but I could not leave Oldmeg to rot in her chair. I fetched in Demetreo and laid them out side by side. I'd no water to wash away their blood and no oil to anoint their fingers or silk to wrap them, as was proper for those who could work magic. And Ciceron death customs were a mystery. So I simply wrapped the old woman in her woven mantle and Demetreo in my cloak and commended them and their dead comrades to the Goddess Mother and the god they called Valo.

When my prayers were done, I sat back on my heels and watched the portal's image shift again . . . and yet again. Once I'd have sworn I saw a crowd of motley women and men with dark braids and dangling earrings, and perhaps one slender girl in a wine-colored cloak. But that was likely a wishing dream.

"Where are you, *serena*?" I whispered, willing my words to penetrate the swirling beauty as I could not. "Forgive me for sending you away yet again, but this was all I knew to do. I swear on the spirits we hold dear, I will find you."

My head sagged to my knees. Weighed down with grief and weariness, I felt very much alone.

But I dared not linger. A whisper of magic restored the portal's shielding enchantment I had ripped away a tenday past. When the smoke-stained plaster looked undisturbed, I snatched up a lamp from the wall, threw a tattered rug over my shoulder, and pulled off my mask. Everyone was looking for a pureblood. I'd best learn how to look ordinary.

CHAPTER 39

Beyond the red door, the hirudo had already become a noisy staging ground for Palinur's defenders. Shouts rang out from atop the wall. Mules lumbered past, hauling in fuel and supplies. Men and boys ran hither and yon, bearing news and orders, shields, water butts, and cauldrons. Serious men counted arrows, honed swords, or used the smoldering embers of the hirudo to stoke blazes for boiling tar and oil. Drums rumbled like distant thunder from the east. Palinur was under siege.

The same young halberdier yet guarded the path. In the smoky shadows of trees and willow thicket, it might have been midnight. "I'm bringing supplies for guards at the slot gate," I said before he could challenge me. "Captain's setting up a permanent guard, as they see it vulnerable. Do you need a lamp? I've extra. Or this flea-bitten rug?"

"Lamp'd be fine. Dark as a sheep's belly down here."

I shoved the enchanted lamp into his hand and hurried on.

Not a sound penetrated the silence around the piggery, so close with rocks and walls, willows and leafless scrub. Perhaps the watchers had been recalled. Concealed behind a protruding boulder, I tossed stones on the path ahead.

No one came. So I scrambled up the path to the slot gate and found two soldiers stretched out on the massive rocks, snoring peacefully. Strange. With the harsh truths of war all around, how could they sleep? Had the Danae enchanted them?

I tossed the rug aside and emerged from the smoky hirudo into a brilliant dawn. The necropolis rose in stark majesty above Plateau Caton. Deunor Lightbringer and his half brother Magrog yet grappled for the souls of humankind atop the gates. The gates themselves stood open as if to welcome me home.

Siege or no siege, the work of the day had begun. A party of diggers trundled barrows between the graves of the unknowns. Two men led three horses across the graveyard as if to join them.

More than anything just now, I wanted to walk through Caton's gates. To hear Constance's squawking voice. To argue with Bastien. To pick up my pens and ink, summon magic, and do useful work. A mug of weak ale, a few dried figs, and a loaf of pignut bread would set a feast, and a few hours' sleep on my straw pallet would be bliss.

On *this* morning, we would more likely face an invasion by Perryn's men wanting us to defend the walls, or Bayard's captains, asking why we should not be conscripted into building siege engines. I might be able to offer some protection—or at least some measure of authority. I had vowed to be at Bastien's side if I walked free, and I hated breaking my word.

But this argument was already settled. To enter those gates would be to compromise the one man who might have the wits to talk himself out of the ill consequences of my situation.

Once safely away where a message could not be traced back to me, I'd let Bastien know why I had failed him. For today I ripped a bit of tattered lace from my shirt and tied it to the slot gate. Maybe Constance would recognize it.

The two horsemen angled toward me, plodding slowly between the hummocks. Wary, I shambled along the wall. A few hundred quercae and I would be out of sight in the gully between the wall and the plateau.

"Lucian de Remeni-Masson?" one of them called from a distance. "Hold up."

They left their mounts and hurried toward me. I smothered the curse on my tongue. My legs certainly had no spring to outrun anyone. Which searchers had found me first? Damon's? Pluvius's? The Albins'?

The two weren't Danae. They wore leather jaques, plain russet breeches, and knee-high boots instead of light-drawn artworks. Nor were they Registry. They wore masks—one brown, one black—not the pureblood half mask, but full masks that fit like a second skin.

Why did that make me shiver so? More even than the coiled whips and well-used swords at their hips.

The threat of pureblood retaliation might be the only means to divert a masked stranger. Though my cloak wrapped a dead man in the Ciceron commons house, I slipped on my mask and extended my open palm to keep them at a distance. "Who dares intrude upon a pureblood at his business?"

One man had the look of a hawk: tough and sinewy, with small, sharp eyes, a beak nose, and short brown hair flecked with sun yellow. The other's sleek black hair, so dark it was almost blue, and long, powerful body put me in mind of a raven.

"If you are the one we name, then we are your only business," said the black-haired man. His words were as smooth as his hair and just as richly dark. "You have the aspect of the person we were told to find. How many tattered, unshaven sorcerers visit a city of the dead?"

"Our coming was told you," said the hawklike man. Coarse and brittle, his voice rasped like footsteps on broken glass. "This is the hour of your choice."

So Damon's strange offer yet stood. Two men would give me a chance of survival, he'd said, yea or nay, never to be offered again. Would he report Bastien's lax oversight if I refused?

"I am the one you name."

"You stand at the crossroads of your future," said the dark one, smoother than his companion. "Do you understand what is offered?"

"A house of healing and reflection, I was told, but heavy with rules and restriction. I've had enough of those, I think. Submission does not entice me."

In no way could I do this, not now that I suspected that acceptance could give my enemies such power over me.

"A house of work and learning," said the man in black. "A house of cleansing, where a man can erase what's past and build his life anew. He can become stronger and more skilled in many ways. A challenging life."

Building anew . . . there was some attraction in that. And gods knew I needed to learn.

"Too challenging for some." The man in brown sounded ready to dismiss me already. "Some wither. Some break. Perhaps you're not as well suited to it as we were told."

"What kind of learning? Magic, art, history? Those are my preferred studies."

"The Marshal will decide what you are taught and in what order. But magic is entwined in all we do."

That surprised me, and yet it was *Damon* had sent them. He had taken risks to set this plan in motion. His search parties had not found me. Of course his protégé had done murder by my hand. Did Pons intend I should have no choice but this? I wanted no bargain bought with blood. Even guilty blood. But how to refuse . . . ?

"What if I don't like what's taught or how or in what order?"

"Your likes or dislikes are no one's concern." The hawk's feathers ruffled easily.

The other was more equable. "Before we take you, you must vow to abide by the judgment of our masters—the Marshal and those he names. You must agree to leave your old life and old concerns behind and begin anew. In return, you will be given nourishment for body and mind, discipline, knowledge, and skills that can take you beyond what you believe yourself capable of. Though magic will be a portion of your training, the goal is not to develop your inborn bent, but rather your physical and magical skills, your will, and your spirit. You will be prepared for whatever the gods have decreed for your future."

I thought that was what I'd done all my life, but then again, my future was not developing in the way I'd imagined. Just now I needed to hide. Though, indeed, any use of my two bents could bring down the Danae and their torments. I shuddered. I wanted to learn a great deal more about the earth's guardians before I asked what use *they* had for me. I scanned the burial ground and the plateau. There was nowhere to run but into the necropolis.

"This would be for a year, I was told."

"Perhaps a year. Perhaps two or three. You will not be a prisoner, though leaving before you are ready will carry consequences. Swords half-forged can be dangerous. Nothing insurmountable if you are so determined. That's all we can say."

"There are attractions in your offer, no question," I said, not wishing to offend men who looked so . . . capable. "But you ask a great commitment on very little information. I need to think on it. I've important things I need to do." Like exploring the mystery of my power. Like pursuing the Path of the White Hand; my only family now lived, I believed, at the other end of it.

"You've no time to think on it," said the man in the brown mask. "We've come a very long way to fetch you and would prefer not to be locked up in this city to starve or die. Choose now. If you refuse, we ride away and you'll not see us again."

Annoyance flared. "And the one who sent you will plague my friends. Do you execute his threats as well as his invitations?"

The raven man shrugged. "We know naught of him. The Marshal heeded a recommendation of you as one who will fit well with our Order. Our standards are very high and very particular."

I should just dismiss them, and yet . . . I delayed again. "What Order? And where is this house of learning?"

The black-masked man laughed—a hearty, honest laugh. "If you decide to go, it doesn't matter. If you don't, we prefer to keep ourselves private."

That made sense. I walked away a few steps and crouched beside one of the hummocks—the grave of an unknown. A man stood in the open gateway of Necropolis Caton, shielding his eyes from the sun as if watching for someone. No way could he see us, deep in the shadow of the wall as we were. The man's shape, his coloring . . . could it be Bastien? Fascinated, I watched as he climbed up the iron gates and mounted something on the tallest spike. He jumped down and vanished inside. The gates slammed shut behind him.

I squinted. It was a very long way. The object on the spike looked like a head, or perhaps it was only that heads had been mounted on gate spikes for a very long time. Or perhaps . . .

How better to warn me away than to spike my other head, the leather mask, on his gate? A laugh bubbled up from inside me, only to die again as quickly. Perhaps it was a sign that I was no longer welcome. I hated to think someone had told my necropolis family about Gilles and Pons, that Bastien might think I had succumbed to petty revenge.

But of course, my embarrassments were unimportant. My only refuge was now barred to me. And even if it weren't, I had to keep away to protect those inside. Running on my own was a daunting prospect. But I was ignorant, not stupid. And perhaps I could keep from starving by drawing portraits, even without magic. Aye, there was the dilemma. How would I learn anything without magic?

What if Pons's talk of hopes and the future was sincere? Damon had said that honor mattered. Magic mattered. Now that I was aware of the risk, was it possible I could hold back whatever consent would allow them to manipulate me?

I was flummoxed. Perhaps after a night's sleep I could weigh such a choice. Perhaps when I was no longer addled from altered portraits and traitorous curators, imaginary rats and spiders, and sending my sister away to who knew where.

"Choose!" A firm *thwup* punctuated the hawk man's command. A dagger with an engraved hilt was buried in the earth beside my knee. "If you would come, cut your palm and offer a blood vow, agreeing to abide by the terms we have described. If you refuse, walk away."

The dagger's hilt was engraved white on black, in a pattern. . . .

I snatched up the knife. The engraving was an archer's quiver with five disparate objects poking out of it—a staff, a sword, a whip, a hammer, and a pen. Not a tree, not a hand, but indeed five branches, white on black.

"Is this the blazon of your order?" I said, excitement pricking me awake.

"It is." They spoke together.

I offered a brief prayer that I was not the lunatic others might name me, and then I stood and wiped the blade on my shirt. An icy sting, and I offered the knife and my bloody palm to the hawk man.

The ancient ritual brought Oldmeg and Demetreo to mind. I hoped these people were as honorable. My own honor must bend and my submission remain incomplete. I would reserve my own will past the swearing; too many enemies were waiting for me to slip. But if this was a step along the Path of the White Hand, I had to follow it.

The hawk man cut his own palm and grasped mine. No smirk of triumph, no gleam of avarice marred his solemnity. *"Dallé cineré."* Aurellian words: *From the ashes.*

I responded. "I swear to abide by these two terms you have set: to set aside the concerns of my life and abide by the discipline of your house as well as I am able. On my family name and blood, on our holy gifts, on the lines of magic unbroken, I swear it. Witness my oath, great Deunor, Lord of Fire and Magic. Witness my truth, mighty Erdru, Lord of Vines."

And then I prayed the gods' forgiveness in advance for the myriad ways I planned to interpret *as well as I am able.*

I had scarce reclaimed my hand when the raven man raised his. "One more step of our rite," he said. "To accept your swearing, I must lay hands on your head."

Before I could think, his large, callused hands lay cool and firm on my temples. They felt solid, substantial. Exhaustion had left me half dizzy.

"Speak your name," he said.

"My name is—Magrog's balls!" His fingers might have been spikes and the slight pressure of his hands a mason's hammer driving them into my skull. I tried to swipe his arms aside, but the slightest movement drove the spikes even deeper.

The bright morning went gray. The circling crows paused in their flight, the sun in its passage.

"Wait!" I cried. Drawings, faces, images, names fluttered like pages torn from a precious book and set flying by a raging wind. As each swept past, I tried to grasp it, but it disintegrated in a shower of dust. I sank to my knees because I could not both stand and reach so deep all at once, and I inhaled great gulps of air because surely breath must be swept away with the dust of my life. . . .

"*Tyro!*" Someone tapped my cheek. "Stand up. At least lift your head so we can give you a drink."

Impossible to obey. My head felt like an anvil, my eyelids like cold lead. I could scarce summon a thought.

The hand lifted my chin and pressed a flask to my lips. Water . . . blessed divinities! I guzzled like a thirsting hound. Rude to take so much. Did he have more?

"They said he'd had a bad evening already and a night on the run," said a second man, "and that was hours ago." An unrefined voice. One that grated on the ear. "I'm thinking his state didn't improve in the hours since."

"Come, *tyro*, we must be going. We've a month's journeying ahead of us, and first we must get through this ham-handed prince's siege. Of all the inconvenient times for a war. The ungifted have a habit of bollixing important work."

Strong hands raised me to my feet. I swayed like a drunkard, but the man in the black mask did not let me fall. "We've brought a mount for you. Are you a capable rider? Our informant didn't know."

"Rider . . . horses . . ." I blotted my wet chin on my sleeve. "Yes. I think so." A stupid answer. But then I felt exceptionally dull just now. Surely I'd ridden a horse, but for the life of me I couldn't say for certain, much less when or where. *Tyro*, they called me. *Beginner.*

"Did I fall and hit my head?" I laced my fingers in my hair.

"A fall, yes, in a way. But you're quite well. You'll feel foggy for a few days. By the time we reach Fortress Evanide, the headaches should be gone." He slapped me on the back. "You are a new man, *tyro*. With work you will make a new life."

I could use some renewal. Dirty, battered, tired, head throbbing, my odd clothes torn and bloody. And hungry. Gods save me, how long had it been since I'd eaten? A glance around looked none too promising. An ill odor came from the temple or whatever it was across the field of hummocks.

"What is this place? I could use a bath and a meal."

"Unlikely to find either close by," said the brown-masked man. "Only dead men get bathed beyond those gates—and then they're burnt or buried. Don't know why we were told to meet you in such a place."

"I can't say, either," I said, uneasy when I turned my thoughts inward and found such a muddle. A deadhouse. What was I doing here? "Perhaps we could go."

"Here, before we go. Your new mask. And we've a clean shirt and jaque that will be better for traveling."

I ripped off the ill-fitting layers gladly and tossed my old mask on the slot gate in the wall behind me. The shirt was good linen. Not elegant, not new, but clean and comfortable. The leather jaque was too big, but it didn't stink of smoke and old sweat.

I felt a fool. My fingers trembled as I laced the jaque. Every time I tried to think what I was doing, the dull throb in my head got worse. The gray mask, though . . . to slip it on and feel its edges form themselves to my features—both sides of my face—was soothing. A full mask of good linen. It felt right.

A belt and knife sheath. Lastly, gloves, sturdy leather. Soft on my sore hands.

"And one more thing before we go." The raven-haired man looped a black cord around my neck. "Tuck this inside your shirt. 'Tis the blazon of the *Equites Cineré* and must remain private, but we'll be able to find you if you should wander off."

Equites Cineré—Knights of the Ashes. The name meant nothing. You'd think I would know my comrades.

Suspended from the black cord was an engraved pendant. It was a rectangular stone, intaglio, a thin layer of black over white, so that the engraving showed white against an ebon field. Portrayed was a quiver, five disparate objects poking out of it: a staff, a sword, a whip, a hammer, and a pen. The device, the same as on the knife strapped to my belt, was new to me. Yet it felt reassuring in a way. I slipped it inside my shirt. "I'm ready," I said.

The hawk man brought up the three horses. I mounted with ease—I had certainly done this before—and the three of us rode out into the bright morning. Surely a brisk ride would clear my head. Enticing, exhilarating, the path stretched out ahead of me.